MW01127292

THE
RUINS OF ARLANDIA

PART ONE

WILLIAM F. F. WOOD

CreateSpace Independent Publishing Platform

North Charleston, SC

CHAPTER ONE

GOING-AWAY PARTY

Calvin Range stood on the deck of his family home, looking out over the river. The sun was setting, turning blankets of clouds the color of fire. It was late fall, and the temperature at night dropped rapidly. The surrounding tree-covered hills displayed their red, orange, and dark purple leaves. He took a deep breath. He loved the cold air mixed with the smell of wood fires. Calvin took it all in, savoring every aspect of his home.

It was a very special evening. The family was celebrating Calvin's graduation from the Space Academy.

Tables and chairs lined the balcony. Silver trays with hors d'oeuvres sat on tables in the back with a server behind each one. A punch fountain stood next to the centerpiece, a large ice sculpture in the shape of a spaceship. A jazz band occupied the opposite side of the deck, and it played lively music.

One hundred and nine guests, dressed in tuxedos, military uniforms, and evening gowns mingled, ate, and drank out of tall crystal glasses. Many stayed warm by sitting around a large fire pit in the middle of the deck. As darkness grew, several torches were lit.

Calvin wore his service dress uniform—black and red with silver insignias. Normally he didn't stress about his appearance. His dark brown hair was too short to have to worry about, and his three years at the academy had made uniform perfection a thing of second nature. But tonight was different; there were senators and senior officers at the party.

"Well, you did it," a voice said. Calvin turned and saw his best friend, Jax, approaching. "For ten years you've been saying you were going to join the Space Command, and you finally did it. The big question is, will you ever go into space?"

"Of course I will, Jax," Calvin said, trying to sound confident. "I know someone who has connections. He says we'll go into space again, someday."

"Calvin, the fact that your father is a senator and a senior member of the space committee isn't going to make a difference," Jax said. "There hasn't been a manned space mission in ten years. Your father doesn't have enough clout to get us back into space. I'm sorry, but I think you've chosen a dead-end career."

"I think you're wrong," Calvin said.

"Definitely the most unpopular."

"Then why did you join up?" Calvin asked.

"It's your fault," Jax said. "I'm still trying to figure out how you talked me into it. Are you sure this is a good idea?"

"Yes," Calvin said, looking up at the stars. "We're going to get back out there. That's where the future is."

"The only people who believe that are at this party. Everyone else thinks we're crazy."

"Your dad still won't talk to you?"

"No. He's still mad that I won't be a farmer, like him."

"Sorry, Jax," Calvin said. "I wish more people felt like we do. But when we report to Space Command next week…"

"When we report next week," Jax interrupted. "We'll serve proudly on the only spaceship allowed to operate, the mighty simulator ship, Defender."

Calvin didn't answer; he just stared at the stars.

The sound of a spoon tapping on a glass rang out. The music and hum of conversation stopped.

"Ladies and gentlemen," a gray-haired man in a dark blue suit called loudly and stepped on a raised platform near the house. Calvin's father, Foster Range, had a smile on his face and looked at his guests with genuine appreciation. "Thank you so much for coming this evening. This is a big day for our family. It is my pleasure to introduce to you, Lieutenant Calvin Range." He was answered with a loud roar of applause. "Come up here, Calvin!" Calvin crossed the deck and stepped up beside his dad.

"Speech!" someone shouted.

"Thank you, everyone," Calvin said.

"Excuse me, Lieutenant," Jax said, jumping up next to Calvin and his father. "I think they mean me. You'll get your turn in a second." Calvin smiled and stepped back.

"Senator Range," Jax said. "I have something to say. I've been friends with Calvin my whole life. His dream of joining Space Command was so strong, he gave it to me. Anyway, Calvin, I just want to say that I'm proud of you. I'm lucky that I can call you my friend. I'd wish you the best of luck in your career, but you won't need it. You're going to be a captain someday, and after that you'll probably be in charge of Space Command. Please everyone, a toast. To Calvin! May there be no limit to your successes. Good luck in your new adventure."

"To Calvin!" the crowd shouted. Everyone clicked their glasses together and took a drink.

"Thanks, Jax!" Calvin said as Jax took a seat. Calvin's father stepped forward again.

"Tonight, we have more than one reason to celebrate. I have the privilege of announcing that for the first time in ten years, the council has approved a manned space mission." There were several gasps, and then a pause. Then everyone clapped and cheered.

"The *Sorenia* has been cleared to fly a training mission around our solar system, and my son will be on it." A wave of exuberance overtook the crowd. There were shouts and cheers with raised glasses. Foster nodded to the band, and it began playing again. Everyone went back to talking, eating, and drinking.

"Thanks, Dad," Calvin said. "This party means a lot to me."

"I'm very proud of you, Son," Foster said. "I'm also jealous. Ten years. Who knows if the council will ever let us go into space again? I doubt it."

"They need to stop letting the past scare them so much," Calvin said. "It's been eighty years. We don't even know what's out there anymore."

"That's true," Foster said. "That's why we need to go find out."

"Right," Calvin said. "The Dark Terror might not even be out there anymore."

Foster was about to reply, but he stopped when a tall thin man in dress uniform approached them. He had gray hair too, and unlike Calvin and Jax's uniforms, his had many ribbons and medals hanging from it.

"Senator," the man said. "Thank you for inviting me to your home."

"Thank you for coming, Captain Delik." The two shook hands. Then the captain offered his hand to Calvin. "Lieutenant Range, it'll be a privilege to have you on my crew. I hear you're a natural at navigation."

"Thank you, Captain," Calvin said, shaking his hand. "At least in the simulator."

Captain Delik laughed, and he turned to Foster. "I'm surprised you got this mission cleared. I thought our days in space were over."

"It wasn't easy," Foster said. "But the backup to the Planetary Disruption Shield needs a new power generator."

"They didn't tell you to use drones?"

"They did, but this time the work is more delicate. We can't trust robots to do it. One wrong move and our planet will be visible for any passing spaceship to see."

"Oh, I see, so that's how you sold it."

"Yes, and it didn't hurt that two senators owed me a favor."

"You make it sound easy."

"Trust me, it wasn't. I had to call in a few favors. Then the security committee threatened me. They said if the *Sorenia* wanders anywhere near the edge of the solar system, I'll find myself in a prison cell. I'm passing that threat on to you."

"Thank you, Senator." The captain's smile faded.

"I just don't want to be alone in that prison cell. Don't worry. Just stay close to home and you'll be all right."

"Can I ask you a question? I heard that the budget for the space program was going to be cut in half next year."

Several people stopped talking and looked in their direction.

Foster's expression changed to a sympathetic smile. "We can talk about that later, Captain. You should enjoy your mission. There's no telling when we will have another opportunity like this one."

The party didn't end until late in the evening. When Calvin finally went to bed, he couldn't sleep. When he got tired of trying, he sat on the balcony and stared up at the stars. What was out there? Was the Dark Terror real or just a story told to scare the population? He had heard the stories his whole life. His father told him they were lies. The problem was that the stories worked. Nobody wanted to go into space. A massive amount of money was spent on the Planetary Disruption Network, a system designed to hide the planet from passing ships. Everyone was scared of space. Maybe Calvin was crazy, but he couldn't wait to get out there.

CHAPTER TWO:

TAKE OFF

Calvin sat in the backseat of the hover car. He stared out the window, lost in thought. It was a beautiful sunny day. There were no clouds in the sky. New Arlandia City was nicknamed the "City of the Sun," because of the sheer amount of glass that reflected the sunlight. The buildings, domes, moving sidewalks, and hover-car lines were all covered in glass.

The hover car made its way downtown on the central line. Calvin was comfortable in his light-grey utility uniform, but his uniform was bare—only a name tag and rank insignia. His career was just starting. He would have plenty of time to add ribbons and decorations. His father and mother sat in the middle seats talking, but Calvin was completely unaware of what they were saying. He was full of conflicting emotions, excited and terrified at the same time. He was excited that after two months of briefings and simulations the *Sorenia* was going to launch. He was terrified that he would make a mistake and let everyone down. Calvin closed his eyes. He was so tired he could feel sleep tugging at him. He couldn't remember the last time he slept well. He opened his eyes, afraid he would fall asleep.

As they got closer, Calvin saw the fields that surrounded the Space Command dome were covered with tents.

"Look at that," Foster said. "Some of them have been camped out here all week."

"It's not every day you get to see a space launch."

There were little tent cities all over, in every open spot. Thousands of people gathered near small fires, sitting on foldout chairs and blankets on the ground. Many were setting up large cameras. Closer to the dome was another group of people. This group held signs and marched along a sidewalk as close to the dome entrance as it could get. Security guards watched them warily. The signs read, "Stop the launch," "You'll kill us all," and "Don't bring the Dark Terror."

The protesters screamed as the hover car passed by. They sounded like an angry, jumbled mess. Calvin couldn't understand what they were shouting. Security quickly waved the car through the gate, and it stopped in front of the entrance to the dome.

Two men in dark blue security uniforms opened the hover car doors. A small reception waited for them outside. One of them saluted Calvin's father.

"Senator Range," The man said. "It's good to see you, Sir."

"Captain Vinder," Foster said, returning the salute. "It's good to see you too. I have to say, though, I didn't expect a reception."

"We don't get distinguished visitors every day," Captain Vinder said. "Or get to witness what could possibly be the last manned space launch."

"So you've heard the rumors," Foster said.

"Just rumors," Calvin said.

"Yes," Captain Vinder said, smiling. "Just rumors. Lieutenant Range, it's a pleasure." Calvin tensed and straightened his back even more than it already was. The captain offered his hand before Calvin had a chance to salute. Calvin shook his hand reluctantly, but with a firm grip. It felt strange to be treated so well by a captain, since Calvin was only a lieutenant. But when your father is a senator, that's what you get.

"It's an honor to meet you," Vinder said. "It's going to be a

7

spectacular launch."

"Yes, Sir," Calvin said. One of the security agents retrieved Calvin's suitcase from the trunk and handed it to him.

Calvin and his parents were escorted into the space center's main building. Calvin half expected to find another group of people waiting to greet them on the inside. He was accustomed to a painful ceremony everywhere his dad went. He was relieved when there was no one there. They stopped in the entryway—a wide-open space in the large glass dome.

Foster looked at his son, and he smiled. "This is it, Son," he said. "We'll say goodbye here."

"OK, Dad," Calvin said.

"We're going to watch in the control room." He looked into his dad's face and saw worry there.

"What's wrong? I'll only be gone for five days. We're not even allowed to leave our solar system." Calvin wasn't able to hide his disappointment.

"I've been trying to change that," Foster said.

"I know, Dad," Calvin said. "It would be easier to change the planet's orbit."

"You're right," Foster chuckled, remembering that he had said that many times himself.

Foster appeared to struggle with what to say. Finally he said, "I envy you. Even if it is only around our system, it's going to be an adventure. Oh, I almost forgot, I want to give you something." He reached into his pocket and pulled out a small gold medallion, hanging on a long gold chain. He held it out to Calvin.

"My father gave this to me, the day I went into space for the first time. I want you to have it."

"Thank you, Dad," Calvin said, taking it from him. He put it around his neck and hid it under his shirt. His mother smiled sadly. Calvin knew that smile; he'd seen it before. She was trying hard not to cry.

8

"Be careful up there," Foster said. "The *Sorenia* is old. You'll get a lot of experience repairing equipment. I'll see you soon."

"Thanks, Dad," Calvin said.

His mom reached out and took his hand.

"I can't believe it," she said. "You're finally going into space." Her eyes started to tear up, so she forced herself to change the subject to something cheerier.

"Don't forget, we're having dinner at our house on Friday. Everyone will be there."

"Thanks, Mom," Calvin said. "I'll be there."

"You can tell us all about your mission," Foster said. "Keep a journal. It will help you remember everything."

"Yes, Sir," Calvin said.

Calvin hugged his mom and shook his dad's hand. Before leaving, his mom reached into her purse and took out a tissue. Then they left, holding hands. It was a sad moment, but it was very hard for Calvin to be sad.

"Hey, did you see all the crazy people out there?" Jax said, approaching Calvin from across the highly polished rotunda. "Ooooo, the Dark Terror is coming. I'm scared." He laughed loudly.

"Yeah, right, let's go find them. Are you ready to go?"

"I'm ready," Jax said. "Just waiting for you." They walked down a glass-covered hallway. "Did you talk to the captain?"

"Yes," Calvin said. "He said it would be no problem. We can share a room."

"Excellent!" Jax said.

"Corridor two, room eighteen," Calvin said, smiling.

The biggest adventure of a lifetime waited for them, at the end of the glass corridor, sitting on the landing platform—the *Sorenia*, a fifty-year-old ship with a dangerously underfunded budget. He'd seen the ship before, both in pictures and even once on a guided tour when he was in third grade, but for some reason, despite its age and reputation as a maintenance nightmare, seeing it sitting out on the tarmac made his heart beat faster and a surge of nearly uncontrollable excitement surge through his veins.

The sun was shining and there were no clouds in the sky. A gentle breeze washed over Calvin and Jax as they crossed the tarmac. It was a perfect moment. The *Sorenia* gleamed in the morning sun. She looked like an airplane, with sleek delta wings, a short stubby tail and a pointed nose. The bridge was all the way forward, on the top.

The ship was a torrent of activity. Vehicles dropped off pallets of food and other supplies near an airlock on the aft end of the ship. Dozens of workers were busy hauling the boxes in by hand.

A fuel truck was connected to the ship with a long hose. A dozens more trucks were lined up behind it, waiting their turn to upload fuel into the ship. There were people everywhere. Maintenance crews crawled across the hull above and below making last minute checks.

Calvin and Jax had to wind their way to the *Sorenia* through the carefully organized chaos. Once there, they climbed a staircase and entered through the main airlock. Calvin had memorized the ship's schematics and found their quarters relatively easy. But the two Lieutenants were too excited to unpack. They dropped off their personal gear and walked back out into the corridor.

"Hey navigator," Jax said on his way to the engine room. "Try not to get us lost, OK?"

"Yeah, well, I'll be impressed if you can get this ancient beast into space."

They both laughed. Calvin headed to the bridge, and could still hear Jax laughing down the corridor. Calvin walked briskly, certain he had never been this excited before.

The ship smelled old, and the metal deck-plates were well worn.

As he walked to the bridge, he passed dozens of young, enlisted crewmen, and all of them looked exactly like he felt, with faces that conveyed nervousness and exhilaration.

10

At the end of the corridor were two stairwells; one that led up to the bridge, and the other led down to the Galaxy Deck, the special area of the ship reserved for the senior officers (the officers that had stars in their rank insignia's.)

Calvin took the stairs to the bridge. He entered casually yet confidently, even though he felt neither.

"Welcome aboard Lieutenant Range," a voice said. At the back of the bridge, standing in a circle with three other senior officers was the Commander of the Sorenia, Captain Delik. Unlike Calvin, the Captain seemed fully calm and relaxed.

"Take your station, Lieutenant,"

"Yes, sir," Calvin replied curtly and turned away. The Room was not very large, all available space was taken up by computer equipment, controls and monitors. To make the situation worse, there were people everywhere; some under computer stations, others sitting at them trying to figure out why they wouldn't work, and some were on tall ladders working above the ceiling plates.

Calvin made his way through the people and boxes of tools to his computer station.

In the front of the bridge was a large window. Right behind that there were two computer stations, facing forward. Those were for the pilot and the weapons controller. Directly behind those were four computer stations, two on each side facing sideways. Calvin's station was second on the left.

"Come on people," The Captain said loudly but calmly. "We're on a schedule."

Within twenty minutes the bridge and the rest of the ship was cleared of everyone except the crew. The last vehicles were driving away. The Captain was sitting in his chair while the section heads worked their way down a checklist.

Lieutenant Calvin Range input the coordinates for launch into the computer, which was then passed to the pilot. He had nothing to do now, but wait, and watch.

11

When it was time to start up the engines, there was the beginnings of a rumble, and then nothing.

"Engine room," Captain Delik said. If he was getting upset, he was doing a great job hiding it. "What's the problem?"

"Standby Captain," a voice said. Calvin could only imagine the panic in the engine room. He'd have to remember to give Jax a hard time. Thirty minutes later, the engines roared to life. The ship shook, the air smelled funny for a second, like burned metal and plastic.

The communications officer requested clearance from the tower. The response was immediate.

"*Sorenia,* you are cleared for launch."

Whether people loved it or hated it, *Sorenia* was lined up at the end of the runway and the entire planet was watching. Even those who were scared and wanted to pretend it wasn't happening were unable to look away. The launch had become the center of attention on every continent. Nearly the entire planet stopped to watch.

Especially the group of ten thousand people gathered around the Space Center to watch the historic event. They were elated out of their minds. Thousands of cameras were there to capture it in vivid color.

Civilian flights in and out of the capitol were cancelled during a two hour window surrounding the launch. The skies were clear.

Calvin had nothing better to do that check the navigation computer. The captain ordered the crew to standby for take-off. Suddenly, the power on the bridge turned off and the sound of oxygen pumps ceased. Everyone looked at each other, and then back towards the captain.

Before he had a chance to say a word, the power turned back on, and Calvin could feel oxygen from a vent above him blowing on him again. Everyone went back to work like nothing had happened. Calvin hoped that wasn't a sign of things to come.

Calvin looked out the front window, the long runway stretched out in front of them. The engines thundered and the ship shook. The noise increased louder and louder, until finally the captain gave the order,

"Release brakes!"

The ship didn't jump forward, as Calvin thought it would. Instead it started rolling forward slowly and increased speed gradually. Even though he knew the runway was one of the longest on the planet – nearly two miles long, it seemed to Calvin they wouldn't get enough speed to actually lift into the air.

At last, when Calvin was certain they were about to run off the end of the runway and into the ocean, the nose of the ship rotated up and the *Sorenia* pulled off the runway and into the air, Calvin felt the elation and couldn't help join the rest of the bridge crew in a cheer. Calvin looked back at the captain. He was sitting in his chair with a smile on his face; no sweat; the man was a rock. *Sorenia* climbed higher and higher into the atmosphere, without a break in engine noise. Once it was high enough in the atmosphere it blasted its way into a low orbit.

Throughout the launch, the *Sorenia* shook violently, creaked loudly, and smelled like burning metal, but the ship made it into orbit without any alarms going off.

"Navigator," Captain Delik said. Calvin turned to look at him. "Set a course for the perimeter of our solar system."

"Yes sir," Calvin answered sharply. He performed the task quickly. He was nervous at first, and afraid of making mistakes, but he had memorized all of the coordinates of their system, and he programmed the computer from memory. Even so, he decided to double check his work, just in case. It turned out he didn't need to—his calculations were right.

There had been some interesting moments on the first day. The ship's sensors showed a very large object appearing and disappearing, somewhere out ahead of them. The captain said it was a sensor malfunction, and he assigned a work crew to fix it.

The most exciting and terrifying thing happened four hours into the mission. There was a power spike in the engine core and a frantic effort to contain an overload. Calvin thought he heard someone acknowledge an order to prepare the escape pods, and he was sure the mission was going to end in a ghastly disaster, but at the last second Jax repaired the computer and saved the ship.

At the end of the day Calvin went to bed, but he found it impossible to sleep. He couldn't stop thinking about almost dying on his first day in space. Images of the flashing red emergency lights, the smell of smoke, and the panic on the faces of his shipmates played over and over in his mind. He was awake for a long time, wondering if the old ship could survive another four days in space. At some point during the night, he fell into a deep, restless sleep.

CHAPTER THREE:

ABANDONED

Lightning streaked across the sky. Calvin stood in the middle of a smoking battleground. Hulks of burned-out battle tanks and the ruins of destroyed cities surrounded him. He couldn't move. A massive fleet of black spaceships circled overhead with laser guns pointed at him. A small group of people stood close by. They all looked terrified. Thousands of monsters with long fangs and jagged claws appeared on the horizon. There were so many they looked like a black cloud. They moved quickly and headed directly toward Calvin and the group of survivors. The monsters screamed as if they were on fire.

Suddenly a beam of light appeared in front of Calvin. It was a beautiful, pure light in the darkest hole in the universe. An old man and woman stepped in front of the light with a young girl. The light shimmered, flashed, and shot up into space. It looked like a bridge. The people walked into the beam of light single file and vanished. The monsters got closer, and the screaming got louder.

The man and woman walked toward the beam of light, but the girl didn't move. She looked at Calvin and stretched out her arm toward him, beckoning him to follow. But the old man pulled her back and pointed his finger at Calvin.

"No!" the old man said loudly. "You cannot come." The old man pulled the woman and the girl into the beam of light and disappeared, but the girl broke free of his grip and fell backward onto the ground. The beam of light disappeared. Darkness closed in around Calvin and the girl. She looked at him with tears in her eyes and said something in a language he couldn't understand. The monsters were almost on top of them. There was no place to go.

*

Calvin woke up terrified. Pain flooded his entire body, but his head hurt the most. The room was lit by a dim red light. It only took a second to realize how quiet it was. No deep hum from the engines or blowing from the oxygen pumps. The only thing he could hear was his own breathing. The silence was so loud it felt like it was crushing him.

Another disturbing thing was the strong smell of burnt plastic and metal. Suddenly a terrible thought occurred to him. The life support system was down! How long could he live without oxygen? He knew the answer—not very long.

Calvin slowly sat up. The pain in his head exploded, but he forced himself upright. For the first time he realized he was lying on the floor in the middle of his room. His blanket, pillow, and personal things were spread all over the floor too. The small gold medallion his father gave him was still around his neck. The emergency light above the door was on, but it flickered unsteadily.

Jax was on the floor under his bed. Only his legs were sticking out. Calvin grabbed Jax by the ankles and pulled him out. Jax was unconscious, and he had an ugly bruise on the side of his head. Calvin checked him; he was breathing, and his pulse was normal. Next, Calvin needed to assess their situation.

During an emergency, all crew members were required to report to their combat stations. As the ship's navigator, his place was on the bridge. He needed to get there as quickly as possible and find out what was going on. Calvin quickly put on his uniform.

He tried to open the door, but nothing happened. He tried four more times—still nothing. There was no power. Why wasn't the backup power working? He was glad he spent all that time studying the ship's schematics. He knew what he was supposed to do. He pulled the manual-release handle. There was a grinding noise, but the door didn't move. Calvin looked around his tiny room desperately.

"This isn't happening! I'm trapped in here!" He beat on the door and shouted for help. When there was no answer he screamed. It was no good. He tried to pull the door open, but it wouldn't budge. The door was too heavy. There was no way he could open it with his bare hands.

Calvin had to get out of his room. He was getting so upset he couldn't think straight. He needed to calm down, but instead he paced back and forth like a trapped animal. He was about to sit down when he remembered something. Every system on the ship had more than one backup. He searched around and found a panel with a small rust-covered crank wheel inside. With each turn the door slid open with a loud grinding sound that echoed throughout the ship. When the door was open enough, he squeezed through.

Calvin cautiously stepped into the corridor and looked both ways. It was dark, lit only by the dim glow of emergency lights.

"Hello, is anyone there?" Calvin called. Something was seriously wrong.

"What's going on?" Jax asked. Calvin walked back into the room and found Jax sitting up, rubbing his head.

"I'm not sure," Calvin said. "But it looks like we've lost power. Are you ok? You look pale."

"My head hurts, a lot, but I'll be all right. I need to get to engineering."

"All right, I'm going to the bridge," Calvin said. He passed several rooms on the way. They were all empty, and the floors were covered with clothes, blankets, pillows, pictures, and computers. Where was the crew? He should have seen or heard someone by now, but he'd heard no answers to his calls. He felt like he was walking in a dream, or a nightmare. He passed six more rooms, all in the same condition. Calvin was getting scared and thought he should stop making noise.

When he walked by the escape pods, he looked through a small, round window on the yellow and black stripped door. He expected to see the interior of an escape pod. What he saw made his heart pound violently and his breath to come in gasps. The escape pod was gone. A wave of nausea washed over him. He leaned against a wall to keep from falling down.

"They left us. The crew abandoned ship and left us here. Why didn't I wake up?"

Farther on he passed sections of the bulkhead that looked like they had been ripped apart and smashed back together. The emergency lights flickered and went out for a second. When they came back on they were noticeably weaker.

In the gloom Calvin saw something that scared him most of all. On a damaged section of the hull, there was a hole. The section he was in was exposed to space. He stared at it for several seconds, not sure why he was still alive and afraid to move.

After a moment he realized, "We're not in space. This doesn't make any sense." The lights flickered again.

Calvin hurried toward the bridge. That's where he wanted to be if the lights went out.

All of a sudden a loud clang shattered the silence. Calvin spun around. It sounded like a hammer was dropped, and it came from outside the ship. The echo reverberated into the distance.

"Hello?" he shouted. "Is anyone there?"

He stood still and listened. There was no reply. Terrified, he ran the rest of the way down the main corridor, up the stairs, and onto the bridge. Calvin walked to the front and checked the pilot's station. The computer was dead. He worked his way around the room, checking all of the computers. None of them worked, except for one. One small computer screen on the arm of the captain's chair was still on. Calvin looked at it.

It displayed the following:

Main power: Offline

Shields: Offline

18

Engines: Offline

Main reactor: Offline

Life support: Offline

Hull breaches: Sections 1, 2, 3, and 4

Escape pod launch sequence: 100 percent complete.

Emergency power level: 2 percent

An icy ball formed in the pit of Calvin's stomach. His fears were confirmed. The crew had abandoned ship and left them behind.

"What are we going to do?" He had a flash of insight. "The answer isn't in here. We have to go outside and find whoever did this to us. This is obviously a mistake. We aren't at war with anyone. If we talk to them, we can straighten this out and ask them to take us home. They have to be reasonable, right?"

He needed to see what was outside before going out. There were several windows at the front of the bridge, which were currently covered with a thick metal blast shield. Obviously the captain had ordered them to be lowered to protect the ship.

Power was needed to raise the blast shield. He looked at the status screen again. Emergency power was down to 1 percent.

He hurried to the windows, found the controls to raise the shield, and pressed the button. There was a very loud click that made him jump, and the shield slowly rose. Halfway up it made a loud grinding noise and stopped. Calvin heard a barely audible beeping noise coming from the captain's chair. Emergency power was depleted.

Ignoring that for the moment, Calvin looked out the windows. He was more than a little disappointed.

"Oh, come on!" There was a large, dark shape in front of the ship, but it was too close to see what it was. He studied it for a while. He looked at it from every angle—standing up, lying on the floor, even upside down. It was no use. He couldn't figure out what it was. Frustrated, Calvin left the bridge.

"Time to go outside." He jumped down the stairs two and a time, but halfway down, in midstep the lights turned off. Calvin was enveloped in pitch-black darkness. Caught by surprise, he missed the next step. His foot slid forward, and he tumbled down the stairs.

He landed on his back. Extreme panic helped him ignore the pain. He quickly flipped over and frantically clambered back up the stairs. The red glow coming from the bridge was just enough to see where he was going. He didn't stop until he was back on the bridge, where for the moment, he felt safe. His heart raced, and his breathing came in gasps. He stood in the doorway and looked into the blackness.

"I'm not doing this!" Calvin shouted. "There is no way I'm wondering around in the dark without a flashlight. I'll have to feel my way on my hands and knees! I'll never make it. Jax, can you hear me?" There was no answer. "Jax!" He wanted to call louder but was afraid to.

The emergency lights on the bridge were slowly dying. Soon he wouldn't have any light at all. He had to act fast. Calvin hurried to the emergency supply cabinet at the security officer's station. He opened it, hoping to find a flashlight. All he found was more disappointment. The cabinet was empty. The crew must have cleaned it out. Then suddenly, his worst fear became reality; the lights on the bridge turned off.

Calvin stood frozen in fear. It was so dark he couldn't see his hand in front of his face.

"What am I going to do now?" He was afraid to move or make noise. "I need to go back and find Jax."

Calvin was afraid of falling down the stairs again, so he got down on his hands and knees and felt his way forward. When he found the stairs he crawled to the bottom. He was terrified and thought he saw gray shapes lunging at him. He realized that his eyes were playing tricks on him.

When he got to the bottom, he stopped for a second. In the dead air his breathing sounded like gusts of wind. He crawled down the main corridor very slowly. He had to feel his way inch by inch. At times he thought he could hear Jax calling from far away.

"Ok, they were right. We should have stayed home. The Dark Terror is real. It's dark, and I'm terrified. Jax, if you can hear me, this isn't funny. You need to get main power back online."

After a while it seemed like he was getting a little used to the darkness. He'd heard that when someone lost his eye sight, the other senses compensated for it. He didn't know if that was true, but at one point he could swear he heard someone walking around outside the ship.

Calvin slowly crawled down the corridor; the only things he was aware of were his own breathing, the stillness of the air, and how loud the silence was.

From the moment he woke up on the floor of his room he had been living in a nightmare. Everything was going terribly wrong. That's why when he saw a light from far away he thought it was his eyes, or his mind playing tricks on him. But then the light got brighter, and it shined directly on him.

"There you are," Jax said. Calvin stood up. "Here, I found these in engineering." He handed Calvin a flashlight. Calvin felt happy for the first time today—happy to see Jax again, but deeply relieved to have some light.

"Did you find anything else?" Calvin asked.

"No," Jax answered. "But I have bad news. The crew is gone. They left in the escape pods. They cleaned everything out when they left. We're lucky they missed these flashlights. Did you find anything on the bridge?"

"No, nothing, and no indication of what made them abandon the ship."

"Why did they leave without us?" Jax asked.

"Our door was stuck. I had to use the manual-release valve to open it. Maybe they tried but felt they didn't have time."

"So they left us," Jax said. "What do we do now?"

"Well, we're not floating in space anymore. Another ship must have captured us. If we crashed there would be more damage. Our first

21

priority should be to find a communications terminal and contact Space Command. With any luck, they will know what to do."

Feeling much safer because of the new source of light, and happy to have a friend, Calvin followed Jax toward the airlock.

Suddenly, a loud tapping noise filled the air. They stopped in their tracks. He couldn't tell where it was coming from, but it was very loud, and it echoed throughout the ship. The tapping wasn't the only sound. They could hear scratching, or clawing. It stopped after a few moments. Calvin held his breath and waited. He heard no more sounds.

"Do you really think it's such a good idea to leave the ship?" Jax whispered.

"Would you rather wait for whatever is out there to come in here and find us?" Calvin said.

"Well, no, not really," Jax said.

Before they made it to the end of the corridor, another loud bang broke the silence. This time it sounded louder and closer. Calvin wheeled around, wildly shining the light in all directions. The sound echoed and then disappeared. He didn't see anything.

"What's out there?" Jax said.

"I don't know," Calvin said nervously. "But I have a really bad feeling we're about to find out."

"I wish we had some weapons."

"Yeah, me too, but we didn't bring any on this trip, did we?"

"Just two, and the crew took them when they left."

"Of course," Calvin muttered. "Jax, I think we should try to be quiet."

"I won't argue with you," Jax whispered.

They made their way carefully and quietly to the airlock. The silence was wearing on Calvin's nerves. Each footstep sounded louder and made him more scared. When they got there, they found the doors were heavily damaged. Although damaged wasn't really the right word for it. The inner and outer doors were crumpled on all sides. Calvin was sure they wouldn't open, but he tried anyway. He wasn't surprised when nothing happened. Jax examined them too, and his assessment didn't take long.

"There is no way to fix this without taking the ship home. Anyway, there's no power."

Calvin felt trapped. He paced back and forth in the corridor, trying to think.

"How are we going to get out? Is there another way?"

"Yes," Jax said. "We could use the escape hatch on top of the ship."

"Great idea."

"Follow me," Jax said, leading the way to the center of the ship, where there was a ladder recessed into the wall. Jax went first; Calvin followed. They only had to climb up three decks to the escape hatch, but it took longer because they had to climb with one hand, and hold their flashlights with the other.

"Ok, this is good," Jax said when they reached the top. "The hatch isn't damaged, but I'll have to use the manual-release lever. It might be noisy." He grabbed the lever and pulled as hard as he could.

The door slid open slowly with a very loud scraping noise that seemed to echo for hundreds of miles. Calvin cringed, and he listened as the echo reverberated. Complete silence followed.

Calvin took a deep breath. This was it. He followed Jax up through the hatch to the top of the ship and was deeply shocked to his core at what he saw.

CHAPTER FOUR:

SEARCH AND EVASION

Calvin and Jax were in the middle of a huge junkyard full of spaceships. There must have been hundreds of them, maybe thousands, all shapes and sizes. They were all piled on top of each other. The junkyard stretched out of sight in all directions except one. There was a large wall that ran off endlessly in both directions. There was a large door built into the wall. The ships must have been pulled in through it. A massive metal arm with long, sharp claws hung on the wall near the door.

"Oh, wow," Calvin whispered. "Look at that. It's a spaceship graveyard."

"Yeah, and look at the *Sorenia*," Jax said, walking to the side and looking down. "It looks like it was grabbed by that arm, and pulled into this ship, or whatever it is."

"So we were attacked, and taken by force," Calvin said.

"And the crew escaped while the ship was being pulled inside. Look, the cracks down the side of the ship were caused when the claws from the arm cut into the hull."

Several large lights above him dimly lit the giant chamber. It wasn't completely dark, but it was hard to see.

Hoping to find a way down without getting hurt, Calvin walked to

24

the edge and looked down.

"It's definitely too far to jump. Or is it?"

"Don't even think about it. I think we can get down on the other side. There is a lot of damage, and there should be a lot of things to hold on to."

They heard a noise that sounded like very loud metallic footsteps.

"What's that?" Jax whispered. "Is that a robot?"

Calvin looked around but couldn't see anything. Whatever it was, it was being careful to stay out of view. There was too much debris and damage in the way.

"Maybe we shouldn't go down there. I don't want to come face to face with whatever that is."

"Then we need to find another way."

Calvin and Jax walked around on top of the ship, and they studied the wall in both directions.

"Do you see that?" Jax asked. Far off in the distance, near the top of the wall, was a row of dark windows.

"They look like windows. Can you see if there is anyone inside?"

"No, they're too dark."

"There could be someone watching us right now."

"Get down!" Jax hissed. They dropped to the deck and lay flat.

"Did you see someone?" Calvin asked, suddenly very scared.

"No," Jax said. "But think about this for a second. Should we be anxious to meet whoever is in charge? If they were friendly, why did they attack us? If it was an accident, or a mistake, why are we trapped down here with the trash? Wouldn't they be down here trying to help survivors?"

Calvin thought about it; Jax had a very good point. The claw that tore into the *Sorenia* was compelling evidence that they weren't friendly.

Lying on his back, Calvin looked up at the ceiling high above.

25

There was a small grate with a ladder under it, and it looked like it was open.

"Jax, look at that. Do you see that vent up there? Do you think we could get up there?"

Calvin examined the nearest spaceship. It was black and was covered with millions of little bumps. Large holes were spread across one side, as if a barrage of weapons fire had hit the ship. It must have put up a fight, but it clearly lost. It had the same claw marks in its hull that the *Sorenia* had. It was a much larger ship, and it was sitting on its end. It stretched up almost to the ceiling. It was extremely hard to see, but it looked like the ship was very close to the ladder that led up to the open vent.

Jax crawled to the edge and looked across at the ship. "We can jump over to that ship," he said, pointing to the other ship. "It's close enough. There's a flat space and a door, just on the other side. It looks like an airlock."

"Can we get across without being seen?"

"No, as soon as we stand up again we'll be in plain sight," Jax said. "But the good news is once we get over there, we should be able to climb to the top on the other side."

"Ok, good," Calvin said. "On three, let's stand up and jump across." He took a deep breath, and got ready to stand.

"One, two, three," Calvin whispered loudly. On three, they both stood up. Calvin took a few steps back and watched Jax cross over. Then it was Calvin's turn. He ran and jumped off the edge. It wasn't very far, and he made it across easily. However, when he landed on the alien ship, there was a loud crack. He felt a stab of fear. Calvin looked down, afraid that the small platform was about to break off and fall. At the same time there was another sound; the metal footsteps moved again, somewhere below. It sounded like it was moving around in a big circle, as if it was trying to find a place where it could see them. Calvin was afraid to move, afraid to make noise. The platform cracked again, and he felt it move.

"Get off of it!" Jax hissed loudly.

The ship was lying at enough of an angle that Calvin was able to climb off of the platform and join Jax on one of the protruding bumps. He sat still for a minute, listening to the footsteps below. They moved very quickly, frantically running in circles. Then they stopped, and total silence returned.

"Is that thing responsible for attacking us and dragging our ship in here?" Calvin asked.

"I doubt it," Jax said. "I think it's more like a guard, sent in here to finish off the survivors."

It was good to be out of view of the dark windows, but Calvin wanted to get out of the open all together. They climbed to the top of the alien spaceship.

Climbing was easy, thanks to the bumps, which weren't very far apart and were easy to get a grip on. They reminded Calvin of the climbing walls he used to train on in the school gym. Calvin was starting to feel confident. The top of the ship looked very close.

"That was easy," he said. "I didn't even break a sweat."

He let out a giant cheer inside his head as he reached the top. He was about to raise his hands in victory, until he found what was waiting for him. His inner cheer died quickly.

"Yeah, that was too much to hope for," Jax said. "It's not going to be that easy." They weren't at the top. There was another ship smashed into the top of the one they were on. They looked identical, and they didn't look very stable. There was another problem. Blocking their way was a giant hole. Debris covered the ground around the hole. Calvin carefully walked up to the edge and looked down, but all he could see inside was pitch-black darkness. He shined his flashlight into it, but there was too much damage to see anything. They would have to jump across.

"What a mess," Jax muttered. "We're going to have to be very careful getting across that. The ground on the other side doesn't look very strong." There were burned cables coming out of the hole, and several large cracks running across the hull.

"We don't have a choice," Calvin said. In his mind the only other option was to go back down, and he really didn't want to do that. "I'll go first this time."

He moved back about ten feet and got a running start. He jumped over the hole and landed on his feet, but the hull disintegrated as soon as he touched it. Calvin screamed as he fell through, and he landed on his back with a loud crash. He was instantly enveloped in darkness. He jumped up, ignoring the pain radiating through his back and legs. Fortunately he was still holding the flashlight. He turned it on, and he shined it around wildly. He was in a long, filthy, dark corridor. When he hit the floor, a cloud of dirt billowed in the air, making him cough violently.

"Calvin!" Jax said loudly. Calvin looked up and saw Jax's face peeking over the side. "Are you all right?"

"I'm fine, get me out of here," he said between coughs. He froze. Far away, down the corridor, he saw two dark red circles. Calvin shined the light toward them, but they were too far away, and dirt in the air was blocking the light.

Calvin stared at the red lights, unable to look away.

"What's that?" he wondered. He nervously dismissed the idea that they were eyes. There wasn't something alive in here, was there? Calvin became aware of a soft hissing sound. Then the lights flickered out for a second, and they were back as solid and as red as before. They were eyes, and they just blinked.

"I'm not alone down here," Calvin whispered. He looked up, desperately looking for a way out.

"Here, use this," Jax said. A thick cable fell through the hole. He turned off the flashlight and stuck it in his back pocket. Then he jumped as high as he could and grabbed onto the cable.

Without looking back he climbed. From down the corridor he heard the sounds of heavy footsteps. It was running toward him. Calvin frantically pulled himself up, higher and higher. The footsteps were getting louder. The thing was getting closer! Calvin pulled himself up to the top and fell onto his back, breathing heavily. The footsteps stopped below him. Calvin didn't move. Was it a robot, or some kind of monster? He didn't know, and he didn't want to find out. From down below they heard a deep growl.

"Robots don't growl, do they?" Calvin asked in between gasps for air. He was tempted to peek over the side, to get a good look at the monster. Instead, he crawled away from the hole and stood up.

"That's not a robot," Jax said.

"We need to get away from here," Calvin said. "Quickly."

Getting onto the second ship was easy. They used debris sticking out of the ship to climb all the way to the top.

An incredible view was waiting for them at the top. Piles of spaceships stretched into the distance, without an end in sight. Some ships looked very old, but all were heavily damaged. They all looked very different. Calvin wondered how far this ship had traveled to collect so many ships. Were there other monsters lurking around in the darkness?

They walked along the top and examined the ladder.

"I was afraid of this," Jax said. Calvin noticed for the first time that there was a five-foot gap between the ladder and the ship, over open air.

"We'll have to jump," Calvin said. "And hope the ladder doesn't break."

"Do you want to go first again?" Jax asked, half joking. He didn't want to, but Calvin was ready. In the back of his mind he knew if the ladder broke he would never survive the fall. It was a very long way down. He got ready to jump, but hesitated. Before he had a chance to go, Jax ran forward and jumped across. He hit the ladder with a loud grunt. His feet slipped, and he almost fell, but he managed to grab middle rungs and hold on tightly. The ladder creaked, but held firm. Jax hurried up the ladder, into the hatch. His head peeked over the side.

"Ok, your turn."

Calvin took a deep breath, trying to work up the courage to jump. Better not to wait too long, he figured. He moved back a few feet to get a good running start, and he ran toward the edge of the ship. He jumped as hard as he could, but too soon. He thought he was going to miss it and screamed. He barely reached the bottom rung of the ladder, and he held on for dear life until he stopped swinging.

The footsteps down below pounded again, like a hammer, and there was a low humming noise. Calvin recognized the sound. It reminded him of a scanning beam. With a great deal of effort Calvin pulled himself up to the next rung, and then the next. The ladder creaked and moved back and forth. Then a loud crack filled the air.

"Calvin!" Jax cried. Calvin's arms were getting tired. Finally he stood on the lowest rung just as his strength was about to give out. Calvin wanted to stop for a few seconds to catch his breath but was afraid to. The ladder continued to crack and shake. He scrambled the rest of the way up the ladder. Jax grabbed Calvin's arms and pulled him up. Just as he got off the ladder, it broke away and fell to the floor with a crash. Calvin got down on his stomach, and he looked down. He could still hear the robot walking around, like it was looking for him. A red light darted across the floor, moving in wide circles.

"Is that the robot?" Calvin asked.

Jax, who was looking down from the other side, said, "I don't know of anything else that can run that fast." The robot ran into the distance. He could see the red light darting away rapidly. Calvin listened for a long time, trying to catch his breath. The sound of the robot mesmerized him. Where was it going?

Calvin and Jax stood up. They were in a long, dimly lit air duct that disappeared out of sight in both directions. The top was just out of reach. The duct was made out of a highly reflective metal. Small, narrow slits on both sides let in small amounts of light, but lit up the duct nicely due to the reflection.

"Which way?" Calvin asked.

"It doesn't matter to me," Jax said. Calvin picked a direction and started walking.

It was eerily quiet, and their footfalls had an odd "trapped in a tin

30

can" sound. Small hatches were evenly spaced in the duct above. They passed one every ten minutes.

Calvin felt his pocket to see if his medallion was still there; it was. They walked for a long time. Calvin wasn't sure how long, maybe thirty minutes. Then they reached an opening in the duct. Calvin looked down into the spaceship junkyard. He still couldn't see the end of it. At the bottom of one pile of spaceships, one silver-and-black one caught his eye. It looked intimidating, but obviously it wasn't a match for this ship.

Suddenly a line in the wall appeared. It spread from the top to the bottom. A huge door, so massive that most of the wall slid apart. The blackness of space spread out in front them. Calvin was terrified of being sucked out into space, but nothing in the cargo bay was sucked out. There must have been a force field keeping the air inside. A giant arm that had been hidden in darkness extended out through the door and into space. Calvin and Jax were shocked, and they stood frozen in fascination. The arm made several rapid movements—left and right, up and down.

Finally it moved back in. At the end of the arm was a series of claws. All of the claws were wrapped tightly around a strange-looking spaceship. The claw pulled the spaceship in through the door, and dropped it on top of a pile of spaceships. There was a huge crashing sound, and thousands of small pieces of metal flew in all directions as the spaceship crushed everything underneath it. The arm moved back into the darkness and disappeared. Slowly, the massive doors slid shut. The edges of the door blended into the wall around it and disappeared.

Calvin looked down, and he strained to see.

"Can you see anything?" Jax asked.

"No, there is too much in the way." All he could do was listen and imagine what was happening. There was a loud hiss from a door opening, a loud bang as the door slammed on the floor, and then the sound of people rushing out of the spaceship. Calvin could hear their boots pounding on the metal floor. A metallic voice shouted in a language Calvin couldn't understand. A laser gun was fired. The voice yelled again. What followed was pure chaos. All of a sudden there was a lot of yelling and shooting. There were several small explosions; the air was filled with black smoke and small metal fragments. The yelling turned to screams. As quickly as it all started, everything went silent. Calvin looked down, but he still couldn't see anything. He was shaking, terrified at what he had just heard.

"Let's get out of here," Jax said, pulling on Calvin's arm.

"Did the robot kill all those people?" Calvin asked.

"Those weren't people," Jax said. "Those were robots too. Couldn't you tell?"

"Their voices did sound funny. This doesn't make any sense, robots killing robots? What's going on here?"

"I don't know, but if we don't move the robots will be after us."

"How do you know they aren't?"

Calvin felt weak, but forced himself to keep going. He had been hoping to find whomever was in charge of this ship and ask to be taken home or at least send a message to New Arlandia. He knew now that wasn't going to happen. Calvin and Jax were going to have to stay hidden and try to get a message home in secret. Now he knew how they treated newcomers. If they were caught, the same thing would happen to them.

After thirty minutes of walking, Calvin stopped for a second.

"This duct could go on forever," he said. "Maybe we should try one of those hatches." He pointed up.

"You might be right," Jax said. "Thanks for stopping. I'm getting tired. All this exercise without food, it's not good. It's just like that time at the academy when you," Jax stopped talking, and Calvin saw why. Farther away in the air duct, he could see a small red light.

"How long has that been there?" Calvin asked. "Did it just turn on, or has it been there the whole time?"

Calvin slowly moved down the corridor, toward the red light, trying to make as little noise as possible. He was strangely drawn to it.

"What could it be?" he whispered.

"Calvin, what are you doing?" Jax asked. "Stop!"

Then Calvin realized what the red light was. It could only be one thing: the robot. Terror gripped him, squeezing his stomach like a vice. The light still looked like it was very far away, but it wasn't moving.

"We need to get out of here," Jax whispered, too loudly. "Let's try one of these hatches." Calvin looked up at the hatch right above them.

The red light changed. The beam narrowed to a small dot. Calvin thought he saw something out of the corner of his eye and looked down. There was a small red dot in the middle of his chest. As he stared at it, the dot got bigger. Then suddenly it disappeared. He looked back up. The red light was still there, but it was moving up and down. Calvin strained his eyes and his ears. There was a soft metallic thump echoing down the air duct.

"It's coming," Calvin said.

Jax jumped up, but he didn't touch the hatch. A loud pounding shook the duct.

"It's running!" Calvin shouted. The red light was very bright, and it centered on Calvin. The robot ran faster. The pounding hurt Calvin's head and felt like nails being hammered into his head.

"I can't get it!" Jax said. "It's too high!"

Calvin and Jax ran the other way as fast as they could. The robot got closer, and the pounding got louder. Calvin frantically looked for another vent. After a few seconds he found one! He was filled with adrenaline as he jumped as high as he could, throwing himself toward the vent. Miraculously he hit the small door. Calvin jumped and banged his fist against the vent cover. There was a loud clang as the cover swung open. The sound of the robot was close now. Fighting the urge to turn and look at the robot, Calvin grabbed a hold of the edge and pulled himself up. Jax grabbed Calvin's foot and helped push him up. When he was up, Calvin reached down and grabbed onto Jax, pulling him up through the hatch just before the robot reached them. Calvin quickly closed the hatch, which slammed shut way too loudly. They sat in total darkness gasping for air and tried to be quiet.

Jax turned on his flashlight. In the gloom, Calvin saw him point down.

"It's still there," Calvin whispered. He fought hard not to breathe too loudly, but he found it very difficult because he was out of breath.

"I'm not sure," Jax whispered. "But I think the robot hit my leg on my way up."

Calvin took the flashlight out of his back pocket and turned it on, relieved he hadn't lost it.

Looking up, he saw that they were standing in a narrow, round tube, under a ladder that ascended into darkness. Calvin stood up and climbed. He was careful to not make any noise.

"You know," Jax said after they had climbed for ten minutes. "I'm beginning to think we should have stayed in the ship. We were safer in there."

"Of course, we would've died from dehydration, or starvation, or the robot would have gone inside the ship and taken care of us."

"It might have been better than dying out here. Now the robot is hunting us."

"But we have a chance to get home," Calvin insisted.

"Not a very good one," Jax said.

"But it's a chance. Try to stay positive. At least we're alive. I was thinking, even if we find a communications room, there's probably a good chance we won't be able to use it. We might be able to find a shuttle bay, and take a small ship."

"And if we can't use their communications gear how do you think we'll be able to use one of their ships? We won't be able to read their language, and I highly doubt the controls will be the same as ours. That's assuming the shuttle bay won't be guarded."

"Right," Calvin said. "We have a problem." He didn't want to talk about it anymore, but his biggest fear now was that the robot was circling around and would be waiting for them at the top of the ladder. But there was no choice; they had to climb up. Calvin hoped he was wrong.

Again, the ascent went slowly because they had to use one hand to hold the flashlight and the other to climb. Calvin never caught his breath, and he gasped for air. The sound of it reverberated throughout the narrow passageway. They climbed for a long time before Calvin stuck his flashlight in his back pocket, with it still on. It was a relief to climb without holding it. They had to stop several times for a break, but in the end, it took an hour to reach the top. Calvin's arms and legs ached, and he was exhausted.

At the top was a closed hatch, with long, thin slits. Calvin tried to shine his light through the slits.

"Do you see anything?" Jax asked, holding onto the ladder just below Calvin.

"No," Calvin said. "It's too dark. I can't tell if the robot is up there or not."

They both listened intently for several minutes but couldn't hear anything. Calvin looked at the handle on the hatch for a long time, debating whether to open it or not. He was terrified that the robot was waiting for them on the other side. Would they be able to run away? He doubted that they could after an hour of climbing. The robot was very fast and didn't get tired. Finally he worked up his courage. He turned the handle and pushed. It was heavier than he thought it would be. Calvin had to push with all of his strength. It flew open. He tried to stop it but was unable to. The hatch fell to the floor with a loud thud. The noise made him jump out of his skin. His first thought was that the robot had found him and was about to grab him. Calvin shined the flashlight around wildly. The robot wasn't there. However, if the robot was anywhere nearby it probably heard the noise, and Calvin had just told the robot where they were. Once they were both out, they closed the hatch. It took both of them, because it was so heavy.

They stood in the dark and shined their flashlights around to see they were in a long, high-ceilinged hallway. The walls along both sides were lined with doors. All of them were closed.

Calvin was still scared, but he was starting to feel a little better.

"Oh thank you," Jax said. "I thought for sure the robot was going to be up here waiting for us. Maybe we lost it."

"I hope so," Calvin said. "But it hasn't been that kind of trip so far. This is the robot's ship. We're lost, and it's not. I just hope it doesn't have too many friends."

"Now who's being negative?" Jax said.

"Sorry."

"So which way?"

"That way," Calvin said. "I want to see what's behind these doors." As soon as he moved away from the hatch the lights turned on. Calvin almost jumped through the roof. He forced himself to relax.

"There must be motion sensors," Calvin whispered.

"Or maybe the crew just found us." They both froze in place and looked around. After a moment it was clear they were alone; nobody jumped out to capture them, and there was no sign of the robot.

"I think we're good," Calvin said. He walked to the closest door, which opened automatically.

It was a small room with a bed, closet, and dresser. The bed was bare, no linen or blankets. The dresser was empty, but the room was perfectly clean—no dust on any surface.

"This is interesting," Calvin said. "Look at the bed. It's normal size. That means the aliens who live here are about our size, and they need sleep just like we do. They're not all robots."

"Right, robots don't need beds. Then what are the robots for, security?"

"I don't know, but the bigger question is, where is the crew?"

They looked through four more rooms. They were all the same.

Calvin was anxious to see more and continued down the corridor. He passed a dozen more rooms on each side. There was a door at the end of the hallway, which opened for them. The lights turned on automatically. Calvin cautiously entered first, making sure the robot

36

wasn't in the next room. He didn't see it. They found themselves in a large room full of long tables and padded chairs. There were small computer terminals evenly spaced along the walls, with small openings next to each one.

"Is this where they eat?" Jax asked. All of the chairs were lined up perfectly. Not a single chair was out of place. They made their way through the middle of the room, toward a set of double doors on the other side.

"This must be a big ship, with a big crew," Calvin said. "They can feed a lot of people at one time."

"Yes, but where are they?" Jax asked. "This is starting to feel like a ghost ship."

Jax followed Calvin through the doors and into another long hallway. The lights came on as they entered. The lights behind turned off when they left.

"This feels very strange," Jax commented. "And a little spooky."

"The ship knows we're here," Calvin said. "I'm not complaining, but why doesn't the robot attack?"

They checked rooms as they moved down the next corridor. They found eighteen more bedrooms. "How big is this ship?" Jax wondered.

Calvin was tired, and he trudged along beside Jax. Their pace was slowing, and because they hadn't seen any people or robots, they were both feeling more comfortable.

"Maybe we should try to find the command deck," Jax suggested. "Obviously the robot is going to shoot first, but if we can get to the people in charge, we can try to talk to them. Maybe they can be reasoned with."

"I don't know," Calvin said doubtfully. "You want to just give up and hope they have mercy on us?"

"No, not really. But I don't want to wander around in this ship forever, either."

"I have a feeling that won't happen," Calvin said. "Let's save that for a last resort."

On the other side of the next door they found a surprise: a huge open room with a ceiling five hundred feet high. It was layered with balconies all the way up and a central staircase that went to the top. Calvin and Jax stopped and stared at it. The walls were mostly white, except for a few dark gray squares.

"Ok, where is the elevator?" Jax said. A brief search turned up nothing—no elevator.

"Sorry, there doesn't seem to be an elevator. We're going to have to do this the hard way."

"Then it's going to take a while."

Climbing the stairs was a painful and eerie experience. The whole way up, their footsteps bounced around in a cruel way. Several times Calvin started to panic inside because it sounded like someone was running down the stairs toward them. He thought for sure they were caught, but it was just the way the sounds were traveling. At every level there were hallways that branched off in different directions, but they kept going up the stairs. After a long, exhausting climb, they reached the top. They were very tired, and Calvin leaned against the railing to catch his breath. While resting, he looked down. It was a very long way down. The ceiling, made of lighted glass, was close now. They went through another set of doors at the top and stepped out onto a grand balcony, completely unprepared for what was waiting for them.

"No way," Jax gasped. Calvin's jaw dropped open, and his eyes got big in total shock. They were on the edge of a huge forest that stretched out in front of them. The balcony was just above the tree line.

"Trees," Jax said. "I don't believe it."

It was an incredible sight. A wide elevated walkway led out over the forest. There were staircases to the right and left that descended down into the trees. They were in a dome, with a single massive light in the middle that was too bright to look at. The light was giving off a lot of heat. If he didn't know better, Calvin would have sworn they were on a planet. The air was fresh, and the artificial light on the dome gave the

38

impression there was a sun in the sky.

Calvin and Jax followed the walkway. After just a few minutes of walking in the sunlight, with the fresh breeze on their faces and the birds chirping in the trees, the fear that had gripped them slowly faded away, and they forget about their problems.

They both lost track of time, lost in the pleasure of the environment. They could have been walking for several hours; they didn't care. Calvin loved every minute of it. There was another balcony on the other end of the walkway. Calvin and Jax took one last look at the trees, one last deep breath of fresh air before leaving it behind.

In the next room, another staircase greeted them. This one seemed bigger than the last. Calvin felt his stomach rumble.

"How long has it been since we ate?" Calvin asked.

"Dinner, last night," Jax answered. "And I'm hungry."

"Me too," Calvin said. "And thirsty. I think that's why I'm so tired." He looked up at the stairs and sighed.

"Better keep moving," Jax said. For Calvin, climbing was a nightmare. His legs hurt, he was tired, and he was starting to feel sick. Each step was harder and took more effort. Every time they stopped for a rest he could feel his legs shaking.

It seemed like an eternity, but they finally reached the top. Both of them sat on the top stair. Calvin felt dizzy, and he was losing hope that they were going to get home. He looked at Jax, and he looked bad. He was pale and looked exhausted.

"I was thinking," Calvin said. "Maybe your idea isn't so bad."

"Which idea is that?"

"Finding the bridge. It's just that, if we did find a communications terminal, there's no way we're going to be able to use it, or even know what one looks like. If for some reason we were actually able to contact Space Command, what would we tell them? Where would we say we are? We have no idea. What we really need right now is to find some water, food, and a place to rest. The mess hall and bedrooms are far away. Why don't we explore ahead just a little more and then head back down to where I know we can find sleep, maybe find food."

Jax nodded, too tired to answer.

Calvin didn't want to stand up again. However, fear that the robot would find them was all the motivation he needed. He groaned as he stood up. His whole body was hurting now. Jax tried to stand but was having trouble, so Calvin helped him up.

"What's this?" Calvin asked. He felt a surge of hope as they entered a section that looked like it could be a weapons training area. Off to the right was a long row of windows that looked down into a practice range. There were small, round targets at the far end. On the closest end were stations where a shooter would fire from. Calvin found a set of stairs that led down into the firing range. Jax sat again and leaned his head against a wall. Calvin left him there and searched the room, looking under every table, but sadly there were no weapons. Sad and disappointed, he walked back up the way he had come. Calvin helped Jax to stand again, and they plodded down the hallway, holding each other up. The pain was unbearable; they were hungry, thirsty, and weak. At the end of the hallway, he stepped out onto another balcony. Just when he thought he had seen everything, he was shocked again with the view in front of them.

The balcony was enclosed in glass and was outside of the ship. A long glass tube led from one part of the ship to another. Even the floor was made out of glass. Calvin was reluctant, but he wanted to see what was on the other side so he pressed forward. He had to tug on Jax to get him moving again. They didn't run, mostly because they were too weak and tired, but also for fear of breaking the glass. Calvin knew it was probably very strong, but it felt strange walking on a glass floor, in a completely glass tube, out in space.

Halfway across, Calvin panicked, losing his sense of direction. Jax hyperventilated.

"Relax," Calvin said. "Close your eyes and think about the trees. We're not floating in space. The ground is firm under our feet." Calvin fought the urge to hold his breath. He kept his eyes focused on the door at the end of the glass tunnel. That helped him to stay calm.

The walk across the glass bridge was an incredible and terrifying experience that he would never forget, but he was very relieved when they reached the other side and the door closed behind them. Calvin took a deep breath, and he tried to find the energy to keep going.

They were on another elevated walkway, over a hangar full of spaceships. They weren't destroyed ruins of spaceships, but perfectly intact and new looking. There were all sizes and shapes—shuttles, fighters, and bombers.

"There we go," Calvin said. "I think we just found a way home."

"Oh, I can't believe it, finally," Jax said. "Let's hurry."

"I don't see a way to get down to them. We could jump, but it's way too high."

"What's that?" Jax pointed to a row of dark windows overlooking the hangar. "They look like the ones near the *Sorenia*."

"It must be some sort of control room," Calvin said. "Come on, let's see if we can get in."

This is it, Calvin thought. All we have to do is get into one of those ships and fly home.

Calvin was very tired and in desperate need of sleep, but he forced himself on. The door at the end was different; it was red with yellow stripes. Calvin took it to be a good sign.

When they reached the doors, they automatically opened up, and they found themselves face to face with the robot.

CHAPTER FIVE:

THE ROBOT

The robot was tall; it towered over Calvin and Jax by two feet. It was silver with thin black lines running the length of its metal body, which highlighted various small panels and strange symbols that were written across its wide chest. Its head and red eyes were round. Its mouth looked similar to a human one, but it was long and thin. Calvin, Jax, and the robot stood still, looking at each other. Nobody moved for several seconds. Calvin was afraid to move, afraid to talk, and afraid to breathe.

Suddenly the robot spoke in a deep, metallic, grating voice. It spoke a strange language that Calvin couldn't understand, and it sounded very angry. When it finished talking, a small panel on the robot's chest slid open, and a red light beamed out of it. The red light shined in Calvin's face and slowly worked its way down to his feet. It did the same to Jax. When it was done, the red light changed to green and shut off.

The robot spoke again, in the same strange language, but its tone sounded completely different. It didn't sound angry anymore. It sounded friendly, almost like the robot was talking to a long-lost friend. After a minute it stopped. It ended its last sentence on a higher note, like it had asked a question.

Calvin was astonished, and he didn't know what to do. He thought they would be killed as soon as the robot caught them. Yet here it was, talking to them. Once again the robot spoke. It spoke for a few seconds and stopped. It seemed to be asking a question. This time Calvin answered; his voice cracked.

Terrified, Calvin managed to say, "I'm sorry, I can't understand you."

The robot spoke again, still in the same unknown language.

"I don't understand what you're saying, please don't hurt us. We don't have weapons, and we can't hurt you." Calvin put his hands up and showed them to the robot. Jax copied Calvin. Suddenly four more robots appeared as if out of nowhere. Calvin and Jax were surrounded. The robots all looked identical, except the new robots were almost all black with silver lines running down their frames. They were just as tall and looked just as formidable.

The silver robot spoke again. As it was speaking it raised an arm and pointed down the corridor. "What is it saying, Calvin?" Jax asked. "It sounds like it's asking something."

The robot didn't seem as scary as it did before, but Calvin was still scared and confused.

"What do you want us to do?" Calvin asked.

"I think it wants us to go with it," Jax said, visibly scared.

The silver robot moved down the hall and motioned for them to follow. Calvin and Jax cautiously followed it. The other four robots were right behind them.

"So you want us to go with you?" Calvin asked.

"Are we prisoners?" Jax asked. "Are you taking us to a cell? I really don't want to get locked up." He groaned. "This isn't fair."

"I don't think they are taking us into custody," Calvin said.

"How can you be so sure?"

"Normally when you lock someone up, you don't politely invite him to follow you to a cell."

"Oh, good point."

They followed the robot to a junction where several hallways met, and they stopped in front of a dark gray section of the wall. The robot reached out and touched the wall. After a moment, the wall slid apart in two sections.

"You have to be kidding me," Jax said. "Those spots on the wall downstairs were elevators? We didn't have to climb all those stairs."

Calvin didn't answer. He was trying to decide whether it was a good idea to go with the robots or not. Maybe it was because he was so tired, but he couldn't think clearly. It was a relief to finally get caught, and Calvin decided it was too late to resist. He, Jax, and the five robots got onto the elevator, and the doors closed.

"I think the silver one is in charge," Calvin said, almost afraid to talk. Even as he said that, the silver robot pressed a button, and the elevator went up. Only dark shadows could be seen through the windows, a blur passing by at incredible speeds. Then all of a sudden bright light poured in, and they had to shield their eyes. When Calvin was able to look through the windows he saw an amazing sight: a city. He had to close his eyes and open them again to make sure, but it was a city.

"Oh, wow," was all he managed to say.

"Calvin, do you see that?" Jax said. "I can't believe it. How big is this ship?"

"Wow," Calvin said again.

Dozens of tall, gleaming white buildings clustered together under a spacious glass dome. In the center was a single building that dwarfed all the others.

"I want to explore the city, go to the top of that building," he said. "Do you see any people down there?"

Jax strained his eyes. "No, I don't see any signs of life. But we're too far away."

They could also see lakes and green areas that looked like parks. The view disappeared when the elevator exited the glass dome. All they saw the rest of the way were dark, blurry shadows. It could have been his imagination, but at times during the elevator ride it felt like they were moving sideways, and then at an angle.

When the elevator emerged from inside the ship, and was moving across the top, Calvin's suspicions were correct. The black emptiness of space was above them, and they were moving toward a tower. At first Calvin thought it was a mountain, because it was so big. At the top of the tower was a large glass structure that was lit with cold blue lights. Both Calvin and Jax gasped when they saw it.

"Do you think that's the bridge?" Jax asked.

"That would be my guess," Calvin said. "And I think that's where we're going. Maybe we'll get to meet the captain."

The elevator moved into the tower, and the view was gone.

"I don't have a good feeling about this," Jax said.

"I think if they wanted to hurt us, they would have done it already," Calvin said. "Besides, there isn't much we can do at this point. They caught us. Now we wait and see what happens."

The elevator changed directions again, this time straight up. Eventually, it slowed and stopped. The doors opened, and the group filed out.

Calvin stepped out of the elevator and into a huge computer-filled room.

"You were right," Jax said. "It's the bridge." The room was a big glass sphere. The elevator shaft was in the dead center of the room. A carpeted circular staircase wrapped around the elevator and led up to a round platform above the elevator. Calvin speculated that must be where the captain sat. The view from the raised platform was perfect. From his seat he could see in every direction. Down below, computer stations and monitors filled every available space. There was just enough room for a walkway down the middle, running all the way around.

There was a view of space in every direction he looked. Around the outer edges of the room the floor was glass, and he could look straight down into space. But there were no people on the bridge, only a handful of robots sitting at computer stations.

As Calvin was admiring the view something caught his eye. There was a small, dark dot floating out in space. He strained to look at it, but he couldn't quite make it out. It was far away and hard to see, but it looked like a small spaceship. Either it was black or dark gray. He couldn't tell. It was just sitting there.

As soon as they arrived on the bridge the robots went to work, moving around the room from computer to computer. Calvin and Jax followed the silver robot up the stairs to the captain's platform. It was an excellent place to see everything that was going on and stay out of the way.

The ship vibrated. They could feel it through the floor. The ship made several small movements, and then in an instant all of the stars became blurry. Calvin gasped. The stars disappeared, and a bright blue cloud wrapped around the ship. For a second, it felt like Calvin was everywhere at the same time. It only lasted for a few seconds, and everything returned to normal, except a blue cloud still surrounded the ship.

"What was that?" Calvin asked, astonished. He looked down, and he found Jax sitting on the floor. "Are you all right?"

"I'll be fine, just give me a second."

"What was that?" Calvin asked again.

"I think I know," Jax said. "We just went into hyperspace. We studied it on New Arlandia, but it is only hypothetical. Apparently it's not for these guys."

"Apparently, but does that mean what I think it does?"

"It means we're moving faster than the speed of light. Oh, I don't feel so good," Jax said.

"Is it from going to hyperspace?"

"No, I don't think so."

"You're probably just hungry," Calvin said and yawned. "And tired." Now that he stopped moving, he realized how tired, hungry, and

46

thirsty he was.

"Excuse me," Calvin said to the silver robot. "I don't suppose you have any food around here, do you?" Calvin looked at the robot. It was staring at a computer screen that was covered with strange symbols and numbers, and seemed very intent on it.

The robot turned to Calvin and said something. Calvin didn't understand, but it sounded like another question. Calvin didn't know what to do.

"I'm sorry. I don't speak your language."

The robot stood up straight, and it spoke a series of short sentences. Suddenly one of the black robots appeared and pointed its arm down the stairs.

"Are you taking us to get some food?" Jax asked. "I hope so. I'm really hungry."

Calvin and Jax followed the black robot down to the main level of the bridge and then down another circular stairwell that was hidden behind the elevator. At the bottom was an intersection of four short hallways. The walls were lavishly decorated with gold and silver.   The light fixtures were encased in crystal shards. The carpet was dark red and very thick. At the end of each hallway was a large window.

The robot led them to adjacent rooms, not far from the stairs. On the side of the door were three lighted buttons: green, red, and white. The robot touched the green button, and the door to the first room opened, then it opened the door to the other room. Calvin walked inside the first one; it was a spacious bedroom. There was a bed next to a window that looked out into space. Thick red curtains were neatly tied to the sides. In the middle of the room was a round table with four chairs. There were also two dressers and a large monitor hanging on one wall. There were two marble columns with a richly carved archway between them. Through the archway was a dining area with a table and chairs. Immediately off to the left of the front door was a large bathroom with a shower and bathtub. Even the bathroom looked like it had been reserved for a king. The fixtures were gold. The tiles were dark red and azure blue. It was obviously an officer's room, maybe the captain's. On the *Sorenia*, the senior officers' rooms were closest to the bridge, so if there was an emergency they wouldn't have to run far.

The black robot left the room while Calvin was looking around. Another robot entered carrying a large covered tray. Quietly, the robot placed the tray on the table and left the room.   Calvin was alone. He approached the table and lifted the cover off of the tray.

"Room service," Jax said, walking into the room with his own tray. Calvin examined his meal with a great amount of nervousness mixed with curiosity. There was a brown slice of meat with some white mushy stuff. There was also a pile of long, thin, multicolored things that looked like noodles or a kind of vegetable. A glass of water was on the side. First he smelled the food. It smelled good, like beef and potatoes. He picked up a utensil. It was flat, like a shovel.

"That's funny," Calvin said. "We're literally gonna shovel it down." He looked at Jax for a response, but he was already eating.

Calvin took a small bite of each item, to test it. Everything tasted extremely good. Then he tore into it like a starving man, which he was.

They ate in silence, savoring every bite, and drinking deeply from jugs of cold fresh water. When Calvin finished eating, he put the cover back on the tray.

"That was delicious," Calvin said. "Whatever it was."

"That could have been because you were so hungry," Jax said. "I thought it was good too. What are we going to do now?"

"I get the impression these robots want to take care of us," Calvin said. "And right now I'm so tired I can't think straight. We've been given these rooms. I suggest we get some sleep, and tomorrow we can try to find a way home, or contact Space Command."

"I'm too tired to argue," Jax said, standing up. "Don't do anything without me, ok?"

"Trust me," Calvin said. "I don't want to wander around by myself."

"Goodnight."

"Goodnight, Jax," Calvin said. The door closed, and Calvin went to the bed and sat. He felt loneliness tugging at him. He turned off the lights and got into bed. The hyperspace field lit his room with a soft blue glow that mesmerized him. He wondered what had happened to the crew of the *Sorenia*, and if they were all right. He closed his eyes and was asleep before he knew it.

CHAPTER SIX:

———◦◦———

THE TOWER

When Calvin woke up he felt rested. He wasn't sure how long he had slept, but the view outside was unchanged; they were still traveling in hyperspace. Calvin sat up and swung his legs over the side of the bed. He stood up and stretched his legs. He was surprised when a robot showed up at his door with more food. The food smelled good, and this time it resembled breakfast food.

There was a knock on the door, and Jax walked in before Calvin had a chance to respond. He was carrying his own tray of food.

"I'm really starting to like this place," Jax said. "The service is really good."

"Yes, it is. But I wonder how they knew I was awake."

Jax didn't respond. He was already eating. Calvin quickly forgot about his questions when he smelled the food. It smelled very good, and there was a lot of it. There were pancakes, eggs, and bacon with toast. There was a glass of something that tasted like orange juice. Also, the robots had left him a new set of clothes—black pants and a purple, long-sleeved shirt. When they finished eating, Jax returned to his room, and Calvin tried on his new clothes. He shouldn't have been surprised, but everything fit him perfectly and was very comfortable.

He was feeling a lot more at ease. He wasn't afraid anymore, but he was still confused about what was happening.

Thirty minutes after breakfast, Calvin and Jax met in the hall outside their rooms, both dressed in clean clothes.

"Ready to go?" Calvin asked.

"Yes, do you think the robots will let us explore the ship?"

"Only one way to find out," Calvin said. They walked down the hall and climbed the stairs to the bridge. It was very quiet except for computer sounds. They stood at the top of the stairs and looked around.

"I don't see any robots," Jax said.

Calvin looked around. "This is the bridge," he said. "They wouldn't leave it unmanned. Look, there's one over there," Calvin said. There was a black robot sitting at a computer terminal.

"Think we can get by without getting caught?"

"Let's go," Calvin said. He quietly led the way around the main ring with Jax close behind. His biggest fear was that the robot would stop them from leaving the bridge, and make them stay in their rooms. But Calvin had to find a way to contact Space Command.

They walked slowly and quietly. Calvin's eyes were fixed on the black robot, but his eyes should have been on where he was going. His foot hit a computer console with a loud thud. Calvin stopped. The robot looked up at him, but then something surprising happened. The robot turned and went back to work, not seeming to care about what Calvin and Jax were doing.

They stood still for a minute, looking around. Calvin half expected a swarm of robots to descend on them and take them back downstairs. When it didn't happen, they casually walked to the elevator and into a waiting car. Both of them took a deep breath when the door slid quietly shut.

"Where to first?" Jax asked. There was a silver, button-covered panel next to the door, with a strange symbol next to each one.

"I've only seen robots so far," Calvin said. "I really want to find some people. Let's try the city."

51

"I wonder which level it's on."

"Let's work our way down, best guess. Go ahead."

Calvin pressed a button that would take them down twelve levels, and the elevator began its downward journey. After a few minutes the elevator slowed to a stop.

Calvin was excited, but that feeling quickly died. When the doors opened, all they saw was a dark blue robot pushing a machine down a long corridor. The machine hovered a few inches over the floor, cleaning as it went.

"A blue robot," Jax said. "Is that the working-class robot?"

"Might be," Calvin said, pressing a button another twelve floors down. "And what, the black robots are technicians?"

"And the silver one is in charge." They watched the blue robot clean the floor until the doors closed. When the doors opened again they found a large empty room.

This wasn't going to be as easy as Calvin hoped. They made four more stops, but none of them led into the city. The doors closed again, and Calvin selected a level much farther down. This time the trip lasted a lot longer.

Suddenly light flooded the elevator. Calvin smiled; they were over the city.

"I still don't see any people," Jax said. "The streets are all empty." Both of them stared out the windows, trying to scan the city quickly, knowing they only had a few minutes until the elevator dropped below the city's ground level. Calvin couldn't wait to get down there and walk around. He wanted to go up to the top of the tallest building. When the elevator passed the ground floor, Calvin saw something that looked like an entry point.

"What was that?" Jax asked.

"It looked like a way in," Calvin said. "Did you see what level it was?"

"That one," Jax said. When the elevator stopped, Calvin pressed the button Jax had pointed to, and they went back up.

The doors opened, and they stepped out. Calvin looked up at the glass elevator tube that stretched up into the vast heights above until it disappeared into the roof of the dome. They followed a stone sidewalk that led away from the elevator. Buildings lined the path on both sides. The path wasn't straight; it wound its way between buildings. They couldn't see anything because of the buildings. It was like walking through a thick forest, but instead of trees, it was concrete and glass. For the most part the path led consistently downward. They passed small shops on both sides. The windows were dark, and the rooms inside were empty except for furniture. The doors were all different colors and were covered with intricate designs. It looked like someone had gone to great pains to put a personal touch on each one.

It was very strange to walk past all the empty buildings and dark windows. The air was still and heavy. It almost felt like Calvin could feel a deep sadness in the air. Even the small saplings that lined the path seemed to droop with despair. Ten minutes later they entered a large courtyard. In the middle was a fountain, surrounded by a circle of white stones. The fountain was off, and the pool was dry. There were brightly painted doors and windows looking over the square. Each window had a small flowerbox under it, but they were all empty.

The path continued on the other side of the square, down and consistently toward the tallest building in the city. The path ended near the shore of a large lake. The surface of the lake was like glass, perfectly reflecting the tall buildings. The path circled the lake.

"Wow," Jax said. "It's beautiful."

"It sure is," Calvin said. "It almost reminds me of New Arlandia City."

"You're right." The tallest building was across from them, on the other side of the lake. They took the left path, for no particular reason. There was an open grassy area between the path and the lake, and a small sandy beach. The parks were very well kept and clean. There were freshly painted park benches facing the lake and nicely cut grass, and the path looked like it had been scrubbed clean.

Calvin tried to imagine a time when this city wasn't empty, when the walking path and park were crowded with people out enjoying the fresh air. There could have been people out with their children, buying balloons from vendors on the street, maybe flying kites.

It was a longer walk than he thought it was going to be. When they started walking around the lake Calvin guessed it would take about twenty minutes. They arrived in front of the giant building over an hour later at the bottom of a long, steep stone stairway. It was very wide, and it went right up to the main doors of the building. Calvin and Jax climbed to the top of the stairs, and they turned around. At this level they were just over the lake, and they could see all of it.

The green park wrapped all the way around the lake, and there were several small docks; two had boats tied up to them. Calvin looked up. The top of the building looked like it was hidden in clouds. The doors were unlocked and slid open when Jax touched them. The room inside was clean, just like everywhere else on the ship. There was no dust, and everything looked highly polished. They walked into a huge open room, layered with balconies that seemed to house offices on each level. Tall, dark red, richly carved pillars lined the walls. In the middle of the room was a large fountain, which wasn't turned on. There were small white tables and chairs around the fountain, and a small café off to the side. On the far right side of the room were several elevators. In the middle of two different sets of elevators was a silent, unmoving escalator that disappeared into the heights above. Calvin walked to the nearest set of elevators, and he pressed the up button. The doors opened instantly, and they both stepped inside. The inside of the elevator was very plush, with deep, soft carpet, and floor-to-ceiling glass windows on three sides.

There was a large control panel that glowed with a soft blue light. There were a lot of buttons, but there was only one place Calvin wanted to go, so he pressed the top button.

The doors closed silently. The elevator moved slowly at first, then picked up speed. Calvin looked out one of the windows. There was nothing to look at until the elevator lifted out into open space. At first he thought the elevator was no longer attached to the building, when in fact it was hanging off the side. The elevator accelerated, climbing the building at an impressive speed. Jax stood in one corner, holding onto the handrails tightly, until his knuckles turned white.

The elevator ride was very smooth, but Calvin held onto the handrail too. The ride up was short. They were so entranced by the view that they barely noticed when the elevator slowed and gently came to a stop. Calvin and Jax left the elevator and walked into a large round room with tall windows all the way around. In the center of the room was a staircase. Calvin ignored the view and went straight for the staircase, intent on finding the highest point of the building he could reach. Jax followed close behind. There was a glass door at the top of the stairs. He pushed it open, and a blast of cold air hit him. There were four more steps to walk up, and then they were out onto an open roof. Calvin was struck with awe and fear at the same time. He slowly approached a metal railing and looked out over the city below.

"Oh, wow," Jax whispered. "This is amazing." Thousands of buildings, green parks, and small lakes filled the city. But one structure got Calvin's attention. It was on the edge of the city, a dark gray building with long, thin windows running down all sides. A gold-colored dome was on top.

"That's an interesting building," Calvin said. "Do you see the dome, right over there?"

"The gold one?"

"I wonder what's in it," Calvin said. "It's the only building that has gold on it."

"That must mean it's important. On New Arlandia only very special buildings have gold on them. We should check it out."

"Good idea," Calvin said. "We can go there next. What's that?" He pointed to a long, thin line that wound its way around the city, circling like a ring about halfway inside.

"It looks like an elevated train."

"How did we miss that? We must have walked right under it." Calvin looked up. From this high up he could see the top of the glass dome, and the darkness of space above him. It was breathtaking, and the cold air blowing in his face felt good. He didn't want to leave. He could have stayed there all day, but he wanted to keep exploring the city. They spent thirty more minutes at the top, admiring the view. When they were done, they headed back down to the street level.

"I think the gold dome is that way," Jax said. Calvin agreed, and they marched off. They hiked for several hours, but they couldn't find the dome. They walked until they were completely lost and wandered around the city aimlessly for several more hours. They passed an uncountable number of shops, restaurants, and office buildings, and they crossed dozens of wide streets that looked like the ones at home that hover cars drove on. They never saw a single person or animal the entire time. The silence that smothered them was eerie and emotionally draining. Several times they went to the top of a building, in the hopes of getting a bearing on where they were, or at least to see the dome; they had no such luck.

They were both tired and hungry, and even though they were together, they felt lonely. Calvin was getting very worried. He hated being lost. He was on the verge of losing hope, when finally they reached the edge of the city and stumbled on a way out. A waiting elevator took them back to the bridge. On the way up, they caught a glimpse of the gold dome.

"We were way off," Jax said.

"And again, we didn't see the elevated train."

They made it back to their rooms without seeing any robots on the bridge.

When Calvin came out of the bathroom he found a covered tray on the table. He lifted the cover to find dinner. He was so happy when steam rose into the air, and the smell filled the room. It was exactly what he needed—a nice hot dinner. He sat and ate. When he was finished he put his tray out in the hallway and went to bed.

Calvin lay on his back and stared at the ceiling. His mind refused to shut off. He couldn't stop thinking about his family. Did they think he was dead? Were they looking for him? He desperately wanted to contact them and let them know he was all right. He also wanted to tell them where he was, but the problem was he didn't know where he was. He needed to keep looking for a communications center. But the ship was so huge, and everything looked strange to him. Everything was written in a strange alien language. The robots couldn't understand him, and he couldn't understand them. Whenever he asked them if he could contact New Arlandia, they replied, but he had no idea what they were saying. He was losing hope of ever contacting home.

CHAPTER SEVEN:

———————◦◦———————

THE GOLD DOME

Calvin awoke the next morning and climbed out of bed. He was anxious to get back out, determined to find a way to contact New Arlandia. Just like the day before, when he got out of the shower he found clean clothes and breakfast waiting for him. He had to admit that even though it was difficult to be away from his family and not know how or if he was going to get home, he was living very comfortably, and all his needs were being met. This was the life. However, there were two questions nagging him. Where were the robots taking them, and what were they going to do with them when they got there? He consoled himself with the thought that if they planned on harming them, they would have done it already, and if they were destined for a prison cell they would be in one now and not be waited on hand and foot. Calvin and Jax ate breakfast together.

"It looks like we're free to go wherever we want on the ship," Jax said.

"They don't seem to be very worried about what we're doing," Calvin said. "At least we have that going for us."

"Do you really think we're going to find a way to contact Space Command?" Jax asked. "Because I'm having serious doubts. Even if we could find a terminal, we don't know how to use their computers. I bet there's a dozen communications terminals on the bridge, but we can't ask the robots to help us, because they can't understand us."

"I don't know what else to do," Calvin said. "We might have to start playing with the computers on the bridge. Between the two of us we might figure them out."

"I wonder how long the robots will let us do that."

"We'll never know until we try."

"Ok," Jax said. "But if we can't, then what?"

"Jax, I have no idea. I still want to find the gold dome. I have a feeling there's something important in it."

"Let's do that next then. If I know you, you won't think about anything else until we get into it. I'm curious myself."

"I was hoping you'd say that."

"Then let's get going," Jax said. "If we get lost again we're going to need a lot of time."

"Time is something we have a lot of," Calvin said.

They finished eating, and they walked upstairs to the bridge. Calvin was relieved when they walked around the bridge and the robots didn't seem to care.

When the door closed, Jax said, "And now we know for sure. They don't care what we're doing."

They took the elevator directly to the city and searched for the gold dome.

"It feels really good to be in the city again," Calvin said as they walked down the walkway toward the lake. "It feels like we're on an alien planet, not on a spaceship."

"We're in an alien city," Jax said. "Have you seen the size of this ship? We might as well be on an alien planet."

They followed the sidewalk for thirty minutes to the first fountain. There, they found another path leading out of it. They followed that to the side of a wide street.

"It's nice down here, even if we're the only ones."

"Not quite," Jax said pointing. As they crossed a street, they saw four blue robots cleaning the sidewalks. So that was why the city was so clean.

Calvin and Jax followed a sidewalk for about an hour, until they passed under an elevated rail track.

"Finally," Jax said. It was at least fifty feet above them and passed between buildings on both sides of the street.

"Excellent, now we just need to follow it. Hopefully we can find a train station."

"It'll be better than walking." There was a path under the tracks that Calvin and Jax followed. It was a very pleasant path, like walking through a garden full of plants, flowers, small fountains, and ponds. They followed the trail for a few blocks and found what they were looking for. Hidden in between two buildings and under several large trees was a platform. Calvin led the way up the stairs to the top.

"Oh, yeah!" Calvin shouted when they reached the top. "What were the chances?" Sitting at the station was a train. It was white with bright red stripes, and it had four cars; the front and back were bullet shaped. They walked to the front of the train, and the door opened automatically. Jax seemed reluctant to go in, but Calvin led the way. They walked past rows of leather seats to the front. Calvin sat down at the controls. Jax sat right behind him. The controls were simple. A large lever sat in the middle of a console. Even though he couldn't read the words on the console, it seemed simple enough. Calvin didn't honestly expect anything to happen when he pushed the lever forward gently. He was extremely happy when all of the doors closed and the train moved forward.

Calvin and Jax both shouted. Calvin pushed the throttle a little more, and the train surged forward. It was a very smooth ride between the buildings and over the tops of the trees. Every ten blocks the train glided through a station. When the train turned a corner, a large building loomed in front of them, and it had a golden dome on top. At the next

60

station, Calvin brought the train to a stop, and the doors opened. Across the station, on another set of tracks, was a second train. Its doors were open, and three orange robots were working inside one of the cars. It looked like they were performing maintenance.

"Hey, look at that, orange robots," Jax pointed out. "That must be the maintenance class."

"I wonder how many other classes there are," Calvin said.

Tall trees surrounded the station. Thick branches hung over rows of benches, where passengers could sit and wait. A faint scent of lilac filled the air. Calvin and Jax took the stairs down to the street. It was a short walk to the dome, which sparkled beautifully in the simulated sunlight. They walked up the stairs and entered through two doors.

Shafts of light streamed through windows, down on rows and rows of bookshelves.

"It looks like a library," Calvin said, disappointed.

"I really don't know what you expected to find in here. Did you think we were going to find a communications center, with signs on the wall saying, 'Come this way if you want to call home?'"

"Yeah, I guess I was," Calvin said. He shrugged and walked toward the nearest rack of books.

"Wait," Jax said. "Where are you going?"

"After everything it took to find this place, I want to look around."

Calvin wandered around, taking down books at random and looking in them. The books were all in an alien language. In the center of the room was a large glass elevator that looked like a big bubble. Calvin took it to several floors, but the only thing he found were books and more books. He even went to the top floor. There was nothing there except more books.

Sad and disappointed, Calvin went back to the main level, near the entrance.

"You were right," Calvin said. "There's nothing here."

"I found some interesting art," Jax said. "Come take a look."

Jax led Calvin to the back, where there was a row of paintings hanging on a wall. They all looked fairly ordinary, except for the first one. It was very dark. A large dark face filled most of the picture.

"That looks scary," Calvin said.

"Do you think that's the Dark Terror?"

"I don't know. It could be." They stared at it for several minutes, unable to look away.

It was hard to see details, because everything in the painting was dark, but after staring at it for a while Calvin noticed the shape of a mountain behind the man.

"Doesn't it look like his eyes are real?" Jax said.

Calvin turned away and shivered. "A little too real," he said, and walked away. "Let's get out of here."

They took the train the rest of the way around the city until they reached their starting point. As soon as they got back to their rooms, the robots brought them dinner. Tired, and a little depressed, Calvin said goodnight to Jax, went back to his own room, and went to bed.

CHAPTER EIGHT:

ALERIA

The next morning, Calvin and Jax worked on the bridge, trying to find a communications terminal. It was slow, exhausting work that yielded very little except frustration. Eventually, Calvin got impatient and went back to exploring the ship, but he was unable to find anything that looked like a way to call home. When he got tired of exploring, Calvin went back to the bridge and helped Jax. Days of agony passed slowly, and they both grew restless and worried. They were completely unable to control what was happening to them, while hurtling through space to some unknown destination.

Finally, on the fifth day, the ship emerged from hyperspace on the edge of a small planetary system. It was early in the morning, and Calvin felt the ship change back to normal space. In fact, that's what woke him up.

He got out of bed and looked out the window. A small blue-green planet floated way off in the distance. He pressed a button on the side of the window, which brought down a small scope. Calvin had discovered it during his days of boredom. He put the planet in the middle of the view finder and enlarged it. He turned on the wall monitor, and the planet filled the screen. It was breathtakingly beautiful. It had deep blue oceans and land masses with mountains, lakes, rivers, and grassy plains. On one southern continent was a large city. The ship moved slowly, heading straight for the planet.

Calvin jumped when the door chimed. It was a robot with a tray of food and new clothes. He was grateful they were feeding and clothing him, but each day he was feeling more like a prisoner or zoo specimen. As usual, Jax showed up with his tray, and they ate breakfast together.

"It's nice to see the stars again," Jax said. "I wonder where we are."

"This might be their home world. I've been dreading this moment."

"Me too. What do you think we should do?"

"I don't know," Calvin said. "But we're at their mercy. Hopefully they're just curious about us, and they are taking us home to figure out what to do with us. If not, we might be in trouble."

"Maybe we'll get to meet the people in charge. I hope so. Then we can find a way to talk to them, and ask them to take us home."

"I love your optimism," Calvin said. "I hope you're right."

"Me too."

When they finished eating, two black robots showed up and escorted them to the bridge.

The room wasn't as empty as it normally was. Calvin counted fifteen black robots, all busy working at computer stations.

The silver robot was standing in the middle of the captain's platform. As soon as Calvin and Jax arrived, it pointed its hand at the planet and spoke. The robot must have known that they were unable to understand because it didn't wait for an answer. The silver robot walked down the stairs, and it motioned for them to follow it to the elevator. Once in, the door closed, and they descended into the depths of the ship. When it stopped, they all stepped out.

"Wow," Calvin said. They were in an immense hangar bay full of spaceships. There were bombers, fighters, and shuttles parked close together. They followed the robots through a maze of ships to a small shuttle resting near the hangar door.

The silver robot entered through a rear door and sat in the pilot's chair. Calvin and Jax sat behind him. Four black robots climbed on board just before the door closed, and they sat in the rear seats. They looked tougher than the other robots; they were black with dark red stripes. They were heavily armed; each one carried a long rifle and a pistol.

"Seat belts," Calvin said, quickly putting his on. The belt crisscrossed over his chest, holding him in the seat firmly.

The silver robot turned on the flight computer. The buttons and dials lit up with a soft white light. The engines hummed to life. The giant doors slowly opened.

Calvin felt a surge of excitement and fear as the ship slowly lifted up and moved out into space.

The small shuttle accelerated toward the planet. It was remarkably fast. They approached the planet quickly. The sky below was full of clouds. The shuttle entered the atmosphere with a loud hiss, and it was briefly enveloped in fire. They leveled out over a large city. Tall buildings stretched off in all directions.

Descending toward the surface, Calvin saw that the city was heavily damaged. Some buildings were completely destroyed, lying in ruins. Large piles of debris were all that remained of them. Huge craters pitted the city surface.

Almost all of the buildings that were still standing showed signs of damage. Some were more heavily damaged than others, but they all seemed to have gaping holes in them. The city had definitely seen better days. It must have been a very big battle.

On the horizon Calvin saw one building that stood out among all of the others. It was extremely tall. At least three times as tall as the other buildings around it. It was thin, and on the top there was a needlelike spire that reached high into the sky. It was a breathtaking sight. He was completely stunned at what he was seeing. One side of the building was severely damaged, like the facade had been scraped off. There were thousands off holes in it. It was amazing that the building was still standing.

The silver robot took them in low and gently landed the shuttle on a large platform near the ground. There was a soft bump as they touched the ground. The engines shut down, and the sound slowly died down and went silent.

Calvin and Jax took off their seatbelts. The robot turned the computers off and got out of his chair. One of the black robots was already up and moving toward the door.

When the door opened, cold air flooded the shuttle. The air smelled very odd. It was a musty, dirty, moldy, old-metal smell all wrapped in one. By the time Calvin got out of his chair and made his way back to the door, all of the robots were outside and were walking across the wide landing platform. The ground was covered with cracks. Calvin and Jax had to run to catch up to the robots, across the platform toward a large gold and purple archway that marked the entrance to the building. The wind was blowing harder out in the open. It felt like it went right through their clothes and down to their bones. Calvin wished he was wearing more than just a light jacket.

The building towered above them. The sides were silver and smooth, and they reflected brightly in the sun. Thin, wispy white clouds floated in the sky above.

"Where are we?" Calvin asked in awe, staring at his surroundings.

"I don't know," Jax said. "But it looks like this place has been dead for a long time. If only my dad could see this. I wonder what he would say."

"He'd say what everyone else would say. 'I told you so. This is what happens when you don't mind your own business.'"

"You're right," Jax said.

As they neared the entrance, Calvin continued to gaze up in the sky. He couldn't stop looking at all of the damaged buildings. Then a small dark object caught his eye. He almost missed it, but there was no mistaking what it was. It was a spaceship! It looked like the same one that Calvin had seen a few days ago on the bridge of the mother ship. He stopped, as if frozen, and stared at it. The robots continued walking toward the entrance. Then he saw something that truly alarmed him; it was moving, coming toward them!

"Um, guys, what is that?" Calvin asked, pointing at the approaching spaceship. The silver robot looked up. When it saw the spaceship it made a loud, sharp noise.

"I hope it's friendly," Jax said. "Please tell me it's one of yours."

The robot replied with a short grating noise, and then it rattled something off quickly to the others in a loud, excited voice. All the robots started running. Calvin got left behind very quickly.

"Wait! Slow down! Wait for me!" Calvin shouted.

"Hurry up!" Jax shouted.

The arch leading into the building was very big and ornately decorated. The robots didn't bother trying to open the door. One of the black robots threw itself into it. The door didn't stand a chance. The robot flew through the door, disintegrating it into a thousand pieces. A loud boom echoed off the buildings. The other robots made the hole bigger as they rammed their way through. Calvin and Jax followed, carefully climbing over the debris that was left behind. They were enveloped in darkness as they ran down a long hallway. Powerful beams of light came out of the robots' eyes, lighting up the whole area. Large puffs of dust and dirt were thrown into the air with every footstep. They followed the main hallway as it led them up and down stairs, down long corridors, and through sections that had lots of turns. Calvin was tired and was having a hard time keeping up with Jax and the robots.

The inside of the building was in an advanced state of decay. Stones were cracked, and debris covered the floor. In many places they had to jump over big chunks of rock that had fallen out of the ceiling, and there were a lot of gaping holes in the floor. The robots went over the obstacles in their path effortlessly, like they weren't there.

Calvin's legs were getting tired. Finally they entered a large open room that looked like a stadium. Rows of empty seats wrapped all the way around and stretched from the ground level up into the heights above. There were cracks and holes in the roof above, letting in shafts of sunlight. The robots turned their lights off.

They ran down a main aisle to the middle of the stadium. In the center was a circle of padded chairs. They looked like they had been rotting for a very long time. One of the chairs in the circle looked bigger than the others. Not too far away was a set of stairs that went down into the floor, where there was a row of computers. They were covered with a thick layer of dust and small rocks. One of the black robots plugged himself into it and fed power directly into one of the computers.

The silver robot followed and activated an intercom system. The silver robot spoke into it. His voice seemed to echo throughout the entire city. It spoke for a moment and then stopped.

Suddenly, people appeared, sitting in the circle of chairs. They looked like they were human, a mixture of men and women. They were glowing and occasionally flickered slightly. The person in the biggest chair, an older man with a gray beard, spoke. He talked in the same language that the robots had been speaking. Calvin was unable to understand it, but he was beginning to hear the same words repeated over and over. The man spoke for several minutes, barely pausing between sentences. At first his voice sounded flat, as if he were repeating facts, then he changed, increasing in emotion and intense pleading.

Calvin was fascinated as he listened to the man. Who was he? He was obviously the man in charge, but what was going on? Was this a recorded message, or was he speaking live from somewhere else? Was he a hologram? When the man was done speaking, he ended his message with what sounded like an emotional plea. Suddenly the images of all of the people disappeared. They were left in silence again. The robots talked briefly to each other and then indicated it was time to leave. The silver robot pointed his hand at the exit and said something.

The robots began running again, back the way they had come, leaving Calvin and Jax behind.

"We weren't supposed to do this much running," Jax said between gasps. Calvin was relieved when the robots stopped suddenly. When he caught up to them he discovered why they had stopped. Calvin stepped out in front to get a better look. He had to strain to see them, but way off down the hallway was a group of shadowy figures. The corridor was dark, lit only by the robots' eye lights, and there was a lot of dust and dirt floating in the air. It was very hard to see, but judging by the way they were moving, it looked they like were running. They were all carrying long, thin black objects, which could have only been one thing: guns. Suddenly the figures all stopped, leveled their guns, and opened fire on Calvin, Jax and the robots.

Everything happened very quickly. Simultaneously, small doors on all of the robots' arms opened, and laser guns snapped out. Two robots moved in front and shielded Calvin and Jax from the laser fire. They took several hits but seemed unaffected. They pointed their arms down the hallway and fired several shots at the attackers. The silver robot grabbed Calvin's arm and pulled him back. The robots turned and ran back toward the stadium. Calvin ran alongside the silver robot. Jax did his best to keep up, but it was clear he was getting tired too. The robots fired their lasers as they ran. Calvin wondered if their shots were hitting anything. He looked back, but he couldn't see anything.

They ran as fast as they could, barely keeping up with the robots. The sound of laser fire echoed throughout the hallway. Explosions hit the ceiling and walls all around them. Blood-chilling screams and shouts could be heard coming from the darkness. It was a frantic, running firefight all the way back into the stadium.

When they entered the stadium, they all ran in different directions. The silver robot stayed with Calvin and Jax. For a brief moment they were out of sight, and they knew it. But the enemy soldiers were right behind them. Calvin ran as fast as he could across the center of the stadium and up a sloped ramp on the other side. Laser shots lanced through the air above his head. The silver robot took a direct hit on its back while trying to shield Calvin. Suddenly a barrage of laser fire sprayed the area. Calvin fell to the ground and crawled behind a row of seats. A loud explosion shook the floor, and a wave of fire passed over the seats. After it passed, Calvin sat up, half blinded by the flashes and confused by the noise of shooting, screaming, and explosions. Jax was lying on the ground near him, but he wasn't moving.

"Jax, get up," Calvin shouted. But he didn't move. Calvin crawled to Jax. Laser shots flew overhead; Calvin kept his head down. When he finally reached Jax, the first thing he noticed was the large wound in the center of his chest.

"Jax," Calvin cried. "No!"

The silver robot grabbed Calvin and pulled him up to his feet. A black robot picked Jax up and carried him.

"Wait, be careful with him!" Calvin yelled. "He's hurt!"

The silver robot shouted at Calvin and pulled him up. Calvin stumbled up the ramp while being dragged along by the robot. Explosions erupted all around them, and entire rows of decaying seats were engulfed in fire. They ran through a small tunnel near the top of the stadium. Calvin wiped tears from his eyes, crushed with panic and fear.

At the end of the hallway they plowed down a flight of stairs. It was dark, and Calvin couldn't see. The robots' lights were on, but there was too much dust and dirt choking the air.

"Wait," Calvin screamed. "I can't keep up!" The robots were leaving him behind again. After he yelled, one of the black robots turned and positioned itself behind Calvin. The robots pressed on. It seemed to Calvin that they were running faster than before. Calvin fought to breathe, desperately pushing harder to keep up. His legs and back ached badly. Each step took more effort than the one before. Fear and adrenalin were pumping through him, giving him energy he didn't really have. Just when it seemed they lost their pursuers, the figures would appear suddenly without warning, blasting the air with uncontrolled swarms of laser fire.

"Hey!" Calvin yelled at the black robot carrying Jax. "Is he all right?" The robot didn't answer. "Jax, can you hear me?" They rounded a corner and entered a huge open room. They were at the top of a steep stairway. There was a row of doors at the bottom. Calvin stopped at the top and looked down. It was a long way down. He felt a moment of dizziness, and he had to steady himself. The robots didn't stop, but continued down the stairs, leaving him behind again.

Calvin ran down the stairs as fast as he could, although it felt more like he was in a controlled fall. Halfway down, he saw several small objects flying through the air over his head. He knew what they were, but there was nothing he could do.

A dozen eye-searing flashes caused him to flinch. He turned his head away from the light and closed his eyes. That was all it took to throw off his balance and miss a step. Calvin's feet slid out from under him, and he fell hard, landing on his side. Pain shot all over his body as he tumbled down the stairs. Ear-deafening explosions burst above him, followed by a wave of fire that seemed to suck oxygen out of the air. Calvin continued to tumble down the stairs, unable to stop himself. He screamed. Suddenly a heavy hand clamped onto his leg, and he stopped. The silver robot picked him up and put him back on his feet.

"Thanks." Calvin said, disoriented. It took him a second to realize which way was up, but the robot didn't give him the time. It issued a few sharp words and pulled him down the stairs. Calvin tried to ignore the pain as he ran alongside the big robot. Bombs continued to explode all around them. They reached the bottom and ran through the doorway. Calvin had to cover his eyes as they ran out into the sunlight.

Calvin followed the robots on a broad walkway around the building. They ran the entire way around the building to the shuttle. When they arrived, they found it lightly guarded by enemy robots. Calvin got his first good look at them, now that he could see them in daylight. They were dark gray, almost black. Each of them carried a long rifle. The big problem was that now there were enemies both in front and behind them. Calvin was terrified. They were trapped!

Then the most amazing thing happened. The silver robot looked at Calvin, and in Calvin's language he said, "Wait."

Three of the black robots moved like lightning and disappeared in a blur toward the shuttle. The silver robot stayed next to Calvin to protect him. The enemy robots were caught off guard. They didn't last long against the black robots. The battle only lasted a few seconds.

With the enemy soldiers bearing down on them from behind, the silver robot grabbed Calvin by the arm and pulled him toward the shuttle. After Calvin started running, the robot let go of his arm, and the two of them ran across the open space at full speed. The black robots had spread out in a circle to protect Calvin and the other robot as they raced to safety. When they reached the shuttle, they scrambled inside. The black robot carrying Jax gently laid him down on a seat in the back. Calvin sat next to him, gasping for air.

The silver robot wasted no time. The engines roared to life, and the ship shook violently before the black robots had a chance to get in and sit down. The back door was still sliding shut when the ship jumped into the air with a force that pressed Calvin into his chair. Laser shots flew past the ship on all sides.

Calvin checked Jax for a pulse, but he couldn't feel one.

The trip back to the mother ship was much shorter than the trip to the planet. The silver robot pushed the engines hard. The gauges on the computer panels were flashing red. The engines were screaming loudly, as if crying from the strain. Unlike the flight down, which was very smooth, the trip back was very rough. There was an extreme amount of turbulence as the ship left the atmosphere. Once they were back in space, they headed directly for the mother ship.

The landing was rough. The ship slammed into the floor of the hanger bay with a hard jolt. It was so hard that Calvin thought they had crashed. The impact caused Calvin to tense all of his muscles, and the shockwave hit him hard. The robots were completely unfazed. When Calvin took his hands off of the armrests, he had to flex his fingers because they were completely stiff. The door opened up, and by the time Calvin had taken off his seatbelt and gotten out of the shuttle, the silver robot and all but one of the black robots were already gone. The black robot gently picked Jax up and carried him off of the shuttle. Calvin followed him down the main corridor, and he watched him lay Jax's lifeless body on a bed in the ship's hospital. Calvin walked to the bridge, and he stood behind the silver robot.

Calvin looked outside and saw another spaceship off in the distance, in orbit over the planet. A small shuttle flying from the surface of the planet entered an open hanger bay.

"Look," Calvin said, pointing.

The silver robot issued a command in its own language. Suddenly the alien ship entered hyperspace, and it was gone. Calvin stared, trying to process everything that had just happened.

"What am I going to do now?" Calvin asked the silver robot. "My best friend is dead."

To his shock, the robot looked at him and said, "I'm going to take you home."

CHAPTER NINE:

ANCIENT HISTORY

When he arrived back on the mother ship, Calvin was lost. He tried to rest in his quarters, but he was too upset. He wandered around the city for hours, dazed and in no particular direction. Eventually he made his way to the top of the tower. He stood near the railing for over an hour, staring out into space. He tried desperately to sort through his feelings and emotions, but he couldn't face them. He wanted to know how he got to where he was, and how he was going to get home. Also, how was he going to explain it all to his father, or to Jax's parents? Later, Calvin wandered back up to the bridge.

Four days passed slowly and painfully. For some strange reason, he found comfort sitting in the captain's chair on the bridge. The blue hyperspace effect was hypnotizing and almost calming. He had a cup of hot coffee sitting in the armrest. At least he thought it was coffee. It was hot, and it gave him energy when he drank it.

But it wasn't all bad, after listening to Calvin and Jax talk for five days, the robot had finally learned their language.

When the robot told Calvin that he was taking him home, Calvin was confused and asked the robot how he knew where his home planet, New Arlandia, was. The robot would only say that he knew where Arlandia was, and they were on their way there. That was enough for Calvin. The trip would take five days. On the first day, Calvin grew bored and asked the robot to teach him how to use the computers. The robot agreed without hesitation. It helped pass the time on the long trip home. The robot taught him the basics of computer control, and how to monitor the status of every system on the ship. Engines, weapons, communication.

The next thing he asked the robot to teach him was how to use the communication system, which was integrated into the main computer, accessible at every computer. Calvin desperately wanted to contact New Arlandia. Calvin had memorized the communications channels for the military command center and also for the planetary control center before he left home. His father had insisted, and Calvin thought it was a good idea. He tried both of them, and a few others that he memorized just in case. Nothing worked. Whenever he tried to contact his home world, all he got was static. It was very strange, but mostly it was frustrating.

He wanted to contact home and tell them what was going on, but there was a new reason to get a hold of them: He needed to tell them that a huge spaceship would be entering the New Arlandia system and not to shoot on sight. He hoped that he would be able to contact them by the time they got there. If he couldn't, things could become interesting, and not in a good way.

Later that night, after Calvin had eaten his dinner in his room, he was sitting on the bridge while the silver robot was doing his rounds checking on the ship's systems.

"How are you doing tonight, Sir?" The robot asked.

"I'm doing good, thank you, Robot," Calvin said. Two days ago, Calvin called him, "Robot," feeling the need to call him something. The robot hadn't said anything, but Calvin still wasn't sure what to call him, or if it bothered the silver robot when he called him that. So Calvin decided to ask, "By the way, what can I call you? Do you have a name?"

"A name?" The robot asked, sounding confused. "I don't have a name."

"Oh," Calvin said thoughtfully. "Well, can I give you one?"

The robot seemed amused at the idea. "You want to give me a name?"

"Well, I have to call you something. I don't want to just call you, 'Robot,'" Calvin stated. "Besides, what would I call the other robots?" Calvin looked at the robot. The robot had letters written on his chest. When Calvin had first seen him, he thought part of the letters said, "Ion." After he had a chance to examine it, he saw that it didn't say, "Ion," but was something in a strange alien language that just looked like "Ion."

"How about 'Ion?'" Calvin said, and he explained why to the robot. The robot thought about it for a second.

"That is acceptable," the robot said.

Calvin sat back in the chair and realized how much he was starting to like Ion. He was far from the scary monster that Calvin thought he was nine days ago. They had spent a lot of time together, and Ion was quickly becoming his friend and guardian. He never got mad at Calvin. He was never impatient. He never made him feel foolish when he asked silly questions, or when he asked for things to be repeated. There was one question, however, that Calvin wanted to ask, but he was afraid to. It took him a long time to work up the courage to ask, and when he started, he became afraid and stopped. Ion looked at him with a quizzical look on his face.

"Master Calvin, is there something bothering you?"

"Yes," Calvin said. "I want to ask you a question, but I'm afraid to."

"Sir, you know you can ask me anything you like," Ion said warmly.

"OK," Calvin said. "I was wondering, when I first got here, you were very hostile. I was terrified of you. You were chasing me all over the ship. Then, after you scanned me you seemed to change. You went from angry to friendly. What happened? What was that big city we were in, and who were the people in the chairs? Why were those other robots trying to kill us? And by the way, why did you capture my ship in the first place?"

Ion answered, "Eighty-four years ago, a very powerful race called the Goremog launched an invasion on their closest neighbors, the Spinarians. The war was over in two short weeks, because the Spinarians were nothing but peaceful farmers. When news of it reached the galactic council, they discussed the issue and could not decide what to do. Many of the delegates refused to believe it had happened. News that the entire Spinarian race had been completely wiped out had reached the council, and they still had not made a decision on what to do.

"But that simple victory wasn't enough for the Goremog, and they invaded another planet, and another. Soon, their conquests were spreading across the galaxy. The council realized too late that the Goremog were bent on conquering the entire universe. Initially, a small group of planets banded together to fight against the Goremog. Eventually, every planet had picked sides, and the war spread to every corner of the galaxy. During the war, your people, the Arlandians, and the Alerians, the people who built me, were very close friends. They united together. The war was going very badly, and the Goremog were winning. Near the end of the war, our two peoples had almost finished working on a super-weapon that they hoped would save them from destruction. Unfortunately, they never finished it, and both races were nearly destroyed. The Alerians were scattered, and they have been hunted down nearly to complete extinction. The Arlandians disappeared and were never seen again. We assumed they were all destroyed.

"When the war ended fifty years ago, the entire universe was in ruins. Hundreds of trillions had died. There was no clear winner at the end. All of the races in the universe had fought until they were out of resources and could no longer fight. What followed after that was a period of relative quiet as planets rebuilt, and races struggled just to stay alive."

"My masters first sent me to your home world, Arlandia. When I got there, I found it was abandoned. When I reported back to my people, they sent me on a mission to find out what happened to you, to see if I could find survivors from your race."

"They sent you in this giant spaceship?" Calvin asked.

"No, I traveled in a much smaller ship," Ion said. "The king ordered the Alerians to hide all ships, to keep them from being destroyed. This ship, *Aleria's Hope*, was hidden in an asteroid field. But we have run out of time. The search for Arlandian survivors was cancelled, and the king ordered that all ships rendezvous. We are leaving this galaxy. All life in this galaxy has been extinguished. Now empires cling to life with only a dozen living beings, while they created armies of robots to continue fighting. But then I accidentally found you. What happened to your people?"

"My father told me stories," Calvin said. "During the war, Arlandia was bombarded from orbit with radioactive missiles. The air was toxic, and the water was poison. My people had to abandon it. The war had destroyed nearly everything we had. All of our colonies had been destroyed except for one. We were forced to move our entire civilization there. It was located near the outer rim. The war traumatized us, and we isolated ourselves, far away from every other species. We are afraid of contact with aliens and stay hidden. My father thinks that we should try to find our old friends. He believes the only way we can survive is if we help each other. He's a senator for one of the most influential continents, and he serves in the military command center, but his views are very much in the minority. It's a huge miracle that he got approval to have a small space fleet. It barely gets any funding, and we aren't allowed to leave our solar system. But he was determined that we not lose our knowledge of space travel and the ability to build spaceships. Our technology is ancient, and our ships are relics, but we do the best that we can."

"So when I picked up your ship, I was very close to your new home?" Ion asked.

"Very close. But you wouldn't have seen it. We take great pains to hide our planet. It's invisible from computer scans so that anyone passing nearby won't know we're there."

Ion didn't say anything.

"So you were roaming the universe, grabbing every ship you came across."

"Yes, after collecting ships, the occupants were scanned."

"And what did you do if the DNA didn't match?" Calvin asked, vividly remembering the sounds of a spaceship being caught and

78

destroyed.

"I was instructed to capture every ship I came into contact with," Ion explained. It almost sounded as if he were trying to defend himself. "My people are desperate. If the DNA didn't match, I was instructed to let them go. However, if they resisted, I was to destroy them. But you are the only living human I found. The universe is full of robots."

Calvin didn't say anything.

"But finally, after all these years, I found you, and your DNA was a positive match. Now there is hope of salvation."

"Salvation?" Calvin asked. "What do you mean? I thought the war was over."

"The Goremog have not been idle. They have rebuilt their planet, built massive shipyards, and have been rebuilding their space fleet. They have made large armies, ready for combat. Of course, like all the other planets in the universe, their armies are made up of mostly robots. But make no mistake, war is coming again. We must finish what we started. The Goremog are most certainly going to try to finish what they started. We believe they are building their own super-weapon, and they may be close to completing it. That's why I said we are out of time."

"So, wait a second," Calvin said, suddenly realizing something. "You're not taking me home; you're taking me to Arlandia, our original home world."

"Correct."

"But if it was destroyed, why are we going there?"

"The weapon was built in ten secret locations. Arlandia was one of them. There is a laboratory with a vault, somewhere on the planet, that contains one of the weapon components. The door to the lab is DNA coded. That is why you are needed," Ion said. "The Alerians, including the high council, will meet us there. They are going to help us search for the lab. Once we have found all of the pieces, and the weapon is assembled, they will need your help to activate it."

"How can I possibly help?" Calvin asked. "I'm not a scientist!"

"The weapon is also DNA coded, to prevent someone else from using it, in case it ever fell into enemy hands. DNA from both races must be used to activate it. All they need are the missing components, and you." Calvin paced around the room.

"Fine," he said. "So you want me to fly around the universe with you, and collect all the weapon segments?"

"Correct."

"How long is it going to take to collect all of the pieces?"

"It is impossible to calculate exactly how long the mission will last, but my best estimation, given the travel time between star systems, is a minimum of at least one year."

"One year," Calvin shouted. "I need to go home! My parents don't even know that I'm alive. You need to take me home, to MY home, New Arlandia!"

"I'm sorry. I can't do that. I have instructions to take you to Arlandia. We need you, and the high council wants to meet you."

A whole year! Calvin paced around the room. He was very upset, and his mind was racing. All he wanted to do at that moment was to talk to his father, but he still couldn't get through. It killed him that his family probably thought that he was dead. He wondered if the crew of the *Sorenia* had made it home safely. What did the captain report? Did they list Calvin and Jax as dead or missing? Were they looking for them? He wondered why he couldn't get a signal through to them. It was making him feel sick. What a nightmare.

After dinner, Calvin sat on his bed looking out the window at the blue hyperspace cloud. It was very beautiful. He deeply missed his family and his home. He closed his eyes and imagined he was there. He could smell the cold fresh air and the smoke from wood fires that gently floated out of chimneys in the neighborhood. He pictured his family sitting out on the balcony by the fire pit, watching the sun go down.

His stomach ached, and he was very tired. With everything that was going on—the urgent need to find and assemble the super-weapon, the Alerians, and the Goremog preparing for war—he couldn't contact home and tell his own people, his own father. It was eating him alive inside.

Suddenly he realized something; he could try to contact his father's office. Why hadn't he thought of that before? What time was it there? Never mind that. He left his room and went to the captain's chair on the bridge. Once there he turned on the communications terminal. He had to pause halfway through setting the communications channel, momentarily forgetting the numbers.

He held his breath as the signal left the ship and was zapped through space at a speed ten times greater than the speed of light. For several moments, nothing happened. He wasn't completely surprised by it. His attempts at contacting home so far had been a complete failure. Why should this be any different? Then, as he was about to give up, the static disappeared, and a face appeared on the screen.

"Dad!" Calvin shouted. "Dad, it's me!"

His father was looking into the computer screen. Calvin could barely hear his father's voice. There was a lot of static. "There is a signal," his dad said to someone out of view. "But it's extremely weak. Can you clean it up?"

"Dad, it's me! Can you hear me? Dad!" Calvin shouted at the screen.

Calvin could hear another voice.

"I'm sorry, Sir, the signal is too weak."

Then his Dad said, "Keep trying."

"Dad!" Calvin screamed as loudly as he could. "It's me. I'm OK. I'm not dead. I'm safe!"

"Wait!" His dad said. "Did you hear that? It sounded like—"

Suddenly the picture disappeared. Static filled the screen. The connection was lost.

"NO!" Calvin screamed. Tears fell from his eyes, and he whispered, "Dad."

Calvin didn't notice that Ion was standing behind him. He put a hand on Calvin's shoulder, but he didn't say anything.

Calvin tried to reconnect with his father's office for another hour before he gave up. Slowly he made his way back down to his room, and he fell into a dark, dreamless sleep.

CHAPTER TEN:

ARLANDIA

The next morning, the ship dropped out of hyperspace. Calvin was exhausted from not being able to sleep, and he had a hard time eating breakfast. He was full of nervous excitement, and he wished that Jax was there. He was still trying to wake up when he stumbled up the stairs onto the bridge. Ion and the other robots were already there.

Calvin stared across space at a small planet way off in the distance. It was a beautiful blue and green planet.

"Is that it?" Calvin asked in awe. "That's Arlandia?"

"Yes, that's Arlandia."

Calvin was amazed. He never thought that he would actually get to see Arlandia, the planet his people originally came from. He grew up hearing stories. It was once a great and powerful planet, back when the Arlandians were respected leaders in the galaxy. They had a huge space fleet and advanced technology. All of that was gone. Sadly, the only thing that remained was the stories.

"Master Calvin," Ion said. "I want you to have this." He handed Calvin a small electronic device.

"What's this?" Calvin asked, taking it from Ion. It was a square electronic device. It was very small, smaller than his thumb.

"Everyone will be speaking Alerian. This will translate for you, so you can understand them.

"Great," Calvin said. "How does it work?"

"Just keep it in your pocket," Ion said. "It generates a special electromagnetic field around your body. Any sound waves that you are exposed to are automatically converted into sounds that your brain can understand. It works both ways. When you speak, it will convert your speech into sounds that others can understand. That's the easiest way for me to explain it."

"Oh," Calvin said. "Wow, that's amazing."

Calvin put it in his front pants pocket. For several seconds, his head swam, and he felt very dizzy. He was glad he was sitting down. After a few seconds, he felt normal again.

"How do I know if it works?" Calvin asked.

Just at that moment one of the black robots came up the stairs.

"Sir, sensors are detecting seven Alerian ships moving toward us. They are requesting docking instructions."

"It works," Calvin said.

"Direct them to hangar bay three," Ion said.

"Yes, Sir."

Ion turned to Calvin. "Sir, the Alerians are very excited about meeting you. We need to go meet them."

Calvin followed Ion to the elevator. "OK, that sounds good."

Nobody talked during the long elevator ride, and Calvin had time to think about the impending meeting. He was nervous and didn't know what to expect. Plus, he felt uncomfortable being the center of attention. They probably thought they were meeting someone who was very important—a prince or a captain. He was afraid that they would be disappointed when they found out it was just Calvin, a lowly lieutenant. They stepped out of the elevator and into a small control room. The walls were covered with buttons, dials, and small computer screens. There was a computer station under a row of large glass windows, which looked out over a massive empty room. The ceiling was very high, and every inch of it was covered with lights. The hanger bay was very bright.

"Sir, will you please open the hanger doors?" Ion asked.

"Sure, no problem," Calvin said. He walked to a computer and studied it. Ion stood behind him, watching. Calvin found a silver panel with a single lever in the middle. It seemed the translation device worked with written words as well. On the top of the panel were written the words, "hangar bay doors." Calvin pulled the lever all the way down. A line of flashing, spinning red lights appeared in the middle of the doors that stretched from the floor to the ceiling. The lights separated, and the giant doors opened to the blackness of space. A faint purple glow lit up the edges.

"What's that purple glow?" Calvin asked.

"There's a force field covering the open door, to prevent all of the air from being sucked out into space."

"How do ships get in and out?"

"Spaceships can easily fly through it. It's a soft force field. Its only purpose is to keep the air inside."

Suddenly a large white spaceship appeared on the other side of the purple force field. Slowly and gracefully it glided in. Large columns of steam erupted from the bottom of the ship, and four large landing gears lowered. There was a very loud whooshing sound as they touched down. The engine noise slowly died away. After Calvin closed the doors, he and Ion got back into the elevator and rode it one level down to the main floor of the hangar bay. It was time to meet the people from Aleria. Ion and Calvin walked across the floor. The floor was white and felt like sandpaper. A hatch on the side of the spaceship slid open sideways, and a ramp extended to the floor. There was a column of steam, and another door opened. Several people emerged from the ship, and they walked down the ramp.

The first two people down wore black uniforms and carried rifles. It was obvious to Calvin that they were guards. When they got to the bottom of the ramp, they took up a position on each side. They both stared at Calvin and smiled.

The next people down the ramp were dressed differently. They wore very nice-looking clothes. There was a woman and a man. The woman had long, dark red hair and wore a purple dress. The dress was beautiful, but it also had a simple quality to it. The man had short black hair, and he wore a uniform, but it was different from the ones the guards were wearing. His was black, but it had a lot of red on it. It looked formal, and it had medals and ribbons all over it.

When they saw Calvin, they immediately smiled and quickly walked over to him. Their arms were stretched out, reaching toward him.

"Hello my friend," the man said warmly. "I'm Lord Fulton, king of Aleria. We have been waiting so very long for this day to come, when we would get to finally meet you."

"We never thought we would ever see another Arlandian again," the woman said. "This is just…" The lady stopped, unable to continue as she fought back tears. Overcome by the power of the moment, the man and woman reached out and touched Calvin. First they took his hands in theirs, and then they embraced him in a hug. It was as if they had found a lost child. After a moment, they stepped back, wiping tears from their faces.

"I'm sorry. I'm Lady Tridara, queen of Aleria. Please forgive us."

"Yes," Lord Fulton said. "We aren't normally this emotional with strangers, but we're not really strangers, are we? We're family, and we just found a long-lost member of our family. What is your name, young man?" Fulton asked.

"My name is Calvin, Sir," Calvin stuttered, choked by emotions. "Calvin Range."

"Range," Fulton repeated in a whisper. "Amazing."

When she heard Calvin's name, Lady Tridara put her hand on Fulton's arm and squeezed. Calvin was so caught up in the moment that he didn't notice Lady Tridara comment to Lord Fulton, "Oh, yes. I see the resemblance now."

"Will you please join us on our ship?" Fulton asked. "We have prepared a small reception for you. Our people are very anxious to meet you, and we want to hear about what happened to Arlandia."

Calvin was feeling a little overwhelmed. "Sure," was all that he was able to say.

"Alpha Seven," Fulton said to Ion.

"Yes, Sir," Ion answered.

"Put *Aleria's Hope* on full alert. Our scouts have reported enemy activity in the nearby system. I want the ship ready for full combat, just in case, and send the word out to the fleet as well."

"Yes, Sir," Ion answered. "I will see you later, Master Calvin." He turned and got back into the elevator.

Lord Fulton and Lady Tridara each took one of Calvin's arms, and they guided him up the ramp into their spaceship. The guards followed them but disappeared once they were inside, and the doors closed.

They walked down a plain-looking corridor and into a room that had a table in the middle and a row of windows looking out into the hanger bay.

Fulton motioned for Calvin to sit down. It didn't take long for the room to fill with people. Some were sitting at the table; others were standing along the sides of the room. All of the people were staring at Calvin, smiling uncontrollably. Several were crying tears of joy.

"I have to apologize again," Fulton said. "Everyone's not here, so you might have to tell your story a few times today, but please tell us, what happened to Arlandia? What happened to your people?"

Calvin told them the story of the defeat of Arlandia, and the exodus from all of their inhabited planets to the only surviving colony in the outer rim, New Arlandia. Fulton and Tridara listened intently the whole time. While he was talking, Calvin felt the ship take off, and he watched out the window as they flew into space. When he was finished talking, the room was quiet. The atmosphere was very somber. Several people were softly crying.

"Now we're scared," Calvin continued. "We're scared of everything in the universe. So we hide on our planet. It's forbidden to communicate with other planets and forbidden to travel outside our star system. Our leaders decided to destroy our space fleet when we arrived at New Arlandia. We have only a very small fleet. It's very old and falling apart. There are a few people that continually work to keep it alive. So I'm afraid if you were looking for an ally to help you in the coming war, you won't find one in Arlandia."

"Does everyone feel that way?" Fulton asked.

"No, Sir." Calvin said firmly. "My father taught me all about our history—the history that they don't teach us in school. He told me that we need to be strong. We need to protect ourselves, not hide in the dark. But our voices are seldom heard."

Fulton sat quietly, considering what Calvin had said.

"Time is running out for my people, and for yours," Fulton said sadly. "Over the last two years the Goremog have systematically hunted us down and destroyed us. There are only a few thousand of us left. We have to find all of the pieces of the super-weapon and put them together before it's too late. If we fail, we're doomed. There will be nowhere in this universe we can hide. The Goremog are building their own super-weapon, and when they are done they will destroy everything."

The severity of the situation shocked Calvin. He had heard the same thing from Ion, but hearing it from the king somehow made it more real. He knew it was desperate, but he didn't know it was that bad.

His voice was shaky, but he managed to say, "Of course I will do what I can to help." Inside he was thinking, "No pressure or anything."

Fulton smiled warmly, putting his hand on Calvin's shoulder. "I know you will, son. There is a reason we found you at this time. There is still hope. But first, we must find the first piece of the weapon. Will you help us?"

"Of course, Sir," Calvin said. "I'll help. What can I do?"

"Commander," Fulton gestured to a uniformed officer who was standing near the door.

"Yes, Sir," the man said and walked to the front of the room. There was a large computer monitor on the wall. It displayed the planet Arlandia in amazingly clear detail.

The man nodded to Calvin.

"My name is Commander Rale. It is a truly an honor to meet you, Master Range," he said.

"Thank you," Calvin said weakly. He was feeling a little embarrassed at all of the attention and respect he continued to receive, sure that he didn't deserve it.

"This is Arlandia," Commander Rale said. "Even though the Goremog devastated the planet over sixty years ago, the atmosphere is still drenched with radiation. Our sensors cannot scan the planet. There is too much interference. So we are going to fly over the surface very closely. We have more ships than we do people, so we would like you to help us search. Alpha Seven has informed me that he taught you how to fly our ships and how to use our computers and communications."

Calvin was confused. "Alpha Seven? Oh yes, I call him Ion." Seeing the questioning expressions on their faces, Calvin explained, "I didn't know what to call him at first, and I thought I saw the word 'Ion' on his chest." The Alerians smiled.

"Ion," Fulton said. "I like that. He's not a typical robot. He is very special—one of a kind. We used our most advanced technology to build him. His brain has the most advanced computer processor that our scientists have ever produced. That's why he seems more alive than the other robots—more real."

"Yes!" Calvin said. "I love that about him. He's my friend."

"Yes, I could see that. That makes me very happy. I think it would be good to keep the two of you together." Fulton looked at Lady Tridara. She smiled at him and nodded.

"Also, my daughter Astra will go with you. She can help you." Several people in the room smiled approvingly.

"Good," Fulton declared. "Then let us begin the search immediately.

We have a perfect ship, prepared just for you. Astra and Ion will meet you on board." Fulton stood. When he did, everyone in the room stood.

"Follow me, Master Range," Commander Rale said. "I'll take you there."

"Calvin," Lord Fulton said. "We are honored to have your help. We finally have hope again. We will stay in contact with you. Please take care of my daughter. The Goremog have been dogging our every move. I will feel a lot safer knowing she is with you."

"Thank you, Sir. I will," Calvin said, and he turned and left the room. Calvin's head swam as he followed Commander Rale down the corridor to a docking port. There they found a small shuttle docked. The doors were open, so they walked right on. Commander Rale walked directly to the pilot's chair and sat. He immediately prepared the ship for launch. Calvin stood at the back, not sure where he was supposed to sit.

"You can sit up front with me," Rale said to Calvin with a warm smile. Calvin sat and pulled the shoulder harness across his chest. It clicked softly as it locked into place. Two guards entered the shuttle and took seats near the exit. Calvin looked forward. He was looking out into space. The shuttle was attached to the outside of the larger ship.

Calvin sat quietly, thinking. He tried to get his head wrapped around what was going on. Did a king just ask him to take care of his daughter? He didn't know Calvin. How did he know he was able to take care of her? Calvin wondered how old she was. He suddenly had an image of a five-year-old girl who wouldn't be able to do anything for herself. Calvin shook his head. No, that didn't make any sense. Did it?

"*Aleria's Crown*, this is shuttle seven, requesting clearance."

"Shuttle seven, you are cleared to depart," a voice said over the speaker.

There was a muffled explosion followed by a loud clang, and the shuttle was floating free in space. They slowly drifted away. Commander Rale gently increased power, and the shuttle glided forward. Clearly Commander Rale was an expert pilot. Once they were far enough away, their speed increased dramatically.

Calvin wondered where they were going and how long it was going to take to get there. There was an uncomfortable silence. Calvin looked over at Commander Rale. He seemed very intent on what he was doing. Then he looked out of the front window. Off in the distance, he saw a very large ship in orbit over the planet. They were heading toward it.

"Is that where we're going?" Calvin asked.

"Yes. That's the *Defender*, our last battle cruiser," Rale answered sadly. "Once there were over a hundred of them. Nothing could stand against them. When they entered a star system, enemy ships ran away in terror. You should have seen them! But the Goremog destroyed all the others. It's manned almost entirely by robots now, with an Alerian crew of seventy-one."

"Wow," Calvin whispered. "How many robots?"

"Over five thousand."

"Wow," he said again involuntarily. Calvin stared at the *Defender*. It looked intimidating. There were hundreds of small and medium-sized laser turrets all over the ship. What impressed Calvin the most were the three massive sets of laser turrets on the front and the one on the back.

They flew into a large shuttle bay. There was only one ship parked in the cavernous bay. It was dark and looked fast. It was a beautiful ship. Commander Rale picked out a spot and gently set them down. They walked from the shuttle to the boarding ramp of the other ship, which had its boarding ramp down and its door open. Once Calvin got closer, he realized just how big the ship really was.

That was when Calvin saw her for the first time. It was a moment he would never forget. She was standing at the top of the ramp, with long brown hair that flowed over her shoulders. She was wearing a white and grey jumpsuit. When she saw Calvin she smiled and walked down the ramp. Her smile captivated him. For a moment he was lost in her gaze.

"Hi!" she said warmly. "Are you Calvin? I'm Astra."

"Hi," Calvin said. "Uh, yeah, I'm Calvin."

Astra stuck out her hand. Calvin took it.

"It's nice to meet you," Calvin said.

"Are you ready to go?" Astra asked. "The search has started already."

"Yes, I'm ready." Calvin followed Astra up the ramp and into the spaceship.

"Welcome aboard the *Azure Frost*," Astra said, smiling. "Let's go to the bridge, so we can get going."

There was an elevator next to the main airlock, which took them to the top level of the ship. They exited the elevator and walked down a long central corridor to the bridge. It was more like a large cockpit than a bridge. There were two seats in the front behind a row of computers, controls, and screens. There was also a row of windows all around the room. Whoever designed the ship made use of every space available. Even the space above their heads had controls and buttons, all lit up with hundreds of lights. There was a smaller computer station in the back of the room. Astra sat in the front right seat, and she motioned for Calvin to sit in the chair next to her.

"This is *Azure Frost*, requesting permission to launch," Astra announced into the communication system.

There was a pause, and a voice answered, "*Frost*, you are cleared to launch."

"Acknowledged," Astra said calmly.

Calvin watched as Astra piloted the ship out of the hanger bay and into space. No matter how many times he saw it, the excitement of flying through space still mesmerized him. He gasped when Arlandia came into view again. There was something amazing about seeing the planet that his people came from, the planet that he'd heard about in all of the old stories. The planet had a strange orange glow surrounding it. He wondered if that was the radiation.

The ride was bumpy as they hit the atmosphere, but it didn't last very long. Soon they were flying over the surface of Arlandia. Astra took them in low. Calvin looked down. It felt like they were very close to the ground, when in fact they were several thousand feet above it.

92

"Our search pattern has been preprogrammed for us," Astra explained. "Our sensors should pick up the electronic signature of the weapon segment." Calvin didn't like the awkward silence. He wanted to talk to Astra but was afraid of saying something stupid. The only safe thing he could think of was, "How big is this ship?"

"It's big," Astra answered. "It's about the size of a light cruiser, but designed to carry important people, like my father and mother. It has more powerful weapons and stronger shields. It has all of our most advanced technologies."

Astra turned on the sensors. A detailed map of the ground below and around them appeared on a small monitor.

"Watch the screen," Astra said. "When we find it, the computer will tell us."

They searched the planet for over an hour. Calvin spent most of that time watching the computer screen, hoping they would see the first segment. The entire time the detector never made a sound. Arlandia was beautiful; they flew over huge snow-covered mountains, deep canyons, thick forests, and an uncountable number of rivers and lakes. There were also ruins of many cities, both big and small. They weren't just ruins; it looked like the cities had been pounded into dust. There was very little remaining of them. Then suddenly, the communication system came to life.

"We found it! All ships rendezvous at our coordinates."

Astra turned off the automatic pilot and turned the ship toward the coordinates given over the radio. The ship was remarkably fast for its size, and soon they were flying over a wide, flat plain. Dozens of spaceships, parked in a circle, were already on the ground in the middle of a small ruined city. Astra set the ship down gently in the center of the circle.

The excitement in the air was electric. Calvin was about to go outside and set foot on the planet Arlandia! Calvin and Astra took off their seatbelts and left the bridge. There was a small equipment room near the main door. There were lockers and benches to sit on, and the walls were covered with various pieces of equipment, hanging on hooks. Astra showed him how to put on a spacesuit. She said it would protect him from the radiation.

Astra opened the door and lowered the boarding ramp.

"This is it," Astra said. "I can't believe it. You're the first Arlandian to return home in sixty years."

"I know," Calvin said. "It doesn't seem real."

"Come on."

Astra walked down the ramp onto the surface. Calvin took his time. He wanted to savor the moment. He stepped through a force field and made his way down the ramp. A hot wind blasted him and nearly knocked him down. He was forced to grab the railing and hold on. When he regained his balance, he looked down at the ground. There it was, right below him, the surface of Arlandia. He was about to set foot on it; his emotions rose, and he took a deep breath. The moment wasn't lost on the Alerians either. Hundreds of them surrounded the ship and watched as Calvin took his first steps on his ancestral home world. They were all wearing spacesuits, and they were all clapping, and some had their hands raised in the air. Calvin was smiling uncontrollably.

"Welcome home," Astra said to Calvin.

"Yes, welcome home," Commander Rale said, walking up to them. "This is a remarkable moment, one that we'll never forget."

Calvin was astonished. After hearing his dad tell him stories about Arlandia, the home world, he never dreamed he would set foot on it. He couldn't wait to tell his father.

"We found the vault," Commander Rale said. "This way." He turned and led the way to a large hole in the ground. Astra stayed close to Calvin. A set of decayed concrete stairs descended into darkness, but they made their way down the broken steps with the help of flashlights. The wind howled outside, sounding scary, like a wounded monster. At the bottom was a rust-covered metal door.

The floor was a combination of eroded concrete and dirt. The walls had large fault lines in them and looked unstable.

"We scanned the room for traps. We didn't find any," Commander Rale said. "We're going to need both of you for this."

Calvin and Astra approached the door. It was flat and smooth except for a long horizontal metal bar in the middle.

"You will each have to place one hand on the bar at the same time," Commander Rale said. "So you'll have to take your gloves off, but the doctor has assured me that a few seconds of exposure should be all right."

Calvin and Astra smiled at each other. Her smile was warm, and Calvin felt a glimmer of light finally piercing through the darkness that had been suffocating him since Jax died.

They both took off their gloves, and they placed their hands on the bar. At first nothing happened. Calvin was about to take his hands off and put his gloves back on when suddenly the bar changed color, from gray to dark green.

There was a collective gasp as a line appeared down the middle of the door, and it cracked open. Calvin grasped the door with both hands and pulled, but it wouldn't budge. Two Alerians rushed forward, one above and one below Calvin, and pulled. It took the combined strength of all three, but they managed to open it. Calvin peered inside, but couldn't see anything. It was very dark. Calvin and Astra put their gloves back on and followed the group of Alerians inside, and the flashlights swept the room.

Broken tables and chairs were spread around the room. There were also computers and lab equipment, but they looked like heaps of corroded, metal-burned wires. Everything was covered with a thick layer of dust. In the back of the room was another set of doors, which was open.

In the middle of the room was a table, with a large silver torpedo-shaped object on top. It too was covered with dust. When the Alerians saw it, they all gasped.

"There it is," Commander Rale said excitedly. "Let's get it moved onto the *Frost* quickly," he announced to the room. Four Alerians moved forward with antigravity equipment and prepared the first segment for transport.

"Everyone else, look around and see if there is anything we should take with us. Pack up all of the computers, and look for books or manuals—things like that."

The Alerians went to work. Large shipping containers were moved into the vault. Computers were packed up in boxes. Everything happened very quickly. Dust was kicked up in the air, making it very difficult to see.

"Remember, we don't have much time!" Rale said loudly. Then he turned to Calvin and Astra. "I'm sorry I didn't mention this to you right away. I suppose I didn't want to ruin the moment. Our sensors indicate that a large fleet of Goremog spaceships is heading in this direction. We need to get done as quickly as possible and get out of here. We can't be here when they arrive, or it will be the end of us." The work in the vault was completed very quickly.

All of the equipment, including the first segment, were taken aboard the *Azure Frost* and placed in the science lab.

As Calvin climbed the steps up to the surface, he felt a deep sense of sadness. When he reached the top, he looked at the sky, and then at the ruined city around him. He wondered if, and when, he would ever come back to Arlandia. He wanted badly to have more time to explore what was left of his heritage. The stories he grew up hearing had a lot more meaning now, and he felt sad seeing what was left and wondering what could have been had things been different. Calvin looked at Astra, who had stopped and was watching him. She smiled at him. It was a smile that conveyed sympathy, as if she knew what he was thinking and feeling. Calvin trudged after her, trying to soak in as much of his surroundings as possible. Commander Rale followed them to the boarding ramp of the *Azure Frost*, and they stopped at the bottom.

"We're out of time. A massive Goremog fleet just came out of hyperspace on the edge of the system. The survival of both of our peoples, and the entire galaxy, now rests with you. I've uploaded the location of the other nine vaults into your ship's computer. You also have everything you will need to complete this mission. The *Frost* is the best ship we have, with every piece of advanced tech that we could put in it. But that doesn't mean you can be foolish with it. The shields are very strong, and the engines are very fast, but you still need to avoid combat at all costs; that isn't your mission. Your number-one mission is to find the other nine segments and take them to the outpost at the center of the galaxy. Assemble them there, and you will save us all. Now take off! Ion and two other robots will go with you. We will cover you until you get off of the planet and enter hyperspace."

"Wait, we're going by ourselves? What about my parents?" Astra asked in a shaky voice.

"Trust me, Miss Astra, we will protect them, and if we had people to send with you, we would, but we can't. Besides, the Goremog will be chasing us, not you. I promise you, they will be safe. We will communicate with you as soon as possible. Now hurry up, get going!"

Calvin and Astra ran up the ramp, and it closed behind them. They took off their protective suits as quickly as they could and threw everything on the floor. They raced up to the bridge and jumped into the front seats. Astra started the launch sequence while she was putting her seatbelt on. There was a loud blast, and the ship jumped violently into the air. There was no smooth transition from lifting off to moving forward, and the ship lurched hard and accelerated. The sudden pressure was incredible. Calvin and Astra were smashed into the backs of their chairs until the inertia dampening system compensated.

"Calvin," Astra shouted, competing with the loud roar of the engines. "Can you take the controls? I need to upload the new map and charge the hyperdrive engines!"

"Sure," Calvin shouted back. He grabbed the flight controls—a half steering wheel with handgrips on each side that worked like joysticks. Both could rotate in all directions and had a trigger and buttons within reach of the thumb.

"*Azure Frost!*" a voice shouted over the speaker. "Activate your cloak. I can see you!"

"It is on!" Astra shouted back.

"There is something wrong with it. I'm telling you, I can see you!"

"We have a problem," Astra said to Calvin. "This will make getting away a little more exciting."

"Astra, head to the coordinates I'm sending you. We can cover you there!" a voice said over static.

"I've got it!" Calvin said as a series of numbers scrolled across a center monitor. He pulled the joystick to the left, harder than he'd intended.

"I'm setting a course to take us to the next segment," Astra said, busy on the navigation computer.

There was a loud hiss. Flames enveloped the front of the ship, and the *Azure Frost* shook violently as they left the atmosphere and flew into space. Calvin gripped the flight controls tightly until his knuckles turned white. He had to force himself to relax his hands.

One of the most amazing events in his entire life was the very first time he flew into space. It was incredible. At that moment, he was certain that he would never experience anything greater. He was embarking on a training mission to learn how to navigate a spaceship. He was intimidated and scared by the idea of it. He was afraid that he wouldn't be able to do it. But today, all that was gone. He was piloting an alien spaceship into a combat zone. It was beyond incredible. It was the most exciting and terrifying moment of his life.

As they left the atmosphere, Calvin saw something that would haunt his dreams and nightmares for the rest of his life. A large cloud of black spaceships was all around them. The spaceships were unleashing a horrific barrage of laser fire on the planet. Hundreds of Alerian spaceships were trying to escape, flying off in all directions away from the planet. Enemy ships were pursuing them, pounding them with their guns.

Suddenly two light gray Alerian ships moved up alongside of the *Frost*, one on each side.

"This is *Broadsword*. We've got you, *Frost*," a voice said over the loudspeaker. "Stay with us, and we'll protect you."

The swarm of Goremog ships closed in on all sides, overwhelming the Alerians as they tried to escape. Several white and red fireballs erupted over the planet, which could only be dying ships. Suddenly several enemy ships appeared in front of them. Calvin yanked the controls hard up and to the right to avoid hitting them. The *Frost* shook violently as it took several direct hits. The ships in formation with them fell behind, taking direct hits themselves.

Bright flashes filled the cockpit, nearly blinding Calvin and Astra. Both had to cover their eyes before the computer darkened the windows automatically. Several of the largest attacking enemy spaceships left the orbit of Arlandia and were headed directly toward the mother ship, *Aleria's Hope*.

"Sorry, *Frost*, we can't stay with you, we just lost our—" There was static, and the speaker went silent.

"*Broadsword*!" Calvin shouted. "What's your status?" There was no answer. "Astra, have you set a course yet?"

"Almost there!" Astra shouted back. Explosions rocked the *Frost* as the enemy poured on the fire. Calvin could barely hear her.

Laser shots flew wildly around the *Frost*. One came so close to hitting the bridge it made him jump in his chair. The room filled with a bright red light for an instant as the laser bolt filled the window in front of them. Calvin pulled hard to the right, trying not to fly in a straight line so they wouldn't get hit. It wasn't working. There were so many ships shooting at them, and most of them were hitting their target.

"I don't know how much more of this our shields can take!" Calvin shouted. He managed to get a quick glance at the shield indicator. It was bright red and flashing.

"That's it. We're set!" Astra screamed. "Calvin, get us out of here!"

Calvin pulled down hard on the hyperspace switch. The ship vibrated, the stars disappeared, and the ship entered hyperspace. Instantly, the noise from space combat was gone, and it was quiet. Calvin and Astra sat quietly for a moment, trying to process what just happened. Calvin closed his eyes and took a deep breath. After a moment, he opened them and looked over at Astra, his new friend and traveling companion. She was sitting quietly, holding her face in her hands. Tears were coming out of her eyes.

"Are you all right?" he asked gently. She didn't answer.

"I'm sure your parents are OK," he offered. "They must have been the most protected ship out there. We can try to contact them later." Astra shook her head up and down.

"How long will it take us to get to the next segment?" he asked, looking at the navigation computer. On the screen was a small white planet. There was a set of coordinates and an estimated time of arrival. The time said five days, six hours.

Calvin put his hand on Astra's arm.

"Let's go get the second segment," he said.

CHAPTER ELEVEN

CONTACT

The next few days were very difficult. There was a heavy, dark depression over Calvin and Astra. No matter how many times they tried, they couldn't contact Lord Fulton and Lady Tridara. They even tried to contact Commander Rale, but they were unable to. How many Alerians survived the attack? Did the ship her parents were on get away from Arlandia, or was it destroyed trying to escape? It was all she could think about. On more than one occasion it drove her to tears. She hid in her room for hours at a time. Calvin tried to comfort her, but since he was feeling depressed too, there wasn't much he could say or do. He was lonely, and he missed Jax even more. The effect of his death seemed much worse now, amplifying his sadness. All he wanted to do was hide in his room. Calvin had tried several times again to contact his own father, but he failed each time. Finally, after two days of trying to contact their parents, they gave up. Astra went to her room and isolated herself for all of day three. Ion stayed on the bridge and kept an eye on things. A second robot was in the engine room, and the third connected itself to the main computer to perform maintenance.

Calvin couldn't sit still. He wanted to explore the ship, to find out where everything was. On the first day, after they were safe in hyperspace, they each picked out a room. There were twenty-five to choose from, and they both picked one near the bridge. For one thing the rooms were larger and nicer, and another reason was that it was better to be close to the bridge, just in case there was an emergency, and given the nature of their mission, that seemed highly likely.

The *Azure Frost* was amazing. Everything about it made him feel comfortable. The ship was obviously not designed as a warship, primarily. When Astra said the royal family used it, she wasn't kidding. It was obviously the king's personal ship. The corridors were wide, with thick red carpet. The lighting somehow felt real, like there was a window with the sun shining through. There were beautiful paintings on the walls in most of the quarters. There were two hanging in Calvin's room. One was a waterfall with an arched bridge spanning over it, and the other was of a man in a dress uniform. Calvin didn't know who he was, but he looked important.

Not too far from his room he found a small library, with bookshelves full of books. The best part of the room was down four steps to a sitting room with two large padded leather reclining chairs, a couch, and small tables with reading lamps. The chairs faced a big window. One press of a button opened the thick red curtains and metal blast shield that covered the window. It was a very comfortable room.

A little farther down was a workout room with exercise machines. The dining room was also located on that deck. It was the most elaborate he had ever seen. It had a richly carved wooden ceiling and comfortable padded chairs.

The ship had five levels. Level five was farthest from the bridge. That whole deck was devoted to engineering—shield and power generators, electrical systems, workshops, fuel and water tanks, and the engine control room. There wasn't much to see, and it was loud down there.

On the fourth level he found a very large raw-material storage tank. Ion explained to him that it was used to synthesize anything they needed, from food to clothing—basically anything. It could even make spare parts. There were also several laboratories and workshops. The shuttle bay was a large room that took up space on the fourth and third levels. There were two small shuttles, and space for a third to park in.

After exploring for several hours, Calvin was tired. He headed back to the bridge to check in with Ion and see what was going on. He could have taken the elevator, but he took the stairs to get a little more exercise. His heart was heavy, and he was feeling very sad. He thought of his family again. Halfway up to the top level, the ship-wide intercom turned on.

"Lady Astra, Master Calvin, please come to the bridge immediately," Ion said. "We are receiving a message from King Fulton."

"I'm on my way up," Calvin said loudly, not sure if Ion could hear him or not. He ran up the stairs two at a time all the way to the top. He walked quickly down the corridor to the bridge. Astra was already there. She was sitting in the pilot's chair, and an image of her father and mother were on the large monitor in the middle of the control console, between the pilot's chairs.

"I'm so glad you are OK," Astra said through tears. "We were very worried about you." Calvin sat in the seat next to her.

"It's a relief to see you, Sir," Calvin said. "You have no idea how worried we were."

"It's OK, son," Fulton said gently. "We're safe. We got away from Arlandia. We lost several ships, but most of us survived. Our communication system was damaged in the escape, but we repaired it. What's important is that you escaped and will find all of the pieces of the weapon. Your success lies in secrecy. The *Azure Frost* is equipped with a cloaking device and a class-ten power generator. Keep the ship cloaked at all times, and you will be safe. Ion, is the cloak currently activated?"

"Sir," Ion answered. "We are having problems with the cloaking system. It may have been damaged in our escape from Arlandia. We are working on it."

The king's smile faded away briefly, and his eyes narrowed.

"That's unfortunate," Fulton said, disappointed. "Ion, repairing that system needs to be your number-one priority."

"Yes, Sir," Ion said.

"Have it fixed before you exit hyperspace, or everything for light years will see you."

"Yes, Sir," Ion said again.

"We love you Astra. I'm sorry I couldn't send more people to help you, but I feel very confident that the *Frost* and the robots will protect you both. I wouldn't have let you go if I didn't think so. The Goremog are more interested in us. As long as their fleet is chasing us, they'll be leaving you alone. Just stick to the plan. We will stay in contact with you. Goodbye for now."

"I love you," Astra said. The screen went dark.

Calvin sat back in his chair. He was very happy that Astra's parents were safe. He looked at her.

She was also sitting back in her chair, smiling. He decided to ask her a question.

"I haven't really eaten anything all day. Would you like to have dinner with me? I know a nice restaurant down the hall."

Astra looked at him. She thought about it for a second, as if trying to decide if she was hungry.

"Sure, I would like that." They got up and walked to the dining room.

"Have you eaten in here yet?" she asked as they entered the room.

"Yes, a few times," Calvin said. "The food is really good, ever since they got that new chef." Astra giggled.

"So you know how to use the food stations?"

"Ion showed me how to use them."

"That's good," she said. "I like that you call him Ion. That's a lot better than Alpha Seven."

The food station was a big, dark glass box, sitting on a table on the side of the room. Calvin and Astra walked to it. The front of it was dominated by a large door that opened downward. There was a large computer monitor sitting on the table next to it that had an onscreen menu system, with pictures of what was available. He was very lucky that there were pictures, so he knew what he was getting. Even though he could read the screen, he didn't know exactly what fried gooble was. It looked like fried chicken, so he ordered it. It only took a second, a small door opened, and the smell of food filled the air. It even smelled like fried chicken. He reached in and pulled out a tray and went back to the table and sat. Astra selected something for herself and joined him.

Neither of them realized how hungry they were until they were sitting down and smelled the food.

They ate in silence for several minutes. When they slowed down, Calvin took a drink and sat back.

"So what was it like growing up on Aleria?"

"Aleria?" Astra said. "Oh, I didn't grow up on Aleria. It was destroyed a long time ago. We've been living in spaceships mostly, moving from planet to planet. Typically we would get a month, maybe two at each place. If we were really lucky, we would get to live on a planet for a year. That only happened twice. But it always ended the same way. The Goremog would find us, and we would have to leave, quickly."

"Wow, that's really sad," Calvin said.

"What about you?" Astra asked. "Where did you grow up?"

"New Arlandia. It was our last surviving colony after the war. It's a beautiful place."

"And the Goremog have never found you?"

"No. Our scientists developed an amazing piece of technology that could hide our planet from all passing ships. Nobody could see us. We're very good at hiding."

"Wow. That sounds nice and sad at the same time."

"I know," Calvin said. "We're afraid of everything. It's sad. If the Goremog ever find us, we won't be able to defend ourselves. We destroyed our military a long time ago. My people believe that if we leave the universe alone, it will leave us alone."

"I can definitely see the appeal of that philosophy. We have been fighting and running so long, we don't know anything else. It would be nice to hide, and not worry about being found."

"But we do worry about being found. We live in fear. Fear that what happened in the past will happen again."

"I hope you don't mind, but I'm really tired. I'm going back to my room and get some sleep." She took one last sip of her drink, and she pushed back from the table.

"Ok. Goodnight," Calvin said.

"Goodnight, Calvin. By the way, thank you for helping us."

Calvin watched as Astra put her dirty dishes back into the food processor. She smiled at him and walked out of the room. Calvin did the same to his tray and walked back to the bridge.

He was tired, but he wanted to do one more thing before he went to bed. He sat in the pilot's chair and turned on the communication system. He tried the usual: New Arlandia planetary control, the command post, and his father's office. The only thing he got was static. He didn't know what else to try. He was about to shut it all down, when suddenly the screen flickered and came to life. His dad's face filled the screen. Calvin's eyes got big, and his mouth dropped open.

"Dad!" he cried. "Can you see me?"

"Calvin! Yes, and I can hear you! You're alive. I knew it was you. I knew it was you." Tears were streaming down his father's face.

"Dad, where are you?"

"That's not fair, Son," Foster said. "You're the one who is lost. Besides, you contacted me."

"Dad!" Calvin said loudly. He had so much to tell his father, and now he finally had his chance. He took a deep breath and tried to calm down. "You aren't going to believe where I've been, and what I've seen, and who I've met!" His father listened intently while Calvin told his dad everything. When he was done, his father just stared in amazement.

"That's incredible, Son. Wow, I had no idea we built a weapon with the Alerians. I'm going to check the old archives to see if I can find any

106

information. I'll let you know if I find anything."

"I've been trying to reach you for days. Is everything all right at home?"

"When you contacted me the first time, I only saw you for a second, and I barely heard your voice. But I knew it was you. When the council found out that an unidentified signal was transmitted to our planet, they ordered a complete shutdown of all communications. There was chaos for two days. The planet went into panic. Everyone was told to go home and stay there. I thought that was bad, but then the planet went dark. Everything was turned off, even the power grid. The government declared martial law. It was terrible. The senate convened an emergency session to figure out what to do. I think they knew I would suggest that we investigate the signal, find out who was trying to contact us. They placed me under house arrest. It made me so angry. I wasn't allowed to contact you. So after everything settled down and things returned to normal, and the politicians were finished terrifying the people, I left New Arlandia, and I went to our secret base in the asteroid field on the edge of our solar system. Son, this is very important; what I'm about to tell you, you can never repeat to anyone, ever. Do you understand?"

"Yes, Dad, I understand."

"Good, I'm letting you in on the secret, because at this point in your life, you obviously need to know. The council does not know about our base. It is known only to a select group of individuals, a small secret group called the Laurites. As of now you are a part of our group. We built the base after the end of the war. The council commanded that all of our space battle fleet be destroyed. Instead of obeying, we brought it here and hid it in the asteroid field. Also, for the last eighty-three years we have been secretly developing new technologies to help us if and when war ever found us again."

"Wow," Calvin whispered. "Good for us. Do you know what the super-weapon is? What does it do?"

"I don't know," Foster said sadly. "And unfortunately, anyone on Arlandia who might have known is dead now."

"What do you want me to do? Do you want me to go after all of the pieces of the weapon, or come home?"

"If what you tell me is true, war is coming. This might be our only chance of surviving. You said you are two days away from the next piece?"

"Yes, Sir."

"Then go get it. I have to return to Arlandia before somebody notices I'm not there. I'm sending you protocols to bypass the security of the Laurite base, so you'll be able to enter the base when you need to. Contact us when you get the second piece, and keep us updated. I will tell the Laurites what you're doing, and that you are now a part of our group."

"Ok. This is a lot of information to digest all at once."

"I know it is. I'm really sorry to hear about Jax. I know he was your best friend. How are you holding up?"

"It's been really hard. I just can't believe he's gone. Would you tell his parents for me?"

"I don't think that would be a good idea right now," Foster said carefully. "We still haven't found the crew of the *Sorenia* yet. If the council was to find out what's going on out there, the panic here would be catastrophic, to say the least."

"That bad?"

"Son, I've never seen this place fall apart so fast. It scared me."

Calvin looked down, and he rubbed his hand through his hair.

"Don't worry about what's happening here," Foster said. "I need you to focus on what you're doing. Be careful out there, Son. I love you. I'll tell your mother that you're safe."

"Thank you, Dad. Tell her I love her."

"I will. I'll talk to you again in a few days."

"I love you, Dad." The screen went dark.

Calvin stood up and took a deep breath. Finally, his parents knew he was alive. He was happy, but now he had so much to think about. He was very tired, but he wondered if he was going to be able to sleep. As he left the bridge, he passed Ion, who had been waiting outside the door.

"Goodnight, Sir," Ion said.

"Goodnight."

Calvin walked back to his room. He put on his pajamas and got into bed. He wanted to sleep, but he was unable to. There were too many thoughts flying around in his head. He lay on his back and stared at the ceiling, trying to process all of his thoughts. Everything he knew about his planet's history had just changed. He had just learned about a secret organization, which he was now a part of. How long had his father been part of it? Everyone knew that the great space fleet was destroyed after the survivors arrived at New Arlandia. They taught it in school. It was a lie? He just found out it was hidden inside an asteroid. What other historical facts were altered? Why were they lied to? Why change history? What were they trying to hide? Could he believe anything that he had learned in school? Maybe the Laurites had the answers. They must be the keepers of the real history of Arlandia. He would ask his dad the next time they talked.

For Calvin, the biggest life-changing news was that his dad wanted him to continue the mission to find all of the pieces of the super-weapon. Calvin wasn't sure how he felt about that. He expected his dad to tell him to come home, that he was worried about him. "The universe is a big scary place, Son. You're not safe out there. Get home as quickly as you can!"

Calvin was shocked. Either his dad wasn't concerned and didn't miss him, or he trusted his son enough to let him handle the biggest mission conceivable. He knew the first one wasn't true. His dad loved him and cared deeply for him. That obviously meant that he trusted him. Calvin had one piece of the weapon and was going after the second, but what was the weapon, and what was it supposed to do? What kind of super-weapon were the Goremog assembling? What would it do? Too many questions. His head was a storm of thoughts and emotions.

Calvin listened to the hum of the ship, and he fell into a light, uncomfortable sleep.

CHAPTER TWELVE

TRAINING

Calvin woke up late the next morning. There was no reason to get up early, so he hadn't set an alarm. He opened his eyes and stared at the ceiling. He felt better, but his worries about home and the mission were still dominating his thoughts. They were only two days away from the second segment, which was on an ice planet. Calvin wondered what was waiting for them. The planet was out in the middle of nowhere, light years from the nearest star. They were too far away to get accurate sensor readings, but from what they could tell it was a big ball of ice floating in space, and not much of a planet.

He took his time getting showered and dressed. Clearly this ship was designed to take care of royalty. Not one single function was without luxury. It took care of all of a person's needs, leaving him or her free to worry about other things. This is how it worked: Each morning Calvin stood in front of his closet door, where a computer would scan him. Once the computer recorded his measurements, he was presented with a program that would allow him to select what he wanted to wear that day. The computer would then make it for him, and it was ready to go. It worked just like the food machine in the dining room, but with clothes instead of food.

Today he decided on a red long-sleeved shirt, with a black pair of pants. Clothes had never fit so well. Even the shoes were a perfect fit. He picked a pair of black shoes that might have been the most comfortable he had ever worn.

After he dressed he walked down to the dining room for breakfast. He ordered eggs and bacon with toast. The computer flashed multicolored lights on the keypad, and the door slid open after five seconds. A wonderfully intoxicating smell caressed his senses.

"This place is great!" Calvin thought, and he sat down to eat. Just then, the door opened, and Astra walked in. Calvin was happy to see she was smiling. There was something else too, in the way she was carrying herself. Her shoulders seemed a little higher, her head a little taller. She got some food and sat across from Calvin.

"Good morning," she said.

"Good morning," Calvin said, looking into her soft brown eyes. "How did you sleep?"

"I slept great," Astra said.

"I did too. I finally made contact with my father last night."

"Oh, Calvin, that's great," Astra exclaimed. Calvin told her about the conversation he had with his father.

"I'm very happy for you, Calvin. I know it's been on your mind a lot lately. At least now they know you're OK."

After days of depression, the dark cloud was gone, and they both felt better.

"So two days till we get to the ice planet?" Calvin said, not knowing what else to call it.

"No," Astra answered. "We'll get there tomorrow night."

"What do you want to do today?"

"I'm going to go down to the lab and study the first segment."

"OK," Calvin said, trying to hide his disappointment. He didn't want to be alone today. "Do you like science? Are you good at it?"

"Oh yes, I love it," she said smiling. "I practically grew up in a lab, taking things apart and putting them back together. It's fun. Plus, the only thing that kept my people alive was the few engineers and scientists who kept our ships flying, discovering and improving our technology that gave us an advantage."

"Oh, I see," Calvin said. "So what does the super-weapon do?"

"It's a high-powered pulse generator," Astra said. "The idea is, once we have all the pieces, we take it to the center of the universe and fire it. It sends a massive pulse across space, literally to every corner of the galaxy, and it destroys all electronics, computers, but most importantly, robots."

"Wait a second, what about planets that don't have anything to do with the Goremog, like New Arlandia? Won't they be destroyed too?"

"Our scientists have done research on that, and they found that Goremog technology has a unique signature. They said they can program the pulse so that it targets only that signature."

"That would be great, if it works like that. Seems like a pretty big risk. How can you be sure all the pieces work after all these years?"

"I'm not really sure," she admitted. "It's old, and the scientists who designed and built it are dead. I have their notes, but they didn't leave behind a manual. The hard part is going to be identifying the pieces, and figuring out how to put it all together. The programming is a whole other story."

"So there's a chance, right?" Calvin asked. "That we find all the pieces, it'll work and not destroy my home planet?"

"Yes, of course," Astra said resolutely. "This ship is small, but it has the most advanced laboratory equipment in the universe. I'm going to analyze the first piece, find out what it is and if it works. Don't worry." She must have sensed that Calvin was worried about it. She seemed to know exactly what to say to him.

"OK, I'll leave it to you then."

"What are you going to do?"

"I want to do some more flight training—how to use the weapons, navigate, and fix basic problems. Ion's been teaching me."

"Ok, that's a really good idea. There's a flight simulator on deck three that you should check out. It starts with the basics and goes all the way up to advanced combat situations. No offense," she said smiling. "But you could use a little more practice. That flight off of Arlandia was a bit rough."

"Thank you," he said dryly. "I'll check it out. Let me know when you want to take a break for lunch. I'll meet you here."

"Ok."

Before going to the simulator, Calvin went to the bridge. He wanted to look at the long-range sensors to make sure they weren't being followed. When he got there he found Ion sitting at the computer station. He was just sitting there, staring into a monitor.

"Hi," Calvin said cheerfully. Ion didn't answer. Calvin looked closely at Ion and noticed a small cable running from the computer directly into the robot's chest. Clearly, Ion was very busy. Satisfied the sensors were clear, Calvin went down to check out the space flight simulator.

The lights turned on automatically as he walked through the doorway. There were two white bullet-shaped pods with black glass canopies in the middle of the room. They each were sitting on hydraulic legs. In the back of the room was a computer station.

Calvin walked to the computer and turned it on. It was extremely user-friendly. It asked for his name and took him through the steps of setting up a profile. A menu screen showed him what training was available and suggested he start with the first lesson.

"I don't have anything else to do," he thought. When he selected the first training mission, the canopy on the first pod opened with a soft hum. A message on the computer screen read, "Please enter Pod One." The interior of the pod looked almost like the inside of an Arlandian space fighter, but instead of dozens of analog computers with dials and switches there was one solid piece of glass, and the chair looked a little more comfortable. The layout looked just like the standard configuration that he had seen in every Alerian spaceship. He appreciated that philosophy—learn on one, able to operate all.

Calvin climbed into the pod and sat down. The central monitor in front of him provided step-by step-instructions. He put on his shoulder seatbelt, and the pod's canopy closed. As soon as it was sealed, all outside sound was completely shut out, and it was dark.

Then suddenly all of the screens around him lit up. He also noticed that the canopy around him, which would have been windows to the outside world in a real spaceship, was actually a series of computer monitors, which displayed stars in all directions. The details on the ultra-definition screens were so clear that it looked real.

"Too perfect!"

The computer began with a simple navigation exercise: fly from point A to point B. Along the way it provided a detailed explanation of the basic ship controls and screen readouts.

The lesson lasted twenty minutes. When it was over, the computer asked if he wanted to begin the next one. Calvin kept going.

The next lesson involved navigating to four different locations, and more in-depth explanation of ship functions. In the third lesson the difficulty increased. He had to navigate through an asteroid field.

During his first run through the asteroid field he thought he was doing well, until a small rock smashed into the side of his ship, disabling him. Unable to control the ship, he floated into a large asteroid and was destroyed. He did much better the second time through, receiving only a small amount of damage after he shot an asteroid that was in his path, and he flew through the debris. He also learned to have a healthy respect for asteroids.

Calvin looked at the clock, and he was surprised to see he had spent four hours in the simulator. It was time for lunch. He turned off the computer, and the canopy opened. His legs felt stiff for a few minutes, but he figured the walk back up to the dining room would stretch them out. He found an intership communications system on the main computer panel.

"Astra, can you hear me?" Calvin's voice echoed through the ship. There was a brief pause, and Astra's voice echoed back.

"Yes, what's up?"

"Are you hungry?" Another pause.

"Sure, I can take a break. I'll meet you in the dining room."

"OK, see you there."

Calvin got there first. He got a plate of food and sat at a table near the food dispenser. Astra arrived only a few minutes later.

"How's it going?" Calvin asked.

"Slow," Astra said, putting in her food order. She took her food out of the machine and sat across from Calvin. She had a bowl of salad and a glass of juice.

"No matter what I do, it defies analysis," Astra said. "First I had the computer scan it, which took over an hour. It couldn't figure out what it is. I'm not even sure it was able to scan the inside. I've been studying it all morning, and about the only thing I know is that it has a massive amount of power in it. It seems dormant, but the energy signature is massive. You know, if I didn't know better I would say that it is fighting me, trying to keep me from knowing what it is."

Calvin wanted to laugh, but her expression said that she wasn't joking.

"What are you going to do?" he asked.

"I don't know. Normally I would take it apart, at least take off the cover. I think I found a hatch on it, but I'm afraid to open it. There is too much power inside it. I need to understand it better before I do that. For now, I'm going to do a search in the database to see if there is anything that compares to this. That's going to take a while. How is your training going?"

"Good. It was boring at first, just flying around. But I had to fly through an asteroid field on the last one. That was a little more exciting."

"Oh, neat," Astra said. "How did you do?"

"The first time...you don't want to know."

Astra smiled. "That's funny. You died, didn't you." It was a statement, not a question.

"Yes," Calvin said sheepishly. "But it wasn't because of my piloting. Well, maybe it was. I didn't use the perimeter sensors or point laser defense. I didn't think I needed them. It seemed like cheating."

"Well, they help, don't they?"

"Yes, they do," Calvin admitted. "I hope I never have to go through an asteroid field without them."

"And you could also try to not run into the rocks." Astra smiled at him playfully.

"I'll try to keep that in mind," he said.

"Just wait until you get to the minefield exercise. That's even more fun."

"Minefield?" he asked. "Really? That sounds cool."

"Cool? Just wait, they don't just crash into you; they explode."

When Calvin and Astra were done eating, they both left the dining room, anxious to get back to what they were doing. Calvin trained in the simulator the rest of the afternoon. He flew the asteroid-field mission again just to make sure he was comfortable with it before moving on. Astra went back to work on the first segment, trying to unlock its secrets.

Later, after dinner with Astra, Calvin went up to his room to relax. It took only ten minutes to realize that he didn't want to relax. He couldn't stop thinking about the simulator. Plus there wasn't anything to do in his room, so he went back down and climbed inside the simulator.

The canopy closed, and the simulator turned on. "I'm addicted to this," Calvin thought.

He was getting very comfortable with the controls, and already he had a standard pattern for turning everything on. Turn on engines and shields, charge weapons to minimum levels so they would be ready faster. He had everything just where he wanted it. The next mission was going to be too easy, another simple navigation exercise. He was supposed to fly to a space station and land—piece of cake.

He loved the simulator; it was very realistic. It was just like flying in a real space fighter. He was lost in thought when suddenly the communications system came to life.

"*Fighter X Two, Fighter X Two*, this is heavy freighter *Blue Tundra*. We are under attack by several unknown ships. We need immediate assistance. We are carrying emergency supplies to the colony on Cordon Four. Please help us! I don't know how long we can hold out."

"This is *Fighter X Two*," Calvin announced. "I'm on my way. Coming in hot!" Calvin pushed the throttle full forward. The hydraulic system built into the simulator made it feel like his speed was increasing, as he was pushed gently into the back of his seat.

He checked the navigation computer. Time to interception was two minutes and ten seconds. He used that time to make sure his ship was ready. He channeled some extra power into his shields and weapons. A small holographic image of his ship floated near the edge of his vision. No matter where he looked, it stayed there. It showed the status of all his ship's systems. A solid blue bubble surrounded the ship, indicating the shields were at full strength.

So much for the simple navigation exercise. He had no idea what was waiting for him. Were those ships more powerful than him, more maneuverable? Calvin didn't know, but he wanted to make sure he was ready for anything. He looked at his scanner. There were seven small red dots, surrounding a big blue dot. He could see them off in the distance, getting larger. Explosions burst around the big freighter. Much closer now, he could see the smaller ships swarming it. They were fighters! The big ship turned and tried to get away. But it was too slow, and the smaller ships continued to pound on it.

Then suddenly four of the fighters broke away from the freighter and headed directly toward Calvin.

"OK, here we go. They know I'm here," Calvin said. He adjusted his course and headed straight toward them. A group of laser shots flew past him, missing him by a large margin. A second later, laser hits splashed against his shields. Calvin fired a few shots back, but the computer reported that they were out of range. Calvin suddenly felt

118

vulnerable and outgunned. The laser fire intensified. The blue circle around the ship had changed to yellow. The shields were failing.

Calvin watched the range display anxiously. Something in the back of his mind was telling him he was making a huge mistake, flying directly toward the enemy fighters and absorbing all of their laser fire.

That's when the ship shook violently. His forward shields were gone! The shield display showed a large gap on the front of the ship. Calvin jerked the controls hard to the right, to get the exposed section of his shields away from the enemy's reach. If just one shot got through the hole it would hit his ship and cause serious damage.

But he didn't move fast enough. The screen went dark, and the canopy opened. He had died, again. Calvin sat in the chair and stared at the black screen for five minutes. He was feeling very tired now. He got up out of the simulator and walked back up to his room. As tired as he was, he had a hard time falling asleep. He replayed the last mission over and over in his mind. What happened? It was a good thing that wasn't real, or he would be dead. He had messed up, badly. He'd waltzed into the battle thinking that he was the most powerful thing flying around. The computer taught him otherwise. He was going to have to adjust his thinking and his strategy.

CHAPTER THIRTEEN

THE ICE PLANET

The next morning he awoke, and he did his usual routine of getting ready. He walked down to the dining room and had a small breakfast of cold cereal, an orange, and a cup of coffee. He was almost finished eating when Astra entered the room.

"Are you all right?" she asked with genuine concern. "What's wrong?"

He looked up at her, and he replied sadly, "I died again."

"Oh," she said, a little surprised. "What happened?" She walked over to the food processor while he told his story. By the time he finished, she had her food and was sitting across from him.

"OK," she said, looking sympathetically into his sad face. "I know exactly which mission you are talking about. You can't take it personally. It's not a reflection of your skill. Well, actually it is. It's the introduction to combat training. See, they designed that mission so that it would be impossible to beat. In fact, when you go back into the simulator it will explain it to you, and it won't let you try again. I know the people who wrote the software and the scenarios. They told me, after I took it, that they wanted the mission to scare me. They wanted me to realize upfront that space combat isn't fun, it's not easy, and that you will not always have a technological advantage. We, as Alerians, were always used to having the advantage, technologically speaking. It had a tendency to make pilots overconfident. Pilots die quickly with that attitude. So don't feel bad. You were supposed to die."

He looked at her skeptically.

"OK," he answered, not entirely convinced. "I was upset about it last night, and I had a hard time sleeping."

"I'm sure you were," Astra said. "Under normal circumstances you would have had an instructor to explain it to you, but you didn't."

"All right, I'll try not to let it bother me," he said, visibly relieved. "I feel better."

After they finished eating, they each went off and did their own thing again. Calvin went back to the simulator. The next group of missions went through the basics of space combat. He started with unarmed drones and learned how to use lasers and missiles, and how to maximize his shields. He learned that there was a way to rebalance them after they were damaged. Later in the afternoon he was fighting one on one with armed ships that shot back. The last mission he completed that day had him take on two opponents at once.

The next morning, Calvin and Astra were sitting in the dining room having breakfast.

"Have you made any progress?" Calvin asked, hoping for some good news.

"No, not really," Astra said. "The only thing I'm relatively sure of is that this piece is some sort of power generator. And not just a regular power generator, it should produce an insane amount of power."

"How much power?"

"OK, you probably won't believe this," she said. "But I checked it several times. This thing, if I'm right, can produce enough energy to power an entire planet."

"Wow," Calvin said. "That's incredible. Really?"

"Yes," she said. Then she briefly looked back at the door, as if she were fighting the urge to get up and go down to the science lab right that second. "You know, if we plugged it into the ship, we would never have

121

to worry about power." Then her eyes got bigger. "Oh, and our shields would be stronger, a lot stronger! I would just have to figure out how to plug it into the ship. I'm really excited about finding the next segment. So how is your training going?"

"Really well," Calvin said. "The simulator is great. I've learned a lot. I feel a lot more comfortable in the pilot's chair now."

"That's good," Astra said. "I'm really glad you know how to pilot the ship."

"Thanks. I hope I get more practice in a real ship."

"Oh, I'm sure you'll get that chance."

"Good."

Later that night, Calvin and Astra met on the bridge. Ion was already there, at his usual place at the main computer. They got there just in time to hear the alarm announce they'd arrived at their destination. Calvin yanked the hyperdrive lever, and the blue hyperspace cloud disappeared in an explosion of color. Way off in the distance was a small, white planet.

"There it is!" Astra said excitedly.

"Do you want to take us in, or should I?" Calvin asked.

"Go ahead, you can do it. You need the practice." Astra smiled at him.

"Thanks." Calvin smiled back. He pushed the throttle forward and put the ice planet in the middle of the front window.

"Warming up the sensors," Astra said. "It's not very big. I don't even know if we should call it a planet."

After a few moments, Astra said, "Scanning." It didn't take very long. "OK, here's what we have. The temperature on the surface is minus three hundred degrees. The average wind speed is eighty miles per hour. The ice is mostly composed of frozen methane. The air is definitely not breathable."

"We'll have to suit up again, obviously." Calvin said.

"I don't see the second segment," Astra said. "The sensors can't locate it, but that could be because we're still too far away."

"How about radiation?"

Astra examined the computer screen. "There is no radiation. We shouldn't have too much trouble finding it once we get closer."

The planet slowly grew larger in the window. Calvin was amazed and ecstatic that he was getting to see another planet. Calvin could feel the excitement in the air. Astra was clearly feeling it too. She had a big smile on her face as she studied her computer screen.

Soon they were flying over the planet.

"I'll put us in a nice high orbit, to make scanning the planet easier."

"Good idea," Astra agreed.

Calvin looked down at the planet below. It was beautiful—mostly white, but it had a tinge of blue on it. The search didn't take very long.

"There it is!" Astra exclaimed. "I found it. Oh, this is interesting. The vault is located beneath the surface—two miles under the ice."

"What are we going to do?" Calvin asked.

"I don't know," Astra admitted.

"What do you think?" Calvin asked, turning to Ion. "Can we drill through the ice? Do we have the equipment to do that?"

"We have a drill on board," Ion said. "But I have a suggestion. Let me go down to the surface alone. The atmosphere won't affect me. You can remain here safely until I'm finished."

Calvin and Astra looked at each other.

"Is that safe for you?" Calvin asked. "It's extremely cold down there. Can you survive in that?"

"Yes, I'm equipped with internal heaters that will keep me warm. I can also survive in the vacuum of space."

"Oh, OK," Calvin said. "You'll probably do it faster than us."

"Yes, I won't require rest." Ion stood. "I'll go and prepare the equipment."

"Please keep us updated."

"Yes, Sir." Ion left the bridge.

They sat in silence for a moment, studying the planet below them.

"Anything on the long-range sensors?" Calvin asked. "See anything out there?"

Astra checked. "I don't see anything. No ships within five light years."

"Good. I would hate to be surprised by someone showing up unexpectedly."

"Yeah, good point. Considering the cloak is still broken."

"I thought Ion was supposed to fix it," Calvin said.

"There was more damage than we thought," Astra said. "Ion has one of the other robots fabricating new parts. I asked him how long the repairs were going to take. He didn't want to give me an estimate."

"This is terrible. I hope he can fix it soon. I feel naked without it."

"Me too," Astra said sadly. "If he can't, we'll just have to be careful."

"Yeah, and keep a close eye on the long-range sensors."

"I have an idea," Astra said. "We could set up an alarm. Anytime the sensors detect a ship, we go to red alert."

"I like that idea."

"Other than the cloak, all the other systems look good, operating in the green."

"That's good," Calvin said. "I'm going down to see if Ion needs help."

"Ok, hurry back." Astra smiled at him. "I'm going to set up the enemy-ship alarm. We can name it something better later," she added when he gave her a funny look.

Calvin left the bridge, unable to suppress his smile. He found Ion in the shuttle bay, loading a large drill into the back of the shuttle.

"Need some help?" Calvin offered.

"Thank you Master Calvin, I'm finished," Ion said. "I'm ready to go down to the surface and get to work."

"Do you have communications?"

"Yes, my communications are built in."

"Ok. We'll watch you on the sensors."

"Thank you, Sir."

Calvin headed back to the bridge.

"How is he?" Astra asked as Calvin was taking his seat.

"He's fine. The shuttle is loaded, and he's ready to launch."

Astra turned on the main monitor so they could watch Ion's progress. The bay doors opened.

"Did you pass all of the simulator levels?" Calvin asked, breaking the silence.

"Yes," Astra answered. "One of my father's rules is that everyone has to learn how to fly and navigate. Since most of our population is gone, we rely on our robots to do everything for us. My father wants us to be able to take care of ourselves, not become dependent on robots. So we all have to learn in the simulator."

"Shuttle one, requesting clearance for takeoff," Ion said.

"Permission granted, shuttle one."

Ion was a perfect model of machine efficiency. The shuttle rose in the air and floated out the door in one fluid motion.

Astra kept the monitor centered on the shuttle. They watched as the shuttle flew down toward the planet. There were little noticeable effects as the shuttle entered the atmosphere.

"I've been having fun with the different scenarios," Calvin said. "They were hard at first, because I wasn't used to the controls."

"It's a lot of information all at once, isn't it?"

125

"Yes," Calvin said. "It's funny, because it was information overload, and a little boring at the same time."

The shuttle descended toward the surface, which looked like a big, blank white emptiness. Ion immediately flew large circles above the area that contained the vault.

"It gets better," Astra said. "The early missions are boring, but the later missions will have so much going on in them, you will long for the early days again."

After completing a few circles, Ion selected a landing site three miles away. Astra had to adjust the camera's view and zoom in to keep the shuttle in the middle of the screen. The video detail was amazingly clear.

As if reading his mind, or perhaps the expression on his face, Astra said, "I think you should keep going—try to finish."

"You do?"

"Yes. The training will turn you into a very good pilot, and I have a feeling the skills you pick up from it will be highly needed on this mission."

A large cloud of snow swirled up in the air around the shuttle as it gently set down on the ice. Astra turned on another monitor. This one showed a view of Ion inside the shuttle. "I've landed," Ion reported. "And calculated the optimal location for drilling. I will start as soon as I get the drill set up."

Calvin hit the communicator and said, "We'll keep this channel open. Please be careful."

"Thank you, Sir, I will."

Ion went to the cargo hold in the back of the shuttle and unpacked the drill. Calvin was amazed at how fast he put it together. Ion opened the rear cargo door and moved the drill outside. Astra changed the view to outside the shuttle. Now they would have to rely on a camera on the *Frost*. Ion was small on the screen, but they could clearly see what he was doing.

126

First he walked around the machine, inspecting it from top to bottom. Then he turned it on, and he stepped back. A large cloud of white powder exploded into the air. It was hard to see from their angle, but they could clearly see the drill sink into the ground. Tiny pieces of ice shot through the air. Ion got behind the drill, and he guided it down into the ground. Within a few minutes he was moving.

"Oh, look what he's doing," Astra said. She manipulated the camera and zoomed in a little more. Calvin was shocked at how clear the picture was.

"He's making it easy for us to get down to the lab, drilling at an angle and then making a flat spot." A thought occurred to her. "We'll still want ropes, though, I would think."

"Yeah, if we start sliding, we won't be able to stop."

"We're going to want to be able to stop," Astra said. "It could be a long slide." They continued to watch, fascinated. Ion continued to work, drilling deeper and deeper until he reached the front doors of the vault. It was remarkable; he never stopped.

When Ion reached the bottom, he contacted the *Frost*. There was a lot of static.
"Master Calvin, Mistress Astra, I have reached the bottom. I'm on my way back up."

"Good job, Ion. We'll meet you in the shuttle bay."

"Are you ready to go for a walk on an ice planet?" Astra asked.

"I'm ready," Calvin said. All the way down to the shuttle bay, Calvin felt the excitement surging through him. He was very excited. He'd been thinking about it for days, and now it was finally time.

When they walked into the shuttle bay, they found that most of the equipment they needed for the mission was already stacked in small cases. Astra was going to inventory the gear, but knowing Ion had set it out she trusted that it was all there. While they waited for Ion to return, Astra showed Calvin how to inspect his spacesuit. When they were done with the suits, they put them on the ship.

127

"Just out of curiosity," Calvin said. "Are these suits going to keep us warm down there?"

"They should," Astra answered. "But just in case, I added extra heating units to them. I trust the suits, but since it's going to be minus three hundred degrees down there I want to be safe instead of sorry."

"Good. I feel better."

They didn't have to wait long for Ion. The shuttle returned and landed gently in the middle of the shuttle bay. When he got out of the shuttle, he walked to Calvin and said, "Everything is ready, Sir. I placed a beacon on the ground near the tunnel entrance. It will guide you down."

"Good, thank you."

"I had to leave the drill at the bottom of the shaft," Ion said. "Unfortunately it used much more power than I anticipated. The power cell was depleted. I will give you a new one for you to take down with you. But there is something else I would like you to take with you."

Ion held out his hand. In it were two small silver objects, each about the size of an ink pen. Calvin and Astra both took one. Calvin examined his. "What is it?" he asked.

"It has a small tracker in it, just in case something happens. It will help me find you if the sensors can't. It does some other things that you might find useful."

"Then you are planning on staying on the *Frost*, right?" Calvin asked.

"Yes. I will stay and monitor you from the bridge."

Astra looked at him with a question on her face.

"Someone has to stay up here, just in case. We'll be OK."

"OK," Astra said, with hesitation in her voice. "I don't really feel comfortable going without him."

"We need more robots," Calvin said.

"I know. We should have brought more with us, but everything

128

happened so fast. We were lucky to get the ones that we did."

"Do you want to take the one in the engine room, just in case?"

Astra thought it over. "Alpha Nine is performing critical maintenance on the hyper-drive engines. We can't use them until he finishes."

"Then we don't have a choice," Calvin said. "I don't think it will be a problem. We'll just run down there, pick it up, and come right back. Do you have the antigravity jacks?"

"Yes, they're on board."

"Do we have a way to heat the door handles?"

She looked at him with that questioning look again.

"If the doors down there are like the last ones, they will be coded to our DNA. We'll have to put our bare hands on the door, and the door will be very cold."

"Oh, I hadn't thought of that. Good thinking. I have something in my lab that will work for that."

Astra ran back up to the lab while Calvin packed up some things in the shuttle. She was slightly out of breath when she got back to the hangar bay. After Ion gave Calvin the spare power core for the drill, he went up to the bridge.

"I'm ready," she said. "You're right. I'm sure everything will be OK."

They boarded the shuttle when everything was loaded. There were two doors to the shuttle. One was a small personnel door near the front, and the other was a wide cargo door in the back. Calvin and Astra boarded the shuttle, and they sat in the pilot's chairs. The cargo door closed with a loud hum. There was a hiss of air as the cabin pressurized and oxygen flowed.

"Do you want to fly?" Calvin asked.

Astra looked at him. She could see it on his face that he really wanted to fly.

"No, you can take the controls," she said, smiling.

"Thanks!" he said, smiling uncontrollably.

Calvin started the engines and went through the preflight check, which included making sure all of the systems were on and that their status was green. They were. Calvin remotely opened the shuttle bay doors, and he put his hand on the flight controls. He gently lifted the shuttle into the air a few feet, and he pushed the throttle forward, moving them through the force field and out into space.

No matter how many times he experienced it, flying out into space always took his breath away and made his heart beat faster. Space opened out in front of them. The ice planet was below them. It was a beautiful sight. The planet was all white, with a tinge of blue. It looked very empty and blank. There were no identifiable marks on the surface at all.

"I'm picking up the beacon," Astra said.

"OK, I see it. Wow, the computer already loaded into the nav system. The autopilot is asking if I want to let it take us down to it."

"You don't have to let the autopilot take over," Astra said. "Just ignore it."

"Good," Calvin said. He was very happy to ignore the autopilot and fly the shuttle himself.

The shuttle descended into the atmosphere of the planet. There were a few small bumps, but because the atmosphere was so thin, it was nothing big. Calvin didn't use the autopilot, but he did follow the course that the computer recommended. It was always tricky entering the atmosphere of a planet. If you went in too steep you would hit the atmosphere too hard. If you did that you could damage and even destroy your ship.

Once they were in the atmosphere, Calvin took them down to the site. All of the ship's statuses were on the glass window in front of him, including his course and speed. There was a small triangle, which told him where he needed to go. He simply followed it down to the ground. Calvin felt more comfortable sitting in the pilot's chair, more confident.

130

The controls felt more familiar now.

Calvin stopped the shuttle a few feet above the ground, and he hovered in preparation for landing. Then he cut engine power. Unfortunately he wasn't as close to the ground as he thought he was. The shuttle hit the ground with a hard bump. He looked over at Astra, and he was grateful that she didn't say anything. Calvin looked up and took a deep breath. The entrance to the tunnel was visible directly in front of them.

It took them ten minutes to put on their suits. After they were dressed they checked each other to make sure everything was hooked up correctly, paying special attention to the heaters and oxygen. Calvin grabbed a pack and put it on Astra's back. She did the same for him. Calvin walked to the backdoor and opened it. A purple force field covered the backdoor before it started opening. The door opened from the top to the bottom, laying down flat on the ground, providing a ramp for them to walk down.

The suits were bulky and forced them to walk slowly down the ramp and onto the ice. Once they were out, Astra closed the door using a set of controls on the arm of her suit. The two of them turned and faced each other. Calvin pulled a plastic wire out of a special pocket of his suit and connected it to Astra's suit. Then he pulled out a little extra to give them some slack. If she slipped and fell he wanted to be able to stop her from sliding down out of control. They turned and walked across the ice toward the tunnel entrance. There was a thin layer of powder on the top of the ice that looked almost like snow, which crunched loudly with each step. They could see Ion's footprints and slide tracks from the drill on the ground.

Calvin looked up into the sky. He wasn't used to the suit, and when he leaned back the helmet was so heavy he almost lost his balance. The sun was shining in the sky, but it was very small. The light wasn't very bright. The area around them was dimly lit. Their suits' sensors detected the low light level and automatically turned on the lights that were in their helmets. The area immediately around them was lit up well enough to see. The suits were amazing, Calvin thought. They also detected how

131

slippery the ground was, and small metal spikes protruded from the bottoms of their boots.

The white flat horizon that surrounded them was remarkable to Calvin. He had never seen anything like this place before. There was nothing to break the flatness that stretched off into what seemed like eternity. It was vast and empty.

Calvin led the way, with Astra close behind him. They approached the tunnel, which was basically a hole cut in the surface of the planet, right into the ice. They descended down a gentle slope. The hole was mostly round, with rough edges all around. It was very nice because it gave them a little something to hold on to if they needed it. Their gloves had rough edges on the fingers that gripped the ice very well.

The tunnel ceiling was only inches above Calvin's head. For some strange reason he couldn't explain, the small space made Calvin feel more secure.

The first descending slope was gentle and about forty feet long. At the bottom of that, the tunnel leveled out for about ten feet. The tunnel kept following that same sequence. It went down forty feet and then leveled for ten feet. It did that ten times. At the bottom of the tenth, the tunnel turned ninety degrees and began again. After the second ninety-degree turn, Calvin and Astra stopped for a rest. They had been walking for nearly two hours.

"Don't sit down," Astra warned, seeing that Calvin looked like he was starting to sit. "You don't want to risk tearing your suit."

"Thanks," Calvin said. "You're right."

Calvin suddenly realized he was very thirsty. There was a small rubber drinking tube, next to his mouth inside the helmet. Calvin grabbed it with his mouth and took a nice long drink of water.

"How are you doing?" Astra asked him.

"I'm doing really well," he said. "The suit is working great. It's keeping me warm. By the way, how much oxygen do we have in here?"

"Oh, these suits have enough air for several days. I wouldn't worry about that," she said casually. "And the battery will last forever. We're constantly recharging our batteries as we walk."

"That's nice," Calvin said. He looked around, down the way they were going toward the vault and back the way they had come. "You know, I'm not usually affected by tight, confined spaces, but this could be the exception. I wasn't feeling it at first, but it's starting to get to me."

"I know what you mean. I'm starting to feel it too." Astra looked down at the computer on her wrist.

"Ion placed a beacon at the entrance to the vault," she said. "It looks like we are almost halfway there."

Suddenly they felt the ground shake a little. It was a mild tremor. Tiny ice particles fell from the ceiling all around them. Calvin felt his heart immediately start racing, and fear gripped his heart and chest like a vise.

"What was that?" he asked. "Don't tell me that was an earthquake. This isn't a good time or place for it."

Astra looked around, and they both stood still, holding their breath. It was quiet, and nothing else happened. The shaking only lasted for a second. The radio in Calvin's helmet turned on, and Ion's voice filled his ears.

"Sir, are you OK? Your heart rate has increased."

"I'm OK," Calvin said, slightly embarrassed. "We just had a small earthquake down here."

"Yes, sensors indicated a very minor shift in the ice. It doesn't appear that you are in any danger."

"I'm OK," Calvin repeated. "It just caught me by surprise."

"I think we should get moving again," Astra suggested, suppressing a smile.

"Good idea. We just took a short break, Ion. We're moving again."

"Very good, Sir."

Calvin led again. The suit was feeling heavier, and his legs were getting very tired, but he pressed on. He kept thinking about how fun the trip back up was going to be.

After two more hours of walking, they reached the end of the tunnel. At the bottom, they found that Ion had cleared out a large space. In the middle of the cleared space sat the drill. It had a large drill head on the front, and sitting behind that was a large square engine. Behind that there was a place for two people to sit, and a flat space behind that for cargo. Calvin smiled, relieved when he saw it, realizing that they wouldn't have to walk all the way back up.

At the back, against a wall of ice, were two silver doors.

CHAPTER FOURTEEN

THE ICE BASE

Calvin and Astra approached the doors and examined them. There was a small panel on the right side. Astra opened it, and she found a simple door control.

Amazingly, the doors opened when Astra pressed a large green button.

"It's an airlock," she said, walking through cautiously. Calvin followed her. Inside they found a small room with white featureless walls.

"No ice in here," Calvin noted. Astra closed the outer doors, and a computer screen on the wall lit up. Large unseen fans sucked all of the air out of the room. When that finished, new air rushed back in. Astra examined the computer screen on the wall.

"It replaced the air," she said. "We should be able to take off our helmets and gloves."

"Should be able to?" Calvin said. "Are you sure? Do you want to trust this old equipment? What if one of the sensors is out of alignment? What would happen if we breathe methane?"

"Any amount would be very bad for us. Most likely we would die instantly," Astra said grimly. Then she examined the computer on the arm of her suit. "According to this, the air is completely breathable. There's no trace of methane."

135

Calvin didn't look convinced. "I still don't know if I want to trust my life to it."

"Well, what's the point of bringing all this equipment if we won't trust what it tells us? And two different computers are saying the same thing. Fine, then we can leave our gear on, at least until we get inside. But we are going to have to take our gloves off so it can read our DNA."

"Ok," Calvin said. "What's the temperature in here?"

Astra looked at the screen again, and then at her wrist computer.

"Both the vault computer and my suit computer say it is fifty-one degrees in here."

Calvin pulled off his right glove. The cool air felt good on his skin. Then he took off his left glove. Astra watched him. She waited for a second, and then she took off her own gloves. Astra turned her attention to the inner doors. There was a metal bar that reached across the door, just like in the first vault. They gave each other a glance and walked up to the door.

"Ok, here we go," Calvin muttered. They both put their hands on the bar. After a second, the handle changed color from dark gray to dark green. There was a loud click, and the door cracked open about an inch. Calvin bent over and looked inside, but it was completely dark on the other side of the door.

"Ready?" Astra asked.

"Let's go," Calvin said. They pulled on the handle, but the door was very heavy and wouldn't open. They had to use all their weight, leaning back and pulling as hard as they could until finally the door inched open. They stopped when they had it open wide enough to fit through.

Calvin went first. His backpack almost came off as he squeezed into the next room. Once through, Astra looked at her wrist computer again, and then she took her helmet off.

"What are you doing?" Calvin asked.

"The air's fine," she said. "I'm going to trust my computer." She pointed at her wrist computer.

Calvin hesitated at first, but he reluctantly decided to trust her. Calvin removed his helmet. The air smelled dusty and old, but otherwise it was ok. Astra moved farther into the room. As she did, overhead lights automatically turned on.

"Whoa," Calvin muttered, startled. They were in a wide room. Tables lined the walls, and rows of large hooks ran all the way down the wall at different heights. There was another door at the other end of the room, which was closed.

"This must be where they kept their gear," Astra pointed out.

"Is that a good idea?" Calvin asked.

"I don't see why not; we'll be more comfortable, and there's no telling how big this place is. Do you want to carry it around?"

"Not really." Calvin didn't argue with her. They took off their spacesuits and laid them down on the tables, along with their backpacks. Astra took her computer off her suit and put it on her arm.

"Let's go look around," she said excitedly. She led the way to the unopened door and opened it without hesitation.

They walked into a much larger open room. In the middle was a large triangular pool with a broken fountain in the center. The small dirty fountain had a large rusted gong suspended over it by a long wire. There was a door in each corner of the triangle. Above them were three other levels. Balconies looked out over the room from each level. The walls were richly decorated and looked like they were made out of marble.

"Which way should we go?" Astra asked.

"Let's try this one," Calvin said, walking to one of the doors. The empty marble halls made each footstep echo loudly. Even their voices seemed amplified. Calvin opened the door and walked through. They found a staircase with stairs leading up and down.

"If you were going to hide a super-secret piece of technology that you didn't want anyone in the universe to find, where would you hide it?" Calvin asked.

Astra thought about it. "Well, I would put it as far away from the

137

main entrance as possible. But would that be upstairs or downstairs?"

"Let's try downstairs first," Calvin suggested.

"Ok. Lead the way."

Calvin went first. The steps were wide and easy to walk down. Small black pipes snaked up and down the walls. They passed several floors before they reached a metal door at the bottom. Calvin opened it excitedly, expecting to find a laboratory with the next segment in it. Instead, there was a hallway leading off in two directions. They spent the next two hours exploring the bottom floors. It was obvious that this was a base. It might have been a research base or a military station, but whatever it was, it had everything needed to support the living needs of a group of people. They found crew quarters, a mess hall, a kitchen, recreation facilities, a power generator, and an empty shuttle bay.

"I've been thinking," Calvin said, as they climbed back up the stairs. "This base must have been on the surface once, don't you think?"

"Why do you say that?" Astra asked.

"Well, the shuttle bay doors are blocked. Nothing can get in or out."

"Maybe they buried it under the ice to hide it."

Finally, after searching the base for hours, they had gone through every level except one: the top floor. Calvin and Astra were getting discouraged. It was looking like the only thing they would find was disappointment. At the top of the stairs they found two doors. When Calvin opened the door on the right, they both breathed a sigh of relief. They had finally found the laboratory.

It was a small room with workstations and tables. Small pieces of broken equipment lay all over the tables and floor. Calvin had been hoping that this vault would be similar to the vault they found on Arlandia, and he wasn't disappointed. In the back of the room was another door. It was cracked open.

Through the next door they found a small square room. The only thing in it was a single table, with a strange-looking object sitting on top. It was round on the front, square on the back, and flat on top. There were several round holes on the sides and several round rods protruding from it. Calvin and Astra approached it slowly, almost reverently.

"It's the second segment," Astra whispered. They both stood in front of it for several moments.

"All things considered," Calvin said. "That was easy."

Astra looked at him with an odd expression.

"You thought it would be harder?" Astra asked. "The location of these vaults is secret, and we are flying around in an invisible spaceship. I don't think the Goremog know what we are trying to do. Really, what can happen to us?"

"I don't know," Calvin said. "But I've noticed that the Goremog have constantly been one step behind me, like they are following me. It could just be my imagination, or a coincidence."

Astra thought about that. "Yes, but *Aleria's Hope* didn't have a cloaking device, and it is a huge ship. The Goremog were obviously able to track it very easily. It leaves a really big hyperspace wake."

"I suppose," Calvin said, unconvinced. "I hope you're right."

Astra gave a crooked smile. "Me too."

"Do you want to look around the lab and see if there is anything else we should take with us?"

"Yeah, that's a good idea," she said.

They searched the lab—every desk, every table, and every corner. By the end of the search, they had found a handful of computer storage devices and two manuals.

"Let's get this stuff back up to the surface."

"Ok," Calvin agreed. He took his backpack off and pulled out four small white handles. He handed two to Astra, and they attached the handles to both ends of the second segment. Each handle had a small button on the end of it. Astra walked around and pressed all of the buttons.

"Ready?" Astra asked.

Calvin and Astra picked the segment up by the handles. The handles were antigravity generators. When they picked the device up, it had no weight. They easily moved it out of the room, and down to the main floor where the fountain was. They had to turn it on end to get it through the doors, but since it had no weight it rotated easily.

As they entered the fountain room, a giant earthquake shook the building. Astra and Calvin were knocked off of their feet and thrown to the floor. The segment was sent floating free in the air. The shaking lasted for several minutes. Dust and dirt broke free from the walls and ceiling and drifted down to the floor in billowing clouds. The shaking eased, but a deep rumbling continued long after. Loud crashes could be heard off in the distance; it sounded like something collapsing. Calvin and Astra sat on the floor, listening to the sounds.

"Are you all right?" Calvin asked, helping Astra to her feet.

"Yes, I'm ok," she said. "That was stronger than before."

"Yeah it was," Calvin agreed. "I think we should get out of here."

After they chased down the segment, they moved it into the entry room and closed the inner door.

They put on their suits as quickly as they could. Boots, suits, gloves, and finally helmets. Then they opened the outer door. They stepped out into the tunnel, taking the second segment with them.

When their lights turned on and illuminated the tunnel ahead, they were met with a big shock. The ceiling of the ice tunnel had collapsed. The tunnel was gone. But the worst part was that the drill car was crushed under the ice.

"Oh no," Astra whispered. "What're we going to do now?"

Calvin stared in shock, realizing they were trapped under two miles of solid ice.

There were three short static bursts, and then Ion's voice filled Calvin's helmet.

"Master Calvin. Are you OK?"

"Yes. There was a big quake," Calvin said. "The tunnel caved in.

140

We're trapped down here."

"What about the drill? The signal stopped transmitting."

"It was crushed under the ice."

"I can come down and dig you out," Ion offered. "Unless you think you can get out of there somehow by yourself."

"No," Calvin said. "There's no way we can get through this wall of ice. We'll wait here."

"Ion, hurry," Astra said. "It's getting worse down here."

"Yes, Mistress," Ion answered. The communication ended.

"What do you want to do while we wait?" Astra asked.

"Let's go back inside," Calvin said. "It's going to be a while before he gets down here. I'm guessing it will be at least two hours, maybe more."

"Ok. We can look around inside some more."

Calvin and Astra went back inside and took their gear off. This time they left it all inside the fountain room.

"I want to go back up to the lab and the vault," Calvin said. "There was a room up there we didn't look in."

"Oh yeah," Astra said, remembering. "The other door at the top of the stairs. Let's go."

Calvin led the way up the stairs to the top of the base. When he opened the door, he found a short set of stairs with a door at the top.

Up to this point, they hadn't found anything dangerous in the base, so Calvin felt no fear in opening the door. A tiny quake shook the base.

Inside they found a room full of computers, which were all off. There were monitors all over the walls, and the ceiling looked like it was made of glass. There was a chair sitting in the center of the room, which was surrounded by four computer workstations.

"It's a control room," Calvin said.

"I was hoping we'd find one," Astra said, following him into the room.

Calvin sat in the chair without hesitation. Nothing happened.

"Where's the on button?" he said, half-jokingly.

Astra was already ahead of him. She found a power terminal on the wall and pulled the power switch until it locked into place. Suddenly all of the monitors came to life, all of the computer panels lit up, and the keyboards glowed.

"There we go," Astra said, looking at information scroll across the monitors. She moved from monitor to monitor, examining each screen carefully.

"These are status screens," she said. "Do you recognize the configurations?"

"They look Alerian," Calvin said. "Like the standard controls in a spaceship. These look like flight controls."

"This is life support." Astra pointed to one monitor. "That one is engine status, and that one is navigation. This isn't just a base. This is a spaceship!"

"And this is the bridge," Calvin said. "Can it be that easy? Can we fly out of here?"

"I don't see how. We're still trapped under two miles of ice."

Another quake rattled the base. This time Calvin held onto the sides of the chair, and Astra grabbed onto one of the computer terminals. The shaking stopped after a few seconds.

"They're getting stronger," Calvin said. "Yes, we're stuck down here. But I think somebody buried this ship down here intentionally. They must've made a way to get it out."

Astra thought about that for a moment. "Yeah, you would think that with something as important as this piece of the weapon, they would have had a way to get it out of here. But first they would have needed a way to get back in. I wonder how they planned to do that."

"That's a good question," Calvin said. "We need to look around some more and see if we can find something. The answer has to be here," he said, pointing to the computers. "Do you want to sit here? You're the computer expert. And it's in your language."

"OK. Move it!" Astra said smiling. Calvin stood up and stepped back.

Astra sat in the chair.

"Master Calvin, Lady Astra," Ion said. "I'm ready to fly down to the surface."

"Ion, wait," Calvin said. "We just found out this base is a spaceship. We're going to see if we can fly it off of the planet."

"That's good news, Sir," Ion said, sounding surprised. "Is it operational?"

"We're about to find out," Calvin said. "Can you remotely pilot our shuttle, and fly it back to the ship?"

"Yes, I can. But there's something you should know. My sensors indicate the ice around your location is shifting, becoming highly unstable. You might encounter more quakes."

"We already have been," Calvin replied. "Hurry and get the shuttle outta here. We don't want to lose it. Wish us luck."

"Good luck, Sir."

Another quake jolted them. This one lasted even longer. Loud bangs could be heard, some close and some far away, echoing throughout the base.

"I found the shields," Astra said happily, "And this is the sensors. Oh, look at this." She pointed at the screen. "There are small objects in the ice all around the ship." She worked the computer. "They're explosive devices. According to this, we can detonate them and shatter the ice. This is amazing. Now I see how they planned to fly the base out. OK, let's get us out of here."

"Just out of curiosity, how much power is left in this old thing?" Calvin asked. "It's been sitting here a long time."

143

Astra checked the computers.

"Calvin, I think this is it. These are the power levels. Oh, this could be bad. It says power is down to 45 percent. I don't know if we have enough to get off of the planet and into orbit."

"It'll have to be," Calvin insisted. "We don't have another option. We definitely can't stay here."

"I agree, but if we launch and don't have enough power to reach escape velocity, we'll fall back onto the surface and crash."

"Is there any way to be certain?"

"No," Astra admitted. "If any of the power conduits or transfer generators are damaged, we could have even less power than the computer says."

"There are no guarantees," Calvin stated.

"No, there aren't."

"So we can sit here and let the power drain a little more, or we can go for it."

"I'm guessing you want to go for it."

"Yes!" Calvin said enthusiastically. "Let's go. At least if we launch, we have a chance of surviving. If we stay here..." He didn't finish the sentence.

"OK, fine. Will you fly us out of here then?" Astra asked.

"Love to."

Astra got up and sat at one of the computer terminals, and Calvin sat in the control chair.

"Put on your seatbelt," Astra said. "I'm raising the shields and powering up the engines."

Calvin quickly put on his seatbelt as the ship vibrated and shook. The engines roared to life; the sound started out as a soft hum at first but quickly got louder.

"The shields are at full power," Astra reported. "I can't believe this stuff still works. Calvin, we have to hurry, or we won't have enough power to get into orbit."

Calvin checked the power levels.

"We're almost down to 20 percent," Calvin said.

"Something's wrong," Astra said loudly. "We shouldn't be losing power that fast."

"Are we going to make it into orbit?"

"I don't know," Astra said, but in her mind she was afraid they wouldn't.

"Get ready!" she shouted; the noise from the engines was getting louder. "I'm detonating the bombs now!"

There was a series of huge explosions that rocked the ship violently. Calvin and Astra both looked up through the glass ceiling. There was a bright flash of light, which caused them both to cover their eyes. Calvin peeked through a small slit between his fingers and saw an amazing sight. The ice above them shattered into a billion pieces. Tiny ice particles rained down on them, bouncing harmlessly off the shields.

There was now a long ice tunnel stretching out all the way to the surface. Calvin could see stars. It was a beautiful sight.

Calvin pushed the throttle forward. The ship vibrated and jerked violently from side to side. A horrific cacophony of loud scraping noises and tearing metal permeated the air as the ship slowly climbed up through the ice tunnel.

Calvin did his best to keep the ship centered in the tunnel, but he realized with horror that the sides of the ship were being scraped along the ice walls on all sides. He could feel the ship slowing, struggling to claw its way toward the surface. Finally the ship cleared the tunnel and slowly began the ascent into space. Calvin urged the ship to climb higher into the atmosphere, forcing it with his will.

Suddenly a red light flooded the bridge, and an alarm, the most annoying sound Calvin had ever heard, rang out. Before he had a chance to ask her, Astra shouted.

"We've got hull fractures all over the ship!" The roar of the engines, the sound of the alarm, and the sound of small explosions were all going on at the same time. Calvin could barely hear her even though she was screaming. "A power generator in the engine room has failed, I think it exploded! There is explosive decompression, but I can't tell where it is. Some of the internal sensors aren't working, but it looks like automatic force fields are turning on. Oh no, power is so low I don't know how long they'll hold!" A few more seconds passed.

"The shields have failed!" Astra screamed. "The ship is coming apart! Automatic force fields are failing all over the ship!"

Then Calvin felt it; they were losing momentum.

"We're slowing down!" Calvin screamed. "We don't have enough altitude yet."

"Every system is failing!" Astra screamed back. "I can't do anything."

"Transfer all power to the engines, even life support! Transfer everything except power to the emergency force fields!"

Astra worked as fast as she could. "That's everything," she yelled.

Now the only thing they could do was wait and hope. They were both very scared and held onto their chairs for dear life. Explosions continued throughout the ship. The vibration got much worse. Calvin felt like he was being shaken to death, and he felt dizzy.

Gradually the ship sped up as it climbed higher into the atmosphere and finally out into space.

"We did it!" Calvin shouted just as the engines died. "We're in a low orbit, but at least we're in orbit."

"But it's not stable," Astra said.

"As long as we can get two or three orbits, we can get out of here."

"We don't have that long," Astra said. "Structural integrity is about to collapse, and life support is gone. We need to get off of this ship right now."

Calvin turned on his communicator. "Ion, this is Calvin, are you there?"

"What is your status, Master Calvin?" Ion asked, without delay.

"It worked!" Calvin announced. "We're off the planet and in a low orbit, but we have a few problems. Our orbit is very unstable. Life support is gone, structural integrity is gone, and the ship is falling apart. We're going to fall back into the atmosphere in two orbits, probably less. We really need you to come over and get us with a shuttle."

"I'll be there as quickly as I can," Ion said. "Once I maneuver the *Frost* behind you, I'll bring the shuttle over and dock. Can you meet me at the airlock?"

"We'll be there," Calvin said. "Don't take too long."

"I won't."

Calvin took off his seatbelt and got up.

"We really need to hurry," Astra said. "We have less time than you think."

They got up and went to the door. Calvin reached out to open the door, but Astra stopped him.

"Wait, I don't think we should go out there." She pointed at the door. "I don't know what's keeping this mess together at this point, but I know for a fact that several areas of the ship are open to space. A couple of the explosions I heard were explosive decompression, areas of the ship being exposed to the vacuum of space. If we rush to get to the airlock, we'll open a door into one of those rooms and get blown out into space. We'll die."

Calvin was about to walk past her and open the door, but he stopped.

"Then what are we going to do?" Calvin asked. "If we stay here we will run out of air. You said the life-support system is down. And if that doesn't get us, our orbit is decaying. We have to get to the airlock."

"I know," Astra said.

"How're we going to know which doors are safe to open?"

"I don't know. The internal sensors are down. I can't even see what's waiting for us on the other side of that door." She pointed at the door again.

Calvin stepped back. The room was feeling smaller. It could have been his imagination, but the air was feeling thin. Astra didn't say anything. She walked up to the door and waved her wrist scanner over the door.

"I don't know why I didn't think of this," she muttered, almost to herself. "Well, I do know why; the oxygen level in this room is getting dangerously low. That's why I'm feeling dizzy. How are you feeling?"

"I feel a little lightheaded. I thought it was just me."

"No, it's not. It looks like there's air on the other side, unless I'm reading this wrong. Here goes." Astra opened the door.

Calvin and Astra walked out of the control room and back to the main stairwell. Calvin followed her down the stairs. The devastation was terrifying. The pipes that ran along the walls were ruptured in a dozen places and were spewing steam into the air, making it hard to see. Even more disturbing were the noises the floor made when they walked—loud cracks and creaks with every footstep. It was even worse on the stairs. If they walked too fast, the floor shook.

"Wow, we really need to get out of here," Astra said nervously.

"Don't stop, keep going." Calvin said.

They made it to the main level but found their way blocked by several large beams that had collapsed and filled the hallway with debris. Calvin could see the door that led to the fountain room, but there was no way to get to it.

"This way," Calvin said, leading her back up the stairs. Astra followed him, holding his hand and anxiously looking at the walls and ceiling. They cautiously walked back up the stairs to the next level.

"We can cross over on the second level, and take the stairs on the other side," Calvin said.

Astra let go of Calvin's hand and waved her scanner over the door.

"There's air on the other side," she said.

Calvin opened the door, and Astra led the way. They found themselves in a long, narrow hallway. The floor made loud cracking noises with each step.

"The floor feels strange," Astra said. "Do you feel it? It feels brittle."

"Yes, I can feel it," Calvin said. The air was full of smoke and dust. The ground shook, causing dust to rain down from somewhere above. They made it halfway down the hallway, when they felt a wave of power pulse through the room. Calvin could feel it in his hair. He looked up at Astra and saw strands of her long brown hair sticking out in all directions. Before he had a chance to ask her what was going on, a bright flash of light split the room between them. Astra felt it too, and she spun around. It only took her a second to realize what it was.

"It's a force field," she exclaimed. Calvin looked at her. He could see a look of resignation on her face. It scared him.

"Now what do we do?" Calvin asked her, trying to get her to focus on their problem and how to solve it. "How can we turn the force field off?"

"Uh, I don't know," she muttered, looking around the room. "Why did this force field turn on, in the middle of the room?"

Calvin watched her face. He watched her expression change from confusion to alarm. She started to say something, but was interrupted. All of a sudden, the room exploded.

Calvin would never forget what he saw at that moment. It would haunt him the rest of his life. The wall behind Astra disintegrated, and the fragments were sucked out into space. Astra's eyes got wide, and she looked at Calvin, pleading for help. Calvin was powerless to do anything. He watched as Astra was violently ripped out into space. She vanished before his eyes.

"Astra!" he screamed. "No!"

Calvin stared out into the blackness of space, in shock and devastated. It felt like his heart was just ripped out of his chest.

"Astra, you can't leave me too," he whispered. "What am I going to do now?" There was a loud crackling noise, and an electric feeling swept over him. Suddenly the force field disappeared.

Calvin was sucked into the vacuum of space so fast he was outside and spinning out of control before he knew what was happening. He closed his eyes and held his breath, knowing that it wouldn't be enough. Being out in space without a suit on was an instant death sentence. He knew he was floating in space. He assumed he was dying, or maybe he was dead already. He didn't feel any pain. He must be dead. But if he was dead, why was he still holding his breath? He held it as long as he could, but eventually, he was forced to let it out. He let the air out and gulped in a deep breath of air!

Calvin opened his eyes. He was still alive! It seemed completely impossible. But where was Astra? He looked around, and he found her floating not very far away. She was alive too! She was very close, but too far to reach. He stretched out his arms, and she did the same. Calvin tried leaning forward, and he tried to push himself, but there was nothing to push against. He tried waving his arms and legs to move closer to her, like he was swimming. Nothing worked.

He strained desperately to get to her, to touch her. Calvin looked into her eyes. He called to her. He could hear his own voice, but it sounded very strange. Astra's lips moved in response to him, but he couldn't hear her.

"I don't mean to sound ungrateful," he said. "But how are we alive? We're floating in space without suits on." She said something again, but he heard nothing.

Calvin and Astra both strained to touch each other, and this time they touched, barely. There was a soft purple electrical flash when they touched. It was a force field! There was a thin force field surrounding each of them. That's why they were still alive. It was protecting them from the cold and airless environment.

They touched fingers again, and this time they managed to hook their index fingers together.

Calvin pulled her toward himself. When they were close enough, they embraced and held each other. Their force fields flickered with small electric currents that coalesced into purple clouds. On the edges, lightning bolts flew off in all directions where their force fields touched.

"Are you all right?" he asked her. She didn't answer. It was a very strange and exciting experience. He felt the urge to shiver, but he wasn't cold. Adrenalin rushed through his body, and he was hyperaware of his surroundings. He had been on pure oxygen once during deep-space training. He remembered how it made him feel, like he was super awake. That's how he felt now.

It was one thing to see space on a monitor or through a window from the inside of a spaceship. It was quite another to be outside floating around in it. The blackness of space was a deeper black than he had ever seen before. The stars were the most brilliant colors. He could see red, blue, green, yellow, and white stars. It was like he was seeing color for the first time in his life. It was also very quiet. He was so entranced by what he was seeing that he almost forgot that he was floating in space. There was no way to know how much time they had left. He had a bad feeling that their force fields weren't going to last very long. When they failed, they would die. At least now he wasn't going to die alone. There was no way of knowing how long they floated in space, holding each other and looking into one another's eyes. It was as if they had both resigned themselves to the fact that there was nothing they could do. Calvin was drawn to her light brown eyes. Her expression was soft, and she had a smile on her face. Was she trying to tell him something? Calvin thought she was, and she seemed to be saying that everything was going to be ok. Focusing on her eyes, in the middle of the blackness of space, he felt peace, and he knew everything was going to be all right.

Calvin relaxed and stopped worrying. What was going to happen was going to happen, and there wasn't a thing they could do about it. So they drifted in space, unmoving.

Then suddenly a large white shape appeared behind Astra. It was the shuttle. The rear hatch was open, and the ship slowly moved backward until they were inside the ship. They were saved. Once inside, the door closed. There was a loud rush of air as oxygen filled the room. Slowly gravity returned, and their force fields blinked out. Calvin and Astra looked at each other again, trying to understand what had just happened to them. Astra hugged Calvin, and she held him tightly.

The door to the forward part of the ship opened, and Ion stood in the doorway.

"Master Calvin, Lady Astra. Are you all right?" Ion asked.

"We are now," Astra said. "Thank you for rescuing us."

Calvin looked out of the front window and got his first look at the base ship. It was not as big as he thought it was, maybe twice the size of the *Frost*. It was shaped like two pyramids, base to base, with large square engines on one end. It wasn't a very elegant design.

"What happened? Why didn't we die out there?" Calvin asked.

"The device I gave to each of you earlier today," Ion explained. "It contained a personal force field and oxygen supply. You could have survived out there for an hour. It also contains a location beacon, so I was able to find you quickly."

Calvin and Astra sat in the crew section behind the pilot's chair. Astra covered her face with her hands. Calvin sat back and closed his eyes.

"We need to get the second segment!" he said suddenly. "We left it onboard the ship!"

"It's all right sir," Ion said soothingly. "I took the base ship in tow with a tractor beam. I'll go retrieve your gear and the segment after I take you back to the *Frost*."

"OK," Calvin said, closing his eyes again. "Well then, wake me up when we get there."

Ion looked at Astra, about to ask her a question, but she was already asleep. Calvin wasn't far behind her. He fell asleep before Ion returned to the pilot's chair and connected his seatbelt.

Calvin woke up and looked out the front window. He expected to see stars, but instead he saw the inside of the shuttle bay. They were back aboard the *Frost*. Astra was still asleep in the seat behind him. Ion walked past them to the back of the shuttle, and he opened the door to the rear compartment. Calvin put his hand on her shoulder and squeezed.

"Are we there yet?" Astra asked, and she slowly opened her eyes.

"We're on the *Frost*," Calvin said.

"I didn't realize how tired I was," Astra said, smiling at Calvin. They both stood and followed Ion out, both yawning.

"Yeah, I guess the sheer terror of being sucked out into space without a suit on kind of wears you out." They both laughed.

"Ion," Calvin said. "Why don't we use the personal force fields instead of spacesuits more often? It would be faster and a lot more comfortable."

"They're very good for what they were designed for," Ion said. "Emergency backup. However, I don't recommend you use them for primary protection, in any environment."

"Don't you trust them?" Calvin asked.

"They are still fairly new and are not entirely reliable," Ion said. "That's why they should only be used as a backup, if everything else fails."

"Well," Calvin said. "I'm glad you gave them to us. We would have died without them. What're we going to do with the base ship?" Calvin asked.

"We shouldn't leave it out here for someone else to find," Ion said. "We should destroy it."

"That's sad," Calvin commented. Astra looked at him sympathetically, understanding how he felt.

"We'll take everything of value with us," Ion said.

"I know, but it's a piece of our history," Calvin pointed out. "There might be something in there that could teach us about our history."

Calvin and Astra went to the bridge while Ion went to the base ship in the shuttle to collect everything that was left behind. When he returned to the *Frost*, Ion took the second segment and everything that was recovered from the base ship to the lab.

On the bridge, Astra programmed the computer with the coordinates for the next segment.

Calvin suddenly felt very tired, and he had a feeling that destroying the Alerian base ship was wrong. "How long will it take to get to the next segment?" he asked.

"Ten days," Astra answered. She looked tired to him.

"The weapons are charged, Sir, ready at your command," Ion said.

"Now you get a chance to practice firing the ship's weapons," Astra said.

"Yup," Calvin said. He turned on a computer in the middle of the console. A monitor displayed the status of all the ship's weapons. "I'm locking onto the base ship." If he hadn't been so tired, he might have been more excited. In fact he was so tired he didn't realize this was his first time firing spaceship weapons.

It took some effort to raise his head to look out the window. The base ship was directly in front of them, hanging over the ice planet. Something inside him was screaming that it was a bad idea to destroy the base ship, even though he understood the need for doing it. He decided not to listen, and he hoped it wouldn't come back to haunt him later.

When he activated the weapons computer, small triggers slid out of the ends of the control wheel on both side, perfectly placed under his index fingers. Two small panels on the top of the control slid open, and two red buttons popped out.

"Firing," Calvin said sadly. He pulled both triggers. Red beams of light lanced out through space and sliced cleanly through the base ship. It was instantly engulfed in a massive fireball. Debris and fragments shot off in all directions. Some burned up in the atmosphere, and some drifted out into space, but hidden behind the explosion, several large pieces of the station landed on the surface of the ice planet, intact. Calvin and

Astra sat in silence for several moments.

Finally, Astra said, "Calvin, the coordinates for the next segment are locked into the navigation computer. You can take us to hyperspace anytime you want."

Calvin pushed the throttle forward and turned the ship away from the ice planet. The *Azure Frost* picked up speed and jumped into hyperspace.

Calvin stared out the front window, mesmerized by the display of lights that flying though hyperspace caused. It was beautiful, and he was so tired he didn't want to move.

"Are you hungry?" Astra asked, shaking him out of his daze.

"I'm trying to decide if I'm hungry or tired," Calvin answered.

"You're probably both," Astra said. "Come eat with me? Please? It will help you sleep."

"That sounds good," Calvin said.

Calvin and Astra stumbled to the dining room like a pair of zombies. Calvin was in the mood for breakfast food, so he ordered eggs, bacon, and toast. Astra got a bowl of soup with crackers. When Astra sat, she sat next to Calvin, not across from him like she normally did. They didn't talk for a little while. They ate in silence. Calvin was trying to process everything that had happened, but his mind couldn't work through it. He couldn't get the image of Astra, being sucked out of the ship right in front of him, out of his mind. Finally he had to say something.

"I thought I'd lost you," he said, with tears filling his eyes. "That was the most horrible thing that ever happened to me. I don't know."

"I know. It's all right," Astra said calmly. She put her head on his shoulder and held his hand. "I was scared too. But its ok now. We're ok." She wiped tears from her eyes. Astra put her hand on Calvin's chin, and she gently turned his head toward hers. They looked into each other's eyes.

"It's going to be all right," she said. "You must be feeling

155

overwhelmed right now, I know. It's dangerous out here."

"This is how you grew up, out here in this nightmare?" Calvin asked.

"Yes," Astra answered. "I've been running from the Goremog my whole life, running from one place to another, from one disaster to another. This isn't the first time I've had to go off on my own. My father had to send me out before, with a squad of robots to protect me. Actually I can't count how many times, but Alpha Seven, I mean Ion, was always there to take care of me. But this time was different. I was scared, yes, but I was afraid of losing you too. Listen, I have to warn you, what happened to us today is nothing compared to what's out there. There are things that will terrify you, things you haven't even imagined, that truly will give you nightmares. You know, after the Great War, all the races of the universe had to rebuild their armies with robots, because all the people were gone. But that wasn't enough for the Goremog. They wanted something more. So they created a monster. They took the most powerful and aggressive robot they had, and they combined it with a living creature. I don't know what it was, but it was at the top of the food chain on whatever planet they got it from. It had long claws and teeth, and It devoured every creature that crossed its path. The result of combining the two was horrific. They wanted to create an army of them, but they lost control of them. Now they're out there, thousands of them, maybe more, devouring everything in their way. I've never seen one, but I've heard the sounds they make. When they scream, your blood freezes, and you know you're being hunted. I still have nightmares."

"Well, thanks," Calvin said. "I should have no problems going to sleep now."

"I'm sorry," Astra said, rubbing her temples. "It's just that, when we were on the base ship, I heard a sound that reminded me of the scream of one of those monsters. It was when the whole place was coming apart, right before we were thrown out into space. It must have been my imagination. It was very noisy in there." She shook her head.

"I think I'll go to bed now," Calvin said. "I can't keep my eyes open."

"OK, goodnight," Astra said. "I hope you can sleep." She smiled at him. Her smile made him feel better.

"You too. Goodnight."

Calvin walked back to his room and got ready for bed. The silence in his room felt heavy, and he felt very much alone. He was so tired that he was shivering as he got under his covers and turned out the light. His thoughts drifted to New Arlandia. He fell asleep, hoping for a dreamless night.

William F. F. Wood

Part Two

THE DARK TERROR

CHAPTER ONE

$$\text{———}\!\!\!\text{▷◦◁}\!\!\!\text{———}$$

ALARM

Calvin sat up and looked around wildly. He had no idea where he was. It was dark, but the room felt familiar.

"Where am I?" he wondered aloud. He quickly realized he was at home, in his bed. "How did I get here, and why is it so dark?" Calvin jumped up and ran to the light switch. He pressed it, but nothing happened. He hated the dark, and his biggest fear was being stuck in the dark without being able to turn on a light. He knew he was having a dream, but that didn't make him feel any better.

"Wake up, wake up. I have to wake up!" But he couldn't.

Calvin cautiously stepped into the hall and stared toward the living room. The hall looked much longer than it was supposed to. In the living room, in his father's chair, was a dark shape and a pair of glowing red eyes. He froze, unsure of what to do. A puff of smoke shot through the air between the eyes. Calvin was terrified. He slowly crept forward and shook with fear. Calvin panicked, turned to run, and found himself face to face with a horrible monster. It opened its mouth and let out a heart-stopping scream. It lunged forward to devour him.

Calvin bolted upright in bed. A multi-toned alarm blared in his ears. He hated waking up that way and didn't care that much for

160

nightmares either. It took a moment for his mind to clear, and he jumped out of bed when he realized why the alarm was going off. The sensors detected an approaching ship. He scrambled into his clothes and ran to the bridge. The bridge was more like a large cockpit. There were two seats in front for the pilots, and a seat in back for the engineer. Every available space was taken up by computers, monitors, buttons, switches, and dials.

Astra was already there, sitting in the right seat. Her hair was a mess, and she wore loose black stretchy pants and a light purple shirt.

"What's going on?" Calvin asked, sitting down in the left seat.

"There's a ship out there, coming straight at us."

"What is it?"

"I don't know yet. Hold on," Astra said.

Calvin switched one of his monitors over to long-range sensors to see for himself. There was a red dot at the top of the screen.

"It's moving really fast," Calvin said.

"It's in hyperspace," Astra said. "Just like us. The computer is trying to identify it."

"Can they see us?"

"I'm sure they can. We're not cloaked."

"Do I need to activate the weapons or shields?" Calvin asked.

"No, wait," Astra said. Seconds passed. "No life signs detected, only robots. It's a Goremog scout ship."

"Should I raise the shields or power up the weapons?" Calvin asked again. He wasn't sure why he asked her. If they were approaching an enemy ship the shields should be up and weapons fully charged. He put his hand on the shield controls and was about to charge them.

"No, they won't work in hyperspace," Astra said. Calvin rested his hands on his lap and watched the scanner carefully. The red dot flashed across the screen and zipped past the Azure Frost like lightning.

"They passed us," Calvin said, taking a deep breath. But he

couldn't take his eyes off the screen. He watched anxiously while the red dot moved away. Would the Goremog ship turn around? If it did, what would they do? The red dot moved quickly to the edge of the sensor field and disappeared off the screen.

"It's out of range," Astra said.

Calvin took a deep breath and relaxed. "Maybe they didn't see us."

"They had to," Astra said. "We were right in front of them."

Calvin yawned. "We really need to get the cloak back online. If that scout saw us, it's going to report our location to the rest of their fleet, along with the direction we're going in."

"Well, there's no way I'm going back to sleep now," Astra said. "I'll go find Ion, see if he needs help fixing the cloak. See you later."

"OK," Calvin said and watched her leave. He sat on the bridge for a while, listening to the computers, and wondered what to do. He yawned again and decided to go back to bed.

It took Calvin a long time to fall asleep, and when he finally did he tossed and turned the rest of the night. When he woke up, he felt as if he hadn't slept at all. He tried to go back to sleep but couldn't. There was no reason to get up, but he was hungry. He took a long hot shower, got dressed, and went to the dining room.

Astra wasn't there. He wasn't surprised, since they hadn't arranged to meet, but he was still disappointed. Calvin ate breakfast alone. When he was finished, he refilled his coffee cup and went to look for her. He was happy when he found her on the bridge.

"Good morning," she said, smiling at him. "How'd you sleep?"

"Terrible," Calvin said. "I couldn't sleep at all. My brain wouldn't shut off."

"I didn't want to even try. I never went back to sleep."

"Any sign of that Goremog ship?" Calvin asked, rubbing his eyes.

"No, but it could be following us, just out of sensor range," Astra said.

"That's a nice thought," Calvin said, yawning. "I'm going to need a lot of coffee today."

"Oh, I forgot, we fixed the cloaking device last night."

"Really? We're cloaked now?"

"Yes, we're invisible. So even if the Goremog wanted to, they wouldn't be able to follow us."

"I wonder if they saw us cloak," Calvin said.

"What?"

"Never mind. What're you working on?"

"I've been thinking about something. You know how every piece of the weapon has a unique energy signature?"

"Yeah."

"Our equipment gets us in the general area, but then we have to search room by room. We shouldn't have to do that. It's been driving me crazy for the last several days, and I finally found a way to program the computer to show the segments in real time and get us within five feet. We won't have to look for the segments the hard way anymore."

"That's great," Calvin said, impressed.

"I was about to test it. Let's see if it works," Astra said excitedly.

Calvin sat down while Astra worked the controls on her computer. A star map appeared on a center monitor, with eight red flashing dots spread in a line leading to the center of the galaxy.

"It worked," Astra said smiling.

"This is great," Calvin said. "So which one we are heading to now?"

"That one," Astra pointed. "That's strange. Our estimated travel time was ten days. Now it's eight."

"Is it because the scanner has an accurate lock on it?" Calvin asked.

"I suppose that's possible, but we already know what planets all the segments are on. The detector will just tell us where on the planets they are. But there shouldn't be a difference of two days traveling in hyperspace."

"Unless the records aren't accurate."

"The records are accurate," Astra said. "Maybe the segment moved."

"You don't think someone took it, do you?" Calvin asked. "But what are the chances of that anyway? An Arlandian and Alerian have to open the vault together."

"There are other ways to open a vault," Astra said. "They're not indestructible."

"You think someone found it and blasted their way in?"

"I don't know, but we'll find out in eight days. Look at this one." She pointed to another red dot. It was surrounded by a blue cloud.

"What's that?" Calvin asked.

"It's a gas giant," Astra said, displaying a picture of the planet on one of the monitors.

"Interesting. It's like they found the most hostile planets possible to hide the segments on. Well, with the exception of Arlandia."

"I don't know. There was a lot of radiation. It seemed like a hostile place to me."

"Good point," Astra said.

Calvin and Astra stared at the image for a long time without speaking. It was beautiful. The planet was a bluish-silvery sphere with huge swaths of white swirling clouds.

"We're too far away for details," Astra said. "But if it's a typical gas giant, finding that segment will be a little more difficult than finding the last one, even with our new detector. Most likely there will be huge amounts of radiation that could prevent the detector from working. So, if the base is floating around in the atmosphere somewhere, it'll be really hard to find. If it's close to the core, I'm not sure our shields will be strong enough to get us down to it."

"Is there a way to boost them, make them stronger?"

"I can try, but the pressure close to the core will be impossible to deal with, even with stronger shields."

"But if that's true, how could the base be down there?"

"It's not that they put a base that far down," Astra said. "But it's been there a long time. Currents in the atmosphere could have dragged it down. I'm only saying it's possible."

"You mentioned before that you might be able to plug the first segment directly into the shields. You said it's an extremely powerful energy source. Are they compatible?"

Astra thought for a second. "I didn't forget about that," she said. "The problem is, I don't know if it's compatible with the ship's power system. I really need to study it some more, but I'm afraid to tamper with it. I don't want to damage it accidentally, but I can't ignore the possible rewards either. If it works, we wouldn't have to worry about power. But if it doesn't work, I could blow up the ship. It might not matter anyway. If someone stole the third segment, we have bigger things to worry about."

"You're right," Calvin said. "But that extra power would come in handy there, too. We're just guessing. Let's wait until we get closer and see what we're up against."

"That sounds good," Astra said. "I'll work on the first segment today. Maybe I can make a big safety switch that can shut the whole thing down if it overloads. What are you going to do?"

"I don't know. I might go train in the simulator some more."

"See you at lunch, then," Astra said.

She slid out of her seat gracefully and left the bridge. Calvin sat alone for a while, enjoying the quiet hum and vibration of the engines. It was very relaxing. After a minute he left to find out what Ion was doing in the engineering workshop. He took his time and used the stairs. When he got there, he found Ion hard at work constructing a new drill.

Ion was busy, so Calvin decided to leave him alone. He spent the rest of the day in the simulator, replaying previous missions. He was so engrossed in what he was doing he forgot about lunch and played through until dinner. He didn't see Astra at dinner and ate alone. Calvin knew she was working in the lab and decided to not interrupt her.

After dinner, Calvin had a headache and blamed it on staring at computer screens all day. He didn't want to be around more electronic devices, so he decided to go to the library and relax. He didn't know if that's what it was called, but it was his favorite room on the ship. He hadn't spent much time there, mostly because he'd been too busy. But now he had time, and he knew he was going to have to give a full report when he eventually got home. He should have taken his father's advice and kept a written record starting on day one. Now he would have to sit and think about it all to make sure he got every detail. But first, he opened the metal shield that covered the window and pulled back the curtains. The blue hyperspace cloud that enveloped the ship while it traveled was very beautiful and calming. It had an almost hypnotic effect on him.

Calvin wanted to write his journal on paper, so he had the computer make a notebook for him. He made a cup of tea, sat in one of the oversized reclining chairs, and began to write. He started at the beginning, just after the launch of the Sorenia, writing down everything he could think of.

An hour later, Calvin was deep in thought and writing furiously. He didn't hear the door open.

"Calvin, are you in here?" Astra called.

"Down here," Calvin said. "What's going on?"

"I've been looking for you."

Calvin put his notebook and pen on the table and stood up.

"I have some interesting news."

166

"Oh, what's that?" Calvin asked.

"The third segment. It was eight days away, but now the computer says we'll be there in four days."

"What, really?" Calvin asked, surprised. "How is that possible?"

"Ion and I think it's moving. How, or why, we don't know."

"That is interesting," Calvin said. "But it doesn't make any sense. If someone else took it, what are the chances they'd be heading in our direction with it? What does it mean?"

"I wish I knew," Astra said. "Just to be on the safe side, I think I'll have Ion check the sensors to make sure they're working right. I'll find you later."

"OK," Calvin said and watched Astra leave the room. He sat down and went back to work on his journal. He took his time. He dreaded recounting the death of his best friend, Jax. Calvin had been very successful in not dealing with it. He was able to block it out of his mind and focus on the mission. But now, alone in the library, he knew he couldn't keep it in the shadows of his mind any longer. For one thing, when he got home there were going to be a lot of questions. His family would want to know every detail, not to mention senior officials in the Space Command. Would there be an inquest? Would they hold Calvin responsible? He was sure the government would never allow another space mission to ever take place. He could see it now—they'd use Jax's death to shut down Space Command.

"I need to stop. It's not my fault," he told himself. He had to force himself to remember the events as they happened, no matter how painful. His tears fell on the paper as he wrote. He put it all down, in excruciating detail: the escape from Aleria, the explosions, the running firefight all the way to the shuttle, and finally saying good-bye while Ion put Jax's body in frozen suspension. Calvin was physically and emotionally tired by the time he finished. He drank the rest of his tea and went to bed. He was depressed, lonely, and exhausted, but he couldn't fall asleep. He kept playing the last moments of Jax's life over in his mind. All he wanted to do was shut his mind off.

When he realized there was no way he was going to be able to sleep, he turned on a small electronic device that was sitting on his nightstand. Ion had given it to him when Calvin complained he was having problems. Ion called it a slumber generator. It emitted highly attuned somatic sound waves that helped balance the chaos within the human mind and help it to rest. It took longer than he wanted, but Calvin finally drifted off.

He woke up nine hours later. He stared at the ceiling for a few minutes and then climbed out of bed. Despite sleeping through the night, he felt half-asleep while he showered and dressed. The hot water did nothing to wake him up. His only hope now was that maybe a cup of hot coffee would revive him. He felt cold, so he put on a dark gray jacket.

He went to the dining room and was disappointed again to find Astra was not there waiting for him. Calvin ate breakfast alone. He missed her and wondered where she was and what she was doing.

After he finished eating, he went off to find her. He didn't have to search long. He found her working in the science lab.

"Good morning," he said. "I missed you at breakfast."

"Sorry," she said. "I couldn't sleep last night. I couldn't stop thinking about the first segment. I have to find a way to make this work. If I can plug it into the power system, we could complete our mission and not worry about the Goremog anymore. I couldn't stop thinking about it, so I woke up at four and decided to get back to work."

"It's no problem," Calvin said. "How's it going?"

"Well," she said cautiously. "Unfortunately, not too good. The computer is still analyzing it. Once it's done, I have to look at the energy patterns to see if they are compatible. If they are, I can connect it to the ship."

"I'll leave you to it, then," Calvin said. "Do you want me to bring you something to eat?"

"No thanks," Astra said. "I ate earlier. I'll call you when I'm ready for lunch, if you want."

"That sounds good." Calvin said and left the room. What was he going to do now? He had no idea. Ion and Astra were both busy. Calvin decided to wander up to the bridge. He hadn't talked to his dad in several days; maybe he would be able to contact him. He needed to tell him about finding the second segment.

Calvin walked onto the bridge and sat in the pilot's chair. He sank into the chair and turned on the communications computer. He had saved several channels into the system and with the touch of a button was sending out a signal toward New Arlandia. He sat back and took a deep breath, expecting it to take a while. Calvin was surprised when the screen changed almost immediately, and a man's face appeared. The man had gray hair and a sharp nose. Calvin recognized him but couldn't remember his name.

"Lieutenant Range!" the man exclaimed, "it's very good to see you again. I'm Captain Vinder. I'm the commander of the asteroid base. I don't know if you remember me. We met briefly the day your mission started."

"Yes, sir," Calvin said. "I remember."

"We've been anxious to hear from you."

"Is my father there?" Calvin asked.

"No, I'm sorry. He's on New Arlandia right now. The senate is in session."

Calvin frowned.

"Is everything all right?" Captain Vinder asked. "Can I pass any information to your father?"

"Everything is fine," Calvin said. He didn't feel comfortable divulging information to a man he barely knew. Captain Vinder looked at Calvin and seemed to know what he was thinking.

"It's OK, you can talk to me," he said. "My clearance is high enough." He paused, as if he were expecting Calvin to laugh. When he didn't, Vinder continued. "I'm also a member of the Laurites. Everyone on this base has been talking about you."

"OK," Calvin said, not sure what to think. He knew that Vinder was going to keep asking questions that he didn't want to answer, so he decided to start asking his own questions.

"Captain, did the crew of the Sorenia make it home?"

"They did," Vinder replied. "The crew limped home in escape pods. They'd been out there for two weeks. Let me tell you, they were in pretty bad shape."

"Oh, good," Calvin said, relieved. "I can't tell you how happy I am to hear that. Did they happen to tell you why they left us behind?"

"As a matter of fact, the first thing Captain Delik asked was if we'd found you, or heard from you."

"You didn't answer my question."

"They tried to get you out," Vinder said. "In the panic, they...I should let Delik explain it to you. He was there, I wasn't."

"They took everything," Calvin said angrily. "Food, emergency supplies, everything."

"Yeah," Vinder said sadly. Calvin could see in his face that Vinder didn't know what else to say.

Calvin wasn't sure what to think, but it did make him feel a little better to vent his feelings.

Vinder looked at him expectantly.

Calvin didn't want to tell this man anything else without speaking to his father first. "If you could just tell my dad I found the second segment, and I'm on my way to get the third." Vinder smiled. "I'll tell him. And, good luck, Calvin. Be safe out there."

"Thank you, I will," Calvin said, trying to sound happy, but not doing it very well. "I'll try to contact him in a couple of days."

Captain Vinder nodded. The screen went dark.

Calvin sat quietly in the chair, staring out into space. Now what was he going to do? He wanted to meet Astra for dinner, but that was still five hours away. There was only one thing that had kept him busy on this trip so far, one thing that he looked forward to doing every day: the space flight simulator. He spent the rest of the day in the simulator, honing his combat skills. He quickly lost track of time.

Five hours later, he was startled by a knock on the canopy. How long had he been in there? He pulled the lever on the side, and the canopy opened. Astra was standing over him, smiling.

"Am I disturbing you?" she asked.

"No, you're not," he said.

"Something bad has happened. We lost the signal from the third segment. It just disappeared."

"What does that mean?" Calvin asked. "Was it destroyed?"

"I don't know. What do you think we should do?"

"We should go to the place where the signal stopped. Hopefully we'll find it there."

"All right," Astra said, visibly worried. "Hopefully we don't find pieces of it instead."

They stopped talking for a minute. Calvin's stomach growled loudly and broke the silence.

"What time is it?" he asked. "How long have I been in here?"

"It's dinner time. I'm hungry, too. Wanna get something to eat?"

That's when he realized he was starving. "Yes."

On their way up to the dining room, Calvin said, "I swear I just went in there five minutes ago. I mean, really, I just turned it on!"

Astra giggled at him. "Was it that much fun?"

"Oh, yeah," Calvin said excitedly. "It's taking me through a campaign. It's awesome."

"Yes, it's one of the campaigns from the war. You fight as an Alerian pilot."

"That's explains why it's so hard. We aren't doing very well."

"Yeah, well, remember we lost the war," Astra said sadly. "But

171

the program is good, because it gives you a lot of practice in combat situations and teaches our history so we never forget it." They both got their food and sat down to eat.

"So, how was your day?" Calvin asked before taking a bite of his dinner.

"Not too good," Astra said. "I hit a wall. The computer finished scanning the first segment, but it's completely incompatible with the ship's systems. It's not all bad news, though. I think I can make a smaller version of it and write its base programming so the power signature will match the Frost."

Calvin was fascinated watching her as she talked. She squinted her eyes slightly when she explained the details of what she was planning to do.

She continued, "It won't be as powerful, but it'll be powerful enough to boost our shield strength by two hundred percent, and increase power ship-wide. It's going to take a little while to do it."

"Time is one thing we have," Calvin said, suppressing a yawn.

"Tired?" Astra asked.

"Yes. The last mission in the simulator was very emotional for me. I was supposed to escort a ship full of people escaping from a colony on Prathix Seven. I tried, but there were so many enemy fighters. The ship was destroyed. Over five hundred people died. I can still hear their cries for help. I tried it three times, but I couldn't win. Please tell me that didn't really happen."

"I'm sorry, it really happened," Astra said sadly, trying not to cry. "All of the events in the scenario happened. Only three fighters were available to escort the ship. It wasn't enough; everyone knew it, but there just weren't enough ships to protect everyone."

"The other two were destroyed at the beginning of the mission. I couldn't do it by myself."

"Hey, it's OK," Astra said, holding his hands. "It happened a long time ago. We just need to make sure it doesn't happen again." There was something in the way she said it.

At first, Calvin was afraid to ask about it. He didn't want to say something wrong and hurt her feelings. But he decided to ask anyway.

"Were you there?"

"I wasn't the one in the fighter, no," Astra said. "I had several close friends on the ship."

"I'm sorry," Calvin said. "That's really sad. I don't understand why the Goremog are so violent. Have you ever seen one?"

"A Goremog? Yes, I've seen them before."

"What are they like?"

"They look like us, but the gravity on their planet is lighter. Their bodies are smaller and very fragile."

"Fragile? They don't sound very scary. How can they be such a danger to the galaxy?"

"If you saw one out in the open, without a battle suit on, it wouldn't look any more dangerous than a baby Tullimar. Oh, and they're not very nice people."

Calvin laughed. "What's a Tullimar?"

"It's a small furry animal with a long soft tail. I used to have one when I was a child."

"They don't sound that bad to me."

"That's because you haven't had to fight them," Astra said. "Imagine you're on an alien planet, and you're being hunted by a Goremog in a full combat suit. He's fast, quiet, and covered with powerful weapons. Oh, and he's not alone. He's going to have several robots with him. But our intelligence people think there are so few living Goremog left, they're more likely to send assassins or assault machines after you, lots of them. The Goremog have the most efficient robot factories in the universe. They can crank out robots faster than anyone else. They don't have the most advanced technology, but they make up for it in numbers, overwhelming numbers."

173

"That's frightening," Calvin said. "But you didn't answer my question. Why are they so hostile?"

"They believe they have a divine right to rule the universe," Astra said. "All other races are unclean."

"Oh," Calvin said.

Astra yawned and rubbed her eyes, which caused Calvin to yawn, too.

"Well, I think I'll go back down and do one more mission before going to bed," Calvin said.

"Have fun," Astra said. "Just try to remember it's just training. I'm going to start building the new power generator."

"OK, I'll see you later."

CHAPTER TWO:

---•◦⊂────

THE FREIGHTER

Calvin thought he was dreaming when he heard Ion's voice over the ship-wide intercom speaker.

"Master Calvin, Mistress Astra, I'm receiving a distress signal. Please come to the bridge immediately." He sat up in bed and looked at the clock. It was five o'clock. Someone out there was in trouble. It could be a mechanical failure, or worse—someone was under attack. He got out of bed and dressed quickly. It was a short walk to the bridge.

"What's going on?" Calvin asked when he got there. Ion was alone, sitting at the computer station in the back.

"Sir, sensors are detecting a distress call, coming from a ship not far from here."

"What does the message say?" Calvin asked, trying to sound relaxed.

"It's an automated distress signal on a repeating loop," Ion said. "Ship in distress. That's all."

"What does that mean?" Calvin asked.

"It's a computer recording," Astra said, entering the bridge. "It probably means they didn't have time to send out a detailed message."

She sat down in the copilot's chair.

"Are there any other ships in the area that could help them?" Calvin asked.

"No, sir. No other ships."

"Ion, please scan the ship," Astra said. "Let's see if we can find out what their problem is."

"Yes, ma'am."

Calvin sat and examined the long-range sensors. There was a small red dot on the screen. Calvin clicked on it, and the image of a spaceship filled the monitor.

"There it is," he whispered.

"I'm not reading any life signs," Ion said.

"No one alive?" Calvin asked. "We're too late?"

"It could be an all robot crew," Astra said. "No humans. But either way, the sensors are having a problem getting a complete scan of the ship. Something is interfering with them."

"I know I'm the new guy out here," Calvin said. "But if our signals are being blocked, doesn't that mean someone is jamming us? It's obviously a trap."

"Not necessarily," Astra said. "The ship is heavily damaged. A radiation leak could be the cause."

"I don't like this," Calvin said.

"Wait, what's that?" Ion said. "I'm reading a weak energy signature. It doesn't match anything else on that ship. Give me a second to analyze it."

"What do you think, Calvin?" Astra asked.

Calvin turned around and faced Astra and Ion. "I don't think we should stop," he said. "Our mission is too important. I don't know what happened on that ship. I feel bad for them, but they weren't able to deal with whatever happened over there. Sensors clearly show no life signs, Therefore, there is nobody to help. We'd be putting ourselves in danger for no reason. I think it's a bad idea. I say no."

"I agree," Astra said. "I feel bad for them, too, but we need to find the third segment."

"I have more information," Ion said. "It's a Tryvellen freighter, and I've identified the energy signature. It's the third segment."

"The third segment?" Calvin exclaimed. "So that's how it was moving."

"The Tryvellen people were good friends of Arlandia and Aleria."

"Did they help create the super-weapon?" Calvin asked.

"No," Astra admitted. "I don't think so."

"Now we have to go over there," Calvin said. "I'm plotting an intercept course."

"I don't like this either," Astra said. "Something is very wrong here. What happened to the crew?"

"Maybe they were playing around with it and killed themselves," Calvin suggested.

"We should stop and think about this," Astra said. "Maybe if we just got close, we could get clearer scans. We need to find out what's going on over there before we rush into it."

"If we can get closer, we should be able to get through whatever is blocking our scans," Ion said.

"Good, but I still don't like it," Astra said, putting on her seat belt. Calvin did the same. "We need to be careful."

"We will," Calvin said, but Astra wasn't convinced.

"I'm taking us out of hyperspace," Calvin said. There was a light storm as the ship returned to normal space. Calvin pushed the throttle forward and changed course.

They saw it immediately, faraway—a light-gray shape against the dark background of space. It was rolling slowly on its side, tumbling through space. The ship was long and thin and was heavily damaged.

Several areas of the ship were open to space, and the inside could be seen through many gaping holes. There was a cloud of debris surrounding it. Calvin was amazed. The ship didn't look like it was defenseless. There were multiple banks of laser cannons along the sides. The engines were large bulky monstrous things hanging off of the back. Calvin brought the ship in closer.

"Scanning," Ion said. "The readings are very strange. Mistress Astra, have you ever seen anything like this?"

"What in the world?" Astra whispered. "What is that?"

"What do you see?" Calvin asked.

"These readings keep changing, flashing back and forth. One second I see two life signs. One is very clear, the other is very strange. It's almost as if it's reading as half a life. Then the next second there are eighty-five life signs, all with crazy readings." Astra looked at Calvin. "I don't know what it means, but I was right, there's a lot of radiation, and it's confusing our sensors. I can say one thing, though, with some certainty, the one life sign that appears normal is Tryvellen."

"How about the third segment?" Calvin asked. "Can you see it?"

"Yes, the signal is very strong," Ion said. "But power levels on the ship are extremely low. Main power is off-line, and life support is failing. If there is a Tryvellen over there, he won't last long. I hate to say this, but if we're going to board that ship, we should do it soon."

"Astra," Calvin said, "I want you to stay on the Frost. Ion and I will go. Stay here, keep an eye on us, and be ready in case we need to get out of there quickly." Calvin was still shaken from seeing Astra sucked out into space in front of him. He didn't want to put her in danger again. It made sense to him to keep her on the Frost.

"What do you think?"

"OK, that's fine," she said reluctantly. "Just be careful over there, all right?"

"I will," he said with a half-smile. He tried to hide his nervousness, but Astra wasn't able to hide hers. "Ion will protect me."

"Ion's not the one I'm worried about." Astra smiled, but she looked unhappy. "I scanned the exterior of the ship. I found several docking ports," she said, centering the screen on one. "They look like standard airlocks. We should be able to dock the Frost with no problems."

"I recommend we take a shuttle," Ion said. "We don't want to expose Azure Frost to whatever might be in that ship."

"Good idea," Calvin said.

"Master Calvin, are you ready?"

"Let's go."

As Calvin stood up, Astra held on to his arm.

"I'm serious," she said. "Be careful. You have no idea what you're gonna find over there, and I can't explain it, but I don't have a very good feeling."

Calvin looked into her eyes. "I'll be careful, I promise."

Their first stop was the equipment room, just outside the shuttle bay. Ion didn't need to prepare or gear up. He was impervious to harsh environments, and all the equipment he needed was built into him. Calvin, on the other hand, needed to get some equipment. First he put a tiny portable shield device in his shirt pocket. On second thought, he decided to take an extra one, just in case. He also took two communication devices. He put on a full space suit but didn't put the helmet on yet. He would put that on when they were ready to go into the other ship. The suit was bulky and caused him to walk slowly to the shuttle.

"Master Calvin," Ion said, handing him a laser pistol. "Better take this, too. Do you know how to use it?"

"No, I've never seen a pistol like this before," Calvin said.

"It's a simple, yet powerful, design," Ion explained. "The safety lock is here, the power pack is here." Ion showed him how to change out power packs.

Calvin put the pistol in a holster, along with several extra power packs. When they were ready to go, they walked out of the equipment room and into the shuttle bay. Ion opened the back door, and they stepped into the shuttle. Calvin made his way to the pilot's chair and sat down. Ion shut the back door and took the seat next to Calvin.

Calvin turned on the computer. The preflight checklist appeared on a small monitor on the side of the console. Calvin ran the checklist. He turned on the power generators, fuel pumps, main computer, auxiliary control system, and compressors. He then waited for the engines to warm up. A green light flashed to tell him the ship was ready.

A high-pitched whine filled the air as the engines started, followed by a deep humming throb that grew steadily.

While he was waiting for the engines to finish starting up, he ran through the rest of the checklist. All systems were fully operational. Calvin pressed a button on the console, which opened the shuttle bay doors. He was normally excited every time he got to fly the shuttle, but this time he was scared. He didn't want to show it in front of Astra, but he was very nervous about what they would find on the disabled Tryvellen ship.

Calvin increased power to the engines and guided the shuttle carefully through the open doors out into space. Once they were clear, he pushed the throttle forward.

The shuttle sped across space toward the derelict ship. Calvin couldn't stop thinking about Astra's last words, about how she had a bad feeling. He hadn't known her very long, but he was learning that it was a good idea to listen to her. When she had a bad feeling, something bad usually happened.

"Master Calvin, slow down. The radiation is interfering with the navigation system," Ion said. "I can't find the docking port. Give me a second."

Calvin pulled back on the throttle. Two thrusters on the front of the shuttle ignited and slowed them down to a crawl. Ion studied an image of the Tryvellen ship on a monitor. Bursts of static lit up the screen. "There are several docking ports, but the two near the bridge are too heavily damaged." He pointed at them on the screen. "There's one here near the engines. It looks like our best chance of getting in."

"OK, looks good," Calvin said, pointing the shuttle toward the back of the ship and accelerating.

"Be careful, sir," Ion said quickly. "There's a lot of debris ahead."

"No problem," Calvin said. "I can do this." But then he saw a huge debris field directly in their flight path. There were pieces of metal everywhere.

"We have shields, right?" Calvin asked.

"Yes, and no," Ion replied. "We have shields, but they're not very strong. I recommend not running into anything."

"Easier said than done," Calvin muttered, steering the shuttle between two large sections of bulkhead. "I can avoid the big pieces, no problem, but there's a million tiny pieces. What about them?"

"Our light shields should protect us," Ion said, "But you should try to avoid them."

"No promises," Calvin cringed as they passed through a cloud of tiny fragments. The shields flickered angrily.

"Can't we go around this?" Calvin asked anxiously.

"I'm afraid not. The debris field surrounds the ship. There isn't a clear path ahead." Calvin dodged a large piece of metal. He flew close around it and almost hit another one hidden behind it.

"Whoa," Calvin exclaimed. He had a flashback of his first attempted flight through an asteroid field. It was in the simulator, but it didn't end well. He slowed the shuttle and carefully turned to avoid another large charred piece of wreckage. He got much closer than he intended, close enough for the shields to flash. He gently and skillfully piloted the shuttle around to the back of the big freighter, weaving through an area with the least amount of objects in their way. It took a long time because they had to go slow, weaving in and out, up and down. Despite slowing down, more than once he hit several small pieces.

Fortunately, they were not big enough to cause damage.

They flew past the big bulky engines on the back of the ship and around to the other side. Calvin tried to scan the hull with the shuttle's sensors, but the screen flickered angrily and filled with static.

"This thing is useless," Calvin complained. He looked ahead out the window, but it was too dark to see.

"This isn't going to work," he said, getting more frustrated. "I can't see a thing."

"Here," Ion said. "This will help." A bright light shot into the darkness, lighting up the side of the alien ship nicely. Calvin piloted the shuttle along the charred hull of the freighter. His heart raced when he saw it—the outline of a door.

"Ion," Calvin said excitedly. "Is that it?"

"Yes," Ion said. "Give me a second to configure the docking connector."

Ion worked the controls for a moment then said, "All right, sir, ready."

Calvin turned the shuttle around, reversed the engines, and backed up slowly until the connection was confirmed with a soft bump.

"Master Calvin," Ion said. "Your piloting skills have improved dramatically. I'm impressed."

"Thank you, Ion," Calvin said. "I've been practicing in the simulator."

"It shows," Ion said. "If you were training at the Alerian flight academy, that performance would have earned you a silver rating."

"I feel comfortable in the pilot's seat."

"If I were your instructor, I would tell you that you are doing very well, your skills are improving and you seem to have a natural ability, but don't become over-confident. You have room for improvement.

"Thank you, I'll try to remember that."

182

Calvin took off his seat belt and was about to shut down the engines, when he suddenly had a thought.

"Ion, should I keep the engines running, just in case? We don't know what's out there, and we might have to leave in a hurry."

"Place the engines in standby mode," Ion said. "They'll stay warm and only take four seconds to restart." Calvin did as Ion suggested.

They went to the back of the shuttle. Calvin put on his helmet. A hiss of air confirmed there was a good seal.

"Ion, can you hear me?" Calvin said, checking the communications gear.

"Yes, your signal is clear," Ion said.

Calvin checked his laser pistol. He turned the safety off and made sure the power pack was locked. It was. He had one hundred rounds available at standard power, fifty at full.

Ion opened the door and went first, into a small square waiting room. There were rows of seats along the walls, and another door on the other side of the room. Calvin and Ion stepped through the next door and into a very long dark hallway. To the left it stretched off farther than they could see. To the right the corridor stopped at a door, not far from where they stood.

Calvin took out a small scanner and turned it on.

"I'm picking up one life sign," Calvin said. "The signal is strong. I think it's the Tryvellen. The other life sign is flickering on and off. It's definitely not human. It's moving around pretty fast. No, wait, now there are eighty-five of them again. Ion, there's obviously more than one of those things here, or the scanner wouldn't keep seeing eighty-five. It hasn't seen more than one Tryvellen."

"Good point," Ion said. "Can you see the third segment?"

Calvin looked into his scanner. He had to change the mode a few times, searching for an energy pattern that matched the weapon segment.

"There it is," he said. "It's right next to the Tryvellen. Does that mean he has it?"

"Possibly. He might be guarding it," Ion suggested. "We need to get to that person. He could tell us what happened here."

Ion led the way down the corridor. It was dark and cold. The readings on the scanner said the temperature was a chilly thirty-one degrees. Fortunately for Calvin, his suit was heated—he was nice and warm. But to Calvin, the most important part of the suit were the lights built into his helmet. Combined with Ion's lights, the corridor was lit up around them nicely.

"According to the scanner," Calvin said. "We need to keep going straight for another three hundred feet. We take a right turn through a door and then a left turn down a major corridor that runs down the center of the ship. We follow that all the way to the bridge." When the scanner flashed, both contacts disappeared, and then white dots covered the screen. "The interference is getting worse."

They slowly plodded on. Calvin carefully watched the scanner for changes. The strange life signs were moving very erratically.

One hundred feet down the corridor, they found a small computer monitor on the wall.

"It's a computer terminal," Ion said. He stopped and examined it carefully. "I hate to add to our problems, but if these readings are correct, the life support system is failing, and oxygen is leaking into space in several sections due to hull breaches. I estimate there is only one hour of air left, and the ship will be completely unable to support life."

"I'm glad I have this suit on," Calvin said. "I hope the other guy has a suit, too, or he's gonna be in trouble."

Up ahead in the gloom, Calvin saw an odd bump on the floor. As they got closer, he saw it was a body. They cautiously walked up to it. Calvin was afraid he was going to see a lot of this. But when they got closer, they saw it was a robot. He felt relieved and sad at the same time. What happened to the crew?

Calvin felt a familiar feeling of dread slowly creep over him, threatening to consume him. He turned and looked around, wildly shining his light in all directions. He was terrified that something was sneaking up on him. He kept hearing strange noises. There was a grinding noise that sounded like metal being pulled apart. But the scariest sound was a tapping noise that sounded like footsteps. It started far away and seemed to rush toward him very quickly.

A short distance away they found two more bodies, both robots. Calvin looked at them carefully. Both were burned and broken into pieces, but one of them was different. The arms and legs on one of the robots looked like they had flesh on them.

"What's that?" Calvin asked, feeling nauseated. The head of the creature did not look like a robot's. There was a metal frame and structure that belonged on a robot, but there was an outer layer made of flesh and blood. The mouth, with rows of razor sharp teeth, looked like it had been crushed inward. Many of the teeth were cracked and broken. Ion stooped down to examine the creature.

"This is very bad," Ion said sternly. For the first time, Ion sounded scared.

"What is it?" Calvin asked.

"The Goremog created these things," Ion explained. "We don't know their real name, but the Alerians call them the Dark Terror."

"What?" Calvin said. "That's the Dark Terror?" He started to breathe faster, his heart pounded, and he began to feel light-headed. "I was really hoping it was just a story. It's real? I can't believe it."

"Yes, they're real," Ion said. "And they're extremely dangerous. This one looks a little different than the other ones I've seen before. We need to hurry."

"You've seen them before?" Calvin asked.

"Yes, several times."

"What happened?"

"They were hunting us," Ion said. "We barely got away. Actually, not everyone in the group survived. Master Calvin, we need to hurry. We're in extreme danger." A blue light came out of Ion's chest. The light started at the monster's feet and slowly moved up the body.

185

When it reached the head, it changed color from blue, to yellow, then red. Then it turned off.

"I scanned it and will study it later," Ion said.

"OK," Calvin said, stepping past it. "Just don't touch it."

"I wasn't planning to," Ion said simply.

Calvin didn't know what was worse—the monsters running around in the dark, the dying ship, or that Ion was scared.

Farther down the corridor, they found a section that was full of robot bodies. Some were normal robots, some were monsters. But all were burned, melted, and torn to pieces.

Calvin looked at his scanner. It had been several minutes since he last checked on what the strange life forms were doing. Suddenly a thought occurred to him. What if the strange life forms were all live robot monsters? He was seeing the evidence on the floor now. What else could they be?

"Something is moving!" Calvin half shouted. Then he lowered his voice. "Coming this way." He moved behind Ion and peeked his head around. Both of them stood still, with their weapons pointed down the corridor. Ion scanned the corridor in front of them. He must have had his scanning intensity set very high; a soft hum filled the air.

Calvin wanted to look down into the scanner but was afraid of taking his eyes off the dark corridor ahead. Another minute passed. Nothing happened. Finally he looked down into his scanner. The red dot on the screen was still there, but the scanner said it was right in front of them.

"Ion," Calvin whispered. "Do you see it?"

"No, I can't see it," Ion said quietly. "But my sensors say it's twenty feet in front of us."

Calvin stood frozen behind Ion and stared intently into the gloom. Ion shined his light directly ahead, but they couldn't see anything. Suddenly an ear-piercing scream shattered the quiet. Calvin jumped. The scream was the most horrible sound he'd ever heard. It crushed his heart like a vice, sapping his strength.

A dark shape appeared out of nowhere and rushed them. It was in their faces before either of them could react. It moved like lightning—arms thrashing, mouth open, flashing rows of razor-sharp teeth. It screamed again, a deafening cacophony of torturous pain and horror.

Calvin and Ion opened fire at point-blank range. The laser flashes were blinding and loud but didn't do anything other than make the creature mad. Calvin stumbled backward. Ion held the monster by the neck to keep it from tearing them apart with its claws and teeth. The monster screamed and grabbed Ion's head with its long arms and pulled. Suddenly a solid, bright-blue laser beam sliced through the air and cut into the monster. It screamed and jumped up, smashing its way into the ceiling. The screaming stopped abruptly, and there was silence.

Calvin stared up at the hole in the ceiling, shocked. He replayed the last few seconds of the attack over in his mind. Did that just happen? He looked down. Lying on the floor at his feet was an arm. There was a metal rod protruding from the end, and a dark colored substance leaking out of it.

"All of that shooting, and we didn't even kill it," Calvin gasped.

"They're very difficult to kill. At least we injured it."

"Yeah, but how much?"

"Not enough, I'm afraid. Are you all right?" Ion asked, running his scanner over Calvin.

"Yeah, I think so," Calvin said. "Please tell me there aren't any more of those things running around."

"Sir, you know there are," Ion said sadly. "Eighty-five of them."

"I know," Calvin said. "And I really don't want to be here anymore."

"Neither do I, sir."

Calvin's hands were shaking as he looked at the scanner. "Speaking of the eighty-five, I don't see them anymore. They're gone. Do you think maybe it was a malfunction after all? They all left the ship or died?"

"Look again," Ion said. "And scan for radiation."

Calvin did what Ion said, and the screen changed. Several areas of the ship were dark.

"What is that?" Calvin asked. "There're several areas of the ship I can't scan."

"The radiation level has been rising since we boarded," Ion stated. "The engine room appears to be the source."

"Yeah, OK. That makes sense," Calvin said. "It's the biggest dark spot on the map. I bet the engines are damaged."

"Clearly, but I should mention the creatures are attracted to heat. They don't like the cold."

"That's good to know," Calvin said. "And I bet it's nice and warm in the engine room. We should stay away from there."

"Good idea. We need to find the survivor and the segment and then get off this ship."

"Come on," Calvin said and led the way. He walked slowly, holding his gun out. His hand trembled, and he breathed in short gasps. Not knowing where the monsters were petrified him. He kept a careful eye on the scanner, hoping the dark areas would clear up, but the static and interference got worse, not better. Fear grew with each step, terror with each thud and echo. It felt like it took a lifetime to walk the length of the corridor. Calvin jumped at every little noise, and there were a lot of noises. The light from his helmet cast shadows on the walls. Occasionally he would catch a glimpse of one and spin around in fright, expecting to see a monster.

After another hundred feet, they stopped in front of a closed door.

"Here," Calvin said. "We need to go this way." He found the controls to open the door, pressed a button, but nothing happened.

"There is no power, sir," Ion said. "I'll open it."

Calvin stepped aside. Ion pulled the door open easily, but Calvin cringed when a loud grinding noise shattered the quiet.

"We have to stop making noise," Calvin said, more to himself than Ion. "Every monster on the ship probably heard that."

"I'm sorry, sir."

Calvin was now completely horrified. The ship was slowly dying, and he could see it on the scanner. He could hear it in the creaks and groans, which sounded like cries of agony.

Calvin peered into the darkness. Another corridor stretched out in front of them, and one that led off to the right and left. There was a loud bang and then the sound of something running away. Calvin was afraid to keep going. He decided to look at his scanner to see what it was.

"Ion, wait!" Calvin whispered loudly. "There's something in front of us. It's moving." His heart pounded as he watched a small red dot move away on the screen.

"I can't tell what it is. There's too much interference," Calvin said. "Is that the Tryvellen? I can't tell, but it's running away from us." Ion stood still. Calvin wanted to shout but was too scared to, and he knew that it would be a mistake.

"I don't think it's human," Calvin said. "The readings are changing. I don't know if it's because we got closer to it. It could be another one of those things." Suddenly the readings jumped again.

"No, wait," Calvin said. "These readings are really strange. Now there are two dots. One of them is the one we saw earlier. It's clear and looks completely human. This other red dot is something else." Calvin's heart froze when he realized what it was. "It's another monster."

"Where is it?" Ion asked. Calvin worked the scanner. "It's one level below us. I bet it's looking for a way up here."

"What is the human doing?" Ion asked.

"He's still moving away from us," Calvin said.

"Is the segment still with him?"

189

"Yes," Calvin answered. "I think he's carrying it. That could explain why he's not moving very fast."

"He must realize how important it is," Ion said. Suddenly a burst of static from the communications gear made him jump.

"Calvin, how's it going?" Astra asked.

"I'm all right," Calvin said in a shaky voice.

"I'm seeing some really strange life sign readings over there, but I can't tell if they're real or not. They keep appearing and disappearing. Are you detecting any kind of radiation that might be blocking your signal?"

"They're real," Calvin said. "We just ran into one a few minutes ago. And yes, there is a lot of radiation coming from the engine room."

"What was it?" Astra said, full of concern. She could hear the fear in his voice.

"It was one of your monsters, the Dark Terror," Calvin said. "Like what you told me about last night." Calvin and Ion walked slowly and cautiously. Calvin watched the signal on his scanner. "Robots on the inside and flesh on the outside. Claws, huge teeth. Scariest thing I've ever seen, and that's saying something now."

"Oh, no," Astra whispered, her voice full of fear.

"It gets worse," Calvin said. "There are eighty-five of them on this ship."

Astra gasped. "Please be careful and don't take any chances. Shoot at everything that moves and get out of there as fast as you can."

"OK. Wish I'd thought of that," Calvin said, sarcastically.

"Funny. Listen, I'll try to help you. The sensors on the Frost are better than your handhelds. I'm trying to burn through the interference and get a better idea of where all the monsters are. I'll let you know as soon as I can."

"Thanks," Calvin said. He was trying to focus on his surroundings. Since his scanner wasn't working very well, he would have to rely on his eyes and ears.

Ion walked forward, with a reluctant Calvin right behind. He used Ion as a big shield. They turned left down the ship's central corridor. Maybe it was because it was dark, he didn't know, but everything in this spaceship looked the same.

"Master Calvin," Ion said. "What's the creature doing?"

Calvin looked into the scanner. He had it fixed on the alien one deck below them. When he checked it again, it was gone.

"It's not there," Calvin said, alarmed. He looked around wildly, half expecting to see it standing behind them. He played around with the scanner and frantically searched for the monster. He could not find it. All he could find was the human, still moving away ahead of them.

"Come on, Ion," Calvin said. "Let's hurry and catch up to that guy." Ion and Calvin started running. At first it didn't seem like it was going to be a problem running in the bulky space suit, but Calvin quickly learned he was wrong. After a few minutes, the suit began to get heavy. He could feel his leg muscles burn, and pain began to creep into his back. After a few more minutes, running became torturous and got worse with each step. After five minutes, Ion began to pull ahead and leave Calvin behind. It brought back memories to Calvin of the harrowing escape from Aleria. Except there he wasn't wearing a heavy space suit. They kept running until they got to the end of the corridor, where they found another door.

"I think he's going to the bridge," Calvin said, gasping for air. He was tired and uncomfortable. His body was covered in sweat. Calvin tried the door, but it wouldn't open.

Ion pulled it open effortlessly and walked through. Calvin followed close behind. The central corridor stretched out in front of them. Some of the lights on the ceiling were flickering. Instead of offering brief flashes of hope, the distant flashes of light scared him. He couldn't tell, but he thought he saw a dark shadow, far up ahead. Was it a monster, watching them? Knowing he couldn't rely on his eyes, Calvin looked into his scanner and watched the screen as he walked. If there was

191

a monster there, it wasn't appearing on the scanner. They continued on but decided to walk instead of run. It felt as if it took forever to walk to the end. Calvin switched back and forth between the scanner and looking forward, terrified of what was in front of them but frustrated that he couldn't see very well. Thankfully he didn't see anything, but he heard a lot of scary noises; scratching sounds like claws on metal; pounding like something big running up to them. But the most distressing noise was a low, deep growl that came from somewhere above. When he looked up and shone a light, he didn't see anything. He sensed that something was there, even though he couldn't see it. It felt like it was following them. At the end of the corridor, they found another door.

CHAPTER THREE:

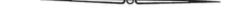

THE SURVIVOR

Ion forced the door open; the screeching sound of tearing metal was louder than before. They stepped through and found themselves on the bridge. The room was full of computer stations, and there was a large star map hanging on the rear wall. Short windows lined the room.

A distant sun cast an eerie yellow light in the room. Long shadows stretched across the floor. Calvin looked out a window and saw the Azure Frost slowly float past. Calvin turned his attention back to the bridge. All the computers, including a dozen large monitors hanging on the walls, were off. Half of the screens were cracked.

"Just out of curiosity," Calvin said. "How long until life support is completely gone?"

"There's twenty minutes of breathable oxygen left," Ion said.

"Hello?" said a quivering voice. "Are you Tryvellen?"

Calvin spun around in the direction the voice came from.

"No, I'm an Arlandian," Calvin said. "My name is Calvin. This is Ion. He's an Alerian."

"How do you know my language?" the voice asked suspiciously.

"I have a translator," Calvin answered. He peered into the

darkness. Calvin couldn't tell where the voice was coming from, but it was clearly a man's voice. "I don't know your language. You can come out. We're friends. We want to help you." There was a row of computer equipment along the wall. Calvin thought the man might be hiding behind it.

"The life support system is failing," Ion said. "There's only twenty minutes of oxygen left. If you don't have a space suit, or a portable life support system, you're going to die."

"I have an extra one," Calvin said. "You can use it." Calvin unzipped a pocket and pulled it out.

"How do I know it's not a trick?"

"We don't have time," Calvin urged. "We have to get off of this ship before those monsters find us."

"You have a way to get off the ship?"

"Yes!" Calvin said. "We have a shuttle. It's docked near the engine room."

"Oh, no," the voice said, clearly upset. "You didn't let them out of the engine room, did you? We had them trapped in there."

"No," Calvin said. "We didn't let anything out. The one we saw was in the corridor."

"Don't tell me that!" the voice exclaimed. "That means they're out again."

"Obviously," Calvin said, feeling sick to his stomach. "And they're everywhere. Look, the Tryvellens and Arlandians used to be close friends. Please come out. Let us help you. Come back to our ship. It's safe there." Suddenly a distant explosion shook the ship.

"Calvin, are you OK?" It was Astra.

"We're OK," Calvin said. "What was that?"

"There was an explosion near the engines," Astra said. "It was huge."

"Astra," Calvin said. "Can you see our shuttle? It was docked

194

near the engines."

"Hold on a second."

A young man stepped out of the shadows from behind a computer console. He was short, skinny, and had medium-length blond hair. He looked like he was about Calvin's age.

"My name's Dev, and I would really like to get off this ship. Can I go with you, please?"

"Yes, good," Calvin said, relieved. "Nice to meet you." Calvin offered his hand. Dev took it, and they shook hands.

"It's good to see a friendly face," Dev said. "I had about lost hope that I would get out of this."

Calvin handed a small shield device to Dev.

"Here, you'll need this," Calvin said. "Just stick it in your pocket. It works automatically."

Dev took it and put it in his pocket. As soon as he did, a force field surrounded him. He took a deep breath. "Wow, that's better," he said. "I can breathe again."

Ion stepped forward and pointed his arm at Dev. Dev was startled and jumped back.

"Ion, what's wrong?"

"Master Calvin, scan him and tell me what you see."

Calvin pointed the scanner at Dev.

"Hey, wait a second," Dev said, trembling. "I thought you said we were friends."

"Don't move," Calvin said. Dev froze, fear reflecting in his face.

Calvin waved the scanner in front of Dev. It emitted a soft beep, and the screen flashed red.

"The segment?" Calvin asked. He waved the scanner across the Tryvellen's chest and followed the signal to a place just under his chin.

"Segment?" Dev asked. "What are you talking about? A segment of what?"

"Do you have something hanging around your neck?" Calvin asked.

"Just this," Dev said defensively. He reached into his shirt and pulled out a silver chain with a small black and silver key attached to it. Calvin moved closer and pointed the scanner directly at the key.

"Ion, that's it!" Calvin exclaimed. "That's the third segment."

"Excellent," Ion said.

"Segment of what?" Dev said again. "Please tell me."

"We'll explain later," Ion said. "When we're safely on the Frost."

Dev looked thoroughly confused.

"That's our ship," Calvin explained.

Ion walked over to one of the computers and quickly began taking it apart.

"What are you doing?" Calvin asked.

"I need to do one more thing before we leave," Ion said. "I want to find the main memory unit. It should contain engineering and sensor logs and possibly personal logs of the crew as well. I'd like to learn what happened to this ship, and with any luck, determine how and where the creatures got on board."

Ion wasted no time. He savagely ripped components out of the computer until he found what he was looking for—a small gray box.

"I believe this is it. We can go now," Ion said, moving to the door. "Master Calvin, are you ready?"

Calvin lifted his pistol so Ion could see it. "I'm ready. Let's get outta here."

Ion opened the door and stepped through, followed by Calvin and then Dev. They left the safety of the bridge and went into the dark, gloomy corridor. Calvin gripped his weapon tightly. He hoped that he wouldn't need it, but if he did, maybe he could find a vulnerable spot on the monsters, if one existed.

They'd only walked five feet, when they heard a loud scream from the darkness ahead.

"Stop!" Ion said. Everyone froze. Calvin and Ion both shone their lights but couldn't see anything. It was too dark.

"Astra," Calvin whispered into his radio. "Any sign of the shuttle?"

There was a second of silence. Calvin could hear his heart beating. There was a loud hiss of static that made him jump.

"I can't see it," Astra said. "There's too much debris in the way. I can't see anything, and I can't burn through whatever is blocking the signal. If I didn't know better, I would say we're being jammed. But, more than likely something is leaking—some radiation or liquid fuel—I don't know. Even the sensors are useless."

"OK," Calvin said, trying to think. He could feel himself starting to panic but forced himself to stay calm. "It doesn't matter anyway. We'd still have to walk all the way back. Hopefully the shuttle is still there."

"I'm sorry," Astra said. "I wish I could help more. Have you seen anymore Terrors?"

"There's one in the corridor with us, I think," Calvin said quietly. "The problem is they're impossible to see until they're right in front of us. We shot the last one several times, but couldn't kill it."

"OK, stop talking," Astra said. "Hurry up and get back here."

"We're working on it," Calvin said.

Calvin turned to Dev. "What's the quickest way to the engine room?"

"The main corridor. It runs the whole length of the ship," Dev said.

"That's the way we came in," Ion said.

"We should go out the same way," Calvin said. "The less time

197

we spend in here the better."

"We should be all right out in the open," Dev said. "I don't think they like it out in the open. I know for a fact the captain said they trapped two in the engine room. I saw two in the shuttle bay and locked them in. Except for the one you saw, I'm fairly sure that's all of them."

"Weren't you listening? This place is crawling with the scariest monsters I've ever seen. Do you know how many of those monsters are on this ship?" Calvin asked.

"No, I don't know for sure," Dev said. "But Lieutenant Ranton thought there were only the five."

"Five," Calvin repeated. "I wish that's all there were. Our computers have tracked eighty-five separate creatures."

"Eighty-five?" Dev repeated, shocked. "That can't be right, but it explains a few things."

"Come on, Ion," Calvin said impatiently. "We have to get out of here."

Calvin was a jumble of conflicting emotions. He desperately wanted to get off the ship but was terrified about going forward. Reluctantly, he forced himself to move. He reminded himself that there was only one way off the ship, and that was down the long, dark corridors. Ion was the first to keep going but stopped almost immediately when a loud thumping echoed off the walls. It was getting louder! Calvin felt a surge of fear and fired down the corridor into the darkness. The flash of light from his laser bolts gave them a glimpse of a horrific sight; a monster robot was charging directly toward them, its mouth wide open and claws reaching out.

"Fire!" Calvin shouted loudly and resumed shooting. The monster screamed, a high pitched heart-stopping scream. The monster dodged from side to side, trying to avoid laser shots from Calvin and Ion. It was difficult to see, but Calvin thought they hit it several times. Finally it jumped and smashed its way through the ceiling. Metal fragments rained down onto the floor. Calvin and Ion stopped shooting and stared down the dark corridor.

"Where did it go?" Dev asked. He looked scared and stood close to Calvin and Ion.

"It went up," Calvin said nervously.

"That's the second time a Terror has smashed its way through the bulkhead to get away from us. Why do they run and not attack?"

"What are you thinking, Ion?" Calvin asked.

"It should have attacked us," Ion said. "But it ran away."

"You were both shooting at it," Dev said. "I'm just guessing here, but maybe it didn't like your laser guns."

They cautiously walked forward. Calvin hurried under the hole in the ceiling, looking up nervously as he passed.

"I didn't believe you," Dev said, as he walked under the hole. "I'm sorry. You were right. I was hoping the monsters were trapped behind locked doors. But they seem to be loose."

"We have to keep moving," Ion said. "Just follow me. If you see a Terror, don't hesitate—shoot it."

Calvin followed Ion and Dev down the corridor. His senses were heightened, and a deep persistent fear caused him to experience a stab of panic with every small noise. Suddenly they heard a loud bang behind them. Calvin spun around and looked for something to shoot, but he couldn't see anything. Nothing happened for several seconds. His heart pounded, and his breathing sounded loud in his space suit.

"Come on, Calvin," Dev said. He and Ion had moved off and were already fifty feet away. Calvin was about to turn around and follow them when he heard a series of very loud cracks above him. The ceiling directly above him disintegrated into fragments and a massive dark object dropped through the new hole. The next thing he knew, Calvin was lying on the floor with a very heavy black shape on top of him, crushing him. It was a Terror! Its open jaws were in his face. It savagely tore into Calvin's spacesuit with its long claws. It reared back, prepared to strike with its teeth. Calvin tried to get free. He pushed, but it was no use. He panicked and desperately tried to cry for help, but the monster's immense weight prevented him from moving or making any sounds. He was trapped.

Just as he was out of hope, the monster reared back, and Calvin quickly saw why. Ion had a firm grip on the monster's neck and back and was pulling it off him. It was enraged and screamed with fury. Ion lifted it into the air. Its arms and legs whipped around, trying to hit Ion. The monster screamed again and inflicted a fierce blow on Ion's right arm, which caused him to release the creature. Calvin tried to stand, but he couldn't get up. He tried to crawl backward, but his arms and legs would not cooperate. Dev darted in, grabbed Calvin by the back of the space suit, and dragged him out of the combat zone.

Ion and the Terror were locked in an intense struggle. The hideous creature thrashed against Ion. It locked around Ion's chest, its claws tore into his metal body. Ion fought back but was unable to stop the creature from biting into his already damaged right arm. Ion shouted something incoherent, picked the Terror up into the air, and hurled it down the corridor. It bounced off the wall and crashed to the floor somewhere in the darkness. The monster wailed in agony and sprinted away.

"Calvin!" Dev exclaimed. "Are you all right?"

"Master Calvin," Ion said. He picked Calvin up and helped him back to his feet.

Calvin felt a wave of dizziness and nausea and struggled to breathe.

"What happened?" Calvin said, gasping for air.

"You were attacked," Ion said. "Your suit has been damaged."

Calvin looked down. The front of his suit was torn and shredded, and blood soaked the white fabric across his chest.

"You're injured," Dev said, pointing to the blood. Calvin began to feel light-headed.

"We need to get back to the shuttle," Ion said. "Now!"

"What…about…my backup…shield," Calvin gasped. "It should

be working."

"It must be damaged, too," Ion said. "Hurry! We may not have much time!"

"What about you?" Dev said. "You're hurt, too."

Calvin looked at Ion. His right arm and leg were heavily damaged. The silver plating was cracked and broken, revealing a damaged interior of broken computer parts and severed wires.

"'I'll manage," Ion said. "But we must hurry."

Calvin faced the long hallway out and wondered if he had the strength to get to the shuttle. Fear of running into more monsters gave him plenty of motivation.

Ion led the way, running the best that he could with one good leg. The other leg, damaged, caused him to limp, stagger, and make an angry, grinding sound.

The other two ran after Ion, but Calvin didn't make it very far. He stumbled and fell to his knees with a gasp and a cry. Dev stopped and helped him stand. Together, they stumbled along behind Ion. It was terrifying and exhausting. Calvin heard loud screams and bangs that seemed to be chasing after them. Twice Ion fired his weapon, and his shots were answered by horrific screams. Calvin turned and looked back once. He saw three monsters chasing them.

"Run faster, Dev," Calvin said loudly.

"I know!" Dev shouted.

Calvin was relieved beyond words to find the shuttle was right where they left it. He and Dev staggered inside, although by this point Dev was doing most of the work. Ion was last. He backed into the shuttle, keeping his eyes and weapons trained down the corridor to protect them until the door was closed. When the door shut, the air pressurized, and Calvin gasped in breaths of fresh air.

Calvin looked around the cabin suspiciously, terrified that one of the monsters got aboard without them knowing. He decided to ask.

"Ion, how do we know one of those things isn't on the shuttle with us?"

"That's impossible, sir," Ion said. "There is nowhere for one of them to hide. We would see it in front of us right now."

"OK," Calvin said, not entirely convinced. He took his helmet off and dropped it on a seat in the back. He hurried to the front. Calvin had the takeoff procedures down to a science. He sat down in his seat, put his seat harness on, and released the docking clamps at the same time. He was dizzy and twice missed a button he was trying to press.

"You better let me pilot the shuttle," Ion said.

"No," Calvin said, still fighting to breathe. "I got it."

He jabbed the maneuvering thrusters to full, delivering a sudden boost of power to push them away quickly. All he could think about was getting away from the monster-infested ship. He didn't check to see if Ion and Dev were ready. He shoved the throttle forward, harder than he was supposed to, but the shuttle's gravity system protected them from being thrown around. They accelerated away from the ship, hitting pieces of debris on the way. Several pieces hit with a loud smash. At the speed they were traveling, it only took a few seconds to clear the debris field. It felt very good to be back out in space.

After a few minutes, Calvin forced himself to relax. He took a deep breath and looked around. Ion was sitting next to him. Dev was strapped into a chair in the back.

Because he was paranoid, he turned on the ship's internal sensors and ran a thorough scan.

He detected only two life signs aboard. That made him feel a little better, but the shock of what he had just gone through was running though his mind and body. He thought he had been scared before, but this could be the most terrified he'd ever been in his entire life. He looked down. His suit was wet with blood.

"Is everyone OK?"

"I'm all right," Dev answered.

"I'm fine, Master Calvin," Ion said. "But you're not. I'm taking you to the medical station as soon as we dock."

Calvin steered them through another large debris field and set them on course back to the Azure Frost. "Astra, we're on our way back." He had to take another deep breath. The dizziness was getting worse.

"Oh, good," Astra said. It was hard to hear her over the speaker. There was a lot of static. "The shuttle bay is open. Is everyone all right?"

"No," Calvin said. "Ion was damaged in a fight with a Terror. I'm hurt, too. I don't know how bad. I'm bleeding." And then he paused. "A lot."

"What?" Astra said. "Ion, is he OK?"

"I don't know, Mistress," Ion said. "There wasn't time to stop and find out."

"Just get back here," Astra said, with concern in her voice. "Hurry."

Calvin carefully guided the shuttle behind the Frost, but his hands slipped off the controls, and he slumped back into his seat. Ion was ready and took over. Calvin was shaking when the shuttle landed and the engines turned off. The sound had not died away completely when the door opened.

Calvin didn't get up. He tried but didn't have the strength. He closed his eyes and tried to control the spinning. He heard Ion take off his seatbelt, get up, and noisily stumble to the back of the shuttle. He felt a hand on his shoulder. He opened his eyes and looked up. It was Astra.

"Hey," she said softly. She looked down at his blood-soaked space suit. "Let's go. I'm taking you to medical." Calvin didn't argue. Astra helped him take off his seat harness. He started to stand up again but was too weak and exhausted. Astra had to help him stand. It wasn't easy. His suit was bulky, and he was sitting at an odd angle. Astra had him sit forward, so she could get her hands under his arms. It took both of them to get Calvin to a standing position.

"Where's Ion and Dev?" Calvin asked, his voice weak and cracking.

"They went to medical," Astra answered. "Ion said he wanted to make sure Dev was OK. You guys were exposed to very high levels of radiation over there." Calvin didn't argue. "Come on." Astra guided him outside the shuttle to a floating chair. She helped him sit and pushed him to the elevator. "Did you meet Dev?" Calvin asked.

"Just for a second. Just long enough to learn his name." Astra answered. It was a short walk from the elevator to the medical station, but it felt like miles to Calvin. When they entered the medical bay, Calvin realized he had only been in there once, briefly, just long enough to see what it was. They found Dev lying on a bed against a wall. Ion was standing behind a computer console. A large scanner on the ceiling was slowly passing over Dev, a multicolored light flashing as it went.

"Let's get you out of your suit," Astra said. Together they carefully removed the space suit. Astra placed the bloody remnants in a hazardous waste container. Then she helped Calvin take his shirt off. A dark shadow crossed over her face as she looked at his wounds. He had large savage scratches in his chest. Blood was oozing from the open wounds. Astra helped him onto another bed, under a scanner. She moved quickly to a control panel and turned it on. The scanner slowly and methodically examined every part of Calvin's body.

On the other side of the room, the scanner above Dev finished. Its lights turned off, and the bar slid quietly to the head of the bed.

"Sir, you can get up," Ion said. "According to the scan, all of your injuries have been healed. Your skin was treated for minor bruising and your lungs for inhaling toxic chemicals. You were also exposed to dangerous levels of radiation. The computer has treated you. Also, you had a broken bone in your arm. The computer has mended that as well. You are perfectly fine now." Dev sat up and swung his legs over the side.

"Thank you, I feel much better." He took a deep breath and dropped down onto the floor.

"You should get looked at, too," Dev said to Ion.

"Yes," Ion said. "I'll go to the repair bay as soon as I know Master Calvin is all right."

204

The medical scanner stopped over Calvin's chest and emitted a purple light. He looked at Astra.

"It's OK," she said soothingly and studied the medical computer screen. "The scratches were deep, and you lost a lot of blood, but it was nothing the medcomp couldn't handle."

"Good," Calvin said. "I feel a lot better. In fact, I feel pretty good."

"That would be the pain medication," Astra said smiling, visibly relieved.

"I can't believe what happened over there," Calvin said. His hands shook, and he felt a multitude of emotions threaten to overwhelm him. He rubbed his eyes. "Those things are the most—" He stopped, searching for the best word to use. Calvin shivered and began to shake.

"Scary?" Dev offered.

"Yes, scary," Calvin said. "But I don't think that word is strong enough. We need to invent a new one."

"That's why we call them Terrors," Astra said, taking a thick blue robe out of a drawer. She wrapped it around Calvin. "I don't know about you, but I can't think of a better word for them."

"Yeah, it's a good name for them. Thank you," Calvin said. He sat down on the bed and looked at Dev.

"I don't know what those things are," Dev admitted.

"How did they get on your ship?"

"Maybe you should start at the beginning," Astra suggested, seeing Dev struggling to answer.

"OK, I can do that," Dev said. "My name is Dev Sorna. I'm from the planet Tryvella, which you already know. Twenty-four days ago, our colony on Sessia Six was attacked by the Goremog. Everything was destroyed. In the chaos, I was separated from my family but managed to get on board the freighter. There were ten people; nine command crew and one hundred robots. We were all going to meet on Ohniah Prime, our last colony. Halfway there we had some serious engine problems and stopped on a planet to repair and refuel. I was allowed to leave the ship but had to stay close by. I don't know what planet it was, but I remember there was a massive castle on the horizon. I stared at it for hours. It was amazing. I loved the fresh air. Anyway, nothing happened. The ship was fixed, refueled, and we took off ten hours later. It didn't start right away. The captain could not get ahold of the engine room. Someone went back to check, but they didn't return. Then two more people went back to find out what was going on. One of them returned and said there were monsters on the ship.

"The captain said they must have got on during our refueling stop. The six remaining survivors organized some robots and went after the monsters. I wanted to help, but the captain said I was too young. I thought when the ship was in serious trouble, you'd want everyone who could hold a gun to help defend the ship. Apparently the captain didn't think so, or maybe he didn't think the situation was as serious as it actually was. But it was. I heard a lot of screaming and weapons fire. Then there was silence. The communication lines all went dead. I figured the crew was dead. I hid in a small locker on the bridge. It was getting cold, and it was getting harder to breathe. I'm glad you came along when you did."

"Yeah, I'd say you were very lucky," Astra agreed. Then to Calvin, she said, "As for you, there are traces of toxic chemicals in your lungs and an unknown strain of bacteria in your bloodstream. You also have radiation poisoning. The bleeding has stopped, and the computer is now regenerating new skin tissue. Then it will administer medication to treat your lungs and blood. You're a mess, but you'll be good as new in a few minutes."

After another minute, there was a flash of light, and the scanner slid back up against the wall and turned off.

"All done," Astra said. "You can get up now." Calvin slid off of the bed and stood up. He felt dizzy almost instantly and nearly fell down.

"Whoa," Astra said, grabbing his arm and holding him. "You still have to take it easy. Your major injuries are healed, but you need rest now."

"Now you tell me," Calvin said. "Hey, wait a second. We forgot
206

the third segment." Then he remembered something else. "Do we have to go back," he asked Ion. "I really don't want to go back there."

"Sir, that won't be necessary," Ion said. "You forgot, Dev still has it."

Dev pulled the small black and silver key from around his neck and handed it to Calvin.

"That's a relief," Calvin said. "Astra look, it's the third segment."

"Segment of what weapon?" Dev asked. "Come on, please tell me."

Calvin explained the mission they were on. Astra would occasionally interject a point or two.

"Where did you get that from?" Calvin asked.

"My father gave it to me," Dev answered. "It's been passed down through my family for generations; sort of a family heirloom."

"Interesting. Ion, did you know one of the segments was taken to Tryvella?"

"No," Ion answered. "No piece of the weapon was hidden there. The weapon was a joint venture between the Arlandians and Alerians. I have no idea how it might have gone to Tryvella. But it's hard to say what could have happened over the last eighty years. Someone must have found it."

Astra examined the segment.

"It does look like a key," she said. "I need to examine it in the lab."

"Can we have it?" Calvin asked.

Dev hesitated. "Sure," he said. "You need it more than I do. It's the least I can do for you, since you saved my life."

"Thank you," Calvin said.

"Now what do we want to do with that ship floating out there?" Astra asked. "Do we just want to leave it there, or destroy it?"

"If we leave it," Calvin said. "Someone else could find it."

"There is a group of nomadic scavengers operating in this area," Ion pointed out.

"If they find it, they'll try to salvage it," Astra said.

"They'll all die," Calvin said. "Those things are a nightmare."

"Then we should destroy it," Dev added. "It's not worth the risk."

"I agree," Ion said. "But may I please make a request, before we do that?"

"Sure, as long as it doesn't involve going back to the freighter."

"No, sir, I think I can do what I need to from here. I would like to scan the ship thoroughly, maybe get a live sample."

"Sample?" Calvin asked. "What are you talking about? Sample of what, a monster?"

"Sir, Mistress Astra, this is an incredible opportunity."

Calvin was horrified. "No, no way," he said firmly.

"I don't know," Astra said slowly. "Ion's right. This is a unique situation. We're always being chased by them. There's eighty-five live Terrors on that ship, stuck there. We can study them safely."

"No, it's too risky," Calvin said.

"I can send a sipper," Ion said.

"OK," Astra agreed. "But why don't you have one of the other robots set it up. You can supervise deployment after you visit the repair bay."

"Yes, Mistress," Ion said. "I'll do that."

"Excuse me," Calvin said. "What's a sipper?"

"Sipper is short for Special Purpose Robot," Ion explained. "It's a very small robot that can be configured for a variety of special jobs."

"In this case," Astra said, "we're going to put our best imagers on it and send it over there to scan the Terrors."

"But you scanned one earlier," Calvin said to Ion.

"Yes," Ion said. "My scanners are good, but sippers are better."

"I think it's a bad idea," Calvin said. "But you two have made up your minds, so while you're doing that, I'm going to get cleaned up and change into some new clothes. Come on Dev, let's go get you a room."

"That sounds good," Dev said. "Thank you." On the way out, Calvin heard Astra say, "Let's go, Ion. I'll help you get down to the repair bay."

Calvin led Dev to the top level by way of the elevator, being too exhausted to use the stairs. Calvin took Dev to a room near his and showed him how to use the computer to get anything he needed, including clothes.

"I'll come get you in an hour, and we can go to the bridge."

"All right," Dev said. "Thank you, Calvin, for taking me with you."

"I'm glad we were able to help."

Calvin went to his room. The door closed and he was immersed in silence. it was nice at first but after a few minutes it started to bother him. He turned on some soft, relaxing music that he found in the computer data base.

His muscles ached as he slowly undressed and put his clothes in the matter recycle unit. He lingered in the shower, letting the hot water soak his sore muscles. He felt like a new man after he dressed. He felt more relaxed but very tired. Calvin walked next door and pressed the electronic doorbell. There was a soft chime. After a moment, the door slid open, and Dev stepped out. He was wearing new clothes and seemed happier. Together they walked to the bridge. He had a thousand questions, but didn't feel like asking them. He assumed that Dev felt the same way, since he didn't say a word. Calvin sat down in the pilot's chair. Dev stood behind him. Ion was already there, sitting at the computer in the back.

"Ion, how long do you need, how long to—" Calvin stopped, and tried to organize his thoughts.

"I'm finished, sir," Ion said. "The sipper returned to the ship a short time ago. You may destroy the freighter now."

Calvin felt a certain amount of grim enjoyment locking the weapons onto the drifting monster infested ship. "Missiles are locked," Calvin said. "Our shields are up. I'm ready to fire."

Calvin heard Dev quietly whisper, "I'm sorry, Captain Frella."

Calvin pressed the firing button. The Azure Frost shook gently as four missiles shot out of their launch tubes. They flew through space and struck the side of the drifting freighter. The ship exploded in a bright flash of light and was gone.

They sat quietly for a moment, until the resulting explosion and fire were gone completely.

Ion broke the silence. "I've set a course for the next segment. You can take us back into hyperspace whenever you want. I recommend putting some distance between us and the debris field first."

Without a word, Calvin complied. He pushed the throttle forward and pointed them away from the debris field. After ten minutes, the ship jumped back into hyperspace.

"So what are we going to do with you?" Calvin asked Dev.

"I don't suppose you'd be willing to take me to Ohniah Prime," Dev said. "I'd really like to get back to my people. Hopefully some of them made it there safely."

"Is that something we can do without losing too much time?"

"I have the coordinates for Ohniah," Ion said. "It's not too far from our next destination."

"Can we drop him off on the way?" Calvin asked.

"I recommend we take him home after we retrieve the fourth segment," Ion said. "Look at this."

Calvin got up out of the pilot's chair and walked to Ion's station. A red line stretched across the navigation screen.

"The next segment is here." Ion pointed. "It is only eight hours away, on this planet. This is Ohniah." It was well beyond the next segment. "Essentially, it's on the way."

"Do you mind if we drop you off after we get our next segment?" Calvin asked.

"That's fine," Dev said. "As long as we stay away from the planet with the castle."

"Actually, I would like to know what planet that was," Ion said. "So we can avoid it."

"Do you think that's where they came from?" Calvin asked.

"Yes," Ion said. "It's likely the Terrors that were on the freighter came from the planet where Mr. Dev stopped for fuel. I'm concerned about this version of Dark Terror. They have several modifications I'm not familiar with. It seems the Goremog have created a new version, a more violent, stronger, and harder-to-kill version."

"Why would they do that, if they are impossible to control?"

"I don't think they meant for the creatures to be difficult to control. They must be attempting to perfect them, make them controllable," Ion said. "I'm going to examine the ship's logs and see if I can learn anything."

Calvin shivered and wondered if he was going to have nightmares. "Are you hungry?" Calvin asked. "I'm starving."

"I'm not hungry," Dev said. "I'm too tired to eat. But if you don't mind, just show me where the dining room is, for later."

"Sure, let's go," Calvin said.

"Before you go," Ion said. "Since you're going to be with us a while, you should have this." Ion handed Dev a small device. "Just put it in your pocket, it will help you understand everyone's different languages."

Dev took it and put it in his pocket. He put his hand on a chair to steady himself for a brief second. "Whoa," he said.

Dev followed Calvin to the dining room. After Calvin showed him how to order food from the computer, Dev went to his room. Calvin walked to the computer and stared at it blankly. He was hungry, but he had no idea what he wanted to eat. The sound of the door opening caught his attention. He turned to see Astra walk through the door. He immediately felt better.

"Hey," she said, smiling. "How are you feeling?"

"Tired," Calvin answered. "And very hungry."

"Where's Dev?" Astra asked.

"He went back to his room," Calvin answered. "He said he was too tired to eat. I almost went to bed myself, but I knew I wouldn't be able to sleep without eating something."

"Are you sure you're all right?" She asked.

"I'm not lying to you," Calvin said. "I've never been that scared before. Nothing seemed to stop them. The weapon I had just seemed to make them mad. We need better weapons."

"I know," Astra said. "Even Ion's beam weapon was ineffective."

"And the suit," Calvin continued. "It was supposed to protect me, but it was too bulky and hard to move in; forget running. Is there a way you can make the portable shield units stronger, so we can go into hostile environments without wearing a space suit?"

"I don't know," Astra said, raising an eyebrow and taking a deep breath. "They're good for what they were designed for—emergencies. Maybe you should work out in the gym a little bit. Anything else? If you have anything else to complain about, I'll need to make a list." She smiled at him.

"Thanks," Calvin said. "I'm done for now. But I'm telling you, we won't survive against the Dark Terror with the equipment we have now."

They got some food and sat down at their regular table. Calvin described his ordeal on the monster-infested ship while they ate. Astra mostly just listened, only asking a couple of questions when she needed more information.

"I don't know what to tell you," she said when he was finished. "The level-five laser pistol is the most powerful handgun we have. The problem is the Dark Terror. They were designed to be very difficult to kill. Their skin is composed of triventian, the strongest known metal in the universe. It's very difficult to penetrate. Their internal organs and vital components are well protected and have multiple backups. Even our best scientists haven't been able to find a weakness that we could exploit. Ion and I are hopeful that the scans the sipper collected might discover something we may have missed."

"That sounds like too much to hope for," Calvin said. "I think the best thing would be to stay away from them." He closed his eyes and yawned. "I don't want to think about it anymore. I need some sleep. It's been a very long day."

"At least we have something nice to look forward to. The fourth segment is on the planet Axia. You'll like it. The database says the lab was built on the coast of big blue ocean."

"That sounds nice."

"Go get some rest," Astra said, smiling. "I'm not staying up too much longer, but there's something I want to try with the first segment. I've been working on a power converter that will allow me to plug it directly into the main power grid." She rubbed her temples. "I'm really nervous about it. It could be dangerous."

"All right," Calvin said. He was so tired, he didn't hear the last thing she said. "I'll see you at breakfast."

"Good night," she said. Calvin felt like he was already asleep as he headed to his room. It was only a short walk, but it felt like it was miles away. He climbed into bed and was asleep almost immediately.

CHAPTER FOUR:

THE CRASH

Calvin woke up late, amazed that he hadn't moved all night or had nightmares. The events on the freighter replayed over and over in his mind, but for some reason the details were hazy.

He took his time and eventually wandered to the dining room, which was empty. He didn't know what he wanted to eat, so he just got a cup of coffee and sat down. He knew it would give him a stomach ache later, but he didn't care. Calvin sat quietly, sipping his hot coffee.

The door slid open, and Dev walked in and looked around. When he saw Calvin he walked over to him.

"Hello," he said.

"Hi," Calvin said. "Are you OK?"

"I just don't want to be alone right now," Dev said sadly. "I was thinking about my family, wondering if they made it to Ohniah."

"We can try and contact them," Calvin offered. "The communication system on this ship is very powerful."

"I already tried," Dev said. "Ion helped me last night. We couldn't get through to anyone."

"I'm sorry. I know how frustrating that can be. It took me a long time to contact my people."

Dev got some food and sat across from Calvin. The smell filled the room and made Calvin realize how hungry he was. He got up and got his own food. They ate in silence for a while.

"I was wondering," Dev said. "I've been trying to figure this out, and it's bothering me. Why are you helping the Alerians? You don't have to. Ion told me your planet is safe, hidden behind some kind of invisibility cloak. Why risk everything on a hopeless cause?"

"You've been out here," Calvin said. "You know what it's like. Yes, my planet is safe for now, but how long will that last? I think it's just a matter of time until the Goremog, or some passing ship, sees New Arlandia, and then it will be all over for us. When that happens, we won't be able to fight back. We don't have a defense force. Even guns are forbidden. I wish they could see what's out here. That might change their minds."

"See, that's why you're better off staying at home and hiding," Dev said. "You're drawing attention to yourself, to your home. What if they catch you and find out where you came from?"

"But we have a chance," Calvin said. "If we can find all the segments, and put the weapon together, we can destroy the Goremog and every other hostile force out there. I can save New Arlandia."

"That's a big risk to take," Dev said. "You've found three pieces out of ten? What if one of the pieces is damaged, and you can't fix it? Or worse, what if one was destroyed or is missing? What will you do then? Will the weapon work with a missing piece?"

"I don't know," Calvin admitted. "But I think it's worth the risk, and so does my father. If I do nothing, then what? We have to live in constant fear that we'll be found and destroyed? I think that would be worse."

"You're lucky you have a home," Dev said sadly. "You should do everything you can to protect it. My people will try to build, but we don't have the ability to cloak a planet. As soon as the Goremog find us, they will simply destroy us again. Just as they have been doing to the

Alerians. We will have to run from planet to planet, while they slowly reduce our numbers. That's no way to live either."

"I agree," Calvin said. "That's why we have to finish this now."

"I hope you can find the weapon," Dev said. "I really do. I would help you, but my people need me. Do you think your people would share their planetary cloaking technology with mine?"

"I'd like to think so," Calvin said. "But if I ever took an alien home with me, I think the planet would explode."

Dev laughed. "That's funny."

"No, really," Calvin insisted. "When my ship went missing, the government declared martial law, shut the power grid off, and went into lockdown mode for days. Trust me, it wouldn't end well."

Calvin took the last bite of his pancake and reached for his coffee. Dev was already finished and took his tray to the recycle unit.

"I'll see you later," he said. "One of the robots is going to do some maintenance on the backup computer core. He said I could watch."

"OK," Calvin said. "Have fun."

"Oh, I will," Dev said and walked out of the room.

When he finished his coffee, Calvin went to the library to write in his journal. He kept the curtains closed and a holographic fireplace turned on. He wanted to pretend he was home, on New Arlandia, not confined inside a spaceship. He tried to recount what happened on the freighter, but he couldn't sort through his thoughts.

The day passed slowly, and twice he fell asleep in the big reclining chair. It felt good to relax, to rest and let his body and mind recover. He skipped lunch, but later in the evening Astra found him and took him to the dining room for dinner.

The next two days followed the same pattern. Everyone kept to themselves during the day, but met for dinner in the evening.

On the third day when he sat to write, whatever was blocking his thoughts was gone. He poured himself on to the paper, recording in detail the events that led to finding the third segment.

Unfortunately, later that night, the nightmares returned as well. Calvin fell into a restless sleep and found himself walking down a corridor on the Azure Frost. The lights were out, and it was very dark. When Calvin found a light switch, he tried to turn on the lights, but nothing happened. He didn't know what was going on. He wanted to find Astra, but he was afraid to move. At the far end of the corridor was a pair of red eyes. Calvin knew what it was. It was a monster. How did it get on the ship? He turned and walked a few steps. When he looked back, the red eyes were closer. Fear gripped him tightly when he realized it was coming after him.

Calvin turned to run. When he did, a dark shape dropped out of the ceiling. A huge set of sharp teeth was in his face. He wanted to scream, but he was unable to make a sound. The monster screamed at the top of its lungs and prepared to lunge at him.

Calvin woke up suddenly. Red lights were flashing in the room, and the ship's alarm was ringing. Ion was standing over him, shaking him.

"Master Calvin, wake up!" he shouted.

"What is it?" Calvin asked, confused.

"Come with me," Ion said. "I have to get you off the ship." Ion grabbed Calvin and pulled him out of his bed.

"Do I need to get dressed?" Calvin asked.

"There's no time!" Ion shouted over a chorus of explosions coming from somewhere inside the ship. Calvin grabbed the clothes he'd left on the back of a chair the night before and put them on as he stumbled across the room. He barely had time to stop and put his shoes on, before Ion pulled him out of his room and into the hallway.

"What's happening?" Calvin asked confused. Then he noticed that Ion was carrying Astra. She was not moving. She was fully dressed, but her clothes and face were burned.

"Astra," Calvin shouted. "Are you all right? Ion, what's wrong with Astra?"

Dev stumbled out of his room. He looked very scared.

"What's going on?" he asked. "Am I still dreaming?"

"We have to evacuate the ship!" Ion said loudly.

"I need to get my shoes," Dev said. He turned and went back into his room.

"There's no time!" Ion shouted. "We have to get off of the ship, *now*!"

Ion turned and started walking toward the stairs.

"No, wait," Calvin said, pulling on Ion's arm. "Dev, come on, hurry up!" Calvin called. Dev ran out of his room, holding his clothes. The corridor was full of black smoke. They ran down the stairs to the shuttle bay. Ion entered the shuttle first, laying Astra down on a row of seats and quickly tying her down with seatbelts. Calvin and Dev stood outside the shuttle, looking confused. Ion took Calvin's hand and guided him to the pilot's seat. Then he made Calvin look him in the face.

"Master Calvin," Ion said. "There's an advanced emergency medical kit on board, as well as several days' worth of food and water. Put your harnesses on, it's going to be a very rough launch. Calvin, you have to take care of them." Ion quickly left the shuttle and the door closed.

As soon as he was gone, the shuttle bay door began to open. Calvin realized what Ion was about to do.

"Seatbelts!" Calvin shouted. When the door was fully open, the force field disappeared. Calvin and Dev were slammed into the backs of their seats. The ship was violently hurled into space, along with anything in the shuttle bay that wasn't secured.

For a brief moment, Calvin was able to see Azure Frost as the shuttle tumbled away. It was severely damaged; floating dead in space. He could see fires raging out of control through the windows. Several explosions erupted from somewhere inside, sending burning pieces of debris flying everywhere and ripping holes in the hull. It was a mess.

218

Why did Ion stay aboard? Explosions continued to rock the ship as it floated away, including another massive blast near the engines.

As he was staring at the crippled ship, he realized something: the shuttle was floating dead in space, too. The engines and life support were off. They only had a few minutes of oxygen! He turned his attention back to the front. Calvin turned on the main computer and began the start up for the engines, completely ignoring the checklist.

"It's going to take a minute for the engines to be warm enough to start," Calvin said.

"Calvin," Dev pointed ahead. "Look out the window."

Calvin looked up. A giant blue-green planet filled the window. The only thing he managed to say was, "Uh-oh."

Dev looked at Calvin, hoping to find some comfort or reassurance that they would be OK, but he found none. "Is there any way you can make the engines warm up faster?" The fear was obvious in his voice.

"No," Calvin answered. "If I try to start them when they're too cold, they won't start, and I could damage them."

"Do you think that would be worse than crashing into the planet?"

Suddenly an alarm sounded.

"What's that?" Dev asked.

"We're falling into the planet's atmosphere. This is bad." Calvin got up and went to the back of the shuttle. He found the emergency medical kit that Ion had left for them. He took a small scanner out of it, and waved it over Astra, who was still unconscious. He read the screen.

"She is suffering from oxygen deprivation and smoke inhalation, and she has a concussion. She has minor burns all over her body, and, oh, some internal bleeding. What happened?"

He plugged the scanner into the med kit.

"Calvin!" Dev said, sounding very scared. "Can you do that

later? We don't have time, look!" He pointed at the planet, which was much closer now. The shuttle began to shake as it entered the upper atmosphere.

The med kit beeped, and a small glass object shaped like an ink pen slid out of a slot on the bottom. Calvin read a message on the screen which read, "Inject into upper arm." Calvin took the device and held it against Astra's upper arm. He felt the device vibrate. A light on the top changed from green to red and back to green.

"Calvin!" Dev shouted. "Get back up here!"

Dev had taken off his seatbelt and sat down in the copilot's chair. Calvin dropped the injection device into the med kit. He covered her with a warm blanket and stuffed the edges under her, hoping it would stay on. He ran back up to the front and strapped himself back into the pilot's chair.

"The engines aren't warm enough," Calvin said.

"You have to try and start them anyway," Dev said. "Or we'll die."

Calvin was glad that Astra was unconscious for this. She would be spared the horror of what was coming. The shuttle began to shake even more. Calvin pulled back on the flight controls, in an attempt to level out and not hit the atmosphere head on. But without engines, there wasn't much he could do.

The shuttle shook violently, and the sound of a thousand tiny explosions filled the air. A small white spot appeared on the windshield.

"What was that?"

"We just passed through some debris," Calvin answered. The computer went crazy. Reams of data began scrolling down. "We've been damaged! Life support, engines, weapons, hydraulics, fuel systems. This is really bad. Wait, fuel leak? That's it, I'm starting the engines." He turned the ignition switch, and the engines began to hum. There was a loud pop, followed by a bump. Everyone was pushed forward as the shuttle hit an invisible wall; the atmosphere. Fire erupted all around them. The flames completely blocked the view out of the windows.

"Something's wrong!" Calvin had to shout over the roar of noise.

"No kidding!"

"Only one engine is working!" Dev grabbed onto the sides of his chair.

"One thing's for sure; this ship will never fly again," Calvin said. He pushed the throttle on the good engine as far forward as it would go, way past the red line.

It was a very bumpy ride. The fire stopped, and Calvin managed to level them out.

Looking up, Calvin noticed a crack in the windshield.

"We need to find a place to land," Calvin said. He turned on the sensors and began scanning the surface. There was a shake, followed by a loud pop. "The engine is dying."

They began to lose altitude. As they got closer to the ground, they could see that they were over a large blue ocean.

"I don't believe this," Calvin said. "It can't end like this." There was another loud bang, followed by a grinding noise. "We're losing altitude. We need to find a good place to set down. Landing in water would not be a very good idea!" They were now flying a scant ten thousand feet over the water and dropping fast.

Off in the distance, they could see land. Then they saw it; a large castle, right on the coast. It was white and had a wall around it. There were a lot of towers in it, but there was one tall tower in the middle that gleamed in the sunlight. There were miles of ruins behind the castle. When Dev saw it he gasped.

"No," he said. "It's not possible."

"What?" Calvin asked, looking at Dev, whose face had turned pale. "What's wrong?"

"I recognize that castle," Dev said. "This is the planet where we stopped for fuel and supplies.

"What?"

Calvin looked from Dev to the castle looming on the horizon in front of them. The realization of what his friend was saying hit him immediately.

"The shuttle is dying," Calvin said. "Assuming we survive the crash, we're going be trapped down there." A new level of panic that Calvin didn't know existed was starting to grow in him. At the same time, the ground was getting closer.

"We're only going to get one chance at this," Calvin said, transferring all power into the engine. "I'm going to try and land in that big open spot in front of the castle."

"Let's hope whoever lives there is friendly," Dev said.

Calvin looked at Dev. "This isn't going to be a soft landing," he said. "Astra's lucky. She's unconscious. I suggest you hold on."

Several moments passed. As they got closer to the castle, they could see the big open space in front was a large garden, full of green trees and colorful flower beds. The vibration became so intense that Calvin's hands, as he tightly gripped the controls, were starting to ache.

"Hold on!" Calvin shouted. Just before they hit the ground, Calvin jammed the thrusters into reverse. The shuttle slowed down, but it wasn't enough. They hit the ground hard.

There was a very loud crashing sound. Calvin tensed his entire body and was crushed against the bottom of his chair. He would have screamed, but the pain was too intense. It seemed to last forever, but after a few seconds, he felt the pressure relax. Both Calvin and Dev took deep breaths. They sat still for several minutes without speaking, grateful but surprised to be alive.

Calvin took off his seatbelt and stood up. Pain shot through his back and spread through his body like lightning. He forced himself to move. He stretched as he moved to the back to check on Astra. He used the seats on both sides as support. He fell on his knees next to her and looked at her. She was still unconscious. Calvin winced at the burns on her face. He gently touched her forehead, which was hot to the touch.

Her breaths were slow and raspy. The medical bag was lying on the floor. Calvin ran the medical scanner over her again. He read the screen. He couldn't understand most of it, but from what he could tell, the machine was telling him to leave her alone for now.

He unhooked the seat belts that were holding her down and straightened the blanket.

Calvin closed his eyes. What just happened? In his mind he could still see the Azure Frost, burning in space. Did it explode? Ion stayed behind. Was he destroyed? The shuttle was a mess; he was certain it would never fly again. They were stranded, and worst of all, there were monsters out there. What was he supposed to do? Ion said it was his job to take care of everyone. He had no idea how to do that. He felt desperate, helpless, and without hope. With the loss of the Frost, how could they complete the mission? The first three segments were lost, and that's how he felt.

CHAPTER FIVE:

———————◦—————————

THE CASTLE

Calvin felt a hand on his shoulder. He looked up and saw Dev standing over him.

"Is she all right?" Dev asked.

"I'm not sure," Calvin admitted. "The medcomp is hard to read, but I think it's telling me she needs rest." He stood up and stretched. He could tell his whole body was going to be sore later.

"Did you see the ship?" Dev asked. "What happened up there?"

"I don't know any more than you do," Calvin said.

"It looked like it was about to explode. What are we going to do?"

"I don't know," Calvin said. His mind raced. What were they going to do? "I'm almost afraid to go out there, but it looks like we're going to be stuck here for a while. We need to go out and introduce ourselves. Ready?"

"Introduce ourselves?" Dev asked. "To who?"

"Dev," Calvin said sternly. "We just crashed in someone's backyard, and they're probably not happy about it. We need to go meet them."

"Wait, should we take weapons?"

Calvin thought for a second. "I bet we're surrounded right now. If we go out there with guns, they'll think we're hostile, and shoot us. We don't want to provoke them."

"What if there're Terrors out there?"

Calvin stopped. "I didn't see any on the way down."

"Then I feel better," Dev said sarcastically. "They couldn't possibly have heard us crash and come to find out what the noise was."

"We don't have a choice," Calvin said. "We can't stay in here."

Calvin walked to the back and pressed the button to open the rear door. He expected to find half a dozen guards with weapons pointed at them just outside. He was fully prepared to be captured and taken into custody. In his mind, there was no way to avoid it. Crashing a spaceship on the castle grounds was certainly not going to be welcomed warmly. When the door opened from top to bottom, it created a ramp.

The shuttle was flooded with bright pleasant sunlight, and they had to cover their eyes briefly. The smell of the salty sea water washed over them, and off in the distance they could hear the sound of waves washing up onto the beach.

Calvin shielded his eyes with his hands but still squinted through his fingers as he looked outside. There were no guards in sight. Calvin walked outside into the sunshine. The warmth of the sun and the fresh air felt very good. The sky was blue with a few white clouds. The sound of the waves was relaxing and peaceful.

"No monsters," Calvin said. "Or people."

Dev handed him a laser pistol. Calvin took it without a word and held it down at his side. They were in a giant garden full of rows and rows of colorful plants and flowers. Calvin walked over to a rock wall on the edge of the garden and looked down. There was a drop-off straight down to the shore, where the waves were breaking on rows of razor-sharp rocks. It was a long way down.

Calvin looked back. They were very lucky. They'd landed very close to the edge. If they had landed forty feet shorter, they would have crashed into the cliff and exploded. He shuddered at the thought. When he turned around, Calvin got a good view of the castle. It was white and massive.

What bothered him was that there was nobody there. Surely the crash was loud enough that every person in the area heard it.

"Since I left home, I've landed on four planets," Calvin said. "And every one of them has been completely lifeless."

"Well, I was here a few days ago, and there were lots of people. I wasn't here at the castle, but I could see it on the horizon," Dev said.

"It couldn't have been abandoned for too long," Calvin said. "Look at this garden. It's clean, the flower beds are well kept, and the grass looks like it was just cut."

"There could be a robot gardener," Dev pointed out.

"I suppose," Calvin said. They both looked around—not a soul to be seen, not even a robot. "But if there were robots taking care of this place, where are they?" Then a dark thought occurred to him. "Maybe the monsters killed everyone."

They walked around. The flowers were in bloom, and there were rows of neatly sculpted bushes. Dozens of fountains sprayed water into the air, and a system of interconnecting streams ran all over the garden. Small wooden bridges crossed over the streams. It made him think of home, of the flower garden his mother used to grow every year.

"There's nothing out here," Dev said. "I guess we can relax."

"I don't think we should relax yet," Calvin said. "We haven't even checked out the castle yet."

"Right, let's go."

"I want to check on Astra first."

"All right," Dev said. "I'm going to walk around some more and make sure we didn't miss anything."

Calvin walked back to the shuttle, and found Astra lying on her back with her eyes half-open.

"Hey," Calvin said softly. "You're awake. How are you feeling?"

"My head hurts," she said quietly. She tried to sit up. Calvin helped her into a sitting position.

She moaned. "My whole body hurts."

"I'll get you some water." Calvin said. He opened a storage locker in the back of the shuttle and found bottles of water mixed in with shelves of other survival gear.

He took one to Astra. She gratefully took it from him and had a few sips.

"Do you know what happened to Azure Frost?" Calvin asked her.

She looked at him, and her eyes began to tear. "Oh, Calvin," she cried. "I'm so sorry. It was my fault. I was working in the lab, and I tried to connect the first segment into the ship. I made a power module that was supposed to convert power into usable energy and a switch that was supposed to break the connection if there was an overload. Instead, it forced the connection to stay open, and all that raw power fed directly into the power grid. I couldn't stop it. I tried to unplug it, but it was fused. It started to smoke; the smell was horrible. It overloaded. I tried to get out of the room, but there was an explosion. Then I woke up here. What happened?"

Calvin looked at her, trying to decide how much he should tell her. He didn't notice Dev walk in, take a hand scanner, and leave.

"Ion woke me up in the middle of the night," he said. "He put us in a shuttle, decompressed the bay, and we were shot out into space. The ship was on fire. The damage was…"

"Was it bad?" she asked, crying softly.

Calvin hesitated. She was hurt and vulnerable. He wondered how honest he should be with her. "It was terrible," he said, knowing there was no point hiding it.

She shook her head and cried.

"It's OK," he said gently. "It's not your fault."

"Yes, it is," she said. "I can't believe I was so stupid. I should have known better."

Calvin tried to console her. "It sounds like you did everything you could. You thought of every safety precaution."

"No, I should have waited. I was so anxious to make it work, I rushed ahead. I'm sorry," she said again.

"It's all right. Everything's going to be OK." Astra had her head resting on Calvin's chest.

"You can't say that," Astra said. "We lost the ship, Ion, and three pieces of the weapon. Oh, and also any hope of contacting my parents. Our mission is over."

Calvin didn't know what to say, so he just held her for a while. What else could he do? He knew from experience that there was very little he would be able to say to make her feel better. That would take time.

"Where are we?" she asked, after several minutes.

"I don't know," he said. "But it's very nice outside."

"I would really like to see it," Astra said. "Please help me." Calvin helped her stand up.

She held onto his arm as they walked outside. First he took her to the wall overlooking the ocean a few feet away. She closed her eyes and took a deep breath.

"It feels so good out here," she said, looking out over the ocean. "It's amazing."

"Yes, it is," Calvin agreed. "But there's something else you should see, turn around." He gently helped her turn around until she faced the castle.

"Wow." Astra gasped. "Incredible." Then her expression changed. "Please tell me we didn't crash on a monster-infested planet. This can't be the same planet with a castle Dev stopped on. That looks a

228

lot like what he described." Calvin had been hoping that she wouldn't notice.

"Yes, he did," Calvin said. "He thinks this is the same planet."

"Oh, that's just perfect," Astra said. "So those monsters could be here?"

"I don't know," Calvin answered. "It's possible."

"It's possible?" Astra asked, getting upset. "Do you understand what's going on? How much trouble we're in? If there are monsters on this planet, there isn't one or two of them. There's a lot. We have to get out of here, now! What condition is the shuttle in?"

Calvin hadn't seen Astra scared until now, and that worried him.

"We crashed," Calvin said. "I doubt we can take off."

"I want to look at it." Astra walked around the shuttle, looking at the hull and engines. Then she sat down in the pilot's seat and tried to turn on the computers. When that didn't work, she opened a panel in the floor and looked inside. When she was finished, they went back outside.

Astra confirmed his fear. "You were right, Calvin," she said, sitting down on the grass. "The ship will never fly again. At this point the only way to fix it would be in the repair dock on Aleria's Hope. But even then, it wouldn't be worth it. It's too far gone."

"So," Dev said, walking up. "What are we going to do? Are things as bad as I think they are?"

"That's what we're trying to figure out," Calvin said. "Can we contact the Frost? Maybe Ion was able to get things under control."

"We can try, but there's no power in the shuttle," Astra answered. "Wait, there should be handhelds in the back. They're low power, but they should be able to reach a ship in orbit."

"I'll go get one," Calvin said. He ran inside the shuttle and came back out with one. He gave it to Astra. She turned it on.

"Ion, this is Astra, can you hear me? Azure Frost, please answer." She tried for several minutes but got no answer.

"We're stuck here," Dev said sadly.

"Ion will come and get us," Astra said.

"I hope you're right," Calvin said. "But in case he can't, we'll have to find another way. Dev, you said you stopped here for fuel and supplies. That must mean there's a star port."

"Of course. What're you thinking?" Dev asked.

"We might find some spaceships there, something flyable. Do you remember where it is?"

"I'm not exactly sure. As I said before I could see the castle on the horizon."

"We need to get on top of one of these buildings," Calvin said.

"How about up there?" Astra said, pointing at the tallest tower. "But there's no way I'll make it. I'll wait for you here."

Calvin started to protest, but Astra interrupted him. "It's OK. I have a weapon, and I'll stay in the ship. You two go and look around inside the castle. We'll each have a communicator, and I'll call you if something happens."

"OK," Calvin said reluctantly. "We won't be long." He looked up at the sky. The sun had moved across the sky toward the horizon. "We'll try to be back before the sun goes down."

"You better be," she said seriously. "I don't want to be out here alone in the dark."

"Sorry. Don't worry, Astra. We'll be back soon."

"I scanned five miles in all directions," Dev said. "I can't see any life signs. Some insects, but no people. Not even animals. But what's even stranger is the miles of ruins around the castle, but the castle isn't damaged."

"That's strange," Astra said.

"I wonder what happened to them," Calvin added.

"I don't see any signs of a battle here," Dev said. "They must have evacuated."

230

"Recently, too, by the look of it," Calvin said. "I wonder what scared them away."

"You don't think it could have been the monsters, do you?" Dev asked.

"A few monsters?" Calvin asked. "No, I don't think so. This place looks easily defendable."

"What about the ruins?"

"I don't know. I don't think so. It doesn't look recent."

"What ruins?" Astra asked.

"There are ruins all around the castle," Calvin said. "But from the air they looked old."

"I'm telling you, if there are monsters here, there are more than just a few."

"Then we need to hurry and get out of here," Calvin said. "I'm really not comfortable leaving you here alone, but I feel better knowing we can keep an eye on you with the scanner."

"If anything gets within five miles, we'll know."

"Speaking of darkness, where are we sleeping tonight?" Calvin asked.

"Right here, in the shuttle," Astra said. "As soon as the sun starts to come up, we can head for the star port."

"There's something else you should know," Dev said. "According to the scanner, there is a big storm coming. I think it'll hit sometime tomorrow. I don't know what the storms are like on this planet, but we can count on high winds and heavy rainfall."

"That figures," Calvin said. "We might want to consider finding shelter here."

"Maybe you can find something for us inside the castle," Astra suggested.

"We'll keep our eyes open," Calvin said. "It might be difficult since we don't have a reservation."

"Very funny," Astra said.

Before they headed off, Calvin and Dev stocked up on supplies and equipment in the shuttle. The equipment locker was in the back near the door. Calvin opened it and found all kinds of equipment.

Astra walked over, amused at the look on his face. She could tell he was unsure of what to take. "Need help? I used to help outfit teams for missions like this."

"Yes, please," Calvin said.

Astra took out a vest and handed it to him. "Try this on," she said and handed one to Dev also.

They each tried one on. Astra showed them how to adjust them so they fit perfectly. The vests had pockets on the front and sides, and had a holster on the side for a pistol. Astra took a pistol out of the weapons rack and handed it to Calvin. "This is a mark seven pistol," she said. "It's the most powerful handgun we have. Good for close-up combat. It has a very quick recharge rate, and computer control guidance helps increase accuracy. And look here. There is a light on the front. Just press this button." She showed him where the button for the light was and how to load and reload power packs. Calvin holstered the pistol and put four power packs in his vest. Then Astra handed him a rifle.

"This is an assault rifle," she said. "It's very powerful and very accurate. It has a light on the front, too, so you can change the intensity of the beam. There is a scope here on top that has an excellent zoom-in capability. And here is where you can select the power of the laser. In single mode, you can fire one single shot. It automatically selects the power level. You can also change it to fire up to four shots at once. But if you do that, the power pack drains faster." Calvin put the rifle on his back. The last things they took were a communicator each and a scanner.

"Please be careful," Astra said. "You're going out there with the best weapons and technology we have. But don't trust that it will keep you safe. Don't trust the scanners exclusively; trust your eyes and use your heads."

"We'll be careful," Calvin said, trying to reassure her. Calvin

232

and Dev walked out of the shuttle. Astra closed the door behind them and lay down on a row of seats in the back to rest. She was beginning to feel sick.

Once outside, Calvin wanted to make sure the communicators were all working before leaving Astra alone.

"Astra, can you hear me?"

"I hear you, Calvin, clear signal. Be careful."

He heard her on both his and Dev's communicators. "We'll be back soon,"

They headed off through the garden toward the castle. It wasn't a straight path to the doors. They had to follow a winding pathway.

The warm sun felt very good. There were a few fluffy white clouds hovering overhead, and a gentle breeze made the tree branches sway. It was very peaceful, yet Calvin was scared. There was a strange feeling in the air. He knew a Dark Terror lurked somewhere, maybe close.

They passed a very large fountain. It looked very clean and was spraying sparkling white water into the air. The drops of water gleamed in the sun. On the other side of the fountain was a large open space, which was covered with a dark-green weedless lawn. They crossed the open space quickly. Calvin felt uneasy out in the open. A wide row of concrete stairs led them up to a set of large doors, which were cracked open. They pulled the doors open.

Calvin wasn't entirely sure what to expect. The previous planets he'd visited had long been abandoned and were in ruins. But everything here was nice and clean. When he walked through the big doors, he was pleasantly surprised. They entered a very large hall filled with richly carved beams that arched across the ceiling. Massive stained-glass windows along both sides stretched from the floor to the ceiling. Dev followed Calvin down the center of the hall. Sunlight beamed through the windows, giving life to the images. The images were impressive, depicting battle scenes and portraits of regal-looking kings and queens. Just like outside, the inside was clean. Calvin noticed that the carpet looked like it had recently been cleaned, and there was no dust on anything. There were large green plants in the hall that all looked very healthy.

"I'm having that feeling again," Calvin admitted.

"What feeling?" Dev asked, staring in awe at the windows as they walked.

"The one where it feels like everyone in the universe is gone."

"You get that feeling a lot?"

"Yeah, but something is different about this planet. This one looks like there were people here yesterday."

Wide open doors at the other end led them into the rest of the castle. For the next two hours, they explored, room by luxurious room. Crystal chandeliers hung from ornately decorated ceilings. The walls were covered with paintings, gold, and jewels, or a combination. There were no plain surfaces. The furniture all looked handcrafted. Where there weren't colorful rugs, the floors were marble and granite. It was also a modern castle. All of the floors were accessible by elevators; spacious elevators with plush carpet and sleek glass elevator controls. Light wasn't a problem either. The castle was full of windows, allowing natural light to flood all rooms. They wandered around for hours, continually checking the scanner for life signs. To Calvin's relief, there were no signs of life.

After several hours of exploring, Calvin and Dev found an unusual door that didn't look like any other part of the castle. It was an oversized metal door, painted red with yellow-and-black stripes across it. They found it deep in a basement, in a far corner on the other side of a concrete maze of storage rooms. They almost missed it, but Dev saw scratches on the floor and wanted to see where they went. They approached it cautiously. Calvin felt strange, as though a voice inside him was telling him they were in danger. He'd learned recently it was good to listen to that voice.

Dev tried to open the door, but it wouldn't open.

"It's locked," he said, sounding disappointed.

"Not just locked," Calvin said, examining the edges of the door. "Look, it's been welded shut from the outside. They obviously wanted to keep people out."

Dev thought about it for a second. "Maybe they wanted to keep something inside." They shared a look, knowing what the other was thinking.

"You think they locked the monsters in there?" Calvin asked.

"I don't know. If they did, let's keep them there."

"Good idea."

"I wonder if the scanner can see what's down there," Dev said, taking out his scanner. He examined it for several moments.

"See anything?" Calvin asked.

"There are miles of tunnels under the castle. Wow, it's very extensive; some of the tunnels go out of range. And they are big. It almost looks like there are roads down there. There are hundreds of rooms. Big, small. Wow, some are huge. There's a lot of stuff down there."

"It sounds like there's a city down there. Any life readings?"

"Yes, I'm picking up a lot of life down there, but I can't tell what it is. It could be bugs, small animals, or monsters. I can't tell them apart. There is a metal shield surrounding the structures that seems to be blocking the signals."

"That figures," Calvin muttered. "Let's get out of here. This place is giving me the creeps."

"Yeah, gladly," Dev said. "The only place left to check out is the tower."

It was a short elevator ride up the tower, but it didn't go all the way up. They had to walk up six flights of stairs to get to the top.

The stairs led through a hole in the center of the tower. A short wall with hand rails ran the perimeter to prevent people from falling over. That gave them a completely unobstructed view for miles in every direction. Calvin smiled when he saw the view. He took out a small pair of binoculars and began to search. Dev did the same. For several minutes they studied the landscape in silence.

"I found the star port," Dev said. "There." He pointed to a spot on the horizon. It didn't take Calvin long to find it.

"I see it," he said. "It looks like it's faraway." The binoculars provided him with a very clear view of a sprawling complex, spread out over half a dozen large buildings surrounded by a concrete ocean. There was a large glass dome in the middle. Then he noticed something on the small digital display on the binoculars. "Oh, there it is. According to this the star port is twenty-seven miles away."

"That's going to be a long walk."

"Is that what I think it is?" Calvin asked. "Are those spaceships on the ground?"

"I think so," Dev confirmed.

"There's a bunch of them. They look like transports. I wonder if we can get one of them to fly."

"Those are definitely flyable. Look at them," Dev said. "I don't see any damage on them."

Calvin hoped he was right, but he had his doubts. Finally, Calvin felt a little bit of hope. Maybe they would be able to get off the planet. Hope felt good. He took a deep breath. The sun, the wind, the fresh air, all felt very good. He looked down at the shuttle sitting near the wall by the sea. Long shadows stretched across the ground. He was about to walk back toward the stairs, when something caught his eye. There was a dark spot on the ground. Fear seized his heart.

"Dev, what is that?" he said, pointing.

Dev examined it with his binoculars. "I don't know." he admitted. "I can't make it out. The trees are in the way."

Calvin took his rifle off of his shoulder and aimed it at the strange dark object. He looked at it through the scope.

"What is it?" Dev asked.

236

"I can't tell," Calvin said. "It looks like a rock. Was there a rock next to the shuttle?"

"I don't remember," Dev said. Calvin pulled his small communicator out of his front jacket pocket.

"Astra, how's it going?"

"Good," Astra said. "I'm feeling a little better."

"Good," Calvin said. "Can you do something for me, please? I want you to peek out the door for me. There is something outside the shuttle on the ground." He was still looking at it through the scope. "It looks like a rock, but I can't tell for sure."

"OK," Astra said nervously. There was silence for a minute. "I don't see anything." she whispered.

"It's about ten feet from the door, just off to the right."

Dev took his rifle off his back and aimed it at the object. "There is a long thin line behind it." he commented. "What is that, a shadow?"

"Yeah, I think that's what it is."

Calvin looked closer and realized, "That's not a shadow. It's going the wrong way."

"Calvin, I think it moved," Dev said slowly. "Look!"

"I still don't see anything! Are you sure it's there?" Astra asked. "You guys are scaring me!"

Calvin made up his mind. "I'm going to shoot it." He gazed through the scope, lined it up in the middle of the crosshairs, and gently pulled the trigger.

There was a loud roar, and the dark object jumped backward. Calvin readjusted his aim and fired again. Dev began firing as well

There was another loud roar, and the thing collapsed in a heap.

Calvin and Dev fired off another few shots, just to make sure it was dead.

"Astra, are you all right?" Calvin asked. Both Calvin and Dev kept the creature in their sights, just waiting for it to move again.

"I'm OK," Astra said. "Did you kill it?"

"Yeah, I think so," Calvin answered. "It's not moving, and we put quite a few shots into it."

"Can you please get down here?" Astra asked. "It's going to be dark soon."

"We're on our way. Be there in a second."

Reluctantly, Calvin lowered his weapon and put it back on his shoulder. They ran back down the stone circular stairs to the elevator and took it down to the main level.

The sun was touching the horizon when they got back to the shuttle. The two ran up and slowed down as soon as they saw the carcass of a very large animal just outside the shuttle. It was much larger than Calvin expected.

"Astra!" he shouted. When she heard his voice, Astra peeked out from inside the shuttle, firmly holding her laser pistol.

"What is that?" she asked when she saw the creature. Calvin and Dev slowly approached it. It was covered with black hair and had a large nose and sharp teeth. Astra smiled when she saw her friends and walked out to join them. She had to walk around the dead beast to get to them. Afraid it might still be alive, she kept her distance.

"Dinner?" Dev asked.

"I don't know about that," Calvin said, looking skeptically at the carcass on the ground. "I wouldn't know where to start. Have you ever hunted before and had to clean and quarter an animal?"

"No," Dev said simply.

"I have," Calvin said. "When I was young my father used to take me hunting. But this is different. I've never seen a creature like this before. How do we know it's safe to eat?"

Nobody answered.

"I'm not too excited about eating it," Astra admitted. "I've never had to hunt for my food. Our ships have always provided our meals. But we should try and conserve the food we have. We don't know how long we'll be here."

"Yeah, you're right," Calvin said. "It's hard to argue with that." He took a deep breath and unhooked the large knife that was connected to the side of his vest.

Dev made a fire, and Calvin did his best to cut the animal up. Astra walked around the garden and found some big sticks. They cooked the meat over the fire, and ate it under the stars. It was nice, and it didn't taste bad at all.

After they were done eating, they all sat by the fire. Their weapons were close by.

"So what's our plan?" Astra asked.

"Our best chance to get off this planet is the star port. It's twenty-seven miles away, and we're going to have to walk."

"Can we do that in one day?" Astra asked.

"I don't think so," Calvin answered. "On flat open ground we might be able to, but there are hills and a forest between us, and I think a couple of rivers. It's probably going to take a couple of days."

"We only have food for a couple of days," Dev added.

"I don't think we have any other choice," Calvin pointed out. Then to Astra he said, "Do you think you can handle the walk?"

"I don't have a choice, do I." It was more of a statement than a question.

"Well, there is another option," Calvin said. "We could leave you here and come back in one of those spaceships. I don't like the idea, but you could barricade yourself inside the castle."

Astra thought about it for a second, but it didn't take her very long to decide. "No, I don't want to be separated from you, and to be honest, I don't want to be alone."

"I don't blame you."

239

"We still have time to think about it," Dev said. "I don't think we should go tomorrow. Remember there's a big storm coming this way. According to the scanner, it's going to be really bad."

"We should move to a new shelter tomorrow then," Calvin said.

"Those rooms we found near the top of the tower would be perfect," Dev said. "And it would be easy to defend, just the one way up."

"OK," Calvin agreed. "That sounds good. We can pack up our stuff and move it up in the morning. Plus we could do some more exploring while we're under the weather."

"That sounds good," Astra said. "Did you look in the tower rooms and see what was in there?"

"No, we were running out of time," Dev said. "By the time we got into the tower, we just went to the top."

No one spoke for several minutes. Astra yawned.

"If you don't mind, I'm really tired," she said. "I'm going to try and get some sleep."

"Go ahead," Calvin said. "I think Dev and I are going to walk around a little bit, make sure the area is secure."

The night passed without incident. Calvin and Dev took turns keeping watch in two-hour increments, letting Astra sleep all night. When it was Calvin's turn, he slowly circled the shuttle. A full moon in the clear sky provided enough light to see by. At one point he thought he heard noises in the distance, but he wasn't sure. It was hard to hear, and it was probably his imagination.

CHAPTER SIX:

THE STORM

It was a long night. Calvin found it almost impossible to sleep. He volunteered to keep watch during the last three hours of the night. The temperature dropped, and he walked around to stay warm. During the long hours, his mind wandered. He jumped at every sound, and all the dark outlines in the garden seemed to be alive. It was a tremendous relief when the sun began to light up the sky behind the castle. Calvin debated with himself about waking Astra up, but he wanted her to sleep as long as possible and left her alone. When Dev woke up, they had something to eat. They decided against eating more of the beast and had some of the dry rations from the shuttle.

Calvin was thrilled to find the shuttle was stocked with survival gear. He found five backpacks, each loaded with food, water, a blanket, a medical kit, and various survival tools. He and Dev also grabbed all of the ammo packs, communicators, flashlights, spare batteries, extra scanner, and all of the medical equipment they could find. Astra was still sleeping when they'd finished packing and had stacked the backpacks by the door.

"What about her?" Dev asked, pointing at Astra.

"I just scanned her," Calvin said. "The med kit made another

241

injection, a combination of pain-killer and something I've never seen before. I think it's making her sleep. I'll carry her."

Dev picked up two backpacks and moved to the door. Calvin picked Astra up gently. Fortunately, she wasn't heavy.

They walked through the garden toward the castle. The sun was shining, but dark clouds were gathering in the sky. Calvin walked slowly, careful not to disturb Astra or cause her pain, but she woke up as soon as they were back outside in the sunlight.

"Good morning," Calvin said, as she opened her eyes. "How are you feeling?"

Astra groaned. "I've been better. Still in a lot of pain." Though Astra didn't weigh very much, she was starting to feel heavy by the time they reached the castle doors.

They were all grateful that they didn't have to climb all of the stairs to the top of the tower. By the time they got to the elevator, Astra was feeling heavier. After the elevator trip, they had to walk up two flights of stairs to where the rooms were. After the first flight of stairs, Calvin sat down on a bench under four tall multicolored stained-glass windows.

"Are you all right?" Astra asked.

"Yes," Calvin said firmly. "I'm fine. I just thought you might want to take a break. Are you OK?"

"I'll be fine," she said. "I'd be in bad shape if it weren't for the pain-killers." Then she paused. "I'm sorry you have to carry me."

"Don't be sorry," Calvin said. "I don't mind."

Astra groaned softly. Calvin thought he knew how she was feeling. She thought this was all her fault. He wanted to tell her that it wasn't, but he knew that no matter what he said to her, she wouldn't believe him. After a short break, Calvin struggled to his feet. He fought as hard as he could to hide his pain the last few steps.

There was an open space at the top of the next set of stairs with a large desk behind a short wall. A hallway wrapped around the perimeter of the tower. The doors to the rooms were spaced around the tower, which were all closed.

"This looks like a security station," Calvin said.

"It's a perfect place to put a guard: in the only way into the tower."

"It almost seems too good to be true."

"What do you mean?" Dev asked.

"Oh, nothing really," Calvin said. "It just seems like there are days when everything goes wrong, and then there are moments like these. Everything's going perfectly. I shouldn't complain."

"No, you shouldn't," Astra said.

Calvin put Astra down on a bench near the stairs, and Dev and Calvin checked all of the rooms to see if they could find a good place to set up camp.

All of the doors were unlocked, and a quick search revealed that all of the rooms on that floor were plush bedrooms. But the best part was, just like the garden, everything was clean. All of the beds had fresh linens on them with blankets and big fluffy comforters. Calvin took Astra to the nearest room and gently laid her on the bed. She was already asleep, so he covered her with a blanket. She looked like she was sleeping peacefully.

He unpacked the medical scanner and slowly waved it over her. The scanner displayed a detailed analysis, most of which he couldn't understand, and produced another injection. He gave her the shot and quietly left the room. Calvin left the door open so he could hear if she made sounds.

Dev met him out in the hall. "How is she?"

"I wish I knew," Calvin answered. "I'm not a doctor. I just do what the medical computer tells me to. She's sleeping, which is probably best for her right now."

Dev followed Calvin to the stairs.

243

"This place is great," Dev said. "There are rooms for all of us. How could we get so lucky?"

"Don't get too comfortable," Calvin said. "I've noticed our luck goes in waves, and we're due for another downturn. By the way, have you checked the scanner recently?"

"No," Dev said, suddenly looking worried. "I'll do it now." He went into one of the rooms and came out with a scanner. He turned it on and waited. After a second, he said, "No life signs, just birds," he said and relaxed. "The storm will be here soon, maybe an hour." Outside, they could hear the wind as it beat against the tower. Calvin looked through the windows. The sky was getting dark.

"OK," Calvin said. "I want to go see what's on the next level." Dev followed him up the stairs.

Just as on every level, there was a bench near the stairs, but this level looked different; there was only one door. Calvin walked through it first.

The first thing he noticed was the tall stained-glass windows all around. The second thing he noticed was the four large computer stations in the middle of the room. They were arranged in a circle, with two large flat monitors hanging above each one.

"Finally," Dev said happily. "This looks promising."

"Some kind of command center," Calvin said. "This is exactly what we need."

"Let's find a way to turn these things on," Dev said, examining the nearest computer.

It wasn't too difficult. There was a large red switch on the back of each one. They walked around and turned them all on. The monitors flickered and came to life.

"Good job," Calvin said smiling. "Do you think we can contact the Frost on one of these?"

There was a soft hum as the computers warmed up.

"Let's find out," Dev said. Calvin walked around the room as the computers were starting up. He looked out the windows. The sky was full of black, angry clouds and the sea was white with swelling waves.

"I can't read any of these screens," Calvin complained, when the computers finished booting up. "I can read the words, but the configuration is very strange."

Dev walked around and looked at it. Then he typed a few keystrokes into one of the computers.

"These are sensors," Dev said. The screen on the left showed an image of the planet and surrounding space. The right screen displayed a close view of the castle and immediate vicinity. "Long and short range," Dev said. There was a trackball, placed prominently in the center of the console, surrounded by keyboards and controls. Dev rolled the trackball and moved the view around the planet. He scanned space until they found a small dot not far from the planet.

"What's that?" Dev asked. He moved a cursor over the dot and clicked on it.

The image of a spaceship appeared on another monitor. It was unmistakable.

"Azure Frost," Calvin whispered. "Can you zoom in on it some more?" Dev played with the controls a little.

"I'm not detecting any life signs," Dev said.

"Of course not, they're robots."

"Right," Dev said, shaking his head. Streams of data began to scroll alongside the picture of the Frost.

"Let's scan for energy signatures first," Calvin said. "Look for robot life signs."

"OK." Dev manipulated the controls like a pro. It didn't take long, and it wasn't what Calvin wanted to hear.

"It's dead, just floating in space," Dev said sadly. "No power at all."

Dev zoomed in on the ship until it filled the screen. Azure Frost, the most beautiful and elegant spaceship Calvin had ever seen, was burned and ripped apart. There were gaping holes where power systems overloaded and exploded through the hull in dozens of places. Shredded pieces of metal floated around the ship in a slowly spreading debris field. Calvin felt his heart sink, as if a dark cloud were hovering over him, suffocating him.

"This isn't happening," Calvin muttered, wondering how he was going to explain to the king and queen that he lost the Azure Frost, and that their daughter was severely injured. He desperately wanted to get onto the ship and find Ion. What was he doing up there? Had he and the other robots been destroyed?

"What do these other computers do?" Dev asked, walking around to the right. He carefully examined the next computer.

"I have no idea what this one does," he admitted. "But according to this, there are thousands of computers somewhere under the castle. There is an option here to turn them all on at the same time or individually. Why would we want to turn on that many computers?"

"Have you seen this kind of technology before?" Calvin asked.

"I've seen something very similar," Dev said. "I can't remember where." Then a menu popped up on the screen. "This is complicated. Each computer can be programmed to perform a specific function. Oh, and they can move wherever we want them. These aren't computers, they're robots. We can control thousands of robots from this console."

"Really?" Calvin said. "That could come in handy.

"Very," Dev said. "And, oh yes, they have weapons. Two heavy lasers on each robot."

"Can we program them to defend us?"

Dev looked through the menu options. "Yes," he said. "We can. That's one of their functions. We can tell the robots to move to any location we choose and then select the level of aggression. The highest setting is, basically, shoot anything that moves."

Excitedly, Dev went to the next computer. "This one controls

246

heavy weapons. All kinds of vehicles—wow, tanks!" Dev quickly moved to the next one.

Air vehicles," he exclaimed. "Look at this! Fighters and bombers. And I have no idea what those are. Or those."

"So this is a war room," Calvin said. "Are you saying all this stuff is out there: robots, tanks, and bombers?"

"Yes. According to the computers, there are several hangars under the castle, and this hardware is down there, ready to use."

"And all controlled from this room?"

"Yes," Dev said.

Calvin walked back around to the sensor computer. He moved the cursor around the castle and around the area. Something caught his eye. On the edges of the screen were several red dots.

"I wonder what those are," Calvin said, trying to click on one.

"Zoom it out a little," Dev suggested.

The screen zoomed out, showing masses of red dots all around the castle.

"I don't know what those are," Calvin said. "But usually on a radar or scanner, red is a bad color."

"Can you click on one and zoom in? We need to get a closer look."

Calvin put one of the red dots in the center of the screen and zoomed in.

Dev and Calvin stared openmouthed at the screen, terrified. On the screen was a horrible image. At first glance it looked like a robot, but the large mouth with rows of sharp, jagged teeth and the claws on its hands and feet were unmistakable. It was one of the monster robots. They stared at it for several moments, unable to look away.

"What is it doing?" Calvin asked. "It's not moving. Is it sleeping?" They both stared for several more minutes. The creature didn't move. Calvin zoomed the screen out again. He changed the screen from a top view to a side view.

"Look," he said. "They're all underground. These are tunnels." He traced light-gray lines on the screen with his finger.

"All of those tunnels go under the castle," Dev observed grimly. "Those connect to the tunnels we saw earlier, that lead to that door downstairs. How many monsters are there?"

Calvin checked the screen. The answer felt like a death warrant.

"Fourteen thousand."

"Fourteen thousand?" Dev gasped. "That can't be right."

Calvin zoomed the screen out. Red dots covered the screen. "The sensors say there are fourteen thousand out there. I guess we know what happened to the occupants of this planet." There was no arguing with that. What else could have happened to them?

"What are we going to do?" Dev asked.

"I have an idea," Calvin said, with a smile. "We can use our army of robots to destroy the monsters."

"Hey," Dev said, getting excited. "That's a good idea." Then a thought occurred to him. "Wait, if that's such a good idea, why didn't the people who lived here do that?"

"I don't know," Calvin said. "Maybe they didn't have time. But I'm fairly certain they weren't here when the monsters attacked."

"How do you know?"

"Look around, this place is clean. If the monsters attacked, I highly doubt they would have cleaned up after."

"Maybe they did what we're planning—escape in spaceships."

"That's possible," Calvin said. "That would explain a few things. But it's strange that they ran away without putting up any kind of a fight."

"I agree, but right now the monsters are leaving us alone. They don't seem to know we're here. We could surprise them."

"All right, how many robots do we have?"

Calvin checked, "Six hundred."

"Six hundred against fourteen thousand?"

"Yes, I'm afraid so," Calvin said. "But remember, the fighting would all happen underground. The robots would have an advantage down there. The monsters would be bottled up and wouldn't be allowed to move around very well. Our robots could pick them off one by one."

"That could also be used against us," Dev pointed out. "And we wouldn't be able to use the tanks or aircraft at all."

"You're right, not underground."

"Well, then," Dev said. "Maybe we should leave them alone. Look at them, they aren't moving. Maybe they will stay that way."

"Maybe, but what if they don't? What if the storm wakes them up?"

Dev didn't have an answer for that.

"At the very least, we can put some robots at the bottom of the tower, to protect us."

"That's a good idea."

They walked around to the robot control panel. Calvin was expecting it to be a very difficult process. The computers he used at home were hard to use and required a lot of time to learn.

But this one, he found to be amazingly easy to learn and use.

There were dozens of large hangars and rooms under the castle. Calvin selected the nearest one, directly under the tower. The computer told him there were twenty in that room, and they were all ready to use. With a simple click of a button, the robot was activated. A small monitor lit up; a view from the robot's eyes. It was dark, but the outline of a door could clearly be seen.

Another click of the device told the robot where he wanted it to go. A small menu gave him the option of selecting the robot's mission and target priorities. Calvin selected guard mode and told it to open fire on anything that wasn't human. In fact, there was a target profile for the monsters already loaded.

"Here's proof," Calvin said. "They did fight the monsters, or they were at least prepared to."

"Yeah, but what happened?"

Calvin clicked "execute" on the screen, and the robot moved forward. It opened the door and moved out into the castle. Calvin and Dev watched in amazement as the robot walked to the bottom of the tower and took up a position facing the way down.

"This is incredible," Calvin said. "Now we can see what's coming."

"We can all sleep tonight, and not have to worry about keeping someone on watch."

"Yes," Dev agreed. "But, I don't think one robot is going to be enough."

"You're right," Calvin said. "I'll put some on the stairs, and a couple right outside the door here."

Calvin activated the rest of the robots in that room. He commanded two to take up a position near the level they were on. He put two more on the stairs halfway down to the main floor. The rest he put down at the bottom of the stairs. Now they had twenty robots guarding them.

Outside, they could hear pounding rain, blasts of wind, and thunder that boomed intensely. Calvin walked back down to check on Astra. She was sleeping peacefully.

"I know the robots are down there," Calvin said. "But I want to see one up close, just to make sure."

Dev started to say something but stopped after Calvin walked down the stairs. Dev followed him.

"You have it set to defend, right?" Dev said, "What if they shoot us?"

"They are only supposed to shoot the monsters," Calvin

answered.

"Right," Dev said. "And you trust them with your life, because computers never make mistakes. Especially the ones you've never seen before."

That made Calvin stop. He turned and looked at Dev. "You have a point," he said. "So you think we should stay away from them, just in case?"

"Uh, yeah," Dev said. "You can go down there if you want to. I'll wait here."

Calvin was very curious and wanted to see one. He believed they were there. The computer said they were. And he saw the view from the robot's eyes as it walked up the stairs and stopped just below the level they were sleeping on. But he wanted to see with his own eyes that they were there. He didn't just want to take the computer's word for it.

He walked down the stairs slowly, taking it one step at a time. When he looked back up briefly, he saw that Dev was not moving but watching him go down the stairs. Calvin stayed close to the inside wall. Finally, he saw the outline of one of the robots on the stairs. He got a little bit closer. He could hear a soft hum coming from the robots. He realized that it was the sound of their scanners.

Calvin still did not have a good view of them and decided to take another step down. When he did, one of the robots turned its head and looked at him. Calvin froze. For a brief second, he was scared that he had made a very bad decision. But, after a second, the robot looked back down the stairs.

Calvin took a deep breath. He turned and walked back up to where Dev was and told him what happened.

"I feel much better now," Calvin told Dev. "Safer."

Calvin and Dev walked back up to the bedroom level. When they passed the security desk at the top of the stairs, Calvin stopped and looked at it. The desk had a computer monitor built into the surface, with a glass keypad. There was also a long black switch off to the side. Calvin didn't know why he did it, but he reached out and pulled the handle

251

down without thinking. When he did, a large metal wall slid down out of the ceiling, blocking off the stairs completely.

"Nice," Calvin said, knocking on the steel wall. "That's solid. I'll definitely sleep better tonight."

"No kidding," Dev agreed.

Calvin yawned. "I can't keep my eyes open anymore," he said. "I'm going to get some sleep."

"Me too," Dev said. "Here, take some food with you." He handed Calvin a food pack. Calvin took it gratefully and headed off to his room.

"Good night," Calvin said. His room was right next to Astra's. He slowly walked into his room and closed the door. He took a deep breath and sat down at the table. He ate his meal in silence, happy to be alone. After he finished eating, he lay down on the bed and fell right to sleep.

The sound of the storm woke him up a few hours later. Calvin walked out into the hall and looked around. Dev was still asleep in his room, and Astra was still asleep in hers. Calvin walked into her room and ran the scanner over her. He was encouraged by the results. It seemed the medicine she had been taking was helping. Her vital signs were more stable.

Calvin walked to a window that had a large flat sill. He sat on it and looked outside, watching the storm. It was impressive. Lightning flashed across the dark sky. Rain continued to pound heavily. He was glad that he was inside, safe and dry for now.

After a little while, he started to get a little antsy, so he got up and walked back up to the computer level. He sat down at the terminal that controlled the ground vehicles, intending at first to just look around.

Two miles away, in a large underground garage, sat rows and rows of battle tanks. They looked as if they had never been used. Calvin selected one. The computer gave him the option to start its engine, which he did. Then the tank revved up, the sounds floating over the speaker. The tank's status showed up. All lines were green.

The interface was the same as the one for the robots. He told the tank to move outside and wait. A large door opened at the top of a ramp, and the tank obeyed his command. It moved up the ramp and outside into the rain. The door closed, and the tank waited for its next order.

Calvin checked its status. The main laser cannon was charged and ready. He told it to stand guard and shoot any monsters it saw. While playing around with the mission settings, he found that he could tell it to patrol any area he wanted. He selected a patrol pattern one mile long, and the tank moved off to obey its new orders.

Amazing, Calvin thought. The best part was, there were more tanks ready to protect them.

He got up and sat down at the sensor's computer, to see what all of the sleeping monsters were up to. When he looked at the screen, all of the red dots were gone. He decided that the settings were probably changed, so he tried to reset them.

There were still no red dots on the screen. An icy ball of fear formed in the pit of his stomach. Where did they all go? The screen flickered, and then all of the red dots were back. That was weird, he thought. Then he looked at the screen again. It looked a little different than it did before. It looked like they were all a little closer to the castle. It might be his imagination, too. What if it wasn't?

He wanted to make sure, so he picked one of the red dots and zoomed in on it. The same ghastly image appeared on the screen. It was one of the monsters. Calvin shivered. But then he noticed something was different. The monster was standing up, and it was moving back and forth slowly. Calvin's eyes grew wide. Calvin zoomed back a little. He stared at the monster for a long time. He had no idea how long he had been watching it before Dev walked into the room.

"What's going on?" Dev asked, looking at the screen. "It's standing?"

"Yes, they all are," Calvin said. "I have no idea why. It doesn't look like they've moved. They're just standing there."

It was hard to look away. The image was so scary and amazing at the same time.

"I was thinking about activating the rest of the robots." Calvin said. "I can put them all around the castle, near the tower, and in the basement."

"That's an excellent idea," Dev said.

"I'll do it now," Calvin said.

Calvin got up and sat down at the robot control computer. He began activating all the rest of the robots. It didn't take very long. Calvin was able to select groups of them at a time and program them. Within thirty minutes all six hundred robots were activated, and strategically placed around the castle. They were all close enough to the tower to provide protection. Calvin sat back, pleased.

Only one big question remained: How effective would the robots actually be? Each one of the robots was equipped with an energy shield to protect it from attack, two heavy lasers, and a dozen or so rockets.

"They should prove to be a formidable defense," Calvin told Dev.

"There is something else we could do," Dev said. "We could blow up the stairs and make it impossible for the monsters to get up here."

"There is only one problem with that," Calvin said. "We would be trapped up here. What if the monsters climb up on the outside?"

"Good point," Dev said, slightly deflated.

"We might want to consider it though, as a last resort, if we become overwhelmed. But let's hope it doesn't come to that."

"Right," Dev agreed.

"I have another idea," Calvin said. "We still have all those tanks. I want to place them around the castle, outside of course, near the base of the tower. They are packing some heavy firepower. Also, look at this map." Calvin took Dev back to the sensor computer. "Look at these tunnels. They all connect at these locations, around the castle." Calvin pointed to several locations on the screen. "There's four of them, two miles away from here on different sides of the castle. If it looks like the robots can't handle things underground, fighting the monsters, we can use the bombers to destroy the tunnels. When the Terrors realize they can't get to us from underground, they will go to the surface."

Calvin looked at Dev. He had a confused look on his face.

"If we force them to the surface, they will have to get through the tanks to get to us," Calvin explained. "And the bombers will be able to see them, too."

"Oh, I see," Dev said, understanding. "Then you should get all of the tanks out there now, don't you think?"

"Yes, I do. In fact, they're all warming up right now. As soon as they're ready, I'll get them out there on the grounds around the castle." Within twenty minutes, all ground vehicles were deployed around the castle. There were one hundred heavy laser tanks and fifty lighter missile tanks. If it weren't for the fact that there were fourteen thousand monster robots, Calvin would feel completely safe.

Calvin walked down to check on Astra. She was lying in bed, staring at a handheld scanner. When she saw him, she motioned for him to come in.

"How are you doing?" he asked quietly.

"I feel a lot better," she said.

"Do you feel like eating something?"

She said yes. He went and got her some food and water.

While she was eating, Calvin explained everything that had been going on.

"Wow, that's a lot of bad news," she said when he finished. "At least we have something to defend ourselves with, but I wonder how much good it will do."

"I wish I could tell you," Calvin said. "I'm not sure, but the tanks and robots have a lot of firepower."

"That's true, but for some reason I don't feel safer."

"I know. My big concern is how to get back to the Frost and find out what happened. We have to repair it and continue our mission."

"I'm glad you're so optimistic," Astra said. "I'm sorry. I'm just not feeling very good about things right now."

"Everything is going to be OK," Calvin said soothingly. "I bet Ion is up there right now, repairing the ship. We just have to wait for him to come and get us."

Astra tried to smile. "I hope you're right."

"Me, too," Calvin said.

"I found something you might find interesting."

"What's that?"

Astra held up the scanner. The screen displayed a map of the castle. There was a small flashing green dot under the castle.

"Is that what I think it is?"

"Yes. It's the fourth segment," Astra answered. "It's located four miles beneath the surface." Calvin stared at the screen in disbelief.

"You've got to be kidding me," He said. "You know what's down there?"

"Yes, I know."

Calvin stared at the ceiling, his mind working at a thousand miles per hour.

"We're going to have to go get it," she said.

"I know," Calvin admitted. Then he turned to her and said, "Dev and I can handle it."

The truth was, Calvin didn't want Astra going down there. She was still not doing well, and they might have to run for their lives. "It would be better for you to stay here, and keep an eye on us. You can guide us, keep us away from monsters."

"I can do that," she said. "I could send some robots down with you to protect you."

"Maybe," Calvin said. "I'm not sure that would be a good idea. I want to sneak down there, as quietly as possible. Get in and out without the monsters even knowing we were there. The robots make a lot of noise. We might as well just tell the monsters we are coming, and where we'll be."

"I understand," Astra said. She felt rejected. The one way she could help, and Calvin didn't want it. But she really did understand. In her opinion, having a few extra guns outweighed the risk of making too much noise. She believed she could find a way of making the robots move quietly. Anyway, she'd been working with robots her entire life. Despite what he said, Astra would find a way to protect him.

Before they went to bed, Calvin got them both some food. They each ate a package of rations and had a bottle of water. They listened to the storm outside, talked, and ate. After eating, Calvin went back to his room. It took him a long time to fall asleep. The thunder and the rain pounding against the window had become very loud. The noise wasn't the only problem. Calvin's mind would not shut off. Just knowing there were thousands of monsters below them, with only a handful of robots for protection, kept sleep from him. He wasn't looking forward to going underground. In the morning, he and Dev would have to descend into the heart of monster territory. The thought scared him—terrified him to his core. Calvin had a restless, dreamless night's sleep.

CHAPTER SEVEN:

DESCENT

Calvin woke up five hours later. He sat up in bed and stared at the room. It took him a minute to realize where he was. Outside the storm raged. The wind was loud as it pounded against the tower. It was still dark, so he lay down again and tried to go back to sleep. He tried for a long time without success. Their impending descent into the dark underground where Terrors were hiding weighed heavily on his mind. But there was no way to avoid it. They had to retrieve the fourth segment. Part of him questioned the need. Why bother going after the next piece when the first three were lost? What were they going to do when they got the fourth segment? Take it to the top of the tower and hope the Terrors left them alone until Ion rescued them? He had to have hope. They just had to find a way to get back up to the Frost, even if that meant looking through the debris to recover the other pieces. Astra would be able to repair them if they were damaged, right? He shook his head and tried to focus on what was next: just go down there, find the segment, and get out. Hopefully they wouldn't run into any Terrors. The clock was ticking. The longer they waited, the more dangerous it would be. After a while, he gave up trying to sleep and got up.

He walked upstairs to the computer level and found Dev sitting at the robot control station.

"Couldn't sleep?" Calvin asked.

"No," Dev answered. "I'm glad you're awake. I think we should go now. I want to get it over with."

"I'm good with that. There's no reason to put it off." They ate some food and then went to their rooms to get ready. They decided to go light; weapons, ammo, lights, radio, scanner, and a portable shield generator each.

Calvin hated to do it, but he wanted Astra to know they were leaving. He softly knocked on the door and was surprised when she cracked the door open.

"What's wrong?" she said in a shaky voice.

"Dev and I are going now to get the fourth segment. Do you want to watch us on the scanner?"

"Yes!" she said, sounding a little irritated. "You should have told me earlier."

"I wanted to let you sleep."

"I couldn't sleep. Don't go yet. I'll be out in a minute." The door closed. Calvin and Dev walked back upstairs to make sure they had everything they needed. Calvin was glad they did, because they forgot to pack water. They each attached a bottle of water to their belts.

A few minutes later, Astra walked into the room. She didn't look very happy. Calvin thought it was because she was still trying to wake up. She sat down at the robot control console and looked at the scanner.

"At least the Terrors haven't moved," she said. "I hope it stays that way."

"Yeah, well, we decided to go find the segment before they wake up."

"That's probably a good idea." She still didn't look happy. Her expression softened, "Please be careful. I'll try to help you as much as I can."

"We'll be careful," Calvin said. "Don't worry." He said that, but he knew she would. He was worried, but mostly scared.

259

Astra walked with them to the door and opened the barrier. She reached out her hand; Calvin took it. She started to stay something, but stopped. He wanted to say something to her, too, but was afraid to. They smiled at each other, and it seemed they both understood without saying anything. Reluctantly, Calvin turned and walked down the stairs. Dev followed him. The heavy metal door closed behind them and shut with a clang that echoed loudly. They walked quietly past the robot that was standing guard. It turned and looked at them as they passed. Calvin could hear the soft hum coming from its scanner. He could feel it staring at him. He knew, or thought he knew, that it wouldn't react, and was relieved that all it did was watch them.

Calvin felt as if a hand were crushing him. All the way down to the basement he felt it. It was sapping the life out of him. There was no getting out of this. They had to find the fourth segment. He knew that if they didn't do this, they might as well just go home and quit. When they reached the door, they stopped and stared at it.

The door looked like it was welded shut, but it wasn't. With a touch of a button, two iron beams slid apart, and the door swung open. A blast of cold, rancid-smelling air hit them, as if the levels below had been pressurized.

Both had their weapons ready. Calvin fully expected to see Terrors at the door waiting to get out. He was relieved that nothing was there. But the steep narrow stairs that led down into darkness caused his fear to rise.

Calvin stared through the open door. Before stepping forward he checked his weapon again to make sure it was loaded and ready. He also made sure his backup pistol was ready, and he could get to it quickly. Dev didn't move. They shared a look, but Dev still didn't move, so Calvin went first.

They quietly stepped down the dark concrete stairwell. Their flashlights cut through the darkness, giving him a tiny hint of safety, but not enough to overcome the tide of his rising emotions. The stairs led down into a narrow hallway. Thick black glass covered the walls on both sides. Calvin shone his light into the glass but couldn't see what was on the other side. They passed through an open door at the end of the hallway and into a large waiting room. Benches lined the walls; a security station blocked their way. They stepped through a tunnel of electronic scanners. They cautiously passed through the center of the room, shining their lights on everything. It was a mess. There was trash, fragments of metal, and pieces of robots all over the floor. The walls were cracked and had holes peppered in them everywhere. The door on the far side was blocked with a mountain of broken furniture.

"It looks like there was a fight in here," Dev said. "And they barricaded the door."

Calvin said what they were both thinking. "To keep the Terrors down there."

"And now you want to remove the barricade and go down there."

"No." Calvin corrected him. "I don't want to." He shone his light around the room. "What's that?" He pointed to two wide elevator doors.

"I suppose it's too much to ask that they work." Dev followed him. Their shoes crunched on broken glass. When they reached the doors, they found the control panels smashed to pieces. Dev played with it for a second but didn't waste much time. "No chance," he said. The disappointment was clear in his voice.

"I'm afraid we're going to have to move all that junk."

It didn't take long. They grabbed pieces of furniture and threw them into a corner. Several of the pieces were large and required both of them to move. The whole time Calvin's mind screamed at him to stop. Once the furniture was removed, they found three heavy iron beams, a stack of stone blocks, and a large metal plate. Calvin wanted to stop to catch his breath but was so anxious to get the segment and get out of there that he didn't even give Dev an option. He pulled the door open, and gaped down another set of concrete stairs that descended into the darkness. Calvin had to force himself to take the next step. It was a long nerve-racking descent down. He couldn't stop thinking; the deeper they went, the more steps they would have to climb back up. What if they were being chased by Terrors? There was no way he was going to be able to run all the way up. That was his worst fear: running up all those stairs. They would be no match against the monsters, and they would be torn to pieces. Several times on their way down, Calvin thought he heard something behind them, but he never saw anything. He kept his gun out, with his finger on the trigger.

It was a long, slow, terrifying descent. Calvin felt suffocated by the confined space. The stale, nasty-smelling air was starting to make him feel sick. He fought to control his breathing, and his heart pounded in his chest. It felt as if it took forever to reach the bottom. Once there, he didn't find relief. Instead, the realization of impending doom threatened to drown him in terror. He knew they were about to enter an area with fourteen thousand monsters, and if Dev hadn't been with him, he might not have been able to keep going. They passed through another doorway, with a thick metal door that was pushed all the way open. They stepped onto a balcony overlooking a small dark city. Hundreds of identical square buildings lined dozens of parallel streets. The city was lit by a strange dim, pale light that radiated from the entire ceiling above. The air was heavy and smelled worse than before. It was bad, but there was something else. He didn't know what it was, but it was disgusting, and it was giving him a bad headache. A staircase took them to street level.

Calvin checked the scanner.

"The segment hasn't moved," Calvin whispered. They hadn't talked on the way down. Calvin was afraid of making noise. His voice sounded very loud in the dead silence. "There are Terrors all around us." Calvin held up the screen so Dev could see. The scanner showed red dots everywhere. There were so many the machine couldn't lock onto one of them. It just kept bouncing back and forth, trying to analyze them all at once.

Calvin led the way down the first street. They walked slowly and cautiously. Calvin felt very uneasy. Monsters were close all around, but not seeing them was almost worse than seeing them—knowing they were there, yet hiding in the shadows. It was an eerie feeling, but one he should have been getting used to, walking through a deserted city, in darkness and deafening silence. They walked for ten minutes, and Calvin spotted an odd shape in the middle of the road, right in front of them. He shone his light on it, but it was too far away to see what it was. It cast a long shadow down the street. As they got closer, Calvin thought it was a person standing in the road. It only took a second to realize what it really was. Dev obviously did, too. He hissed something and ran to the side of the road. Calvin panicked and ran the other way. He pressed himself up against the side of a building and dropped to his knees. The ground was cold and hard. He turned around, thinking Dev was behind him, but he wasn't there. Calvin looked around rapidly, and saw him on the other side of the road. He waved at Dev until he got his attention. They stared at each other for several moments without moving.

"Now what?" Calvin mouthed. Dev looked at him. He looked scared. Calvin glanced back down the street the way they'd come and saw something even more alarming; two more dark shapes in the street. They weren't far away, and Calvin knew what they were.

The Terrors had them boxed in! Calvin stood. His heart pounded in his chest. Slowly he inched his way forward. He held his gun tightly, ready to open fire. He thought about blowing the monster to pieces now, but he was afraid to. Every monster in the area would hear it and converge on them. He looked back over his shoulder nervously. Did the monsters see him? He took several steps forward and stopped, carefully watching the monster ahead. Dev watched him and moved forward a little, too.

Calvin desperately wanted to get out of there. Something was telling him to get moving—maybe it was his brain—but his fear wanted him to ignore it and stay still. They couldn't sit there forever. He knew that much. So he got up and walked forward. He looked back at Dev, whose eyes were wide open, clearly shocked at what Calvin was doing. He mouthed some words and shook his head. Calvin ignored him.

As he got closer, all doubt was removed; it was a Terror. Its mouth was open, rows of razor-sharp teeth clearly visible. The monster's chest was moving slightly, and he could hear a soft metallic breathing sound. He looked at its eyes. It had a dark face, covered with black leathery skin. Its eyes looked closed. Calvin turned and motioned to Dev to follow him. At first Dev didn't move, but slowly got up the courage to stand and move in Calvin's direction. The two of them walked forward slowly, trying to make as little noise as possible.

Calvin held his breath as he passed in front of the monster. He didn't pause or wait for Dev, who followed close behind him. When they had gone half a block away from the Terror, they turned and looked back. None of the monsters had moved, but Calvin couldn't relax yet. He knew they were going to have to go back the way they came.

The scanner guided them to a distant corner of the underground city. The screen clearly showed that the street continued ahead of them, but it was blocked with a tall spike-covered barricade. It was a dead end. Calvin looked up and let out a breath. Then he looked at the scanner again.

"It's that way," he said, pointing.

"There's no way we're getting through this," Dev said. "Or over it. Look at those spikes. Is there anyway around it?"

Calvin examined the scanner and changed the settings.

"No, here's the problem. It's still below us. There it is. You've got to be kidding me. It's still a about a mile down. We need to find the stairs."

"Stairs? How about an elevator?"

"Whichever comes first," Calvin said.

"Do you want to split up and look for it?"

"No way," Calvin said quickly. "That's a very bad idea. We're better off together."

"All right," Dev agreed. "Which way then?" They looked around.

"Let's follow the wall along that way," Calvin said, pointing off to their right. "If we keep to the edges, maybe we'll attract less attention."

"And what if it's in the middle?" Dev asked.

"I hope not," Calvin added. "Let's take it one step at a time."

Calvin started to move and looked back. Dev was standing still.

"Are you OK?"

"Yeah," Dev said and slowly started to follow. Calvin looked at him. He could see the fear in Dev's face very clearly.

"And you wanted to split up?"

"Not really. I just want to get out of here."

"I do, too," Calvin said. "But those monsters take a lot of fire to take down. I don't think either of us can do it alone."

"You're right. Forget I said it."

The light in the massive room was very strange and seemed to come out of the ceiling in a thousand different places. It was a dim-yellow, unnatural light that cast their shadows in all directions. Each of them had four shadows.

They followed the dark gray wall for a long time. Calvin jumped at every sound, every shadow that seemed out of place. It was nerve-racking. When they reached a corner on the far side, they stopped.

Calvin was starting to panic and had to fight to stay calm. He turned around to ask Dev a question, and when he did, he saw three large shapes slowly approaching them down the street.

He gasped. Dev spun around to see what he was looking at. When he saw the monsters, Dev gasped, too, and started moving backward.

"They're moving!" Dev hissed and turned to run.

"Wait," Calvin whispered. "Look!" They both stood frozen in fear. The monsters were moving toward them, but very slowly. "What are they doing?" It was mesmerizing.

"Let's get out of here," Dev pleaded. "Please."

They walked down the street, passing within a few feet of the advancing monsters. Calvin held his breath as they walked by them. The monsters didn't seem to notice. Once past, they quickened their pace.

Calvin and Dev hurried forward and found a place to hide in the shadow of an overhanging building.

"This isn't working," Calvin said, quickly scanning the area. "We're not going to find it on the edges. We need to go to the center."

"The center," Dev said. "So they can surround us?"

Several dark shapes appeared in the gloom down the street in both directions. They were moving faster now.

"They're already surrounding us," Calvin said. "It's like they're waking up. I don't think we have much time."

They ran from one building to the next, trying to stay out of view. The streets were filling with large, slow-moving shadows.

"Calvin, wait," Dev whispered loudly.

"Hurry up, Dev," Calvin snapped. "They know we're here, run!"

Calvin checked his weapon again and held it out in front, ready. Dev followed him for several blocks, running at full speed until they reached a round glass building in the middle of a wide open area. There was a single door, which was open. In the middle of the room was a stairwell leading down. Calvin was so scared, he couldn't think straight. He rushed ahead, plunging down the stairs without even looking at what they were rushing into.

The stairs were metal, and their footfalls banged loudly as they pounded their way down. At the end of the first flight they reached a landing. A tremendous banging thundered on the stairs above them. Calvin spun around. Four large monsters were pushing their way toward them, moving much faster than before. The stairs shook, and dust trickled down from above. Dev grabbed onto Calvin's arm and pushed him to move.

Terror filled Calvin's brain. They ran down the steps at lightning speed. The thunderous sound that filled the stairway was deafening. The pattern was constant, stairs, landing, turn. Stairs, landing, turn. Calvin found it easiest to grab onto the railing as he was turning each corner, pull himself around, and push off toward each new flight of stairs. He didn't dare stop and look back. He could sense the monsters were close behind.

A burst of static filled Calvin's ears.

"Calvin," Astra said. "You have—behind you—closer—"

"Astra!" Calvin shouted. "Say again, you're breaking up! Astra!"

She didn't answer.

They ran down flight after flight, not pausing, gasping for breath, driven by cruel fear. When they finally reached the bottom, they found a large metal door. Calvin quickly looked at his scanner. The segment was just ahead. They charged through and closed the door. It was very heavy, and they had to use their legs to push—legs that had turned to jelly and were aching. The door shut with a loud click. Calvin found and slid a large dead bolt.

Sounds of heavy pounding footfalls rushed to the door and stopped. Calvin held his breath and took a few steps back. What were the Terrors going to do? He was snapped back to reality by Dev, who pulled on his arm again.

"We have to keep moving," Dev whispered.

Calvin's nerves were frayed. He tried to forget for the moment that they were trapped, miles beneath the surface. Another thought occurred to him: What if the segment was too big to carry? How would they get it back up to the surface? How would they get past the Terrors that were now almost fully awake?

They passed doors on both sides, which were closed. They were in a long tunnel that seemed to have no ending. Unlike the deserted science city above, there were no lights. Only the bright beams of their flashlights cut through the darkness. Calvin kept an eye on the scanner. The segment was straight ahead and a mile away. It was a long walk. Dev kept looking back over his shoulder nervously.

"Can we take a break?" Calvin asked after they had walked half a mile. "My legs are killing me."

"Sounds good to me," Dev said, but he sounded unsure. They sat

267

down on the floor, each facing a different direction, holding their guns out defensively.

"It would be nice if we could find an elevator," Dev said. "I am not looking forward to walking back up the stairs. My legs hurt. And how are we going to get past the monsters. Any ideas? Are we in as much trouble as I think we are?"

"Hey, an elevator," Calvin said. "There must be one down here somewhere. You can't tell me they hauled heavy equipment up and down the stairs. We just need to find it."

Suddenly there was a loud bang. Calvin and Dev looked at each other and had the same thought.

"Time to go," Calvin said. It was painful to stand. Every muscle in his body was in distress.

At first, Calvin was content to walk, but after hearing several more loud bangs echo down the hallway, he picked up the pace. He had to force himself to run, to ignore his pain. After a few minutes, the banging stopped, and he began to relax slightly. He even slowed down, thinking maybe the door would hold.

"Hey," Calvin said. "We're gonna make it."

Suddenly there was a very loud crash. Dev screamed and ran past him. Calvin pushed himself on, fighting to keep up with Dev. The fear reached hysteria as the sound of heavy footfalls echoed loudly, pounding in his ears.

At the end of the hallway they were stopped by a locked door. The pounding was getting louder, closer. A loud heart-stopping scream cut like a knife through the air. Calvin and Dev frantically pulled at the door, but it wouldn't budge. With panic fully in control, they both pulled as hard as they could. Ignoring all pain, they pulled until they heard a loud crack.

Calvin sensed the Terrors were nearly on top of them. He and Dev pulled the door open just wide enough to get through and then pulled it closed from the other side. It shut with a loud click. Immediately there was a massive bang on the door. Calvin jumped away.

There was no time to rest. Calvin checked his scanner and led the way through a room full of lab tables. In the back they found a closed door with a bar across it.

Calvin stopped and stared at the door. In the midst of the banging on the door, dust falling from the ceiling and filling the air, he realized that it took two to open the door, and Astra was not there. Calvin looked at the door and then at Dev. Fear gave way to desperation, and then he felt all of the hope drain out of him. They were trapped in the small lab with no other way out. Small cracks were beginning to appear in the door where the monsters were pounding on it. Dev was shouting something at Calvin, but the noise from the pounding on the door was all he could hear. Calvin felt weak. All of his strength was gone, just like his hope.

Suddenly there was a loud explosion. Calvin was sure that his life was about to end. He sat on the floor with his back against the door. Dev was on his feet, frantically searching the room for another way out. Calvin raised his rifle and pointed it toward the door.

"Dev, I could use your help here!" he shouted. He heard Dev yell back but couldn't understand what he was saying. Calvin focused on the door. Whatever came through that door was going to get the full force of his weapon. Grimly, he knew, that didn't mean a lot.

"You're not getting me without a fight!" Calvin shouted at the door. He set his weapon on overcharge and prepared to fire one massive bolt at whatever came through the door first. Then he took out his pistol and made sure it was ready. Large cracks ripped across the door. Several loud screams wailed outside.

"This is it!" Calvin shouted. He was gratified to see Dev standing beside him, pistol ready.

The door exploded into a thousand fragments. A wave of heat and pressure forced Calvin back and knocked Dev off of his feet. Calvin held onto his weapon tightly but had to turn his face in order to shield his eyes from the flying debris.

Four large creatures smashed their way into the room. Calvin

269

aimed his weapon at the first one, put his finger on the trigger and started to pull. Before he could pull the trigger, he saw something that made him stop and lower his weapon.

"Astra!" he shouted, a wave of relief washing over him. "I can't believe it." Four large robots were standing in front of him. Astra was on the back of the first robot. Down the hall he could see the bodies of several monsters, lying on the floor.

Astra climbed down off the robot's back. She had a small controller in her hand. Calvin climbed off the floor and walked to her. Before he had a chance to say anything, she hugged him.

"You forgot it takes both of us to open the vault doors," she said with a mixture of scolding and playfulness.

"Yeah, I completely forgot," was all he could say.

"I did too," she smiled. "I followed you down as soon as I remembered. I brought a few friends with me. Look, I can control them with this. It's a remote control." She showed him the scanner.

"I don't mean to be rude," Dev said. "But I thought you said the weapon segment was down here."

"It is here," Calvin said. "This way." He led Astra back to the vault door. There was a strong sense of urgency in the air. Calvin and Astra walked up to the door and put their hands on the opener. The metal bar glowed dark-green, and the door clicked open. They pulled the door open and walked inside. There, sitting on a table in the middle of the room was a large, strangely shaped object.

Astra used her robot control scanner to order one of the robots to pick up the fourth segment and take it out of the room. Astra climbed on to the back of her robot and smiled.

"Come on," she said. "Grab a robot. It's the quickest way out of here." Calvin walked to the nearest robot and began to climb up on its back. Amazed, he found several places that fit his feet, which he could use to climb up. There seemed to be an indentation on the back of the robot, in the shape of a human body, that he could press himself into. There were two handles on the back, perfect for holding onto. It quickly became obvious to him that he was going to need them.

Once they were all mounted up, Astra input commands into her controller. The robots took off at a run that almost gave Calvin whiplash. The robots sprinted down the long hallway. Calvin felt the wind on his face. At the end of the hallway, the robots began the climb up the stairs. Calvin caught sight of at least six robots out in front, leading the way. The robots were surprisingly fast, and Calvin was extremely grateful he didn't have to climb the stairs himself.

Flashes of light lit the darkness like lightning bolts. Laser beams fired. It was hard for Calvin to see what was going on, but he heard several screams and saw the bodies of several monsters tumbling into the darkness below. At the top, they burst into the streets of the old city. The robots didn't pause. Once out in the open, their speed increased markedly. They made a direct line for the exit. The rush of air on his face felt really good, even though it was cold, stale air.

Several groups of robots converged on them, forming a robot shield all around them. For a brief moment, Calvin felt safe. That feeling quickly faded when he looked behind them and saw six monsters chasing them. Six became eight, and then eight turned into twenty. More and more monsters joined the chase with each street they crossed. One of the monsters shot a cable out of its chest. The cable attached to one of the robots in their formation. A shower of sparks and blue electrical currents wrapped around the robot, and it fell to the ground. Calvin could do little more than watch. He wanted to take his rifle off his shoulder and fire at the monsters, but he was afraid to take his hands off his robot. Three more robots were taken down before they reached the end of the street.

At the end of the street, the robots carrying Astra, Calvin, and Dev ran up the stairs to the balcony. The remaining robots created a barrier around the stairs to give them time to get away. They opened fire with their beam weapons, cutting down the approaching hoard. Dozens of monsters were cut in half. Calvin could hear the screams as they passed through the next door and into the security waiting area. Five robots followed them up the stairs. Astra set them up to cover the doorway behind. The monsters began to pile in immediately. The robots opened fire with everything they had—beam weapons and light laser fire. Astra didn't wait. She moved the three robots they were riding and the one carrying the fourth segment out of the security room and began a furious climb up the next set of stairs toward the basement of the castle. Calvin was surprised at how smooth the ride was up the stairs. When they reached the top, Astra commanded her robot to close and seal the door.

Calvin gave her a questioning look. She held her scanner up for him to see.

"The robots were all destroyed," she said with a hint of sadness. "None of them made it."

Astra had the robots take them up to the top of the tower. The fourth segment was placed outside her room, and she sent the robots to the bottom of the tower to stand guard. Everyone had the same thought: it was better than having nothing to protect them, but they didn't prove very effective in their first encounter. The monsters clearly won the first battle.

"How many robots did we lose?" Calvin asked.

"Sixteen," Astra answered. "But I'm not sure they were destroyed."

"What do you mean?"

"I've been looking at the scanner readings. The monsters attached a cable to each robot, and if I'm reading this right, they rewrote their code. I think they are being controlled by the monsters now."

It took a second for that to register with Calvin. When it did, he took a deep breath and looked at the ceiling.

"So the monsters increased the size of their army," he said. "Oh, that's just great."

"Do you think they will attack us?"

"I hope not."

"I'll go check the computer, and see what they are doing," Dev said, leaving the room.

Calvin helped Astra upstairs. It didn't take long for Dev to return.

"The monsters aren't doing much," he said. "Their energy signatures keep disappearing, but I think the computer is having a hard time seeing them. They're still surrounding the castle and aren't moving."

"That's good," Calvin said. "How do our defenses look?"

"Everything is still in place. The tanks and robots are still outside and ready. The bombers and fighters are warmed up and ready."

"Good," Calvin said. "Maybe we'll get lucky, and the monsters will leave us alone."

"I hope so," Astra said. "But just in case, I put an alarm on the robots at the bottom of the tower. If the monsters try to break in, the alarm will go off."

"That's a good idea," Calvin said.

"We agree though," Dev said. "That we're just trying to buy time until the storm is over."

"Of course," Calvin said. "We need to get off this planet. I don't want to spend any more time here than we need to."

"OK."

They ate a meal together and then went to their rooms to sleep. Calvin lay down on his bed after getting cleaned up. The storm still raged outside, but the sheets of the rain hitting the window lulled him to sleep. It helped that he was exhausted.

CHAPTER EIGHT:

THE ASSAULT

Calvin woke up abruptly when a bolt of lightning flashed outside the window. It was immediately followed by a deafening crack of thunder. Since he was wide awake, he decided to get up. He got dressed and walked up to the computer level to see what the Terrors were doing.

He sat down at the sensor computer. The red dots that represented the monster robots were all gone. He wasn't worried. He was sure that they were there. Calvin was sure it was a computer problem. He tapped the screen. Nothing happened. He tapped it again: nothing. He zoomed the view out and back in again. The Terrors were nowhere to be seen. That's odd, he thought. Where could they be?

He walked around to check the other computers. The robots were still in place inside the castle. The tanks were still outside surrounding the castle. The bombers and fighters were still in their hangars. Everything was just as it was when he went to bed, except that the monsters were gone. That worried him. A lot. He walked back to the sensor computer and searched for the Terrors again. The computer still couldn't find them. Then he increased the search range to three hundred miles.

It took a few extra minutes, but the result was the same: nothing. Calvin looked at the screen not sure what to do. He wanted to think the monsters were gone, but he knew better. Maybe the storm was interfering with the scanner. He got up and went back to his room. He had a feeling in the back of his mind that he chose to ignore. He didn't see, after he walked away, the flickering red dots on the screen.

Calvin was able to fall back to sleep without too much trouble. He fell asleep listening to the rain hitting the window. He felt safe and relaxed.

He woke up several hours later, to the sound of another explosion. He opened his eyes, startled. He assumed it was another lightning strike. The blast reverberated throughout the castle. It shook his bed. Something was different this time. He didn't see a flash. He had a very bad feeling. Calvin jumped out of bed and put on his clothes as fast as he could. If there was an emergency, he wanted to be dressed for it. He found both Astra and Dev waiting for him in the computer room.

"What's happening?" He asked.

Astra was sitting at the sensors computer. "The Terrors are attacking!"

"How many?" Calvin asked, looking at the screen.

"All of them," Astra replied. A sea of red dots surrounded the castle and slowly moved toward the tower. Calvin felt a surge of excitement and fear.

"This is it," Calvin said. "Let's get everything going."

"I'll take the bombers and fighters," Astra said.

"I've got the robots," said Dev.

"Then I'll control the tanks," Calvin said.

Everyone hurried to their seats. They performed checks on the bombers, fighters, robots, and tanks to make sure they were activated, powered up, and ready to fight. The monsters surged forward. A sea of individual dots merged together into one big red mass, converging on the castle.

In a hangar under the castle, rows of bombers were lined up and ready to take off. Three large doors slowly opened in the cliff wall over the ocean. Engines roared to life. Computers calibrated bombs and armed their explosive cores. More lined up behind them. When the doors opened, three bombers shot into the air. As soon as they were clear the process repeated. The monsters had reached a wide open field just outside the ruins of the city. Astra had the bombers programmed to begin dropping their bombs on the front of the approaching mass as soon as they were able.

The storm had decreased, but instead of thunder and lightning, the air was filled with the thunder of explosions. Halfway across the field, Calvin ordered everyone to open fire. The robots charged headlong into the approaching tsunami of monsters. The tanks launched a bombardment of artillery. The bombers swooped down from above and released a torrent of small but powerful bombs. Huge fireballs shot into the sky. The power of the bombers' attacks was exciting and terrifying at the same time. Large clusters of monsters were consumed. When the monsters got closer, the tanks unleashed volleys of high-powered lasers into the approaching mass. It wasn't enough. When they reached the tanks, the monsters tore them apart.

There were too many of them. They ran through the ruins, jumped over broken walls and flattened buildings, heading directly toward the castle. The Terrors went insane with rage. They smashed everything in their path. When they reached the massive wall that wrapped around the castle—a barrier Calvin thought would slow them down—they went right through it, almost as if it wasn't even there. Explosions rocked the castle. Out of bombs, Dev instructed the bombers to crash into the invading army; one last desperate act. A thousand monstrous screams filled the air in one terrifying roar.

That's when the monsters reached the second line of tanks, which were positioned near the outer wall. They were able to get several shots in but were overwhelmed and quickly destroyed.

The situation was clear to Astra, who was staring in terror at the sensors screen. The monsters were coming, and nothing was slowing them down. The horrible screaming got louder.

"Calvin, how about that plan B?" she shouted. "You might want to get it ready!"

Calvin felt instant panic. He knew what that meant. Astra didn't think they were going to stop the Terrors.

"OK!" Calvin shouted back. "I'm on it!"

"Calvin, you better hurry up!" Astra shouted, sounding very scared.

"Dev, I have an idea!" Calvin said. "Put all of the robots in the stairwell. It's small and narrow. The monsters will have to fight their way up to us, and our robots will slow them down. It might give us an extra minute."

"Good idea!" Dev said loudly.

"Hurry, Calvin!" Astra shouted.

"It's on the way."

From down below, the sounds of the doors being smashed to pieces reverberated up the stairwell.

Calvin and Astra looked at each other.

"We can't do anymore here," Astra said. "Let's get out of here!"

Calvin, Astra, and Dev scrambled out of the room. They ran downstairs and grabbed their backpacks, hurriedly stuffing them full of their things as quickly as they could and tore back up the stairs. From down below, the screams from the monsters were very loud now. They ran up the stairs to the very top. The door was open and they ran through it. Dev closed the door behind them and fastened the bolt, knowing there was no possible way it would hold. A robot was waiting for them on the roof, holding the fourth segment.

The sounds from downstairs were horrifying, even through the door. The monsters were screaming loudly, there were shots of laser fire and small explosions. The tower shook and began to sway from side to side slightly. The noises were getting louder, closer.

"Hurry, Calvin," Astra whispered. "They're coming!"

The sound got so loud, so fast, Calvin worried that the robots they placed on the stairs either were not fighting back or were no match for the horrible Terrors. Suddenly a large shape flew up over the top of the tower and hovered just above them. It was a ship! A side door opened, and the ship slowly moved down until it was low enough for them to jump in. As quickly as they could they all threw their backpacks through the open door. Astra commanded the robot to put the fourth segment into the ship. The screams of the monsters had reached a deafening level.

Calvin took Astra by the hand and guided her toward the ship. He put his hands around her waist and lifted her up into the open door.

"You're next!" Calvin shouted.

Dev got a running start and jumped into the ship. He cleared the distance with no problem. The door holding the Terrors back splintered into a thousand pieces.

"Calvin!" Dev and Astra screamed.

Calvin wanted to look behind him and see how close the Terrors were, but he knew he only had seconds to escape. He ran and jumped, but the ship started pulling away before he landed.

Calvin reached out but missed. He was able to get ahold of one thing. Dev was lying on the floor with his hands out. Calvin caught them and held on for dear life. The ship rose higher into the air. Calvin looked down, just as a dozen Terrors swarmed onto the roof of the tower and tore the robot apart.

Seconds later they were flying over the ruins of the city. Hoards of Terrors destroyed what little remained of the ruins and converged on the castle. Several fires burned.

He looked back. There was a monster hanging off of the back of the ship! It clung to a maintenance hatch. Its eyes glowed dark red, and it opened its mouth to show its teeth.

Calvin tried to pull himself up, but he was stuck, unable to move.

"Dev!" he screamed. "Pull me up!" But the high-pitched whine from the ships engines was very loud. "Help!"

The monster glared and swiped its arm at him, but it was too far away. The creature roared, jammed its fist through the skin of the ship,

278

and grabbed onto something on the inside. Then again with the other hand, it punched holes through the ship to slowly make its way closer to Calvin.

Calvin was horrified and desperately wished he had a way to shoot the thing. Then he realized he had a laser pistol strapped to his thigh.

He was going to have to let go of Dev with one hand. The monster kept coming.

Quickly, Calvin let go. It wasn't easy, but as he pulled away, Dev tightened his grip and would not let go.

Finally he was free with one hand. Dev almost lost him altogether, and he grabbed Calvin's hand with both of his.

Calvin grabbed his laser pistol off of his leg and fired at the monster. The first few shots seemed to do nothing but make the monster scream. Then he adjusted his fire and started firing at the monster's arms.

Calvin kept firing, making several direct hits on the monster's arms and hands. Finally one arm blew off and the monster hung, unable to move. Calvin kept firing. The monster must have realized it was about to fall, and the seriousness of its situation. It swung itself back and tried to throw itself at Calvin. It fell short, barely touching his boot. The monster fell with a horrifying scream.

Calvin almost lost his grip on Dev but somehow managed to hold on. He dropped his laser pistol and grabbed hold of Dev with his other hand. It took all of his strength, but Dev pulled Calvin up into the ship. They both stayed on the floor for a moment, trying to catch their breaths.

Calvin felt the ship turning. He climbed to his feet and walked to the front. Astra was sitting in the pilot's chair.

"That was close," he said, sitting down next to her.

"Yes, it was," Astra said. "I didn't think we were going to make it."

"We're not there yet. Can we use this ship to get into orbit and find the Frost?"

"No," Astra answered with disappointment in her voice. "The ship has sustained too much damage."

"What are we going to do now?" Dev asked, standing in between the two seats and looking out of the window ahead. The lights on the control console flickered several times. There was a loud bang from somewhere in the back of the ship.

"We're going to crash," Astra said simply, as if she didn't believe it herself.

"What?" Dev asked. "This can't be happening."

"Why can't we catch a break?" Calvin asked, disbelieving. The ship started to lose altitude. "Astra, can we make it to the star port?

She played around with a bunch of knobs and buttons. "We can put everything into the engines. We don't need shields, life support, or weapons." She turned it all off.

The ship stopped losing altitude and leveled out.

"Can we make it?" Calvin asked.

"No," Astra admitted. "Before the computer died, it said the star port was forty-seven miles away. The Terror broke several fuel lines and made a hole in one of the fuel tanks. We are leaking fuel. We're still going to crash. Dev, you better sit down. Put a harness on."

"OK," Dev said. He walked back to a seat and sat down. They were over a thick forest.

It wasn't long before the shuttle started losing altitude again. Calvin sat down next to Astra and quickly buckled his own harness.

"That's it, we're out of fuel," Astra said. "We're going down."

The engines choked and sputtered. The shuttle began to lose altitude again.

"I'm sorry, Calvin," Astra looked at Calvin and tried to smile. Calvin reached out and took her hand, smiling back.

"Thank you for being my friend," he said.

Astra channeled every last volt of battery power into the engines. The ship slowed down, but Calvin didn't think it was enough. The ship dropped into the trees. Branches and leaves beat against the glass windows. They collided with a large branch and tumbled end over end, landing upside down on the forest floor.

The sounds of groaning metal, falling trees, branches, and leaves, and the last gasp of the engines died away. Silence took over. For a moment, nobody spoke. Calvin, Astra, and Dev were hanging upside down, securely harnessed in their seats. Calvin and Astra looked at each other. Her hair hung straight down around her face.

"Are you all right?" he asked.

"Yes," she said. "Whoever put this ship together did a good job."

"Dev, are you all right back there?" Calvin asked, turning around. Dev's eyes were open, and he was rubbing his shoulders.

"I'm OK," he said, giving a crooked smile.

Calvin unhooked his seatbelt. He held onto the seat to prevent himself from falling, but his hand slipped. He fell anyway and landed on his head. Fortunately, it wasn't far, just six inches. He got up and helped Astra. She unhooked her seatbelt. Calvin caught her as she fell and gently set her down on her feet.

"Thanks," she said, and gently touched his head. "That looked like it hurt. Are you all right?"

"I'm OK."

"How close did that monster get to you?"

"Too close," Calvin said. Astra held his hand, and together they stumbled outside. The ship was in the middle of a clearing, surrounded by tall trees. Dark smoke poured from the engines and billowed up through the trees. Calvin led Astra to the nearest tree, and they sat down on the ground. Astra lay on her back and closed her eyes. When Calvin closed his eyes, the world spun around him.

"I don't feel very good," he said.

"We just crashed," Dev said, sitting on the ground next to

Calvin. "I have a feeling that might be part of your problem."

No one spoke for several minutes. There was a cool breeze blowing through the trees, but he could tell the wind was blowing harder above the forest. The sound was relaxing.

Finally Calvin spoke. "When was the last time we ate? I think I'm hungry."

"You think you're hungry?" Dev asked. "I'm not having that problem. I know I'm hungry."

"I don't know when we ate last," Astra said. "But I'm starving."

Nobody moved. Eventually, Calvin became too hungry to wait. He groaned as he stood. He must have tensed every muscle in his body during the crash, because every part of him hurt. Calvin retrieved a backpack from the ship and gave Dev and Astra some food and water.

After they finished eating, Calvin and Dev collected all of their gear from the ship and put it in a pile. The fourth segment was very heavy, and it took both of them to move it. When they set it down on the ground next to the rest of their stuff, Astra got up and inspected it.

"At least we didn't lose any gear," Calvin said.

"The segment seems to be undamaged," Astra said.

"Now what are we going to do with that?" Dev asked, pointing at the fourth segment. "We can't carry it all the way to the star port. It's too heavy."

"It won't be that bad," Astra said, "because we have these." She took four black round devices out of a pocket of her backpack. "I found them in the castle, in an equipment room."

"Are those what I think they are?" Calvin asked.

"Yes." Astra smiled. "Antigravity generators!"

"Oh, thank you!" Calvin exclaimed. "You're wonderful."

Astra smiled. "Just trying to help." She handed the devices to Calvin.

"What are those?" Dev asked.

282

"They create a bubble of zero gravity around an object," Astra explained. "So even though the segment weighs two hundred pounds, you can carry it on your back and not even know it's there."

"It's amazing you've been able to make them so small," Dev said. "We have something similar, but much larger."

It only took three antigravity devices to make the fourth segment weightless. Dev strapped it to a backpack, along with the other backpacks stuffed with the rest of the gear, and put it on.

Astra stood next to Calvin. She looked tired.

"Will those things work on a person?" Calvin asked.

"I don't see why not," Astra said, with a confused look.

"Here," Calvin said. He turned one on and handed it to her.

"Oh, I get it," she said. Calvin picked her up. She was very light. Calvin let her climb on to his back, and they started off on their hike to the star port.

CHAPTER NINE:

THE STAR PORT

They left the crash site and headed east, picking their way through a thick forest. Astra had her scanner resting on the back of Calvin's neck and was reading it.

"We're closer than I thought," Astra said. "The star port is only nine miles away."

Calvin carefully stepped over a moss-covered fallen tree. "That's better than twenty-six," he said.

"What if we get there and none of the spaceships are flyable?" Dev asked.

"I'm more afraid of what we'll find when we get into orbit," Astra said.

"Or what we won't find," Calvin said. He was worried about both of those things, but at the present, he was worried about running into Terrors out in the open. They walked for two hours over rough terrain, over small hills and across a shallow ravine. But generally the path forward led downward at a gentle incline. Calvin kept his eyes and ears open, but he never saw or heard any Terrors.

They took a short break on a large flat rock in the center of a clearing. Astra stretched out on the rock and warmed herself in the sun.

She looked happy.

Calvin stared up into the deep blue sky and wondered what was waiting for them up there. If they found nothing but a debris field, what would they do?

The sun felt good, but it was starting to get hot, and he was ready to get back to the shade under the trees.

They rested for ten minutes, and when they were ready to continue, Astra turned her antigravity generators back on and climbed on Calvin's back.

Thirty minutes later, under a canopy of green leaves, Calvin listened intently for the distant scream of approaching Terrors. He was happy that he didn't hear anything except for the gentle wind in the trees and an occasional bird overhead. He also heard several almost imperceptible beeps.

"Oh, come on," Astra exclaimed. More beeps and a bang.

"Something wrong?" Calvin asked.

"I downloaded the database from the castle before we left," Astra said. "Most of the files are unprotected, but I found a locked area. I'm trying to get in, but no luck so far."

Calvin walked around several large rocks. "What have you found so far?"

"I found a bunch of personal journal entries," Astra said. "The people who lived in the castle were called the Myantes. They were displaced by the Goremog sixty-one years ago and found this planet. They built the castle and the city. That's all I know so far. There is a set of files I can't get in." There were more beeps. Astra groaned.

"Can I try?" Dev asked.

Astra hesitated and then said, "Sure, I'm not getting anywhere."

Dev took the handheld scanner and worked the controls.

Astra looked up at the trees above and took a deep breath. "It feels so good out here," she said.

Dev furiously worked the scanner. There was a steady stream of beeps.

"Here you go," Dev said smiling, after twenty-five seconds.

"What?" Astra took the device from him. "You got in?"

"Yes," Dev said. "That was a little tricky; whoever designed that code knew what they were doing."

"Are you sure?" Astra said. "How did you do that?"

"I can't explain it," Dev said. "I'm just good at breaking code."

"That's a handy skill to have," Calvin said.

Astra read for the next thirty minutes, while Calvin climbed down a steep rocky hill and over a cool mountain stream.

"No," Astra said. "I can't believe it. It says here that the Myantes people found the Goremog lab deep underground. They moved in and continued research on the Terrors. They made their own modifications and created an army of them to protect themselves from another Goremog attack."

"What kind of modifications?" Dev asked.

"They wanted to make them smarter, so they worked extensively on their brains," Astra said. "I think that's why they lost control of them. The Terrors went insane."

"What happened?" Calvin asked.

"There was an accident, and the Terrors got out. The Myantes were forced to evacuate the planet."

"I wonder why they didn't use the army of robots to defend themselves," Calvin said.

"They did." Astra quickly corrected him. "They fought for days. That's how the city was destroyed."

"And they destroyed themselves," Dev shook his head. "They should have made sure their creation was a little more stable before they made fourteen thousand of them."

"Fourteen thousand?" Astra said. "No, they didn't make fourteen

286

thousand. According to this, they made over three hundred thousand."

Her last statement hung in the air. The pleasantness of the sun and sky was suddenly gone. The shadow of the Terrors descended on them again. Calvin quickened his pace.

They walked all day under the shade of the trees, taking short breaks whenever they needed to. Calvin looked back a dozen times. Each time he expected to see Terrors rushing toward them.

Six hours after they crashed, they reached the top of a small hill and emerged from the trees. Calvin helped Astra down, but before she was on the ground the antigravity device popped, and she fell the last few inches. Fortunately she landed on her feet.

"Whoa," she said. "I guess I'll have to walk the rest of the way." She leaned against him for a second, her head against his chest. They sat down on a rock, and Calvin gave her a bottle of water. They were running low on water, but he didn't stop her. He let her drink as much as she wanted. Calvin was exhausted. He stretched his legs. Dev stood next to them and admired the view. They were at the top of a hill overlooking the star port below, which was in the middle of a wide valley.

Miles of concrete stretched out before them. In the middle of the concrete sea were rows of glass buildings. A deep chasm circled the star port, like a moat. There was only one bridge visible. Several large spaceships were parked on the ground near the buildings. There were also several hundred smaller ships.

"Only one bridge?" Calvin asked.

"There must be another one on the other side," Dev guessed. "Behind those buildings, maybe." He pointed to several tall glass buildings that blocked their view of the canyon.

The wind blew on them, and now that they were out of the shade, it was becoming hot. On the wind, Calvin heard a distant scream. He wasn't sure. It could have been a bird. Or a Terror. He was going to ask Astra, but her expression told him everything he needed to know. Without a word, she was up.

"Time to go," she said. Calvin jumped up. He took a drink of water and tossed the empty bottle. Dev was already up. Astra sat on the log and looked at Calvin as if she were trying to send him messages with her thoughts.

Calvin thought he knew what she was thinking and tried to imagine how she must feel. She didn't feel very good and wasn't sure if she was going to be able to make it all the way to the space port.

Calvin, Astra, and Dev walked down the hill. Dev jogged straight down to the bottom and got there first. Calvin and Astra walked slower and crisscrossed their way. When they got to the bottom, Calvin desperately wanted to take another break, but he knew it would not be a smart thing to do. It was a long, grueling walk. The sun beat on them mercilessly. Calvin was drained. Each step took more effort, strength that was rapidly failing. Astra held on to him. He couldn't wait to find a cool place to rest.

Finally, tired and thirsty, they reached the bridge. Astra sat down on the grass. Dev sat down next to the edge of the canyon and looked down. Calvin slowly and cautiously approached the bridge. It looked solid. He put his foot on the first step up and put some of his weight on it. It felt solid. It was metal and had grated floors. A cool wind hit him in the face when he stepped out over the edge, which felt very good. He smiled and took a deep breath.

"Astra," Calvin called. "You need to feel this air, it feels really good." He walked back and helped her stand.

"I'm so tired," she said. "And hot."

"It's nice and cool over here," he said. "Come on." He helped her to walk to the bridge. She closed her eyes when the air engulfed her.

"Wow, you're right," she said. Instead of stopping, Calvin kept walking with her. Dev looked up and saw them crossing the bridge. Reluctantly, he followed. Halfway across, Calvin stopped and looked over the side. It was a long way down, and it was hard to see the bottom, but it looked like there was a small stream. Several birds circled around. Calvin could see their nests in between the rocks.

Suddenly a loud familiar sound shattered the quiet. It was the scream of a monster, and it sounded close. It was followed by a superloud chorus of screams, from many monsters. Calvin was instantly terrified. Astra grabbed on to his hand and squeezed. He looked into her eyes, and he could see the fear in them. Her expression reflected desperation and hopelessness. In her current condition, would she be able to run away? Calvin didn't think so. He frantically tried to think and came up with only one option.

"We have to blow up this bridge," he said quickly. They hurried to the other side and put down their gear. Calvin pulled a small block of explosives out of his backpack.

"Calvin," Astra said. "That's Borenite; we use it to blow open doors, or small holes. It won't be enough to take down the bridge."

"It's all we have," Calvin said. He didn't wait for a reply. He and Dev ran to the center of the bridge.

"I'm not an expert," Dev said. "But I think we need to put this on the bottom of the bridge for this to work."

Several monsters emerged from the tree line. They immediately saw them on the bridge and began sprinting toward them. A steady stream of Terrors followed.

"We don't have time," Calvin said. "We have to put it in the middle of the bridge and hope it's enough to bring it down." The monsters were getting closer.

"Hurry," Astra called to them.

Calvin set the timer at five seconds, and then the two of them ran back away from the bridge. They grabbed their stuff. Calvin tried to ignore the shrieks from the monsters. He helped Astra to her feet, and they ran as fast as they could in the direction of the glass buildings.

There was a bright flash and a loud boom. The force of the explosion threw them both to the ground. Calvin landed on his stomach. Debris flew over his head. Small pieces of rock and stone rained all around them. Calvin rolled over and sat up. A cloud of smoke hovered over the bridge. Calvin and Dev were on their feet quickly.

"Did it work?" Calvin asked.

"I can't see anything," Dev said.

The ground shook, and the screaming got louder.

"We need to get away from here," Calvin said. "Fast!"

They turned and ran to where Astra was waiting. Calvin looked back and saw that the smoke had cleared. The bridge was not destroyed. There was a large hole in the middle, and several cracks running through it in both directions. Calvin was certain they were going to die. There was no way they could outrun the Terrors, and the star port was too far away. There was only one thing they could do.

Calvin took the weapon off his belt and pointed it toward the bridge.

"We're not going to run," he said. "We're not going to die without a fight. We're going to stand our ground!" Astra and Dev stood next to Calvin, their weapons ready also. A mass of screaming monsters charged onto the damaged bridge.

Calvin opened fire first. His first shots missed. He forced himself to relax and focus on his aim. His next set hit the lead monsters directly. Astra and Dev began firing, but none of their shots seemed to do anything. It only seemed to make the monsters angry. The monsters crowded onto the narrow bridge. That's when Calvin got an idea.

"Shoot the bridge!" he shouted. Instead of shooting at the monsters, all three of them concentrated their fire on the bridge. At first it looked like their shots were completely ineffective. All of the laser bolts bounced off harmlessly. Then suddenly the bridge broke into two pieces and collapsed into the canyon below, taking the monsters down into the depths. The monsters not yet on the bridge stopped, and something very strange happened. The monsters separated into two groups, each running off in a different direction around the canyon. The screams faded away as they ran off into the distance. Calvin, Astra and Dev stared in shock. It was Dev who broke the silence first.

"Either they are looking for another way to get across, or they already know there is one, and that's where they are going."

"That's not a very comforting thought," Astra said. "Let's hurry and get out of here."

It may not have been a pleasant thought, but it gave them, even Astra, the motivation to escape and a burst of energy. They began a slow jog toward the nearest spaceship. It looked closer than it was, but it was not a short walk. Halfway there, Astra stumbled and fell. Calvin picked her up, put his arm around her, and helped her to keep going.

It was a relief when they finally made it. The ship was big, silver, and had a rounded hull. They jogged the whole way there, two miles across the concrete landing pad. So many things had gone wrong since the dreadful accident on the Frost. Calvin was expecting the worst when they got to the spaceships. He was sure that they would all be too damaged to fly, or they would be sealed shut, so they would not be able to get in. He was surprised to find the boarding ramp on the first ship was down, and the main door was open. Calvin had a very bad feeling, but he chose to ignore it.

They rushed up the ramp and jumped over a small gap at the top. Before he went into the ship, Calvin turned and looked back the way they had come and scanned the area. Off in the distance, he heard a scream.

"Calvin, come on," Astra pleaded.

Once inside, they found themselves in a very long corridor that seemed to run the length of the ship. Dev and Astra were leaving him behind. Calvin hurried after them.

"Do you know where you're going?" Calvin asked.

"The bridge, hopefully," Astra answered. "I'm guessing the bridge must be at the front of the ship." She was right. At the end of the corridor was an open door.

The layout felt familiar. Then Calvin realized what it was. It looked like the bridge on the Frost, only bigger. There were two chairs in the front for pilot and copilot, which were surrounded by banks of computers, screens and controls. In the back were four other computer stations. Calvin went to the front and sat down in the left chair. Astra sat next to him. Dev stood by the door and faced down the hallway.

291

"I don't like this," Dev said. "Something isn't right." He aimed his laser pistol down the corridor, ready just in case.

Calvin turned on the computer and was shocked when the screens came to life.

"This is an Alerian ship," Astra commented. "How is that possible?"

"I don't know," Calvin said. "I'm wondering why there is still power. Not that I'm complaining."

The controls were laid out the way that Calvin was familiar with and understood. He turned on the compressors, and then the engines roared to life.

Astra thought she heard a noise and looked into the shadows behind her. There was a small door, which was open. That wasn't too unusual, but what was unusual was that the door was still moving, as if it had just been opened.

Calvin looked back too, but he didn't see anything. He went back to what he was doing. The engines were running at full power now. He was just about to take off, when he heard Astra say, "Hello, there."

Calvin turned and looked back again. There was a small robot standing in the middle of the room, looking at them with wide eyes. It looked scared. It wasn't very big, only three feet tall.

"It's all right," Astra said. "We won't hurt you."

The little robot looked back and forth from Calvin to Astra. Dev turned around and started to walk toward it. When the robot saw Dev, it jumped back.

"No, Dev, don't move," Astra said quickly. "It won't hurt you."

Dev moved back slowly toward the door. "What is that?" he asked quietly.

"It's an 'N' series robot," Astra answered. "Nanny class."

"Nanny class?" Dev said. "Really?"

"Yes." Astra said. "There weren't that many built. A lot of

people didn't like them. They were built for children to play with. But this one is all alone. I wonder what happened."

The robot stared at Astra as she talked. Suddenly the robot smiled and said, "Teelala?" He slowly began to walk closer to Astra. "Teelala, oonna tay?"

"I don't understand you," Astra said.

Calvin decided it was time to take off. He closed the main door and increased the throttle to full. The ship slowly began to rise into the air. As they got higher, Calvin got a good view of the glass buildings and four wide bridges that crossed over the canyon. All of them were intact.

"Calvin, can you understand him?"

"No, I can't," Calvin said. "That is strange, now that you mention it. My translator can usually understand everyone."

"Teelala!" The robot exclaimed, running up to Astra and hugging her.

"It likes you," Calvin said.

The robot jumped into Astra's lap and hugged her tightly.

"Yi anorna mi tronso," the robot said. It sounded like it was crying.

She held onto the robot as they left the atmosphere. Calvin put them in orbit and started looking for the Frost using the sensors. During the whole trip into orbit, the little robot didn't move.

"We're in a stable orbit," Calvin announced. "Are you OK?"

"I'm fine," she said. "This is interesting."

"It's strange," Calvin said, concerned. "Do you think it will hurt you?"

"I don't think so," Astra said. "I wonder what happened to the child it was taking care of." Then a dark shadow passed over her, as a thought occurred to her. "I wonder if it died."

"The robot thinks you are the child."

293

"So it was a girl."

"Must have been," Calvin said. "That's sad."

The robot sat up and looked at Astra, smiling. "Torna Yi sona!" The robot said. A small panel on the side of the robot opened, and it pulled out a small pink bunny and held it out to Astra.

Astra sighed. "How cute." She took it. The robot smiled a big smile.

"It looks like we have a new member of our crew," Calvin said.

The robot took out a small notepad and a crayon and began to scribble something. After a moment it held it up to Astra.

"Oh, nice," Astra said. The robot held it out to Astra. "What's your name?" she asked it. The robot just stared at her.

"We should call it Fina," Calvin said. "That's what the writing looks like on the front." Calvin pointed to its chest.

"No, I don't think so." Astra said, shaking her head. "You got to name the last robot."

"That doesn't count," Calvin said. "You weren't there when I named Ion."

"Yeah, but I'm going to name this one. Besides, it likes me best. I think I'll call you Scribbles." When she said Scribbles, the robot smiled at her.

Calvin returned his focus to the ship's computers. He decided to check the status of the ship's systems. What he saw caused him to be instantly concerned.

"We have a problem," Calvin said. "It may not be serious, but the internal sensors are not working. I wanted to make sure we are alone on the ship, but I can't see anything."

Dev walked back into the room. "That's perfect," he said sarcastically. "Can you use the external sensors and redirect them into the ship?"

There was a pause. "Hold on," Calvin said. He turned on the

external sensors, which filled one of the monitors in front of him. It displayed the planet. It was surrounded by little red dots, which were moving. On the other side of the planet was one small black dot. Calvin clicked on the black dot, and it filled the screen. It was the Azure Frost!

"There's the Frost!" Calvin said, excitedly. He ran a quick scan of it.

"There are no power readings. It's just floating in space, dead," he said sadly. He pulled back to the view of the planet. Then snow covered the screen. "Whoa," Calvin said. "What's this?"

Astra looked at the screen. "Either there's a problem with the sensors, or we are being jammed."

"Jammed?" Dev exclaimed. "Who would be jamming us?"

Suddenly the lights flickered, and the engine sounds died away.

"We have another problem," Calvin said. "We just lost the engines."

"What?" Dev asked, completely shocked.

"The computer is showing faults all over the ship," Astra said, checking the computer. "This obviously wasn't a good ship to take."

Calvin took out his communicator and turned it on. "Ion, this is Calvin, can you hear me?"

Static was the only reply. He tried again, but did not get an answer.

"What now?" Dev asked, with a little bit of fear in his voice. "Are we ever going to get away from this planet?"

"Our orbit will decay, eventually," Astra said. "We're going to fall back into the atmosphere and burn up." Suddenly the lights flickered again. This time they stayed off for several seconds.

Calvin looked at Astra. "I think we have a bigger problem than the ship falling apart."

"Bigger than crashing into the planet?" Dev asked.

"I think we've got Terrors on board," Calvin said. "They must

295

have circled around and got on before we took off." Astra and Dev looked at him. There was silence for several moments.

"I should have seen this coming," Dev said. "The door was wide open."

He walked back to the door and looked down the corridor again. It was empty, but he couldn't see all the way down. The lights on the other end were off, and it was bathed in darkness. Suddenly there was another flicker, and the soft hum of the oxygen pumps died away.

"We just lost life support," Calvin announced.

Dev walked back into the room. He closed and locked the door.

"What's next, main power? We need to stop them."

"How many are there, do you think?" Astra asked.

"Remember the big group we saw outside?" Calvin said. "They could all be on the ship. We can't go out there. You know how well our weapons work on them."

"But if we get rid of them, we could repair the ship."

Calvin stood up and began to pace. "That's a good idea, it really is, but exactly how do you propose we get rid of them? There are probably a hundred of them out there—and by the way, they are impervious to our weapons."

"I don't know," Dev said, getting upset. "But we have to do something. We can't just sit here and wait for them to come get us."

The lights flickered again, and this time they stayed off. The emergency lights turned on. The room filled with a soft red glow.

"We can't go after them," Astra said firmly. "I won't let either of you go out there."

"Then what are we going to do?" Dev demanded. "This is exactly what happened before. We took off, and the ship started falling apart. The monsters were tearing the ship to pieces. Then people started dying."

"Exactly," Astra said. "And the only reason you stayed alive was because you stayed on the bridge. Isn't that right?"

"Yes, I guess that's right," Dev said reluctantly. Just then all the computer monitors turned off.

"We have to get off this ship," Astra said. "There has to be a way."

"Escape pods," Calvin said. "This ship has to have escape pods."

"I don't think we're that lucky," Dev said. "They're probably all gone."

Suddenly there was a massive bang on the door to the bridge. They all looked and saw a large new dent right in the middle. Then they all looked at each other.

Dev turned and moved away. "I'll look over here." Calvin went in the opposite direction. Astra stood up and tried to help. Scribbles stayed next to her the whole time. There was another loud bang on the door. They moved faster. The pounding got louder and faster. The sound of tearing metal filled the room.

"Found one!" Dev cried triumphantly. "Hurry!"

Calvin and Astra hurried to where he was. When they got there, Dev already had the door open. They rushed inside, and Dev closed the door. Astra went to the front. The escape pod was very small. Just room in the front for one person to sit, and there were two benches along both walls in the back. There was a loud bang on the door to the escape pod.

Fortunately, the makers of the escape pod realized that if someone was in the pod, they must have had a great need to get away. There was a large red button in the middle of the console, which was surrounded by small computer screens. Astra hit the button, before they had a chance to put on seatbelts. The escape pod shot out into space. Astra was pressed into the back of her seat. The little robot held onto the back of her chair. Calvin and Dev were thrown to the back of the escape pod, and pressed into the door. After a few seconds, the pressure stopped, and they were able to stand up.

"That was close," Dev said, plopping down on one of the padded benches and taking a deep breath.

"Again," Calvin said, sitting across from him. Astra sat back in the chair and closed her eyes. The little robot climbed up into her lap.

Calvin, Dev, and Astra sat quietly for a moment and didn't speak. After a few minutes, Calvin walked up to the front of the pod and examined the controls. The robot eyed him suspiciously.

Astra sensed that he was standing over her and looked up. She smiled at him. Her smile was very warm. She had a calming effect on him, like a patch of calm sea in the middle of a storm.

"Well, the good news is that when we ejected from the mother ship, we were placed in a pretty high orbit. We should be fine here for a while."

"What's the bad news?" Calvin asked, sensing it in her voice.

"The bad news is that we are stuck in orbit around the planet," she said. "Obviously."

"Is there anything we can do?" Calvin asked, retaking his seat on the floor in the back.

"The flight computer is damaged," she said. "I think I can run a bypass. Then we can fly the pod manually. On the positive side, we should be able to stay in this orbit without risk. We'll run out of food long before then."

"How about the oxygen supply?" Dev asked.

"That looks like the one system on this thing that's not damaged," Astra answered. "We have at least a week of oxygen."

"And we have food," Calvin said. "If we ration it carefully, I bet we can last a week or two."

"I'm sure it we'll be OK," Astra said. "Do you mind if I rest first, before I start working on the pod?"

"No," Calvin said. "I'm really tired, too. Let's have something to eat first and then get some rest."

Calvin and Dev opened the backpacks. They ate and had something to drink. There wasn't very much space, but they spread out

298

on the floor. They used the backpacks as pillows. Calvin fell asleep listening to the sound of the oxygen pumps. Scribbles curled up next to Astra and began softly humming what sounded like a lullaby. The song was soothing. Everyone was asleep in less than a minute.

CHAPTER TEN:

———————◦◦C———————

DISTURBING DISCOVERY

Calvin woke up seven hours later. He opened his eyes, lay still for a moment, and stared at the ceiling. He heard the soft sounds of the oxygen pump and an occasional tapping sound. Someone else was already awake. He slowly sat up. A dull ache flooded his body. Every muscle in his back and legs hurt. He looked around, once he was sitting up. Dev was still asleep, and Astra was under the computer console.

"Good morning," he said.

"Good morning," Astra answered, her voice muffled. She put a tool down on the floor and climbed out. "It wasn't as bad as I thought," she said. "I was able to bypass a damaged power generator. We should be able to maneuver now." She sat down on the floor next to him, picked up a nutrient bar, and took a bite.

"How did you sleep?" he asked.

"I slept really well," she said. "I was so tired."

"Me, too," Calvin said. "I don't think I moved all night. As soon as I closed my eyes, I was out." Calvin reached into his backpack and took out a nutrient bar. He removed the silver wrapping and took a bite. "I didn't like these at first," he said. "But they're starting to grow on me."

"They take some getting used to, don't they?" Astra asked. "They were designed to be able to fulfill all of your nutritional requirements." The last part she said in a mocking tone of voice. "That's what the scientists say, anyway." She giggled. They ate for a moment in silence.

"Can I ask you a question?" she asked. "Is your planet really untouched by the Goremog?"

"Yes," Calvin answered. "The planetary disruption network shields the planet completely. My people regard it as our greatest achievement. It allows us to hide from the rest of the universe."

"Wow, you are so lucky. If our mission fails, do you think your people would let us hide with you, on your planet?"

"I don't know. If I were in charge, I would let you," Calvin answered, smiling. "I've been imagining my homecoming. In my dream, there is a parade, fireworks, and a lot of food. Everyone is happy to see me. But in reality, what I think is going to happen is nothing short of panic. They will lock me away and interrogate me for a very long time, although they will call it a debriefing. They will want to know everything I did, everything I said, and if I told anyone where our planet is. They will be terrified that someone followed me home."

"Wow," Astra said. "But I can understand why they feel that way. You know what it's like out here. It's dangerous. If I could hide my people away safely, I would do whatever it took to keep it that way."

"Yeah, you're right," Calvin said. "I should be happy my people are safe. I never thought I would say that. I always thought the rules on our star fleet were way too strict and unfair. But now I understand why."

"So how do you think they will react to seeing us?" Astra asked.

"Not well, I'm afraid," Calvin said, choosing his words carefully. "It will have to be handled delicately. My father will know what to do. I'll ask him the next time we talk."

"OK."

"Let's go find Azure Frost," Calvin said.

301

"That brings us to our next problem," Astra said. "The scanners aren't working, and I have no way of fixing them."

"Can we use our handheld scanners?"

"Their range is too short." There was a stirring behind them.

"Does Azure Frost emit a homing signal?" Dev asked, sitting up.

"No," Astra answered.

"How about a distress signal? Maybe Ion activated a distress beacon."

"No," Astra said. "He would never do that. It would attract the wrong kind of attention."

Calvin picked up a handheld scanner and turned it on.

"That's crazy," Dev said. "If you don't call for help, you'll never get it."

"What good is it to call for help, if you're picked up by the Goremog?" Astra asked. "My people are being hunted down and destroyed at an alarming rate. There are less than two thousand of us left! We can't afford to lose any more. We're going to have to solve our own problems."

"All right," Dev said, backing off. "Then what are we going to do?"

"I'm not picking up any signals," Calvin said. "And the last time I was able to scan the Frost, it was completely dead. There was no energy coming from it at all."

Dev looked up and took a deep breath. "Can I see the scanner, please?" he asked.

"Sure." Calvin gave it to him.

"I've done this before," Dev explained. "I had to find a small spaceship that was lost in orbit of my planet. If I can find the right setting, to make it look for fabricated metal alloys, I might be able to find your ship. It won't give the exact location, but it should at least tell us what direction to go."

302

Dev sat, adjusting the scanner. Astra stood up and sat in the pilot's chair. Calvin stood behind her and looked over her shoulder.

There was a soft hum from the back. The lights on the console lit up. Calvin noticed none of the lights were red. That was good. Astra eased the controls forward, gently testing the repairs. The escape pod slowly moved forward.

"The engines were stressed but seem to be OK now. I'll keep our speed down, just in case," Astra said.

Calvin and Astra scanned the horizon, looking for Azure Frost. It would look like a dark spot, against the black of space. It would be extremely difficult to find it visually. The planet rotated below them. It was beautiful. Most of the surface was covered with a deep blue ocean, with small islands sprinkled haphazardly. They were on the sun side of the planet. Calvin hoped that would make it easier to see the Frost.

"I'm getting a reading," Dev said. "Port side, thirty degrees."

"Turning," Astra said. She took the pod in a wide, gentle turn. A dark object appeared in front of them, in a low orbit, almost touching the atmosphere. Dev stood behind Calvin, staring out the window.

As they got closer to it, its shape became clearer.

"That's not the Frost, is it?" Calvin asked.

"No," Astra said. "That's the ship we were just on."

"Smashed," Dev said. "Its orbit is decaying. It won't be long until it falls into the planet's gravity."

"Good," Calvin said. "It will take the monsters down with it." He stared at it with distaste. Then he saw something strange. "What's that?" Calvin asked, pointing to a dark cloud around the dying spaceship.

"It's a debris cloud," Dev said, staring into his scanner. "I see over two hundred small pieces of metal."

Something small floated by the left side. At first Calvin thought it was a person. It had arms and legs. When they passed another one, Calvin saw that it was moving.

"What are they?" Astra asked.

"No, they can't be," Dev whispered. "Please tell me they aren't what I think they are."

"They are!" Astra shouted. She shoved the throttle full forward and yanked hard right. The pod jumped forward, and there was a loud pop.

"We just lost an engine," Calvin said, holding on to the back of her chair. They passed through a small group of floating Terrors. Several of them banged against the hull as they passed. Calvin closed his eyes, and hoped one of them wasn't clinging to the hull of the escape pod.

Astra pushed the pod as fast as it could go, well past the safe level. Red lights flashed on the control panel.

"Look out!" Dev shouted, as a small group of Terrors appeared in front of them. Astra yanked hard on the controls, the pod dived down and hard to the right.

Dev stepped back and sat down on the floor, his eyes on the scanner.

"I think we're clear," he said. "Give me a second. I'll see if I can find the Frost."

Astra reduced speed, and the angry sounds from the engines quieted.

"It'll be OK," Astra said, reading the concerned look on Calvin's face. "The engines will cool down." Calvin took a deep breath.

"Wait, I think I found something," Dev said. Several minutes passed. The engines pulsed softly, and the red flashing lights on the console changed to yellow.

"I think I found it," Dev said. "Turn to starboard, thirty degrees."

Astra turned in the direction Dev indicated. Five minutes later, "Turn starboard, five degrees."

Astra complied. Ten minutes later, a dark object loomed in front of them. Its shape was unmistakable. Calvin and Astra gasped at the same time. Azure Frost looked dead, tumbling slowly end over end. The hull was burned and blackened. A debris cloud surrounded it.

"Look at that," Astra said quietly. "Look at that." There were several large gaping holes near the engines. "What did I do?" Tears rolled down her cheeks. Calvin desperately wished there was something he could say, but even in his mind, everything sounded hollow and empty. He simply put his hand on her shoulder.

Astra slowed the shuttle to a crawl, so they could have more time to examine the hull of the Frost.

"Let's see if we can get into the shuttle bay," Calvin suggested.

"Would you please take the controls?" Astra asked, starting to shake.

"Sure," Calvin said. Calvin sat down in the pilot's chair after Astra got up. She sat on the arm of the chair and leaned against Calvin. He could feel her shaking.

Calvin piloted the shuttle to the back of Azure Frost and was relieved to see the bay doors were open. He carefully aligned the escape pod's attitude with the Frost and slowly entered the shuttle bay. He landed gently on the floor and shut down the engines.

"The shuttle bay seems to be intact," Calvin said. "Is it possible to use the handheld to contact the Frost and remotely close the bay doors?"

"Let me have it, please," Astra said. "I'll see what I can do."

Dev handed the scanner to her. Astra took it and began working. The machine emitted several angry beeps. It didn't take her long to come to a dismal conclusion.

"I was afraid of this," Astra said. "The Frost has no power. I can't connect to the computer." Her mood was very dark. "But even if I could, there's no reason to think we'd be able to create a safe room, with breathable air."

Calvin tried to think quickly. He had to get them through this.

"We still have the portable shield generators," he said. "We can use them to go out there, search the ship, and find Ion."

"That's not a bad idea." Astra considered the plan. "But they're unpredictable. There's no guarantee they will last long enough to do what we need to do."

"How many do we have?" They went through all of their supplies and piled them neatly on the floor.

"We have ten," Astra said.

Silence fell over them, as they each contemplated what they should do next. Astra seemed depressed and didn't speak. Dev had his eyes closed and his head down. Calvin looked from Astra to Dev, hoping someone would say something, but no one did.

Calvin knew what they were going to have to do. They had to use the unreliable shield generators to go out and look for Ion. Waiting wasn't going to change anything—unless Ion heard them land and suddenly showed up, which he had a feeling was not going to happen.

"OK," Calvin said. "Here's what we should do. We each take three shield generators. We all go outside, search the ship quickly, and then get back here. Hopefully that will give us enough time to find Ion. Whoever finds him, bring him back to the pod. I'm hoping, if we can find and fix him, he can finish repairs that we need to survive: power, life support, hull breaches. What do you think?"

"That's a good idea," Astra said, perking up a little. "We should each take a different area, so we don't waste time looking in the same places twice."

"Good idea," Dev said.

"And," Astra said, "keep an eye out for anything that might be useful—specifically tools and more portable shield generators."

With that, they each picked a search area. Astra decided to look in the engine room, since she believed Ion was more than likely down there. Calvin took the bridge, and Dev was to take the middle decks.

"When we open the door," Astra said. "All of our air is going to be sucked out. If I don't let the air out first, everything will be sucked out violently, including us."

"How long will it take to remove the air?" Dev asked.

"About twenty seconds," Astra answered. "What do you want to do with that?" She pointed to the fourth segment, which was now blocking the door.

"Let's put it in the back of the shuttle bay," Calvin said. "For now."

"That'll work," Astra said. Then she looked at Scribbles.

"Scribbles," she said. "I want you to stay here in the pod, OK?" While she was talking, Astra pointed at the robot, and then at the chair. "I want you to stay here." Astra picked the robot up and set it down in the chair.

Scribbles nodded, seeming to understand.

"You guys ready?" They both nodded. "Here we go." There was a loud hissing sound as Astra let the air out. After a few moments, a purple light surrounded them when their portable generators sensed there wasn't enough air for them. When the air was completely gone, Astra opened the backdoor.

Calvin went first. He pushed the fourth segment out the door and left it next to a wall. He quickly removed the antigravity handles and dropped them on the floor. That would keep it from drifting away. Then he looked around. The shuttle bay was a mess. There was equipment strewn across the floor. The walls were burned, but there were no holes in the sides of the ship. He walked out of the shuttle bay into the main corridor. Astra and Dev silently followed. In the middle of the long corridor, they separated. Astra took the stairs down, Calvin took the stairs up. Dev stayed on that level and began a room-by-room search.

Calvin climbed to the top of the stairs and walked out onto the first deck. It looked like a massive fire had burned everything. The carpet was gone, the walls were black. He went straight to the bridge. The computers had all exploded, and the glass windows were all blown out. The room was exposed to space. Calvin turned and left. He couldn't look at it any longer. He walked down the corridor, looking in each room as he passed.

"I found Ion," Astra said over the communication system. "In the engine room. Calvin, Dev, can you guys come down here and help me, please?"

"Be there in a second," he heard Dev say.

"On my way," Calvin said. He took the stairs all the way back down to the engine room. He was shocked and deeply upset about the level of destruction he saw, convinced there was no way they could repair the ship. The Frost was a lost cause. How in the world would they survive this?

Halfway down the stairs, there was a flicker of purple, and the light went out. He felt a stab of intense pain before the purple light turned back on. He had just lost his first portable shield generator. Better hurry, he thought. He jogged the rest of the way to the engine room. When he got there, he saw Dev helping Astra stand up.

"One of my shield generators just died," she said.

"I lost one on the stairs a minute ago," Calvin said. "What did you find?"

"Ion's power supply is completely dead," Astra said, pointing across the room. There was Ion, standing in front of the power transfer system. He had his hands inside it. "He shut down while he was trying to restore power."

"How did his power run out?" Calvin asked. "He can function for months without recharging, can't he?"

"Yes," Astra said sadly. "The ship was bleeding power everywhere. He transferred his own power into the main system to stabilize it. It didn't work, because there was too much damage to the ship."

Suddenly Dev's shield went out and was quickly replaced by another one.

"That was my last one," Dev said. "Can we go back to the escape pod now?"

"Yes," Astra said. "I can't do anything here." They walked out of the engine room and headed for the stairs. Calvin's force field flickered and went out. He fell to the floor in pure agony. It felt like he was being squeezed to death. Blood red filled his vision. Mercifully, it stopped after a second when his last force field turned on. Astra and Dev ran to him and helped him to stand. Calvin stuttered and tried to speak, but he couldn't get the words out.

"Dev, we have to hurry," Astra said. "We're almost out of time!" Together, Astra and Dev, one on each side of him, helped Calvin down the corridor to the stairs. Try as he might, Calvin could not get his legs to move. But he found that by focusing all of his energy in a single force of will, he could help them carry him forward. He didn't know that he wasn't actually doing anything. It was all in his mind.

At the top of the stairs, they tried to be careful and take it easy, but the sheer terror of losing their only protection to the vacuum of space made them move faster, and they all fell down the first set of stairs. It was panic that moved them now. Astra and Dev let gravity help them down the stairs and did their best to hold on to Calvin the whole way down. At the bottom of the stairs, they were using energy they didn't really have. Calvin was aware of what was going on around him, but he still couldn't move. He felt very bad that they had to carry him and wished he could move his arms and legs. They made it to the shuttle and closed the door. The three collapsed on the floor. Just at that second, Astra's force field turned off. She gasped for breath, but there was no air in the pod to breathe. She forced her way to the front. In the midst of losing her sight, her arms were getting extremely heavy and hard to move, but she managed to turn the oxygen back on. She fell to the floor, completely out of energy and on the verge of blacking out. She lay on the floor until she felt her lungs fill with oxygen.

Calvin had his eyes closed—his only defense against the pain that was filling his body. When the pod filled with oxygen, he took a deep breath and sat up. His entire body still was flooded with pain, but at least now he could move.

Calvin looked up to see Scribbles standing over Astra.

"I'm OK," Astra said. Scribbles took out the pink bunny and

gave it to Astra. Astra smiled at the little robot, who smiled back.

"Is everyone all right?" Calvin asked.

"That was scary," Dev said. "My last shield generator died just as the door closed."

"Mine, too," Astra said. "That was very close."

"The fourth segment!" Calvin exclaimed. "It's still out there."

"It's...fine," Astra said, struggling with her words. She sounded very tired. "It's out there with the other three. Just having the one doesn't do us any good."

"Now what do we do?" Calvin asked. "Is there any way for us to repair the ship?"

Astra closed her eyes. "No," she said. "No way. Ion and the robots couldn't do it. The ship is too badly damaged." She started crying again and wiped her eyes with her hands. "We need Aleria's Hope to find us. There is a repair facility in it that could repair the ship. That's the only way."

"There's nothing for us here," Dev said. "We should go find that ship then. At least if we're out there looking for it, there's a small chance we could find it, right?"

"Well, sitting here isn't going to do us any good, I agree," Calvin said.

"If we stay here, we'll eventually run out of food," Astra said. "There is a large radiation cloud surrounding this planet. It will block any communication signals we send out. If we can get away from it, we might be able to contact the Hope."

"I'll take the controls," Calvin volunteered. "I feel fine now."

"Go ahead. I don't feel too good now."

"I just need to take us out into deep space?"

"Just get us away from the planet."

"All right." Calvin sat down in the pilot's chair and turned on the computer. There was a delay. The system did not turn on right away.

When it did, the little screens flickered, and there was a soft pop, followed by a burning smell. Calvin didn't know if the others noticed, but he decided to keep it to himself. No reason to alarm them. When the engines were ready, he slowly and carefully lifted the pod up into the air a few feet and backed out into space. When they were far enough away, he kicked the engines forward and turned away. He felt a deep sense of sadness as they left Ion and the Frost behind. Calvin wondered if they would be able to contact the Hope, or if they would die in space.

They would either die from dehydration, starvation, or asphyxiation. He could always lower the pressure in the escape pod until they all passed out. Then they would die without pain. These thoughts rushed around in his mind. Something was telling him they should stay alive as long as they could. There might be a small chance, even a minuscule chance, that they would be rescued. He didn't want to see Astra suffer. He sat, staring out at the stars ahead. When they were far enough away from the planet, he turned to tell Astra but saw that both she and Dev were asleep.

Calvin turned on the distress beacon. He made sure it was working and hoped that the Alerian's would hear the signal and come for them. There was nothing left to do. He went back, lay down on the floor next to Astra and Scribbles, and fell asleep.

He couldn't see through the dark, foul-smelling smoke. He didn't have to look around to see where the smoke was coming from; he already knew. The smoke came from everywhere. It came from the burning cities that were on the horizon. It came from the army of burning battle tanks. He looked up at the beautiful beam of blue-and-white light that shot up into space, right through the fleet of angry-looking spaceships that were overhead. It all felt so familiar. He'd been told since he was little, that if you really wanted to, you could take control of your dreams. He could never control this dream, no matter how many times he tried.

The group of people stood before the beam of light. They slowly walked into it and disappeared.

Astra stood at his side, holding his hand. An old man and woman

311

stood near the beam of light.

"Astra, come with us." She shook her head yes and walked in their direction, pulling Calvin along with her.

"You can't come with us," the old man said, looking directly at Calvin. "You have to stay here."

"I can't stay here," Calvin protested. "I'll die here."

"This is where you belong,"

The old man took hold of Astra's hand and pulled her along with him. But Astra broke free of his grip just as the old man and woman walked into the beam. She stood and walked back to Calvin and held his hand. The darkness closed in around them. A sea of monsters ran toward them. There was a loud explosion that shook the asteroid they were on.

"I love you, Calvin," she said.

Calvin woke suddenly. The escape pod shook violently. Calvin, Astra, and Dev jumped to their feet. The memory of the dream was still lingering in his mind. It felt so real. When did Astra become the girl in that reoccurring dream, he wondered. Suddenly a bright yellow light filled the escape pod.

"What's happening?" Astra asked, looking out of the window in front of her. She couldn't see anything but space. All of a sudden the stars disappeared, and everything went dark.

"It's a tractor beam," Dev said. "Someone is pulling us into their ship with a tractor beam!"

"Weapons!" Calvin exclaimed. Calvin and Dev scrambled, quickly riffling through their stuff. "We're going to be boarded soon." They found their weapons and loaded them. Calvin's hands shook, and his heart raced.

"Stay back there, Astra," Calvin said. "Stay behind us." Astra moved back to the chair and sat down, holding a pistol firmly in front of her.

"What are we going to do?" Dev asked. "Do we have a plan?"

"What do you mean?" Calvin asked.

"Are we going to start shooting as soon as the door opens, before we know who they are? What if it's Astra's people, here to rescue us?"

"Then we have to wait and make sure we know who it is," Calvin said.

"What if it's the Goremog?" Astra said. "They won't hesitate. They'll shoot as soon as the door is open."

The shuttle was jarred sharply. There was a loud boom, and the sound of something very large connecting to the pod and locking into place. Calvin and Dev looked at each other, not sure what to do.

The door opened, and a small object was tossed into the pod. Before Calvin had a chance to do anything, there was a bright flash. In the blink of an eye they were all unconscious.

CHAPTER ELEVEN:

———◦———

THE GOREMOG

Calvin was vaguely aware of being awake, but he was in a dense fog. He had no idea where he was, couldn't open his eyes, and couldn't speak. Slowly he was able to crack his eyes open. At least, he thought his eyes were open, but he still couldn't see anything. His head felt strange; groggy. In the darkness before him, a blue object appeared. It was a planet. After a second it cleared up and got bigger. Calvin thought it looked familiar. It was New Arlandia, his home planet! What was he looking at? Was it a dream? The vision zoomed into the planet's atmosphere, over massive glass cities, deep lush valleys, and tall, snow-covered mountains. Then he rocketed into space, just above the planet. He became aware of intense pain growing in his head, and he was dizzy.

He started moving around the planet very fast then out high above the New Arlandian planetary system. He could see all seven planets. The view zoomed out farther, and he could see the surrounding star systems. He remembered looking at them through his telescope and studying them on forbidden star charts. He moved out a little bit farther away, until everything went black. Calvin sensed puzzlement. He flew back into the star system then out again, just over the threshold where everything went dark. It went back and forth four more times, and then his eyes were opened, as if a curtain had been pulled back.

314

Calvin found himself sitting in a metal chair with two small round robots floating around his head. Two figures stood in the shadows, next to a row of computers. He couldn't see them clearly enough to know what they were. Several computers flashed images of star systems and compared them to the image of New Arlandia.

What just happened? he asked himself, completely panicked. Did they just find New Arlandia? Do they know where it is? What have I done?

"He doesn't have the information," a voice said. "His knowledge is incomplete."

"How is that possible?" another voice asked. "He must be deceiving us."

"Impossible, he's an Arlandian. That species doesn't possess the intelligence capable of blocking our probes."

"Arlandian? I thought they were all wiped out."

"Obviously not. Lord Killith will not be happy. What do we do now? Can we dispose of them?"

"No," the first one said. "I have my orders. Use the probes on his friends and see if we can get any data, but we have to take them to the lab on Doonterria."

"Merciful deaths for them? I don't understand."

"Merciful deaths? No. Humans can't survive the mind processor. But if they are hiding anything, we'll find out."

"Isn't the planet going to explode soon?"

"Yes, but there is plenty of time to completely analyze their brains before the evacuation."

"I don't like this."

"Lord Killith has ordered it this way. Look, the creature is awake. Put him out, so we can finish. We have enough information on his star system, we'll find it."

"Wait!" Calvin tried to shout, but nothing came out. His vision went dark.

When he woke up later, his senses quickly returned. His head still hurt. He tried to sit up, but he was too weak, so he leaned on one elbow. Astra was already awake, and she helped him sit up. They were in a small cell. Dev was still asleep on the floor. In the corner, on a bench, was a young man with black hair and big muscles. Calvin looked at him. He looked unhappy and bored.

"Are you all right?" Astra asked.

"No," Calvin whispered. He looked at Astra as the memories of what just happened crashed down on him. "No, no, no, what did I do? Oh, Astra, they scanned my mind. They saw my planet. I tried to stop them, but I wasn't strong enough. I couldn't stop them." Calvin tried not to cry, but he did. Astra wrapped her arm around his shoulder and wiped tears from her own eyes.

"They saw everything."

"I know," Astra said. "They did it to me, too. Unfortunately they learned from me how many of us have survived, and what ships are left. They know they've almost won."

"They?" Calvin asked. "Who are they?"

"They're Goremog," Astra said. "We've been captured by the Goremog."

Calvin's heart sank. "How long have we been here?"

"I don't know. A few hours."

"We keep going from bad to worse," he said dejectedly. "And honestly I didn't think it could get worse, but it did."

"Much worse," Astra agreed.

"Who's that?" Calvin said, nodding in the new guy's direction.

"We haven't spoken yet," Astra whispered.

"I'm Wexton Zite," the young man said.

"I'm Calvin. This is Astra, and that's Dev."

"Hi," Wexton said, with a sad smile. "How did you get so lucky to get caught by the Goremog?"

"Just in the wrong place at the wrong time, I guess," Calvin said. "We were trying to get home, and they caught us." Calvin didn't feel comfortable with the stranger, not sure if he could be trusted or not. So he decided to not say anything about their mission.

Wexton nodded. "The Goremog are everywhere now. It's next to impossible to travel in the universe and not get caught by them."

"So what's your story?" Calvin asked. "How did they get you?"

"They invaded my home world, Celdostra," Wexton said. "I was training to be a special combat space soldier at the military academy. I would have graduated in two months." He laughed sadly. "We fought hard and held our ground for a long time, but in the end the Goremog's robot army overwhelmed us. Celdostra was destroyed. A few of us were captured and taken away. I don't know how long I've been in here. It feels like forever."

"I'm sorry," Calvin said. "They destroyed my home world, too." Calvin suddenly realized something. "Where's Scribbles?" He looked around the cell.

Astra quietly said, "She's standing behind me." Calvin looked behind her. The robot wasn't there.

"She?" Calvin asked.

"Of course," Astra said. "She's obviously a girl." Calvin looked carefully, but still didn't see anything. Then a voice whispered from behind Astra, "Yi'n lorna." Calvin looked at Astra.

"When I woke up, I noticed she wasn't here," she explained. "I freaked out. The poor little robot, what happened to her? Before I had a chance to dwell on it too much, I felt a tug on my jacket. I looked down, but there was nobody there. Then she started whispering to me, and I realized she can make herself invisible."

"Oh." Calvin stared back behind her. "That's a nice trick. I wish I could do that."

317

Calvin closed his eyes and massaged his temples. His head still hurt a little, and he was very worried. After everything they had been through, to find four pieces of the superweapon, only to get caught by the Goremog. There were still six pieces left to find, and it was looking very much like the adventure was over.

"We have to get out of here," Calvin said. "Your father is going to kill me."

"My father?" Astra asked. "I'd be more worried about the Goremog right now, if I were you."

"Do you have a way to escape?" Wexton asked. He didn't give Calvin a chance to answer. "Take me with you. They're going to kill me. I have to get out of here, too. I can fight. I can help you."

"I don't know how we're going to get out of here," Calvin said. "But when we do, you can come with us."

"Thank you," Wexton said. His smile looked a little warmer this time.

"Any ideas?" Calvin asked.

"I've never been captured by the Goremog before," Astra answered. "So, no. I don't have any ideas." It was clear that she felt, like him, very upset about being locked up, not knowing what was going to happen next.

"I wonder how long we'll have to wait in here."

"Oh, don't worry," Wexton said. "You won't have to wait long. You see, the Goremog will gas us and put us to sleep. That way they don't have to feed us or guard us."

"I see," Calvin said, feeling the familiar stab of fear. "Then we won't have to find something to do to pass the time."

At that very moment, there was a loud hiss, and a white vapor streamed out of the ceiling.

"You may want to lie down," Wexton advised. "At least sit down." Calvin and Astra took his advice and lay down on the icy-cold floor, facing each other.

318

"Astra," Calvin said. "It's going to be all right."

"Are you sure?"

"Yes, I really think so." Calvin said, trying to convince himself, not just Astra. He felt dizzy, and his vision went black. "Wait," his mind said loudly. "I'm not ready." He fell into a dark unconsciousness.

When Calvin woke up, he was lying in the same position. He hadn't moved. He was instantly aware of severe pain in his head. He tried to sit up but found he couldn't move his arms or legs. He opened his eyes and looked at Astra. She was still out. He tried to say her name, but nothing came out. Calvin wondered how long they had been unconscious.

The door to their cell opened, and a group of robots walked in. They were all black and had red symbols on their arms. They had dark gray helmets, with dark visors covering their faces. Each of them had long black pistols attached to their belts. A robot picked up Astra and carried her out of the cell. Calvin tried desperately to move, to kick, to scream to do something. But he couldn't. He was completely paralyzed.

More robots entered, one for each of them. They were carried out, one by one. Calvin was wide awake the whole time, and he was beginning to feel a tingling sensation in the tips of his fingers. They were carried down a series of hallways. Calvin tried to memorize the route but couldn't see very well, and after a few minutes he was totally turned around. He lost track of time. The only thing he could see were the light gray walls and an occasional doorway.

Finally they walked into a room. The robots sat them down in big, wide padded chairs and stood next to them. Calvin looked up. It looked like they were in a courtroom. At the front of the room was a large podium. A man in a black uniform stood behind it. His hair was black, with a lot of gray mixed in. It didn't take Calvin long to realize that he was looking at his first Goremog officer. His stare was icy cold.

Calvin was able to glance sideways in both directions. He saw Astra, Dev, and Wexton were all awake and were looking at the judge. The man stared at them for a second, and then he began to talk. His voice was low and gravely. Calvin kept wanting to clear his throat just listening to him speak. What he had to say put fear into his heart.

"You're accused of stealing a space cruiser from the quarantined planet Axia, a ship that was being prepared for use by the king of Traxia, ally of the Goremog Empire, to escape the plague happening on that planet. As a result of your actions the king and his entire family died. I find you guilty of theft and murder of the royal family of Axia. I sentence you to death on the prison planet of Doonterria. If you survive the interrogation process, you will live out the last days of your lives as you choose, because the planet has become unstable and will explode soon. There is no escape from Doonterria."

He banged a gavel on the podium and unceremoniously walked out of the room. The robots carried them back to their cells and put them on the floor. The door clanged shut, and they were left alone again. They lay there on the floor for a long time before the paralysis wore off, and they were able to speak.

"What was that?" Calvin asked.

"They didn't even allow us to say anything," Dev complained. "We didn't get to defend ourselves."

"That's because they had already decided what to do with us," Wexton said sadly. "They were just going through the motions in there."

"I don't understand," Calvin said. "Why did they have a trial for us? I thought the Goremog were ruthless killers. Whey waste time like that, if they already decided what they were going to do with us?"

"In the past," Astra explained, "the Goremog were a just race. They believed in right and wrong and fought hard to protect the innocent. Maybe that was a leftover from the old days."

"Or for some strange reason they feel a need to justify what they're doing," Dev said.

"But even if that's true, we didn't kill anyone," Astra objected. "Our scanners clearly showed that there were not any life signs there. They're basing their justification on lies, unless they really believe those things they said about us."

320

"It was clear, at least to me," Dev said. "That the Terrors killed them before we got there."

"That must be why the ship was ready to take off," Calvin realized. "They had the ship ready to go, and the Terrors got them before they had a chance to escape."

"And we are being blamed for it," Astra said. "This isn't fair!" Then she shouted to the door. "We didn't do it!"

"It's no use," Calvin said. "They won't listen. They just want to get rid of us."

"That's the way they are," Wexton said. "They did the same thing to me. They accused me of treason. They didn't let me talk. They just said I was going to die on a planet that was going to explode soon."

"And that's where we're going now," Astra said angrily.

"Don't worry, Astra," Calvin said, trying to sound relaxed but not doing a very good job. "As long as we're alive, there is hope."

"I don't know what hope we have of getting off that planet," Dev said angrily.

"We made it this far," Calvin said. "We should have died a few times over."

"I'm with you, Calvin," Wexton said. "If there is a way off the planet, we'll find it."

"I like your attitude," Calvin said. He had to believe there's hope, or they might as well give up. There was a loud hiss, and gas was pumped into the room. Calvin put his head down on the floor and waited. Before the darkness took him, he thought about his mother and father. He wondered what was going on at home. He hoped they were all right.

When Calvin woke up, he had no way of knowing how long he had been unconscious. His head hurt, and it took several attempts to even open his eyes. His ears popped, and he became aware of a loud sound. The sensation of sight and sound hit him at the same time, and he was completely disoriented. Where was he? It took a second for him to realize what was going on, and where he was. He sat up and looked around. They were in another cell. Astra was sitting up, too, but both Dev and Wexton were still asleep on the floor.

"They moved us," Astra said. "We're on a different ship."

"How can you tell?" Calvin asked.

"I can feel it in the engines." Astra said. "I'm guessing, but I think we arrived at Doonterria. We're on our way down to the surface."

There were no windows in the shuttle, so Calvin couldn't confirm what she said, but the bumps and sounds of the engines led him to believe she was right. During the trip down, Dev and Wexton sat up. Dev rubbed his eyes, and Wexton stretched his arms and legs. They knew when the shuttle landed. There was a hard bump. The door opened, and four heavily armed robots walked in. They weren't harsh or rough but kept their weapons pointed at them.

"Come with us," one of the robots said in a metallic voice. They followed the robots down a corridor to a boarding ramp. When the door opened they were hit with a blast of cool air.

"Proceed down the ramp and go out," a robot commanded. At the bottom of the ramp, they stepped outside into a clearing surrounded by tall trees. The ground was hard and dry, the trees were black, brown, and only partially covered with leaves. Two robots followed them outside. One of them kept its weapon pointing at the humans, but it felt to Calvin like he was the primary target. The one robot that didn't have a gun spoke into a small communication device.

"We have arrived at the coordinates. Why are you not here?" There was a pause and no answer.

"I repeat. This is GX two. I am ready to hand over the prisoners. Please answer."

"We could take them down," the other robot suggested.

"No, I don't have the access codes."

Before the other could answer there a roar from overhead, and a dark shadow flew by at high speed. Several small explosions burst all around. The robots looked up at the sky. The one with the gun fired into the air. GX two ran inside the ship, leaving the other robot all alone. Calvin was stunned, feeling that they were missing an opportunity. That thought was not lost on Wexton. He threw himself at the Goremog robot. Its laser fired, missing Calvin's head by mere inches. Wexton hit the side of the robot's head, and the robot quickly retreated inside the ship. Lasers bolts from the air hit the ground, and one hit the ship. The boarding ramp retracted, and the door closed.

A blast of air from the engines created a huge dust cloud and almost knocked them down. The shuttle lifted off the ground and accelerated into the sky with a high-pitched whine.

Calvin, Astra, Dev, and Wexton watched the ship leave them behind. The spaceship flew up into the sky against a very beautiful sunset. The sun reflected off its metal body. A smaller ship followed closely, shooting at it with bright lasers.

"That was our only way out of here!" Dev said angrily.

When it was gone, and the only thing they could hear was the wind in the trees, they all stood still for a moment, looking at each other. Scribbles was visible now and was holding Astra's hand.

Calvin thought to himself, 'Wow, that little robot must have a strong power source to stay invisible for so long. I wonder how long we were unconscious on the Goremog ship. Then he looked into the faces of his companions. He saw sadness, and a complete lack of hope, which was exactly how he felt. He was hungry, thirsty, and tired, and worse, he had no idea what they were going to do. He looked around again to take in their surroundings. They were on top of a mountain, surrounded by half-dead trees.

There were several rivers flowing into a large lake, but the water levels were very low. Dozens of tall mountains were on the horizon

"Who was the other ship?" Wexton asked.

"Enemies of the Goremog," Astra said. "Take your pick. They have a lot of enemies."

"It could have been the No'Rath," Dev suggested.

"Who?" Wexton asked.

"The Nuh Wrath," Dev pronounced the name slowly.

"Oh, right," Wexton said. "That makes sense."

"Who are the No'Rath?" Calvin asked. "Or, what are the No'Rath?"

Wexton looked at Calvin with a surprised expression. "Seriously?" He said. "You don't know about the No'Rath?"

Calvin felt foolish. "Sorry, I haven't been out here very long," Calvin said, trying not to sound defensive.

"The No'Rath and the Goremog are ancient enemies," Astra said. "They fought long and hard during the hundred year space war."

"When Ion told me about the war, he said it was the universe against the Goremog," Calvin said. "But anyway, it's good that someone is out there fighting against the Goremog, right? They'll keep 'em distracted."

"Unless we get caught in the middle," Wexton said.

Suddenly something caught Calvin's eyes. There was a light. It was a small white light, down in a valley below them. Then another light turned on. He looked closely. It was a small village, on the banks of a river. One by one, dozens of lights turned on. Then a thought occurred to Calvin, like a light switching on in his brain.

"Why did the Goremog bring us here?" Calvin asked. "They were meeting someone. There must be a base close by, or something."

"You're right," Dev said. "I wonder why they didn't show up."

"That's a really good question," Astra said. "But remember, this is a Goremog-controlled planet."

Suddenly Calvin felt very unsafe.

"Do you think they know we're here?" Dev asked. "I mean, we haven't exactly been quiet, and they were supposed to be here to meet us."

"Something isn't right," Astra said. "It's just doesn't make sense that they were going to transfer us out here in the middle of nowhere."

Everyone looked at Calvin. "All right, let's get away from here, before the entire area is covered with Goremog robots."

Calvin led the way out of the clearing and into the trees. The ground was dry and covered with dead leaves and broken branches, which crunched loudly as they walked. Fifty feet away they found a heavily damaged concrete foundation and a set of broken stairs descending into darkness. The ground was charred; even the trees nearby were burned. They all froze and stared at the stairs, except for Wexton. Slowly and cautiously he stepped to the stairs and peered into the darkness. He turned and made several hand motions that Calvin didn't understand, but he had a very bad feeling Wexton was saying he was going down into the ruins of the building to see what was down there. Calvin shook his head, but Wexton crept forward and made his way down the stairs. Calvin waved his hands and wanted to shout at him to stop, but to Calvin's alarm, Wexton disappeared into the darkness.

He wasn't gone long.

"Calvin!" Wexton shouted. "Come down here. You have to see this," Calvin's heart started beating faster. "What did you find?" Calvin said on his way.

"Just get down here."

What they found was the remains of a security station. It was dark, but cracks in the ground above let in shafts of light, dimly lighting up the room. There were pieces of broken computers spread across the floor. Another stairway led down even farther, but the way was blocked. There was an elevator, but it, too, was damaged and had no power.

"Was this the Goremog base?" Dev asked.

"That would be my guess," Calvin said. "I wonder what destroyed it."

"Do you think the No'Rath destroyed it?"

"I have no idea," Calvin said. "Is there anything down here we

325

can salvage, anything usable?"

"I'd like to look around," Dev said.

"Calvin," Astra said, her voice full of fear. "Look." Calvin
looked and saw something that froze his blood; a severed arm was lying
on the floor. It had a metal rod through the middle and several robotic
attachments on the outside. Calvin and Astra shared a look. Astra looked
terrified.

"No," Calvin whispered. "Not here, too. We just can't get away
from them."

Astra shivered. "I'm freezing."

"Do you think it's safe to make a fire?" Wexton asked.

"It's safer than freezing to death," Calvin said.

"Then I'm going to make one," Wexton said and left. Calvin and
Astra and Scribbles followed, the sounds of the little robot's arms and
legs moving echoing on the stone walls. Back in the clearing, Wexton
began gathering all the dry wood he could find. Calvin and Astra helped.
They didn't have to go far to collect wood for the fire. There were dead
branches lying on the ground everywhere. They made a big pile near the
tree. Wexton had a roaring fire going within five minutes.

The sun disappeared behind the mountains, and darkness began
to grow. One bright star appeared in the sky. Once the sun was down, the
temperature dropped even lower, and a blanket of stars spread out across
the sky. It was beautiful. Everyone huddled around the fire to stay warm.

"What are we going to do?" Astra asked.

"We could try and make it to the village down in the valley,"
Dev said. "I assume it's a village."

"What if it's a Goremog base?" Wexton asked.

"I don't know," Dev said. "We can't live in the forest forever.
Do you have a better idea?"

"We'd never make it off of this mountain in the dark," Calvin
said.

"We don't have to," Wexton said happily. "We can sleep here, on the ground, or better yet, over there, under that tree."

Everyone looked at him with a variety of expressions. Calvin was unhappy with the thought of sleeping under the stars, on the hard ground, but he figured it would be better than sleeping in a prison cell.

"It's already cold," Dev observed. "How cold do you think it will get?"

"It's hard to say," Astra said, "since I don't even know where we are. I've never heard of Doonterria before."

When the sun went down, they were smothered in darkness. Not even the vast array of stars in the sky overhead provided any light. If there was a moon, it was hidden behind clouds. Their small fire created a bubble of light that was unable to penetrate the night more than a couple of feet. The trees around stood like dark-gray sentinels. The temperature plummeted rapidly. Calvin, Astra, Dev, and Wexton huddled close to the heat. Scribbles stayed close to Astra.

"How are you feeling?" Calvin asked.

Astra smiled. "I'm OK, I guess. Just really tired; worn out."

"Is anybody hungry?" Wexton asked.

"I'm starving!" Dev answered.

"Then I have bad news for you," Wexton said. "We don't have anything to eat."

"No kidding," Dev said sadly. "We need to find something to eat soon. I can't burn energy I don't have."

After a three minute lull, Astra asked the question everyone was thinking.

"Do you still think we're going to find a way off of this planet?"

They all looked at Calvin. "I have to think so," Calvin said. "I refuse to just give up."

She nodded and tried to smile, but it was a sad smile.

"I like your optimism," she said. "I hope it's not misplaced."

327

Astra yawned and lay down next to the fire. Scribbles stayed close to her. After a few minutes, the robot laid its head on Astra's arm and closed its eyes. Calvin wondered if it was recharging its batteries.

Calvin, Dev, and Wexton searched the nearby trees for more wood. They each carried an armful back to the pile. When he walked back to check on Astra, Calvin found she was asleep. He decided to lie down near her, on his back, and stare up at the stars. They were beautiful, and he longed to be back out in space again. He thought about Azure Frost, and Ion, floating lifeless in the blackness. He thought about Jax and wished his friend was there to help him. But Calvin was grateful that he wasn't alone. The situation was desperate; they were lost on a Goremog-controlled planet, where Terrors could be running wild through the woods. He had hope, but he wasn't sure how long he would be able to hold on to it. Calvin eventually fell asleep, listening to the wind blowing gently through the trees, the dry leaves blowing across the ground, and the crackling fire.

The story continues in book two: Inferno!

ABOUT THE AUTHOR

William F. F. Wood is the author of the Ruins of Arlandia, an exciting science fiction series set in the aftermath of a galactic war. He has worked for the United States Air Force for twenty-five years. William was raised in Sandpoint Idaho, and currently lives in Illinois with his wife and two daughters.

66552201R00183

Made in the USA
Middletown, DE
12 March 2018